Anyush

'A beautiful, haunting and very important work.
It's quite an achievement to recount a part of history that
has remained shamefully occluded in such a compelling and
illuminating manner, through a story filled with love and life.'
Donal Ryan

'A deeply touching, powerful and vividly described love story set
amidst the barbarism of the Armenian genocide.'
Julia Kelly

'A vivid and elegantly written page-turner, a haunting love story
set against a background of sweeping historical events that shaped
the modern Orient.'
Conor O'Clery

Martine Madden was born in Limerick and worked in Dublin before moving to the United Arab Emirates with her husband John. In the oasis town of Al Ain she came to meet two Lebanese Armenians who were the first to tell her about the Armenian Genocide. Their stories and the much later discovery of Armin Wegner's genocide photographs prompted her interest in Armenian history and formed the basis of the novel *Anyush*.

Martine returned to Ireland in 1990 and now lives in the Midlands with her husband and family.

Anyush

Martine Madden

BRANDON
AN IMPRINT OF O'BRIEN

First published 2014 by Brandon,
an imprint of The O'Brien Press Ltd,
12 Terenure Road East, Rathgar,
Dublin 6, Ireland.
Tel: +353 1 4923333; Fax: +353 1 4922777
E-mail: books@obrien.ie
Website: www.obrien.ie

ISBN: 978-1-84717-566-3

1 3 5 7 8 6 4 2

14 16 18 19 17 15

Layout and design: The O'Brien Press Ltd
Cover photograph: Armenian dancers perform during a rally to mark the 90th anniversary of the
Armenian genocide, on Syndagma Square in central Athens, 20 April, 2005. Hundreds of Armenians
living in Greece marched to the Embassy of Turkey demanding the massacre to be acknowledged by the
Turkish authorities. FAYEZ NURELDINE/AFP/Getty Images
Map: Keith Barrett, Design Image
Author photograph: Brian Redmond, AIPPA, Roscrea, County Tipperary

Printed and bound by ScandBook AB, Sweden
The paper in this book is produced using pulp from managed forests.

The O'Brien Press receives assistance from

Dedication
For John

Acknowledgements

I am indebted to many people who helped make this book a reality. In particular, I would like to thank all the team at The O'Brien Press, especially Michael O'Brien, who took a chance on an unknown, Ivan, Ruth, Clare, Gráinne, Jamie, and Emma, who designed the beautiful cover. Huge gratitude to my wonderful editor, Susan Houlden, for her keen eye, insight and considered suggestions.

Heartfelt thanks to my triumvirate of miracle-makers: my dearest friend, Eileen Punch, and Conor and Zhanna O'Clery, without whose kindness and generosity this book would never have been published.

Many thanks to Zarmine Zeitounsian, who corrected my shaky Armenian, and to Keith Barrett, who designed the map of the Ottoman Empire.

To Melissa Marshall and Gillian Stern, who read very early drafts and liked it nonetheless. Your kind words and encouragement underpinned everything I wrote.

Sincere love and thanks to my team of family and friends, whose enthusiasm and support for this book equalled and sometimes exceeded my own. I can never thank you enough. And in memory of my father, Percy O'Kennedy, who told me my first stories.

To my darling husband, John, and five wonderful daughters, this book is dedicated to you.

Finally, to two remarkable Armenians, Houry Belian, and in memory of Salpy Godgigian.

'History will search in vain for the word ... "Armenia".'

Winston Churchill

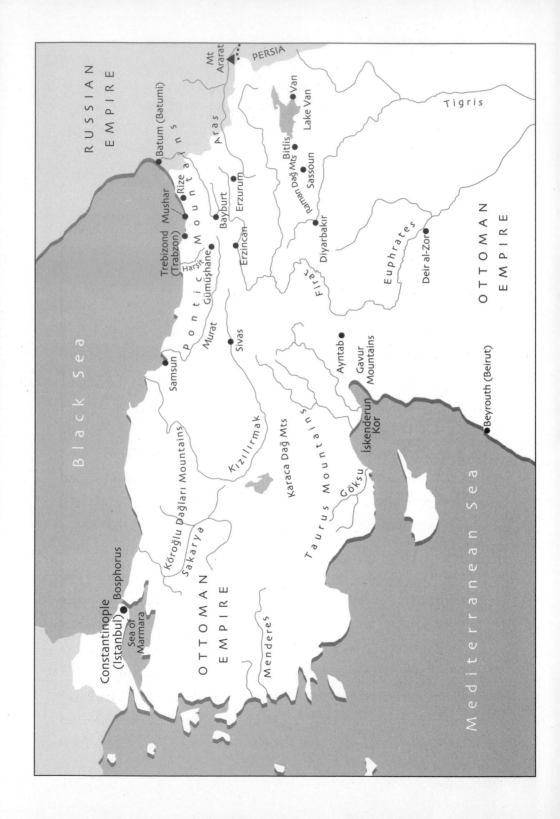

Anyush

Trebizond, Ottoman Empire, Spring 1915

Change came to the village in the form of Turkish soldiers - a whole company of them, marching down the street as though they would flatten it. Women pulled their children close and old men looked away as the sound echoed around the stone walls. The soldiers had come to Trebizond in October of 1914 and to the village six months later. The world was at war and all anyone talked of was unprotected borders and a Russian invasion. The young village men had been put in uniform and marched away many months before, and their families still mourned the loss of them. These soldiers were not local, not Armenian, and the air blew cold in their wake.

Two young Armenian girls watched from the foot of the church steps. They followed the progress of the soldiers as they turned into the square and took up formation along the southern side. The smaller of the two girls, Sosi Talanian, was carrying a loaf of black bread which fell from her hand when the lieutenant shouted his command. A hundred rifles hit the ground, rising clouds of dust around the soldiers' boots. The bread was snatched by a hungry dog, and it was only the dog which seemed untroubled by the stamping feet. Anyush Charcoudian, the taller of the two girls, turned to look back along the street. On the other side of the street, standing in the doorway of Tufenkians' shop, a small woman, Anyush's mother, looked on. She was old for her thirty-nine years and thin like everyone else. She watched the soldiers defiantly, but her narrow face was white as flour beneath the headscarf. It was a moment Anyush would remember. One she would never forget. She understood then that her mother was afraid.

Ŭ Ŭ Ŭ

Through a rusty gate and down a lane overgrown with weeds, Anyush walked to the Talanian farmhouse. The farm once had a goat, a pair of pigs with a yearly litter of piglets, a milking cow and a proper hen-house full of laying hens, but by 1914 that had all changed. Sosi's father and her two older brothers had been called up to join the Turkish army and Mrs Talanian tried to run the farm as best she could. Nine months after the letters and money had stopped coming there was no news of the men, and she had given up trying. The pigs were gone, one sold, one eaten, and the sty lay empty. The goat had disappeared and the horse was too old to be of much use for anything. The farmhouse, like Mrs Talanian herself, looked as though it had given up and fallen in. The roof of the long red-tiled building sagged in the middle and a creeper invaded the soffits and crept in under the eaves so that green tendrils hung down over the window of the bedroom Sosi shared with her sister Havat. Mushrooms grew in a damp corner of one of the downstairs rooms, and the shutters on the windows were coming loose or had fallen off altogether. Anyush tried to push one back on its hinge as she passed by, but it was rusted through and fell to the ground. In the yard the youngest of the Talaninans, eleven-year-old Kevork, emerged from the cow byre, pitchfork in hand.

'*Barev*, Anyush,' he said, his eyes on the koghov can she was carrying.

'*Barev dzez*, Kevork. Where is everybody?'

'Sosi and Mother are gone to the village. Havat's over there.'

Havat got up from where she was sitting on the swing in the hay barn and walked over.

'What is it?' Kevork asked, nodding at the koghov in Anyush's hands.

'Taste it and see.'

The boy lifted the lid and inhaled the delicious smell. He scooped some out with his finger and ate it, his face breaking into a smile.

'Your grandmother makes good *kamsi köfte*,' he said, holding some out for his sister.

They sat under the oak tree, eating with their fingers until every scrap was gone. The fishy smell hung in the air and the Talanians' goose lifted its head.

'None for you.' Kevork laughed.

'More,' Havat said, traces of anchovy meatball on her chin.

'There isn't any, Havi, and stop drooling.'

The boy wiped his sister's mouth brusquely with the end of his sleeve.

'We'll check the hens later. There might be an egg for supper.'

But they all knew the hens weren't laying, and the Talanians were living off the last of the chickens and whatever their neighbours could spare.

'I'll bring something tomorrow,' Anyush said. 'Pilaff maybe.'

Havat smiled, her tongue pushing against her lower lip and her eyes blinking in her wide face. In the village Havat was known as the Mongol because she resembled the Mongolian horsemen who rode into Rizay and Trebizond from the Russian steppes. The villagers said her mother had been too old when she had given birth to her, but, to everyone's surprise, Mrs Talanian had become pregnant again and had produced a healthy boy, Kevork.

'Bayan Stewart was asking for you,' Anyush said to him. 'She wanted to know why you weren't at school.'

'I'm working on the farm now. I have to help my mother.'

'The prizes are being given out tomorrow. I'm not supposed to tell you, but I think you got one.'

Kevork squinted up at her.

'A medal?'

Anyush nodded.

'You came first.'

He thought about this for a moment.

'Give it to Sosi. I have work to do.'

'I think your father would like you to have it.'

'My father would want me to look after the farm.'

Mr Talanian couldn't read or write like many of the village men but encouraged his children to learn. He had been a childhood friend of Anyush's father and a distant relative of her mother. Anyush's father was a man she had never really known. There was only his portrait hanging by the door to remember him by and a shaving brush she kept in her room. In the picture he posed in a stiff collar and suit, standing beside her mother, who was seated and wore a traditional Armenian dress. They stared solemnly into the camera, like the two strangers they were. The daguerreotype had faded in colour from brown to a hazy green, giving them an otherworldly pallor, but it did not diminish the kindness in her father's eyes or the lustre of his thick brown hair. Anyush adored the man in the picture with the love only a child can feel for a father she has never known. They looked alike, not in height, because he was unusually tall, but with the same dark eyes and hair. Her likeness to him was a source of great comfort, and when the other village girls put their hair up at the age of twelve, Anyush wore hers in a thick plait hanging beneath her scarf and swinging like a cat's tail between her shoulders.

'Push me,' Havat said, taking Anyush's arm and pulling her towards the barn.

She settled herself on the seat and Anyush stood behind, pushing gently against her back.

'Higher.'

The ropes creaked and the rafters groaned as Havat's feet swung through the cool air.

'Higher,' she said, leaning back against the ropes. The old barn seemed to heel against its foundations, joists lifted from the earth with every swing.

'Push harder.'

'You'll fall off, Havi,' Anyush said, giving one hard shove.

A loud metallic screech startled the swallows in the rafters. Anyush caught the ropes and brought Havat to a sudden stop. In the yard Kevork dropped the pitchfork and went to look down the lane. Since the trap had been sold, the gate was never opened and access to the road was through a gap in the crumbling stone wall. The hinges had rusted in the salt air and complained loudly when the group of soldiers pushed it open. They came into the yard as Anyush and Havat emerged from the barn. The men looked mean and dangerous. One of them walked over to the boy. He was thin and short, not much taller than Kevork, with a narrow head and ferret-like darting eyes. One brown eye and one hazy blue were sunk too close together either side of a long nose.

'You live here?'

Kevork nodded.

'You?' he asked Anyush.

'I'm a neighbour.'

The Ferret turned to the soldiers at his back.

'A visitor! Well ... I like to make time for visitors.'

The soldiers laughed as he turned to the two girls.

'We're here for food. All of it. Go into the house and bring it out.'

'There is no food,' Anyush said.

'You're lying.'

'It's true. There's nothing here.'

'Search the house,' the Ferret said to the others, and they disappeared inside.

'The place is a wreck,' one of them said, coming out empty-handed. 'Not a fucking thing to eat. Even the cool room's empty.'

From an upstairs window a flutter of clothes drifted to the ground, followed by the double thud of heavy boots.

'I'm taking the boots,' the face at the window shouted.

At Anyush's side Havat began to cry.

A third soldier appeared in the doorway with a photograph frame in his hand.

'No!' Kevork shouted. 'That's my father.'

The soldier pushed the boy away, but Kevork kept reaching for it.

'Give it to me.'

'Get away.'

'It's mine.'

'Have it then.'

He smashed the glass against the barn wall and took the silver surround. Kevork picked the torn photograph from amongst the shards of broken glass.

'Look in the outhouses,' the Ferret said, and two soldiers disappeared into the pigsty and the barn.

'Empty,' one soldier said. 'Old pig shit, that's all.'

'A few hens in the barn. Not much else.'

'Start with those. Take Sanayi and wring their necks.'

Two soldiers closed the barn door behind them and, in the yard, everyone could hear the sound of flapping and clucking which stopped abruptly. The door opened again and the soldiers appeared with four limp-necked chickens in their hands.

'Where are the other animals, boy?' the Ferret asked.

'There's nothing here,' Anyush said. 'There's nothing left to take.'

'I didn't ask you. I asked farmer boy. You look like a farmer. Are you, boy?'

Kevork nodded.

'So where are the animals?'

He didn't answer.

'Look,' one of the soldiers said. 'A goose.'

With arms spread wide, he hunched towards the bird, but it spat at him, hissing loudly and beating its huge wings.

The soldier jumped away and the others laughed.

'You're not afraid of a goose, Hanim?'

'You catch it, then.'

'Just watch me.'

'Don't take the goose,' Anyush said. 'Please ... they have nothing else.'

'Here goosey goosey,' the soldier said, taking off his tunic. 'Come on ... that's the way.'

The goose spread its wings, lowered its head and advanced on the soldier, but he held his ground and threw the jacket over it. Suddenly, he was on top of the struggling bird, calling for the others to help. Kevork ran over, screaming, but a hand grabbed him by the collar and threw him halfway across the yard.

'Get me that axe,' the Ferret said.

He pulled the jacket off the goose and two of the soldiers stretched its neck over a block of wood.

'Hold it steady.'

Lifting the axe over his head, he brought it down on the goose's neck, and warm blood spurted out like a living thing. It covered their clothes, their hands and faces. A soldier opened his mouth and drank it as the Ferret held up the headless body triumphantly. But Kevork ran towards him again, biting and kicking for all he was worth.

'Little bastard!'

With the full force of his fist, the Ferret hit the boy in the face. Havat screamed as Kevork fell backwards but struggled to his feet. The boy staggered towards them, but his knees gave way and he began to retch. Anyush ran to help him, but the Ferret launched himself at the boy, punching him again and again.

'Stop it! Leave him alone!'

'Hanim ... calm down ... he's only a boy.'

The Ferret grunted, and as he drew back his arm to hit the unconscious boy once more, Anyush grabbed the pitchfork and rammed it into the heel of his boot. The Ferret roared, turning to lash out at her and pull the pitchfork away. He fell on his backside, clutching the boot and straining to see what damage had been done.

'Armenian bitch!' he swore, blood staining the leather. 'My fucking ankle!'

He stood up and tested his weight. The boot had protected him, and he discovered he could still walk.

'I'll show you. I'm going to teach you a lesson you'll never forget.'

Hobbling over to the barn, he went inside and came out carrying a length of rope.

'Hold her!'

'Hanim—'

'I said hold her.'

He fashioned the rope into a noose and threw the free end over a bough of the oak tree. 'Bring the boy here.'

'No ... please God, no.'

Anyush's knees began to buckle, but the soldiers held her upright. Kevork groaned when he was pulled to his feet and dragged over to the tree.

'Please ...' Anyush begged. 'Please, I'm sorry ... I beg you.'

By the barn, Havat screamed her brother's name. 'Kevo ... Kevo!'

The Ferret tied the boy's hands behind his back and put the noose around his neck, pulling it tight. Pressure from the rope brought the boy to his senses and he swayed on his feet, the breath rasping through his mouth.

'Are you watching, bitch?'

Holding the other end of the rope, the Ferret pulled harder so that Kevork was balanced on the tops of his shoes. His face turned red and then began to darken. Yanking the rope again, the Ferret watched Anyush's face as the boy struggled to breathe.

'Don't like what you see? Not so brave now, are you?!'

Kevork's mouth was open and his tongue was pushing past his lips. Anyush sobbed as Havat covered her eyes.

'This is only the start of it, bitch. Your turn next.'

'Hanim!'

Two soldiers on horseback rode into the yard. The Ferret dropped the rope and Anyush ran to Kevork who collapsed on the ground.

'What's going on?'

'We were attacked, Captain Orfalea. We only wanted to take the goose, but they turned on us with a pitchfork.'

The captain looked around. He was younger than some of the others and noticeably different. His uniform was neat and well cut, and his boots were polished. He didn't wear a moustache or beard, and his straight black hair was unusually long.

'You were attacked,' he said contemptuously. 'Five of you. By two girls and a boy.'

The soldiers looked uneasy, but the Ferret stared sullenly. 'I wasn't going to hurt him. Just scare him a bit.'

The captain went to where Kevork lay on the ground. The boy's nose was broken, his face bruised and swollen, and red rope burns ringed his neck.

'Lieutenant, escort these men back to base.'

'She attacked me,' the Ferret said. 'I've a right to defend myself.'

'And throw Corporal Hanim in detention until I decide to let him out.'

The soldiers left, following the lieutenant down the lane, and the captain walked over to where Anyush was crouched over Kevork.

'Is he alright?'

Anyush nodded. She helped Kevork to sit and loosened the collar of his shirt. The captain looked around the yard, at the broken glass and the mutilated goose.

'Keep the boy indoors for a while and maybe stay away from pitch-forks next time.'

Anyush got unsteadily to her feet. 'Next time I'll put it in his belly.'

We arrived in Constantinople two weeks ago as the rain pelted down and I thought I was back in wintry New York. Hetty and I were both exhausted from travelling but we were relieved to see Elias Riggs waiting for us at the quayside. I'm not sure what I had been expecting of an ageing American missionary, but I really didn't think he would be so energetic or so tall. He's been working as a doctor in the Empire for over forty years, and when I told him about my plans for trachoma research, he seemed more interested in telling me about the times of religious services in the area. The man is very devout which makes for a certain awkwardness between us. I did of course take this job as a 'missionary' doctor but, as Hetty pointed out when I first proposed coming here, I'm an atheist and she's Jewish. We do go to services occasionally, some of them at least, but I think Elias already suspects I'm not what he thought I was. For a while, it looked like he was going to send us home, but it turns out he badly needs help at the clinics and he's already very fond of Hetty.

Our final destination is to be a small village in the Trebizond area on the Black Sea coast. From what I've learned, the place is pretty remote but not that far from Trebizond city, a large town and an important sea port. The village is at the centre of one of the most badly infected trachoma districts in the country, so a lot of hard work awaits us.

For the moment, we're living on Istiklal Avenue in Pera. It's not exactly luxurious, but it is clean and serviceable and on the European side of the Bosphorus. Just three rooms which come with a Greek kitchen maid, a Turkish hamal (or jack of all trades) and a Polish cook. Hetty, my khanum or lady as she's called here, is in her element. She cannot practise as a doctor because women doctors are only allowed work in the harems, but she's up early most mornings sketching the ruins in old

Constantinople. Her fascination with the city is understandable. The Whore of the Orient certainly lives up to her name and is magnificent and tawdry in equal measure. On any given street there are sights to take your breath away, the grandeur of the Hagia Sophia church or the opulence of the Topkapi Palace, while around the corner vermin-ridden slums spring up in the ruins of buildings levelled by the earthquake of 1894. Paris in miniature extends along the elegant boulevards on the European side of the Bosphorus, while on the eastern side women in full purdah walk three paces behind their husbands and the Prophet reigns supreme. As Elias says, it is a city of contradiction and contrast.

We've already made good friends in Henry Morgenthau, the American Ambassador, and his wife, Josephine. They're Jewish, so Hetty feels right at home, and Henry is a stimulating and interesting character. He entertains royally and has a very fine cellar, so it amuses him that a 'poor missionary doctor' should be partial to a good claret. The Morgenthaus know everyone in Constantinople, from the diplomats to young men on the Grand Tour, and they seem intent on introducing us to all of them. We will be seeing more of the Morgenthaus in the immediate future now that Hetty is expecting in the autumn and our travel plans have been put on hold. The delay is unavoidable but frustrating, although it seems we would have had to wait for travel permits anyhow. In this country it is impossible to work, build or do the smallest thing without them. Elias counsels me to be patient. He tells me that when he first came here the old Sultan would not allow foreign reading material or gas lighting for fear of corrupting his subjects. He bids me to remember that I, at least, can read and have lamps to see by. Amen to that!

Anyush

Where the trees thin out on the northern promontory the river bends in a wide arc towards the sea, and the flow of water slows to a pool. The surface is broken by jutting grey boulders like bathing giants, and it is here the village women come to do their laundry. Anyush and her mother walked in silence towards the river, each carrying a basket. Voices and the sound of wet clothes slapping against the rocks drifted towards them as they rounded the bend.

'*Barev*, Anyush. *Barev dzez*, Bayan Charcoudian.'

Parzik Setian was standing in the shallows beside Sosi, her arm waving in salute as she called out to Anyush and her mother. Both girls had their skirts tucked into their waistbands and clothes in the water under their feet. On a rock nearby Havat sat by herself, her legs dangling in the water. Anyush's mother barely acknowledged them and upended the clothes from her basket onto the bank. She took off her boots and stockings and hitched up her skirts as she waded into the river.

'What are you gawping at them for?' she snapped at her daughter. 'You think those clothes will wash themselves?'

Anyush tipped out the contents of her basket and sat down to take off her stockings and boots. The clothes belonged to their landlord, Kazbek

Tashjian, and his son, Husik. They were filthy and reeked of things Anyush didn't like to think about. Taking a cake of soap and a shirt, she dipped it in the cool water, scrubbed it, beat it hard, then laid it out on the high rocks to dry. Mother and daughter worked side by side for a time, without speaking, Anyush struggling to match her mother's pace. Khandut Charcoudian was wiry and strong, with a strength belied by her small size. Since her husband had died, it was she who hammered and sawed and climbed the roof to repair the wood tiles. She took pride in her ability to dig trenches, and hang gates, and take on whatever task needed to be done. Gohar, Anyush's grandmother, looked after the small vegetable garden, and Anyush took on whatever chores brought in extra money and most of those that didn't. In her mother's eyes, it was never enough. If it were not for Khandut Charcoudian, she liked to remind them, they would be walking the roads and they were lucky to have her. What Anyush felt about her mother had little to do with luck. Nothing satisfied the woman or gave her any pleasure. She was vexed by life in general and by her daughter in particular.

'Pssssst …'

Parzik beckoned. Anyush nodded and looked over to where her mother was wringing soapy water from a pair of trousers.

'I'm going to wish Parzik luck,' she said. 'Her mother's started on her wedding dress.'

'Make it quick,' Khandut replied, without looking at her.

Parzik stood in the water, hands on her hips, looking like a half-submerged colossus. She was very tall for a girl, her height accentuated by her thinness and her unusually long neck. Her thick black hair was wound around her head in girlish braids, but her beak-like nose had earned her the nickname '*t'Rchun*', the bird. She was not pretty as Anyush and Sosi were, but she had full breasts and wide hips that had appeared, as if by magic, two years before. Parzik was the only one of Anyush's friends engaged to be married, and Vardan Aykanian, a local plasterer and her second cousin, was to be the groom. Spared conscription and the army because of his work on the local barracks, he was one of the few young men left in the village.

'I heard what happened,' Parzik said.

'Shhh! My mother doesn't know. How's Kevork?' Anyush asked, turning to Sosi.

'All right.'

'And Havat?'

The three girls looked over to Sosi's sister staring at her reflection in the water.

'She cries a lot. I haven't told her yet that Kevo is gone.'

'Gone? Where?'

'My mother is taking him to my uncle in Ordu. They left for Trebizond this morning.'

Anyush looked at the river, the slow-moving water broadening its reach towards the sea.

'What will you do?' Sosi asked.

'Me?'

'That soldier knows what you look like. It's not safe for you either.'

'The captain seemed fair,' Parzik said. 'Lucky for Kevork he came when he did.'

'He's a Turk,' Anyush said. 'They're all the same.'

'I'm only saying, if he's around then you don't have to worry.'

'My brother was almost hanged,' Sosi said. 'You think we don't have to worry?'

'That's not what I meant. Look ... Anyush will be fine and I'm going to be married. We need to celebrate a little.' She grinned, pointing to herself. 'Bayan Vardan Aykanian, that'll be me.'

'If Vardan will have you,' Sosi said.

'He'll be lucky to have me! A laying hen, unlike certain chickens I know.'

Sosi splashed Parzik and started to laugh. It caught her friend by surprise. Cold water ran down Parzik's chest and drenched her blouse. Recovering quickly, she skimmed the surface of the river with her large hands, wetting Sosi and Anyush into the bargain. They were laughing now, and Havat got up from her perch on the rocks to join them. River water splashed everywhere and, in the excitement, Anyush forgot about her mother. But Khandut was already drenched, the sleeve and skirt of her dress soaked. With the noise and the laughter, it was a while before Anyush realised someone was calling her. She turned to see her mother whirling a wet shirt above her head which she flicked in her direction. But Parzik had crossed in front of Anyush, and the wet sleeve coiled like a snake around her long neck. Her hands flew to her throat, to try and loosen it, and she lost her footing, falling helplessly into the river. Gasping for breath, Parzik struggled to her feet, thoroughly soaked.

'*Khoz!*' she spat at the older woman. 'Pig!'

Khandut turned her back to them.

'Madwoman! You're mad!'

'Parzik—'

'Leave me be,' she said, pulling away from Anyush.

With Havat on one side and Sosi on the other, Parzik waded over to the bank, wiping water from her face. The three girls gathered their things and left. Anyush wanted to weep with shame. Her mother *was* mad. Cruel and twisted and spiteful. She cursed wilful fate that chose her for her mother and deprived her of the father she loved. Leaving the washing on the stones, Anyush ran from the water and headed towards the coast road. Taking the track down to the small bay, she walked across the beach in the direction of the cliff. The wind was in her face as she paddled in the shallows, and her hem quickly became soaked. Beside her, the sea broke over the rocks, a dull sullen grey. After a time, the tightness in her chest began to ease and her breathing became calm. The wind whistled in her ears and the waves pounded on the sand, drowning out her mother's carping voice. She wanted to keep walking, to follow the shoreline until there was nowhere left to go. As far as Constantinople maybe, far enough that she would never have to see her mother again.

She didn't notice him until they were quite close. Her first instinct when she saw a soldier in the uniform of the Turkish army was to turn and run, but there was something familiar about him. His walk. The way he held his head. From a long way off she could feel him watching and her heart quickened. They drew abreast of each other, and, to her surprise, the captain greeted her in Armenian and walked on. They were now moving away from each other, but Anyush soon reached the foot of the cliff and could go no further. With no other option, she turned back, but there was no one behind her – nothing to see only the restless ocean and the empty beach. One set of footprints disturbed the yellow sand – her own.

Jahan

What struck him at first was the contradiction. The girl from the farm seemed young and yet old at the same time. With her childish plait and defiant air, he couldn't make up his mind about her. The events at the farm troubled him and he had no doubt what would have transpired had he not come upon them when he did.

At times he felt helpless to control the men under his command in a way he never had with his old company. Since the passing of the Amele Taburlan decree, all Armenians in the Ottoman forces had been demobilised and assigned to unarmed labour battalions. The captain's company had lost roughly a third of its men in this way, soldiers he had come to know and respect, unlike their replacements. Most of the new recruits had minimal military training, and others, such as Corporal Hanim, had been released from prison. Aside from his lieutenant, there were few the captain could trust. They spoke cruelly about the fate of the Armenian soldiers, claiming they had been shot because of their allegiance to the Russians, or set free and used as target practice. Whatever the truth of the matter, Jahan had neither seen nor heard of his Armenian soldiers since, and every newspaper article, every proclamation issued by the government was rife with anti-Armenian propaganda.

In the evenings the captain had taken to walking the long stretch of beach lapped by the waters of the Black Sea, and it was here he came in contact with the girl again. She was coming towards him, her skirts flapping noisily and her hair blowing in wisps around her face. Despite the ugly headscarf and tattered clothes, he could see she was attractive and possibly beautiful. It fascinated him that she should walk alone, especially after what had happened. On the pretext of asking after the young farm boy, the captain made discreet enquiries about her in the village. He discovered that she worked for the local doctor, an American missionary by the name of Stewart, and helped out at the school run by his wife. This was unusual as Turkish girls married young and were not allowed work outside the home. He found himself looking out for her and began to discover just how unconventional she was. There were times he noticed her clothes and hair were wet, as though she had been swimming, but he never actually saw her in the water and was careful never to approach That first time he had passed her on the beach he had made an effort to say hello in his few words of Armenian, but she didn't acknowledge him, and her hostility was like a cold breeze blowing against him. He didn't blame her. He could hardly have expected her to be in any way approachable, but he was sorry for it nonetheless.

Today was one of the longest, most irritating, back-breaking days I have ever spent in a saddle, and one I hope not to repeat for a long time. But I'm running ahead of myself.

Some months have passed since we came to Constantinople and much has happened in that time. Hetty and I have made good friends; we've learned Turkish and a smattering of Armenian and Greek; and we are the proud parents of a baby boy, Thomas George Stewart. Three weeks ago, we said goodbye to Elias Riggs and the Morgenthaus, before setting out for Trebizond. Hetty was sorry to leave, and I suppose it is daunting bringing a small baby into the wilds of eastern Turkey, but, I have to admit, I was impatient to get started. We've had to bring almost everything we need with us, and I spent weeks organising the shipment of furniture, medical equipment and supplies, as well as provisions for the journey. It was the usual exhaustive round of permits and bribes, but finally it got done and we were under way.

A small coastal frigate by the name of *Mesudiye* brought us along the Black Sea to Trebizond. The Circassian captain told us that the town derived its name from the Greek word *trapezous* meaning 'table', and, as he guided the boat into the bay, we could see the ramparts of the old city, built on the flat hilltop, surrounded by a buttressing medieval wall. It was a surprisingly large town and not the backwater I had been expecting. At the dock, a crowd gathered on the quay, and a line of mules and their handlers stood to one side. Waiting for the boat were pedlars, customs officials, baggage handlers, caravan hamals and hangers-on of every description and persuasion. A full head and shoulders above these was a tall, foreign-looking man, whom I guessed to be our contact, an Englishman Elias had arranged would

28

meet us. But in pride of place, standing at the foot of the gangway, was a local dignitary. He was dressed in a long khameez, with a green girdle wound around his substantial waist, and traditional Turkish slippers. On his head was a turban like a miniature minaret, and his fingers sparkled with a dazzling display of jewelled rings. Two servants held a striped awning above his head, and a rug had been unrolled beneath his feet. He barely glanced at Hetty, but his black eyes never left my face. I was used to people staring by this time, but under this man's gaze I felt like the dish he was about to eat for supper.

'*Selamın Aleyküm,*' I said.

'*Aleyküm Selam,*' he replied.

He said no more, and I was unsure if I should bow to him or pay him *bahşiş* or simply walk past.

'Let me introduce the Vali, His Excellency, the Governor of Trebizond,' a voice said. The foreign-looking man removed his hat. 'Sorry ... I should introduce myself. Paul Trowbridge.'

Like Riggs, he was tall and thin, his linen suit looking a little the worse for wear and hanging in creases at his elbows and knees. He towered over Hetty and patted Thomas on the cheek.

'You're welcome to Trebizond. The Vali was anxious to meet you.'

The great man said something to Trowbridge in a dialect I didn't understand, and left. It all seemed a great to-do about nothing, but Paul assured us it was otherwise. 'It's a mark of honour. Of respect. The Vali doesn't usually meet foreigners at the quayside.'

'Does he always behave oddly?' I asked. 'Staring like that?'

'Only when he likes you.'

Paul laughed at my expression and told me a rumour had spread that I had some skill as a dentist. 'He wants you to pay him a visit. Our esteemed Vali has very bad teeth.'

It took an age for the luggage to be unloaded and repacked onto the mules, so while we were waiting Paul suggested we eat at the local hotel. It was surprisingly good, run by two French brothers from Bayonne. Over dinner Paul told us a little about himself. After qualifying as a doctor, he decided to travel through Europe, spending time in most of the major cities, before moving on to Athens and then Constantinople. Elias Riggs was his only contact, so he stayed with him in the city and worked there for a couple of years.

'Not as a missionary,' he said. 'I never believed in all that "my God is better than your God" nonsense.'

He apologised then, and said he hoped we didn't think his views were offensive, but, in fact, I found myself liking Paul Trowbridge more and more. It was Riggs who offered Paul the position in Trebizond when a friend of his, Dr Fred Sheppard, died of typhus, and the authorities were looking for somebody to replace him.

'How many years are you here?' Hetty asked.

'Too many,' he said. 'I've stopped counting. My parents are dead, and I have only one brother in England, so I rarely go back. This is home really. I hope you'll come to feel about it as I do.'

I assured him that we would give it our all, and I meant it. During the long trek across Europe I did have doubts about my decision to come to Turkey. From a career point of view, leaving the medical hierarchy was disastrous. Certain people, Hetty's mother to name but one, thought that from all points of view it was disastrous, but Paul Trowbridge convinced me otherwise. By the time the food and wine arrived, I was congratulating myself on having made the right move.

Before we had finished the meal, Hetty had told Paul a little about what we'd been doing in New York, and I could see they had hit it off immediately. She was charmed by his old-fashioned manners, and he was clearly taken with her unflappability and good humour. I should have taken against him since he is everything I am not: tall, handsome and charming, but it is impossible to dislike Paul Trowbridge. He is amiable, easy company, and we might have been there yet, had the time had not come to leave for Mushar.

The last part of the journey proved to be the most difficult. Paul had warned us about the army of flies in the mountain pass into the village, but nothing prepared us for them. We had brought wide-brimmed hats with netting and a floppy bonnet for the baby, but they were useless against the onslaught that descended as we rode in single file through the pass. As soon as we hit the treeline, they appeared, and no amount of swatting or netting kept them away. I spent the journey batting at the cloud above my head, and noticed that few of the little bastards appeared to be troubling Paul. After the caravan of horses and mules jangled up the mountain and down the other side, the village of Mushar finally came into view. What a contrast to the glory of Constantinople and the elegant harbour at Trebizond! Dusty, foul-smelling streets, full of yelping dogs and ragged children, buzzed with flies and mosquitoes.

'*Şapka giyen insanlara gel!*' the children chanted, which Paul translated as 'Come see the people wearing hats!'

Black-eyed, brightly dressed children crowded around us, while their mothers drew their scarves over all but one eye and ambled through chickens, lambs and dogs to see for themselves. Many of the children had swollen eyes covered with clusters of black flies and I asked Paul why they didn't shoo them away.

'Because they believe that to do so would bring on the eye-sickness. Trachoma. It's rampant in these parts.'

Trachoma, caused by flies, leads to chronic infection and, if left untreated, would cause blindness in at least half of these children. I watched them run after our horses, clouds of black flies following them. The adults were no better off, and they didn't try to brush away the flies either. Instead, they made us gifts of fruit, goat's milk and grapes, huge bunches of them that they pressed into our dusty hands. A woman carrying a baby pressed a bit of blue cloth, with the shape of an eye embroidered on it, into Hetty's hand, nodding to where Thomas dozed on her back.

'It's called the *atchka ooloonk*,' Paul explained. 'People carry them to ward off the evil eye.'

The children were wearing blue beads, shells or triangular bundles of cloth, which had the same symbol and verses from the Koran sewn inside. Hetty leaned down to touch a dark-eyed baby wearing one around her neck, but the woman pulled away, covering the child with her veil.

'Don't take it personally,' Paul said. 'You must never praise a child because it draws the evil eye to him, and if you forget you must say *Maşallah*, "God has willed it".'

Mushar, it turns out, is bigger than I first thought, running east to west along the Black Sea coast. Heavily wooded hills reach down almost to the shoreline where pristine, undisturbed white sand gleams in the midday sunlight. The centre of the village is more developed than the outskirts with wooden two- and three-storeyed houses looking onto a reasonably sized square. A Christian church and a mosque dominate either end, and the only other building of note is what looks like a store, with a haphazard jumble of items spilling from an open doorway. Paul led us down a small street, behind the Armenian church, and we turned onto an overgrown, cobbled pathway. At the end of this narrow lane we saw a neat, biscuit-coloured stone house, which looked as though it had been transported fully formed from the English countryside. It was a house such as a child might draw, with a central wooden door surmounted by a small, arched fanlight and two mullioned sash windows on either side. This arrangement is repeated on the second floor, with the addition of an extra window in the middle. The remnants of a garden were visible in the overgrown borders both sides of the door, and old fruit trees blossomed in a little orchard to one side.

'It's just wonderful,' Hetty said.

'Who on earth would build such a house here?' I asked.

Paul looked at it as he got down from his horse. 'It's called *usuts'ch'I tuny*, "the teacher's house". Jane Kent had it built when she taught at the school here.'

'It reminds me of a house from an English novel,' Hetty said.

'That was the idea. It's supposed to be a model of Jane's home in Surrey.'

I asked Paul why the teacher had left, but he was preoccupied with unloading the mules and didn't seem to hear. Inside we walked from room to room.

A small parlour and drawing room look out either side of the front door, while the dining room has a view of the orchard to the rear. A tiny maid's room leads off one side of the kitchen, and a scullery, pantry and cool room off the other. Upstairs are four modestly sized bedrooms, a dressing room, a bathroom and an airing closet. The privy is in the yard. As you might expect of a building that hasn't been lived in for some time, it is full of dust, damp and musty odours, but it has a definite charm and could be transformed with a good clean and the appropriate furniture into a comfortable home.

Sometime later, when everyone had gone and we were finally alone, Hetty and I sat exhausted in our two chairs.

'It's odd, don't you think?' Hetty asked.

'I thought you'd like it.'

'I meant that Jane Kent should have left. I had the impression that Paul didn't want to talk about it.'

'Oh?'

'Did you notice that he used her first name?'

'Are you saying there was something between them?'

'I'm saying that he knows the house better than one might expect.'

'Perhaps he stayed here?' I suggested. 'Or looks after the place?'

'Perhaps,' Hetty said. 'Even though he works in Trebizond, a three-hour journey away.'

I laughed, wondering what Paul would think of our speculations.

It is now well past midnight, and Hetty is urging me to blow out the candle and put my pen away, but I know I won't sleep. My mind is turning over, making plans. There is so much to learn about this place and so much to do. The small maid's room off the kitchen would be the perfect spot for my laboratory, and tomorrow I'll move my equipment in there. It is at least a start.

Jahán

The captain's second encounter with Anyush happened on the same beach some time later. He saw her in the distance, but this time she was distracted and didn't notice him. Carrying a boot in each hand, she pitched them into the air, throwing them furiously along the curved line of sand as though aiming at someone's head. The boots sailed past his ear and landed in the shallows at his feet. He picked them up and brought them to her.

'You missed,' he said, 'but I'll give you another shot if you allow me the pleasure of walking with you.'

Holding out the wet boots, he smiled apologetically, and she began to laugh. Her eyes were filled with the brightness of the sea, and when he came to think about that day down the years, he remembered it as the day he fell in love with her.

They walked towards the eastern end of the bay along the shore. Her smile quickly disappeared and she became wary of him. The beach was screened by the cliff and the woods, but every so often she glanced over towards the track and the road leading to it. The captain didn't think she was afraid of him but understood that she was reluctant to be seen in his company. He wanted to find a way to put her at ease. More than once, he tried to catch her eye, but she stared fixedly ahead. Her cheeks had pinked up prettily, but it was only when he pretended to stumble that he had a full view of her face. It was a perfect oval with a wide brow, a small straight nose and pale complexion that was more cream than milk. Her eyes were widely set and the colour of liquid sugar, but it was her mouth that caught his attention – full, slightly protruding lips, the colour of persimmons, with a downward droop at the corners. He was staring, and she looked away.

'This is a difficult place to find,' he said. 'The track is almost invisible.'

'*You* found it.'

'So I did. Well, actually, I followed you.'

A look of alarm crossed her face.

'I couldn't find my way down here from the main beach. You were walking on the road ahead of me and turned off in this direction so ...' He shrugged. 'I apologise if I've imposed myself on your hideaway.'

'It's not mine,' she said, walking on again. 'Anyone can come here.'

'It's really lovely. In an odd way it reminds me of home.'

'Constantinople.'

'How did you know?'

'Your accent. And you use French and English words.'

'Do *you* speak English and French?'

'Some. Bayan Stewart teaches them at the mission school.'

The captain's interest was piqued. 'So you grew up here? You have family here?'

Unexpectedly, she clamped up again.

'That's rude of me,' he said. 'Why don't you ask me something in return? A sort of trade.'

There were things she wanted to ask. He could feel her curiosity and also that she wouldn't give in to it.

'I'll tell you about myself, then. I'm the oldest and only son of four children. My eldest sister, Dilar, is a terrible flirt and will make some poor fellow very unhappy. My middle sister, Melike, is shy and bookish with a talent for painting, and my youngest sister, Tansu, could charm every snake in the Empire. My father is retired from the army, due to ill health, and has ambitions for his son, that is to say myself, to take over in his stead. And my mother? Well, she wants to marry me off as soon as possible. There. Now you know everything. Your turn.'

'I didn't make any promises,' she said. 'Seems to me you were entertaining yourself.'

He laughed, and her colour deepened.

'At least tell me what it is you do when you're not wielding pitchforks.'

He had the satisfaction of extracting a small smile.

'I help Bayan Stewart at the school. And I'm a nurse's assistant at Dr Stewart's hospital.'

'I've met Dr Stewart. He's a serious man.'

This, he could see, was easier for her, safer than talking about her family, or anything concerning herself. She spoke for a time about the Stewarts, and he learned how they were in the village as long as she could remember. How Dr Stewart was respected and how he had set up a hospital in the village, which people travelled to from as far as Trebizond, and beyond. The American spoke Turkish, Armenian and Kurmanji badly, she said, but people made allowances for him because he worked hard. Mrs Stewart, or Bayan Stewart as she was known, was a doctor for women and had taken over the running of the school after the previous teacher left. She had also set up a sewing and embroidery cooperative for girls and was much loved by the village women.

By this time, they had come to the end of the beach, and the base of the headland loomed before them. They could only go back, but the captain found that he didn't want the conversation to end.

'What's that?' he asked, pointing to the cliff. 'At the top?'

'A ruined church. And a graveyard.'

'Is it possible to get up there?'

Pointing out rough-hewn steps cut into the side of the cliff, she said that it was, but that few people went there because some believed it was haunted by ghosts.

'Can you show me?'

She hesitated, and he thought she would refuse, but she turned and climbed up the slippery stone, telling him to watch where it was eaten away in places. Picking his footing carefully, he followed her, struck by the ease with which she climbed. It was clear she had done this many times before, and ghosts did not deter her. At the top, the wind blew directly in their faces and whined between the headstones in the tiny graveyard. Some stones had fallen into the sea, and others leaned over like stumps in an old man's jaw. The church itself was a small beehive-shaped building, with part of the roof missing and the main doorway skewed slightly to the west so that it looked out over the sea but away from the prevailing wind. Inside, the render had long since fallen away, revealing the stone-mason's ingenuity in constructing a circular wall with layers of chiselled granite blocks. The stone floor was speckled with bat and bird droppings, and the place smelled of must and salt. He walked around the walls, grit cracking beneath his boots, while she watched from the entrance. There was nothing else to see, no ornament, no icons, nothing of any religious nature, except a short transept at the apex of the circle opposite the door. A swallow flew over his head and darted out into the sunlight.

'Only a bird would find this homely,' he said, his voice competing with the moaning wind. 'I feel as though I'm standing at the centre of a drum.'

'Go to the back,' she said. 'The very back.'

He moved to the darkest part of the church, to the wall opposite the doorway. In the space of a few paces, the noise of the wind dropped, and the place became eerily quiet. He stepped back towards the door, and there it was again, the wind whistling and sighing.

'Extraordinary!'

But she hadn't heard because she had gone outside. He could see her dark-blue skirt and light-coloured blouse moving among the gravestones, her head bent and the sun shining on the plait hanging below her scarf.

'I have to go,' she said when he joined her.

'Let me walk with you.'

'No. I can go home this way.'

He tried to insist, but she wouldn't hear of it.

'You never told me your name,' he called after her.

She stopped and turned around. 'Anyush.'

'Very nice to meet you Anyush. My name is—'

'I know your name.'

Quickly, she crossed the headland and disappeared into the hazel wood beyond.

We are finally something like a proper medical practice, if 'proper' is the right word. The small maid's room is now furnished with microscope, specimens and slides. I've been obliged to use the kitchen as an operating room and our downstairs parlour has become the consulting room. The patients I find waiting for me every morning come in all shapes and sizes: men in salvar trousers, tent-like kaftans and Western suits; women veiled, cloaked and burquaed; children standing at their mothers' sides and one or two sitting in the branches of the fig tree. In the beginning they liked to stare sullenly at me, as though I do not measure up to their idea of a doctor and they are already regretting abandoning the local chekeji, but I think finally we are reaching an understanding. They have had to adjust to my ways, and I must adjust to theirs. The local ideas of rank and influence, for example, were familiar to me from our time in Constantinople, but, if anything, are more pronounced here. There is a system of caste, a pecking order of those who must be seen first, no matter who is the most ill or infirm. It is related to the country's long and troubled history and can neatly be summarised as Turk, Kurd and lastly Armenian. The Turks are the ruling class, the oppressors, if you like, even though historically the Armenians were here first. And the Kurds are fierce hill tribes who think nothing of killing a man for his horse or his money. They command respect even from the Turks. That leaves the Armenians, who are viewed by the government as being sympathetic to Russia, the old enemy, and so have little chance to improve their station in life. Paul and I have had many discussions on the subject. He believes the Armenians are unfairly oppressed, but, as I've often told him, the Turks are a territorial race and all outside alliances are viewed with mistrust.

Meanwhile, I've acquired a guide. A personal bodyguard probably describes him best, and he comes with me whenever I leave the village and sometimes when I'm still here. Hetty says she expects to find him eating breakfast with me any day now or sitting with his rifle in our bed. He's a Kurd by the name of Mahmoud Agha, who brought his youngest son to see me with one of the worst cases of trachoma I've seen. The boy was almost blind, but after I had successfully treated him, Mahmoud assigned himself the job of my guide and protector. Like most of the mountain Kurds, he's a farmer, and spends his time with his flocks of sheep and horses. He has three older sons, a wife he referred to as 'kuldeoken' or 'ash-dumper', and many 'children', as he calls his daughters. Hetty has been allowed treat his girls when they're ill and many of the local women also, but the men will only see me, Doktor Stippet as I'm known. I was telling Paul about this and about some of the unusual cases I had seen when he came to dinner this evening. In particular, the numerous and distressing incidents of children with burns and branding-iron scars to the neck and belly.

'Burning is thought to cure trauma,' Paul explained. 'Or any kind of fright.'

I told him I thought that kind of ignorance was appalling, but he advised me not to dismiss the traditional cures.

'You're not seriously promoting them?'

'No, but you'll find the old remedies are as important to them as the new. If you force people to choose, they'll return to what they're used to.'

'Even if it's misguided and dangerous? Our role is to educate as well as to treat.'

'Education by example, Charles. Once they see that western medicine is effective, more effective, you'll win them over. Although never completely.'

We talked on in this vein, and I told him about a six-year-old child I had seen in the surgery this morning called Anyush Charcoudian. She had not been burned or forced to ingest some horrible concoction, but I suspected she had been beaten and probably by her mother. Paul thought this was unusual. He said that Turkish children are generally well behaved and their parents moderate in matters of corporal punishment, but in this instance there can be little doubt. The child was sitting outside my surgery with her grandmother, bleeding from a cut over her eye when I called her into my room. She glanced apprehensively at the old woman but walked in obediently. The cut was deep, requiring several stitches, and although it was difficult and took a while to suture, not one word escaped her during the whole procedure. Afterwards, she stared at the instruments and charts on the wall and I asked her grandmother what had happened and where was the child's mother. The old woman's refusal to meet my eye was not that unusual, but something about her put me on my guard. It is a wariness every doctor feels when he realises he is hearing only a version of the truth. A fall from a tree had caused her granddaughter's injury and the mother was too busy to come. It was entirely possible of course that when the child hit the ground she made contact with something sharp, but I noticed red linear marks along her cheek and bruising near her ear. Although the story did not convince me, the old woman seemed genuinely concerned, and the child was obviously very attached to her. On the pretext of listening to her lungs and palpating her belly, I looked for other signs of trauma. There was nothing much to see except a fading, yellowish-green bruise above her left elbow. Accident or pulling injury? I could not tell. She was a striking child with huge brown eyes and chestnut-coloured hair. Quite an unforgettable little girl, so that I found myself wondering what kind of person would do her harm. I offered her one of Hetty's cookies, which I keep in a jar on my desk, but she seemed reluctant to take it. Her eyes flicked to her grandmother for permission before she took one and bit into it. The shock and delight on her small face when she tasted the sugary cookie made me smile. The old woman smiled too, and for no other reason than the obvious pleasure she took in her grandchild, I asked no more questions.

Anyush

The early morning sun hung low in the sky, and the part of the meadow bordering the wood was in deep shade. From the trees came the melodies of the dawn chorus and the rustlings of animals foraging for the coming day. A light mist lay suspended on the burnt grass, wetting Anyush's boots and the hem of her skirt. As she walked the track, she was thinking of the soldier and their conversation on the beach. She hadn't been able to sleep thinking about the stupidity of what she had done. Anyone could have seen her with him. Someone from the village. Her friends. Her mother. If Khandut had even the smallest suspicion Anyush would be thrown out of the house, or worse. She had been beaten many times for less. Why had she brought him to the church? The trick of the wind was her discovery and hers alone. Every moment she had been with him her heart was in her mouth but she hadn't been able to walk away. He'd talked and talked, clever words meant to impress, and to her own ears she sounded like a peasant girl with a thickened peasant tongue. Why had she risked her reputation to walk with a soldier? If Sosi found out, she would never forgive her. And for all Parzik's talk, she would never look at another boy, except Vardan, and certainly not a Turk. *Himar, himar,* fool! Never again. She would stay away from the beach and avoid him altogether.

At the end of the clearing, the path turned to skirt around the wood and link up with the main road into the town. She looked around for soldiers or gendarmes and, seeing none, began to walk in the direction of the hospital. Close to the village, she saw someone she knew walking ahead of her.

'Sosi ...Wait!'

Her friend stopped as Anyush ran to catch up with her.

'Where were you yesterday?' Anyush asked. 'I brought pilaff for Havat but I couldn't find you.'

'Planting potatoes for Vardan's father.'

'You're working for old man Aykanian? Where was Vardan?'

'Keeping his fingernails clean for the wedding.'

Anyush laughed. Vardan was the most vain peacock ever to wear trousers.

'Parzik and Vardan have settled on a date, then?'

'Day after the Easter ceremonies.'

Sosi held up the basket of straw she was carrying.

'I'm starting on the wedding braids.'

'Parzik will be pleased. I'd better go,' Anyush said, 'I'm late.'

'Just to tell you ... Husik is hiding over there.'

Anyush's landlord's son was good at hiding. She had seen Husik cross the forest floor, without breaking a twig, and slip his body into the smallest of places. Most often, he hid from his father, who had a quick temper, but he also stayed away from the soldiers who wanted him for the army and the gendarmes who treated him like a fool. The villagers called Husik 'the wild boy' because he lived in the wood and ate what he caught in his traps. His boots were made from cow leather he had tanned himself and smelled of the manure he used to cure them. His old, patched trousers were tied to his legs with cat-gut, and his shirt, many years too small and without sleeves or collar, strained across his chest. In the past few weeks he had started working for Dr Stewart, and Nurse Manon had given him a long white coat to wear over his clothes and a pair of shoes which she kept for him at the clinic. She made sure he washed at the pump and combed his wild hair, and Husik meekly complied. She was one of the few people he would take direction from and there weren't many. He had a temper like his father and wasn't afraid to use his knife, but there was a quieter side to him. From when Anyush was very small, Gohar had told her to be kind to Husik because his mother was dead and his father neglected him. Kazbek was a dangerous man, who mistreated his son and beat him often. It made the boy angry, and it was only with the Charcoudians that he was in any way calm. He followed Anyush like a lamb, waiting for her, every morning, to let out the hens and help with her chores. They didn't talk much and were companions more than friends. 'He's lonely,' Gohar used to say, 'be kind.' But Anyush spent her time by the sea, which Husik had a fear of, so they weren't together as often as he would have liked. As they grew older, Husik began to change. He stopped speaking to Anyush and no longer called to the house. She saw him in the distance, herding his father's cattle or bringing a brace of rabbits to the town, but she sensed he was never very far away.

'My mother says he's possessed of a *jinn*,' Sosi said, shivering.

'Ignore him,' Anyush said. 'Tell Havi I'll bring some pilaff later.'

This is the first free moment I've had in many months to write in my diary and there is much to relate. The practice is thriving and I'm finding very little time for anything else. Earlier this week, I received news that my paper on 'The Causes and Treatment of Trachoma in the Eastern Ottoman Empire' has been accepted by the *American Journal of Medicine*, and I am more than pleased. It is only the start of my research but a promising one.

Turkey, as ever, exerts its many demands. I've had to learn the skills of a surgeon, an anaesthetist, a physician, a pathologist and a dentist. People here believe I can do everything from lancing a boil to determining the sex of their babies, and I haven't managed to disabuse them of it. I'm not complaining though. I enjoy the work and need the income, and the thorny old question of money is never very far from my mind. If Hetty and I had never considered ourselves to be missionaries on arriving in this country, our state of penury means we certainly live like them. The villagers are too poor to pay, or pay with chickens and whatever else they can spare. The wealthier patients often don't bother, or wait to see if they are cured before even considering it. We receive a small monthly stipend from Elias Riggs which is spent mostly on medical supplies and doesn't go very far, and we'd probably starve but for Hetty's thrift and ingenuity. She has planted maize and vegetables behind the house and we keep a few chickens and a goat. These are the mainstay of our existence and at certain times we live almost entirely on goat's milk and turnip. Paul never calls without gifts of French cheese, or bottles of Italian wine, or Turkish delight for Thomas and baby Eleanor, even though I know he doesn't have much himself. He also brings plenty of gossip from the town and from Constantinople. Hetty really looks forward to Paul's visits and I think at times she misses the mental stimulation of New York. Politics has always been a huge interest of hers, and when Paul comes to stay we sit up late into the night discussing world affairs, or whatever gossip he manages to pick up in Trebizond's bazaars. I enjoy these evenings but Paul's opinions sometimes surprise me. He has a particular bias towards Armenians and believes, wrongly in my view, that they are subject to all sorts of harsh rules and regulations at the hands of the Turks. I've seen no evidence of this discrimination and find the Turks to be a fair-minded, tolerant sort of people who love nothing better than to talk. But Paul is a soft-hearted man, the kind who always shouts for the underdog. He has a very English sense of fair play, but it is not terribly balanced.

Anyush

The light softened in the early evening, but the heat remained, and the path along the road was dusty and hot. Anyush took the short-cut through the wood where the low red sun flashed between the trees and the birds roosted noisily. She was thinking of the conversation she'd had a few days previously with Dr Stewart.

'You should be a proper nurse,' he said. 'Your talents are wasted as an assistant. Nurse Manon and I have discussed this, and we would like you to train.'

Anyush's work at the hospital was long and sometimes unpleasant, but she never thought of it as a waste. Training as a nurse would mean moving to the Municipal Hospital in Trebizond for two years and leaving the village. Anyush had always thought she would be a teacher, like Bayan Stewart, but Dr Stewart had Nurse Manon on his side, and it was impossible to argue with her.

'It is the correct path for you. You will have money and food and excellent training. Of course you will go.'

On hearing the news, Anyush's mother had not been happy.

'Dirty work! No better than a hamal.'

In the village, nursing the sick was thought to bring bad luck, but, in the end, Khandut knew her daughter's chances of making a marriage were poor and money was scarce, so she had reluctantly agreed to the training. Anyush would leave the village at the beginning of autumn for two years.

Following the track until it joined the road, Anyush left the wood behind her. On the seaward side, the setting sun had dipped towards the ocean, and she turned to catch the last of the light on her face.

'*Barev*, Anyush.'

'*Barev*, Husik,' she said, without opening her eyes.

'How did you know it was me?'

'Because it's always you.'

He walked along beside her, smelling of sweat and animal blood and newly turned earth.

'I saw you at Parzik's shordzevk last night,' he said. 'With the other women.'

'What if I was?'

'I heard the Mongol is to be allowed sew the hem of the dress.'

'You seem to know a lot about the wedding, Husik.'

'I was there to slaughter the goat. That's all.'

Eznmortek usually involved slaughtering a cow, but Parzik's mother couldn't afford a cow and could ill afford the goat.

'You stayed too late,' he said.

'That's none of your concern.'

'It's not safe to be out alone.'

Anyush opened her eyes and looked at him. It was the first conversation of any length they'd had in a very long time.

'Of course I was safe. There were lots of us there.'

'They won't protect you. There are soldiers everywhere.'

'What if there are?!' Anyush snapped.

Husik stared at her, his mud-coloured eyes taking in the heightened colour of her face.

'Anyway,' she said. 'I knew you'd be around.'

He half smiled then so that she could see the gap where he had lost a tooth after one of his traps recoiled in his face.

'Will you be at the wedding?' he asked.

'Of course.'

The entire village would be there. A celebration the like of which hadn't been seen since before the war. Every family felt the loss of their men, but it would be an excuse to think of something other than loneliness and empty bellies. A reason to dance. Anyush shivered.

'Go home, Husik,' she said.

Husik stood at the entrance to his father's farm, watching until she rounded the bend.

Today is a red-letter day in the history of our village. This morning, in the presence of the townspeople and many dignitaries, including the Vali himself, we opened the doors to our new hospital. After ten months waiting for permits, and lumber, and stone, the village hospital is finally finished. People queued to see it from early in the morning and Hetty set up a table inside the main door with sweet treats for the children and rice pilaff for the adults. Many of the villagers brought gifts of their own, grape butter in little goat-hair bags, cheese and goats' milk. The general consensus was that the hospital was most magnificent, and Doktor Stippet and his khanum had done very well. The oddest aspect of the day was my own sombre mood. I couldn't shake the feeling that this had somehow fallen short. Paul was first to notice.

'Cheer up, Charles,' he said, my son's legs draped around his shoulders. 'If the wind changes and all that.'

'I am perfectly cheerful.'

'You look miserable.'

'Apparently I always do.'

He laughed and set Thomas down to run over to his mother.

'So why the long face?' he asked.

I looked at the new building, a small, two-storey stone structure built around a service courtyard to the rear and divided into male and female sides. Fully finished, it is more or less as I imagined it, but only on the outside.

'We ran out of money,' I told him.

From the fund Elias Riggs had given us, large portions were spent long before the foundation stone was laid. Bribes and permits, greedy builders and thieving workmen. By the time the structure was built, there was no money left to furnish it.

50

'Looks very impressive from here,' Paul said.

'Until you look inside.'

I told him how the operating room consists of our kitchen table covered in a sheet of zinc and a mop bucket to catch the blood. How there is no way of sterilising instruments and how we're boiling them in the kettle. How we have no X-ray apparatus, no heating, no dry room for clothes in winter, no separate rooms for contagious cases or TB cases, and most of my operating instruments I've had to make myself.

'Work as usual then,' Paul laughed.

A line of villagers was coming and going through the main door, some eating pilaff from vine leaves with their fingers and others stopping to talk to the khanum. Watching Mahmoud Agha's wife putting pilaff into the pocket of her dress, I tried to explain to Paul that I had wanted to build something exceptional. A modern facility. He reminded me that things happen very slowly in Turkey and that everything would come together eventually. I just needed a little faith.

'Faith?' I said. 'Maybe that's where I went wrong.'

Over by the table of food Hetty was holding baby Robert in her arms while trying to prise a fistful of cookies from Thomas's and Eleanor's hands. She had worn her blue silk dress for the occasion and had taken extra trouble with her hair. Her cheeks were a little flushed, and as she bent to whisper in Thomas's ear I was struck by her girlish prettiness.

'Why don't you give yourself a break?' Paul said, watching her. 'Come to town for a few days.'

For once, the idea was appealing. I couldn't actually remember when I had last been to Trebizond.

'Bring Hetty to the hotel for a night or two. Spoil her a little, Charles. She doesn't see enough of you.'

I turned to say that I would, but my friend's attention was elsewhere. He was looking at Hetty with such undisguised longing that for the first time I began to wonder if Paul Trowbridge was not in love with my wife.

Anyush

Night had fallen outside as Anyush looked at her reflection in the darkened glass. There was no mirror in the cottage and she had to stand on a chair to see in the window. Craning her neck around, she looked at how the dress fell in two graduated layers at the back. It was a little too long, but when she stood on her toes the effect was perfect. An elegant woman in a beautiful, American dress. Bayan Stewart had made her a gift of it, but Anyush had to wait for her mother to leave the house before she could try it on. Parzik would have given her entire trousseau to be married in a dress like this. It was made from a fine white material, light like clouds and delicate as sea-spray. The hem was a little dirty from Bayan Stewart's last outing but Anyush had never seen anything like it, especially the hand-sewn flowers and lace cuffs. Pulling her hair from her plait, Anyush piled it onto her head the way Bayan Stewart arranged hers. The doctor's wife was very beautiful, perfect as a woman in a painting and very different to Anyush's mother. Khandut pinned her hair tightly to her head and kept it hidden beneath a scarf. Beauty was a weakness, she said, a flaw like vanity itself. Bayan Stewart was not vain. She dressed plainly and wore no jewellery except a pair of emerald earrings which made tiny tapping noises whenever she moved her head. She had large grey eyes, skin like honey and hair the colour of wet sand. Anyush had often wondered why a woman like Bayan Stewart would live in a village such as theirs, but then her life was different from the other village women. She could work as a doctor and speak to her husband as if she was his equal. Dr Stewart, with his dark skin and beard, might have been born in Turkey. People said there was no disease he couldn't cure but that his spirit was restless. He was a man with his eye on tomorrow when today was barely done. A good man, but a strange and difficult giaour.

Anyush's reflection stared back at her in the glass, and something else – a dark figure creeping away towards the wood. She jumped down from the chair and pulled open the door.

'Husik!'

The trapper's dog was barking somewhere in the distance.

'Husik, I know you're there.'

There was no answer, only the distant wash of the sea and the blood pounding in her ears.

'Stay away from me, you hear? You mean nothing to me, Husik Tashjian. Nothing!'

Going back inside, she pulled off the dress and hid it in a corner of the loft.

Two more TB patients arrived at the hospital today. They were both children, so I've put them on the female ward which is almost empty, but this is a situation which cannot continue. An isolation unit was included in the original hospital plan, and I haven't given up hope on finding some way to fund it. Elias Riggs is slow to respond to my letters, but his answer is always the same: we will have to make do. Since the hospital opened there is more pressure than ever to bring in income, especially now that we have our first member of staff. Manon Girardeau is Matron and Head Nurse, the only nurse in fact. She arrived to my office from Trebizond one morning, a substantial presence blocking my exit through the door-way. She's of French Lebanese background and came originally to Constantinople with her mother's family. Roughly the same height as myself and with the frame and physique of a blacksmith, she's an imposing figure and commands instant respect. It was Paul who told me she was looking for a position and that she had worked with him in the Municipal Hospital as a theatre nurse for many years. I knew he thought a lot of her, but I wondered why she would move to a small, badly equipped, underfunded hospital in the sticks.

Yesterday, during a visit to the Vali to extract one of his teeth, I happened to mention our new arrival and he grinned knowingly, saying there had been an incident.

'*Un scandale*,' he told me.

I pressed him for details, but he would say no more. Paul knows something but is clearly uncomfortable talking about it, so I let it go. I did however decide to interview Manon, before taking her on, and she left me in no doubt as to which of us would be in charge.

'The hospital is run by me and the staff they will answer to me. You are told only if there is a *problème*.'

'Well, I *am* the—'

'We choose new staff together and all must have my agreement before a decision is made.'

'I haven't actually decided—'

'*Alors*, the roster is written at the beginning of the week, and if there is a change, you talk to me.'

'I see.'

'I am paid every Thursday and in full before my *vacances* of six weeks to France.'

'Six weeks ...!'

'Otherwise, I work all days, except Friday.'

I chose not to tell her that aside from Hetty and myself there was no other staff, and hired her immediately.

Manon, it turns out, is exactly what the hospital needs. She's taciturn and sometimes brusque to the point of rudeness, but a better commander-in-chief I cannot imagine. The wards are running like clockwork, and, best of all, she has put manners on our more difficult patients. Even the Circassians bow before her impressive bulk. It means I have more time to devote to my neglected research, and Hetty has reopened the school, which has been closed since Jane Kent's time. I'm also discovering that Manon has very definite opinions about this country, and is not reticent when it comes to sharing them. Hetty was telling her recently about how I've increased the number of calls to patients a distance away because of *ayak teri* or 'foot-sweat', one gold lira for every hour of caravan time, which all goes into the hospital coffers. Manon expressed surprise, saying that the hills are full of bandits waiting to rob me and slit my throat. I don't think she appreciates how these people have accepted me, bandits included, and that I am in no danger. In fact, I look forward to these outings away from my normal routine, and with Mahmoud Agha at my side I have taken to this country as my own.

Two evenings ago the subject arose again with Manon over dinner.

'Do not fool yourself, Dr Stewart. You may like this country and it may like you, but it will never be your home. It is foolish to become sentimental about it.'

'I am not in the least sentimental,' I said. 'You are forgetting that your experience and mine may be quite different. As a woman that is.'

'The village is not Paradise, Dr Stewart. You think you are accepted here? *Non.* You will always be a giaour in this country, an unbeliever and a foreigner. For the Turks you will always be so, *rien de plus.*'

'My children know no other home,' I protested. 'What about them? You think America is their home? A place they have never seen?'

'Missionary children are not the same. You do not like to think so, but your children will not belong here *or* there. *Pas de problème*, they are young. They will adapt. But you ... you, Dr Stewart, should be careful.'

I told her I thought the Turkish opinion of women had left her rather biased, at which point Manon changed tack.

'For Jane Kent the village was home,' she said, looking at me over the top of her glass.

'Yes, but she didn't stay. We've no intention of leaving.'

'Jane and Paul were lovers. You knew this?'

Hetty said we'd guessed, and Manon proceeded to fill us in on the passionate and sometimes foolhardy nature of the affair.

'Are we to presume,' I asked, 'that since Jane is no longer here they were discovered?'

'Discovered? *Non.* Jane was attacked. Beaten very badly and ... the worst kind of attack.'

I was deeply shocked. Seeing my phlegmatic nurse on the verge of tears was as shocking as the story itself.

'Jane would not see anybody,' she said. 'Not me. Not her friends. Paul once ... twice *peut-être.*'

'Poor Paul,' Hetty said, looking through the dining-room window as though he was standing beneath the fig tree. 'And poor Jane. But are you saying this man assaulted her because he knew about their affair?'

'Of course not. He was evil, that is all. *Un criminel*! In this country there must be two witnesses to a crime. Two witnesses who are men. No witness ... *Alors! Le crime n'existe pas.*'

I remembered then the day of the hospital opening and the wistful look I had seen on Paul's face. I begin to wonder if what I saw was not so much a longing for my wife as a yearning for someone else.

Anyush

Parzik was standing beneath the trees at the start of the wood waiting for Anyush to pass by.

'Over here.'

'I was just going to see you,' Anyush said. 'Everybody's talking about the shordzevk.'

Parzik smiled. 'I wish I could do it again, but at least the dress is finished.'

'It was good of your mother to let Havat sew the hem.'

'I had to fix it though. A lot of it came undone.'

'Havat was happy.'

Parzik linked her arm, and they walked along the path skirting the wood. 'In one week I'll be a bride.'

'I'll have to call you Bayan Aykanian.'

'You'd better! Won't that be strange? It'll be your turn soon, Anyush. Wait and see, it'll happen. You just have to find the right boy.'

'I'm not going to get married, Parzik.'

'Yes, you will. There has to be someone in the village who doesn't mind your crazy habits and your mad mother.'

The girls smiled.

'A boy who's just as odd. I know ... Husik Tashjian!'

Anyush dropped Parzik's arm and pulled away.

'I'm joking ... hey, you know I'm joking.'

She caught Anyush's arm and they walked on. 'You have to be at my house early on the day. You and Sosi. You'll come early?'

'You know I will.'

'Before I'm awake? Promise, Anyush.'

'I promise.'

'Just so Vardan doesn't find me asleep.'

Parzik was making an effort to smile, but there were tears in her eyes. 'I don't want to leave the house, Anyush. There's been so much leaving. My mother is putting on a brave face, but I know she'll be thinking of my father and the boys. Stepan especially. It broke her heart when he joined the others. Not knowing where they are is killing her. Maybe I should stay.'

'Why would you think such a thing?'

'It feels wrong, Anyush. Whenever I think about the wedding, I'm afraid.'

'Don't think too much, t'Rchun. You love Vardan, and your mother likes him. She wants you to get married, doesn't she?'

Parzik nodded.

'Of course you're afraid. Who wouldn't be? Every daughter weeps when she leaves home. All weddings have tears.'

'I know, but I've been having terrible dreams.'

Parzik wiped her hand across her eyes. 'My father used to sing to me when I had bad dreams. He had a beautiful voice, remember? I wish he was here. I wish the boys were with me.'

A faded wedding picture came to Anyush's mind and a father who was known to her only from a photograph.

'Listen to me, Parzik, your wedding will be wonderful. You're nervous because brides are always nervous. Who wants to see a laughing monkey strutting down the aisle?'

'Or a big beaked bird!'

The girls laughed.

'Until the morning then?'

'Until the morning,' said Anyush.

Parzik nodded and walked back towards the village.

Diary of Dr Charles Stewart

Mushar

Trebizond

April 9th, 1915

I missed Thomas's birthday, and the boy will not speak to me. For the eldest of five children he sometimes behaves like the youngest, but then Hetty has always indulged him too much. She claims he's a sensitive soul and needs a little understanding. I tell her the local children would never have that luxury, but she doesn't listen. Robert and Milly are hardy creatures, although Robert has become a little wild of late. He and his older brother are returning to America in the Fall to finish their schooling, which will be something of a shock. Grandmother Fincklater will not tolerate sensitivity, or any other eccentricity they may have acquired. Privately, I am happy the girls are staying. Hetty of course believes it is unfair to educate our sons when the girls are just as clever, but I couldn't bear to be parted from them, especially Lottie. I suppose every father reserves a corner of his heart for his baby daughter, and I am no exception. Eleanor tends to whinge, and Milly only ever wants to be with Robert, but Lottie's smile would gladden the weariest of hearts.

Odd to think how time has passed. Hetty and I are now the old hands, veterans like Elias Riggs, who is still running the mission in Constantinople at the grand old age of eighty-two. It is difficult to believe we've been living in the Empire so long, and yet, at times, it feels like an eternity. I find myself thinking about it a lot these days. In fact, I can hardly think of anything else. My research has ground to a halt, and I can't seem to concentrate on anything to do with trachoma. Every evening I go to write up the patients I've seen that day, but my mind wanders. The smallest things distract me. Birds sound like foghorns and the noise of the schoolchildren across the road irritates me beyond belief. I went back to making slides and tried to concentrate on titration of sulphonamide, but it is no use. Hour after hour, day after day, I sit staring at pages written only in my head. Hetty thinks I'm tired and that I'm doing too much.

'Take Mahmoud Agha and go to the hills. A change is what you need.'

But I'm wary of the hills, fearful of what might come under an empty blue sky. I *am* tired though and it worries me. Trachoma research is the work of a lifetime, and if I fail at this juncture then what am I doing here? For the first time since coming to Turkey I'm wondering about the wisdom of what I've done. Marvelling at the casual manner in which I threw over my career for an idea I had never given much thought to. And Hetty's career. It bothers me most of all to think of it. She doesn't begrudge the missed opportunities, or the loss of family and friends. I know she forgives my impatience with the children and intervenes on my behalf with them, but there are times I feel she's watching me. At her sewing, or reading a book, her eyes come to rest on my face, and I have to be careful not to look at her. I busy myself with whatever I'm doing because I'm afraid of what I might see. Worried that I'm pushing her away but incapable of doing anything about it. To avoid these wordless confrontations, I stay longer at the hospital. I've doubled the number of operations and have taken on two extra clinics in the week. Manon thinks I've lost my reason, but she remains by my side and never leaves the hospital before me. Work has become my mistress and my obsession. My days are filled so completely that I have no time for introspection, or indeed anything else. Only my patients occupy my thoughts and a couple of hours of dreamless sleep.

April 11th

Stayed up most of the night trying to make the accounts balance. This hospital is like an amorphous beast, rabidly devouring whatever money we make. Even the staff seems to grow in a manner I have little control over. Manon has taken on two student nurses, Mari and Patil, on secondment from the Municipal Hospital. She had previously employed Anyush Charcoudian as an assistant nurse and Husik Tashjian as an orderly. I was committed to taking on two medical students, Bedros

Bezjian and Professor Levonian's son, Grigor, for training in eye surgery, and we've had Malik Zornakian running the dispensary since last year. All excellent staff, all needing to be paid. Malik is constantly in my office complaining about supplies. Because of the war, thirty cases of medicine on their way from America were taken by the government in Alexandretta, and a second shipment could not get beyond Egypt. All new shipments have been grounded at the ports because every available horse and wagon has been commandeered by the army. Even Mahmoud Agha is afraid to leave his village in case his horses are requisitioned. And if that wasn't trouble enough, the country is experiencing the worst famine in years. It is depressing to see this once fertile land look as desolate as the Sahara. The grain withers from the root, as if it has been burnt by fire, and people are subsisting on wild mustard and turnip. Whole populations have deserted the outlying villages, looking to us for help. Hetty's soup kitchen is working to the limit of its capabilities, but food supplies are dwindling. Most of it we are growing ourselves, or try to on the mission farm, bought with money Hetty's parents sent. Arshen Nalbandian lost the farm when he couldn't pay the taxes on it, and I persuaded him and his two sons to stay and run it for me. A small herd of Guernsey cows arrived last year from England and we were managing well enough, but we've since lost one of the calves, and Arshen is finding it difficult to keep the herd watered now that his boys have gone to war. This morning he arrived at my door, wide-eyed and agitated, saying that soldiers had come to take the cattle. I went to see their commanding officer, a Captain Orfalea, whom I found stationed at the old grain store on top of the hill overlooking the village.

'My apologies, Dr Stewart,' he said, shaking my hand. 'I can only offer you bad coffee.'

The captain was a young, good-looking fellow who spoke excellent English and was obviously not from these parts. His assessment of the coffee was accurate, but we both tossed it off as though it was the finest brew. We spoke about my work and local matters generally before he asked the question I am in dread of hearing.

'I've heard you're a missionary, Dr Stewart. Is it true?'

I attempted a non-committal gesture.

'I'm always fascinated by the Western urge to impose Christianity on the heathen Turk,' the captain smiled. 'During my training I spent time in the Military Academy in Paris and saw more godlessness on the streets there than in the slums of Constantinople.'

'Captain Orfalea,' I said wearily, 'a number of years ago I might have attempted to convince you of my missionary credentials but not any more. My interest lies in saving lives, not souls, and I'm under no illusion that your countrymen had the measure of me before ever I stepped off the boat.'

'I like your honesty, Dr Stewart,' the captain smiled. 'Now let me be honest with you. You've come about the cattle I presume?'

I told him that I had, and that they were missionary property.

'I'm under orders, Dr Stewart. Soldiers must be fed or they cannot fight.'

'Even if it means the villagers starve?'

'There are other sources of food. The sea is full of fish.'

'The fishermen are gone and their boats with them. You've been here for some time, Captain. You've seen the failed crops and dead animals in the fields. The cow's milk is the only nourishment some of the children have in the entire day.'

He listened without comment, and I pressed on. 'If you take the cattle, they will probably die of starvation anyway. It won't make a huge difference to you, but it could mean the life or death of a child. For many of the villagers. Think about it, Captain. Do the people here seem well nourished to you?'

He looked out through the small barred window set into the stone wall. Through it the spire of the Armenian church was just visible over the tops of the trees.

'Very well, Dr Stewart,' he said. 'I will not requisition the cattle. But if I discover you're hiding food or animals from me, I will take the lot.'

Anyush

A hazy, opal-coloured sky cleared to a cloudless blue on the morning of the wedding. Preparations were well under way by the time Sosi, Havat and Anyush got to the Setian house. At the stove in the yard Parzik's sisters were preparing food for the arrival of the groom's party, and the bride was sitting at the kitchen table where Bayan Setian was painting her hands with henna. Mother and daughter were singing softly to each other:

'Colour one hand with henna
Don't colour the other
To take the cares of your mother.'

Parzik looked up when the girls came in and held out her hands.
'Today's the day,' she said, smiling.
'Today ... today.' Havat nodded.
The small house had been decorated with wildflowers, ribbons and Sosi's straw braids, which hung in garlands above the holy pictures and around the windows and doors. A photograph of Parzik's father and two older brothers in uniform, and another of her youngest brother, Stepan,

sat among bunches of white daisies and poppies.

'Go on. Off you go,' Bayan Setian said, shooing the girls upstairs to the bedroom Parzik shared with her sisters. 'Vardan will be here, and there'll be no bride waiting for him. And take your veil, Parzik.'

The house quickly filled with the village women who brought trays of food and small gifts. Parzik's godparents, Elsapet and Meraijan Assadourian, had arrived earlier and, as the family elders, would give her away. Elsapet was a small, dark-eyed woman lost in the folds of her many black layers. Her head trembled on the stalk of her thin neck and her bony hands plucked constantly at the fabric of her skirts. Her husband Meraijan was very tall for an Armenian, and it was from him that Parzik inherited her height and beak-like nose. For the occasion of his god-daughter's wedding he was wearing a white side-buttoning shirt, dark wool trousers and a cotton arkhaluk, the brightly embroidered traditional Armenian tunic tied about the middle with a large-buckled belt. Meraijan was the village elder, the man who settled disputes, negotiated with the Jendarma and officiated at all Armenian ceremonies. Nothing happened in Mushar without his permission or his blessing.

The single girls had started to arrive in twos and threes, and the married women gathered in a huddle of black by the tables of food, their small children running at their feet. The Tufenkian sisters had closed their shop for the day and only Khandut Charcoudian had not come.

From an upstairs window, Anyush looked down on the crowd in the street below, a sea of brightly coloured waistcoats, silk breeches, embroidered caps and red fezes. Everybody was waiting for the sazandar, the wedding band that would announce the groom's arrival. Behind her, Sosi and two of Parzik's sisters were finishing the bride's hair.

'She wanted me to wear her old arkhaluk,' Parzik was saying, 'the one *she* got married in.'

'I'd like to wear my mother's wedding costume. If she offered it to me.'

'You haven't seen it, Sosi. It's so old it looks like a Persian rug. *And* she wanted me to put tassels in my hair and cover my face.'

'I think it's a nice tradition.'

'That's exactly what I *didn't* want. Look at us,' Parzik said, spinning around and upsetting the hairpins onto the floor. 'We live in a new century. We're from a different age. We'll never be like our mothers.'

'She made a nice dress,' Havat said, nodding to herself.

'Yes, Havi. A beautiful, modern dress like you might see in Constantinople or Paris.'

Anyush thought it *was* beautiful, and that Parzik would look beautiful in it. Everyone stood back and admired t'Rchun when she went to the mirror by the window. Her braids were wound into a coil at the back of her neck, and her mother's pearls gleamed softly at her ears. Kohl ringed her green eyes so that they sparkled like emeralds, and her high colour lent a feminine softness to her face. Parzik had never looked as happy, or as well.

Faint strains of music drifted in through the open window.

'They're here!' Anyush said. 'The sazandar is coming.'

The music grew louder as the wedding band rounded the corner at the end of the street. There was only a handful of old men playing the instruments as all the younger men were in the army. The lead musician, Arshen Nalbandian, who ran Dr Stewart's mission farm, played the kamanche and the duduk, and behind him came the Zornakian twins, who were married to the Tutenkian sisters and ran the shop in the village. They played the daf and the doumbek, beating out the rhythm on a tambourine and drum. At the rear came Nayiri Karapetyan, a close friend of Parzik's father, who played the tar and the oud. Behind them all, strutting like a peacock, was Vardan the groom.

The girls crowded around the window.

'Where's the basket?' Parzik demanded, pushing one of her twin sisters out of the way. 'He's supposed to be carrying the basket with my shoes in it.'

'His father has it. Look … he's coming along after him,' Sosi said.

Slightly stooped and thin as a whippet, old man Aykanian walked behind his son, dressed in a worn-looking arkhaluk and carrying a covered basket in his hand. He was waving and smiling, no trace on his bony features of his customary frown. Aykanian looked more like Vardan's grandfather than his father, because he had married a young bride in his middle years and lost her after the birth of his son.

'What are you doing, Parzik?'

Bayan Setian gripped her daughter firmly by the arm and pulled her away from the window.

'You are not supposed to see the groom before your godparents, and certainly not in your underwear.'

Her eye fell to the hairpins on the floor.

'Am I mistaken? Has old age deprived me of my few remaining senses or is it really my middle daughter who is getting married today? Perhaps it is you, Monug? Or you, Aghavnik? You at least have clothes on!'

The twins giggled as Sosi helped Parzik into her dress. Seranoush, Parzik's older sister, put her head around the door.

'Elsapet and Meraijan are asking for you,' she said to her mother.

Bayan Setian smoothed down her skirt and glanced at herself in the mirror. 'Finish your hair, Parzik. And make sure your feet are clean.'

While Sosi and the twins put the finishing touches to the bride's dress, Anyush watched Vardan make his way to the Setian house. His dark hair was shiny with oil and slicked back over his ears. He wasn't dressed traditionally as his father was, but wore a white shirt and stiff collar, a new-looking jacket and trousers and shiny brown leather boots. He was clean-shaven, except for his trimmed moustache, and his light brown eyes were seeking out every good-looking girl in the crowd. Anyush glanced over at Parzik who was smiling to herself.

'Come on, Anyush!' Sosi called. 'Parzik's ready.'

They moved downstairs just as Meraijan opened the door on a bowing, smiling Vardan.

'I come bearing gifts,' he said, taking the basket from his father.

Inside was a bottle of vodka, a flask of perfume and the bridal shoes. The sazandar resumed playing, and the house was suddenly filled with music and clapping. On cue, a barefoot Parzik came down the stairs, and Seranoush followed, carrying her veil. Bayan Setian nodded approvingly as Meraijan took the wedding shoes from the basket and handed them to his god-daughter. But before Parzik could put them on, each of the twins grabbed a shoe and ran around the crowd.

'*P'rkagin, p'rkagin*, ransom, ransom!'

The old men pulled out their empty pockets and the women turned up their bare palms, and just as the strains of the sazandar slid into a minor key, Vardan's father stepped forward and dropped a five-livre note into a twin's hand. Everybody clapped as Parzik was escorted to a chair and handed her shoes. The single girls gathered around her, waiting in turn to write their name on the soles. As each girl married, her name would be crossed off.

'I hope yours is the first to go,' Parzik whispered to Anyush when her turn came.

'I hope not,' Anyush said with a laugh.

'Ay, ay, ay...' everybody chanted, as the men tossed back large glasses of vodka.

'Again!' Vardan called, holding out his empty glass.

'The church,' Bayan Setian said, taking it from him.

Vardan and Parzik stepped outside to a cheer from the waiting crowd. The bride was fully veiled, her face and dress covered, and her hennaed hands hidden in white gloves. She was smiling, but kept her eyes modestly cast down. The sazandar led the wedding procession in a long line towards the church, and, in the confusion, Anyush got separated from the others. Husik stepped off the street into the crowd at her back, his pale face bearing down on her like a stormy moon. They had almost reached the church steps when Anyush noticed the gendarmes. Everywhere. More of them, it seemed, than usual. They didn't approach or interfere but stood beneath the trees, their faces in shadow.

'I lost Sosi,' a voice at her shoulder said. Havat grabbed a fistful of Anyush's skirt, flower petals falling from her hair. 'I want Sosi.'

'She's just there, Havi. Up ahead, see? Behind Parzik.'

'I want Sosi.'

Taking her by the hand, Anyush skirted around the procession towards the front. Up ahead she could see Sosi's dark hair, and she was trying to catch her attention when a man in uniform bowed to her. The captain was standing beside the lieutenant and smiling, showing all his teeth like a woman might show her pearls. His hat was under his arm so that the sun shone on his shiny black hair, and his buttons gleamed like polished diamonds. Anyush turned away, pretending she hadn't seen him.

'Havi ... there you are!' Sosi reached behind her and took her sister's hand. 'Come on, Anyush. We're supposed to go in together.'

An entire afternoon's work had to be put on hold today to attend the wedding of
Parzik Setian and Vardan Aykanian. There was no question of not going as weddings are something of a rarity, and everyone in the village including the hospital
staff were there. We left our shoes in the large pile inside the main door of the
church, and nodded and salaamed to the congregation sitting on the floor or kneeling by the side walls. The nave was divided into a sea of red fezes and turbans on
the left where the men were sitting and black veils and headscarves on the right.
Our seats were at the very front, directly behind the groom's family where the
children had a bird's eye view of the proceedings. Father Gregory waited at the
transept, mopping his face and adjusting his headpiece. It was already very warm,
the muggy heat intensifying under the blaze of candles from the chandelier hanging over the choir and the sconces along the walls. Everybody fanned themselves
with paper screens or the loose ends of veils, or anything else that came to hand.
My suit felt as if it was made of the thickest fleece, and the stiff collar I was wearing threatened to choke me. Heads turned constantly towards the door, wishing
the whole business would get under way. In the seat behind me Manon fanned her
flushed face and whispered that Paul had sent word he couldn't come.

'O glorious crown ...' the choir sang, and everybody rose to their feet.

A nervous-looking bride walked down the aisle on her godfather's arm to where
Vardan waited at the transept. Meraijan's wife, Elsapet, tied Parzik's and Vardan's
wrists together with ribbon, and the ceremony was under way. Finally, when the
heat had become unbearable and drops of sweat fell like a dripping faucet from the
priest's nose, the newly married couple walked down the aisle into the sunshine.
Everybody followed them outside.

'*Le mariage est vraiment l'enfer,*' Manon said, looking like she had been basted on a spit.

In front of us the bride lifted her veil and salaamed to her husband before setting off on a circuit of the square behind the local band.

'Doesn't everything look lovely?' Hetty said.

Colourful awnings had been strung across the lemon trees and tables set out beneath. A few chairs had been put in place for the wedding party, but everybody else would sit on rugs and cushions. Anyush's grandmother and some of the older women were putting the finishing touches to the food, and I spotted Father Gregory licking his lips in anticipation. I was thinking to slip away and go back to the hospital, but my stomach rumbled and I realised I was hungry. The smell was tantalising, but nobody was allowed eat until Meraijan had made the toast.

'To my god-daughter, Parzik, and her new husband, Vardan,' he said, raising his glass. 'May you grow old on one pillow.'

It was only as I drank that I noticed the line of gendarmes on the opposite side of the square. These were not local men, not patients of mine. We had a small coterie of Jendarma in the village, more or less unchanging from year to year, and I wondered at the need for so many of them. Just then, Meraijan announced that the feast would begin and everybody tucked in to the food: shish kebabs, rice pilaff, hummus, baba ganoush, and bourek. There were also plates of anchovies cooked in every conceivable way. Manon had brought some concoction of raki-soaked pigeon and my own children had made iced lemon cakes which went down well. It was a display such as hadn't been seen for years and, for which, many would go hungry in the weeks to come. Meagre rations had been pooled and it was a matter of pride that everyone would give something. After Fr Gregory and the bridal party had been served, the villagers fell on the food, filling their bellies with the concentration of the starved. As a habit, I like to eat alone, but I ate with enthusiasm, glancing every now and then at my wife, who looked particularly lovely in a large hat trimmed with roses.

Anyush

Anyush didn't want to dance. The pairing was the part of the day she had been dreading and had hoped to avoid. But when the duduk player stepped forward and announced the tamzara, Sosi pulled her onto the dancing ground after her. A hiss of excitement rippled through the crowd. For the tamzara unmarried men and women could mix and this was what Husik Tashjian had been waiting for. On one side, Anyush stood with Sosi, Havat and the other single girls, and, on the other, Vardan lined up with the two Stewart boys, Bedros from the hospital and Husik.

'Stop frowning, Anyush,' Sosi whispered. 'It'll be fun.'

Bedros smiled shyly at Anyush, and the trapper glowered at the young doctor. Anyush ignored them both.

'Really, Sosi... I don't want to.'

Gripping her friend by the hand, Sosi held her on one side and Havat on the other. The opening notes of the dance were played, and Husik made to push up the line opposite Anyush, but somebody else got there first.

'You'll have to teach me,' the captain said. 'And I must warn you my dancing is a little rusty.'

Anyush's mouth fell open and everybody grew silent. The musicians stopped playing and Meraijan gripped the arms of his chair. Parzik's face was frozen, and some of the women blessed themselves. Anyush stood in the line, her gaze fixed rigidly ahead. The wedding cloths flapped in the breeze and the seabirds wheeled closer to the food. Finally, Arshen Nalbandian took matters into his own hands. He put the duduk to his mouth and began to play again. As the strains of the tamzara drifted across the square, the dancers took up their positions. The music had a heavy, circular rhythm, repeating over and over as the dancers linked arms. To each beat they bent their knees and then straightened, leaned forward and then straightened again while stamping their feet and turning on their heels. The soldier's arm gripped Anyush's, but she refused to catch his eye. Nobody looked at anybody else, and only the captain seemed unaware of the atmosphere he had created. He fooled around and danced like a donkey as though he was completely alone. Whenever the others leaned forward, he leaned back, and as the entire line bent their knees he straightened his. Havat giggled as he tried to turn and bumped into Sosi and stood on the toes of the dancers opposite him. People began to smile. His dancing, if anything, was getting worse. They laughed as he pulled this way and that, throwing everybody out of line and deliberately making a fool of himself. After what seemed like an age, the music stopped and the dance came to an end. The captain bowed, Anyush nodded curtly, and they walked to opposite sides of the square as the musicians tuned up for the next dance.

It was to be performed by the village girls but Anyush would not take part. She had retreated to the shade with her grandmother to recover from her ordeal. The dance had only begun when the gendarmes made their move. The square was suddenly full of them, walking quickly towards the wedding party. They descended, guns drawn, on the table where the bride and groom and other family members were sitting. The leader of the group, a short, ginger-haired man, singled out Vardan's father.

'Mislav Aykanian ... by the authority of the Empire and the Committee of Union and Progress you are under arrest for treason.'

Two gendarmes moved either side of the old man and lifted him bodily from the chair.

'What? Wait ... what are you doing?' Vardan pushed past his bride to where his father was being dragged from the table. 'That's my father ... he hasn't done anything.'

'He's guilty of treason,' the gendarme said.

'Treason? No!'

'Rifles, bayonets and two rounds of ammunition were found on his farm.'

'We have no rifles. This is a mistake. My father owns nothing except hay forks and shovels. He's never held a rifle in his life.'

'Stand back or I'll arrest you too.'

The old man hung limply between the hands that held him, his eyes wide with fear.

'Take me,' Vardan said. 'Arrest me. It's my farm too.'

The ginger-haired gendarme moved his face close to Vardan's.

'You have a job to finish on the police barracks. But don't worry, when the time is right we'll come looking.'

They marched away, half dragging the old man as Vardan ran after them.

'He's innocent. Where are you taking him? He's innocent I swear!'

Dr Stewart caught Vardan by the arm.

'There's nothing you can do right now. Let me talk to them. We'll find out where they have taken him and decide what to do from there.'

The square was eerily quiet. Anyush looked at Parzik. She was standing behind her husband, her face white with shock. Vardan had slumped into a chair, his head in his hands, weeping. Everything was in disarray. People looked helplessly at each other, not knowing what to do. Dr Stewart whispered something to his wife and then followed the gendarmes along the street. On the opposite side of the square, a laneway led down to the river and Anyush saw the captain and his lieutenant disappearing into it. Without thinking, she ran after them.

'*Efendim*!' she called. 'Captain Orfalea!'

Both men turned around. The alley was dark and rank and not the place for a girl to be alone with Turkish soldiers.

'*Efendim*, may I speak with you?'

'Go on ahead,' the captain said to the lieutenant. 'I'll follow.'

'It's old man Aykanian,' Anyush said, struggling to find the right words. 'The groom's father ... they've arrested him.'

'Yes, I was watching.'

'They won't say where they're bringing him, but it must be some-where outside the village. It would mean a lot to ... to Vardan and the family if you could find out where they have taken him.'

'I can't interfere with local policing.'

'You have authority, *efendim*. More than any Armenian.'

'We have no influence over the gendarmes. They are completely inde-pendent of us.'

'You are someone they would respect, *bayim*.'

He shook his head and sighed. 'We do occasionally hear things but I can't promise you anything. I'll keep my ears open. It's the best I can do.'

'Thank you, *efendim*. I am in your debt.'

'Somehow I doubt that. Meet me in the ruined church in two days. Same time as before.'

She nodded and ran back to the square, hoping nobody had realised she was gone.

I went to see the Vali in Trebizond today. It is Bairam, the Muslim feast day, so there is a better chance of catching him in a favourable mood. The gendarmes who arrested Mislav on the day of the wedding would give me no information about the old man, only that he was to be tried for treason, which leaves me no option but to appeal to the governor himself.

Since our first meeting that day on the quayside at Trebizond, the Vali and I have become friends. I have been summoned to the mansion at all hours of the day and night to tend to his bad teeth and, as I come through the walled garden, I hear him bellowing like a bull and cursing the giaour who takes so long to arrive. When he sees me at the gate, he becomes meek as a lamb, opening his mouth wide and begging me to pull out the rotten tooth. Once it is extracted and oil of clove administered, I am usually invited to join him for supper or breakfast, or whichever meal he feels he is at the lack of.

Despite outward appearances, the Vali is intelligent and well educated, a man who generally deals fairly with his subjects but can be capricious and ill-tempered. Remaining in his fickle favour is crucial to the smooth running of the hospital and is one of the reasons I am willing to ride for three hours in the middle of the night to look into his mouth. The Vali pays handsomely but also in kind. Disputes with the gendarmes are settled, permits come through relatively quickly and many other favours are granted to me. It takes only a discreet word and the problem magically disappears. The Vali is my lucky card, my ace to trump the many frustrations of living in the Empire. So I rode to Trebizond in an optimistic mood.

I arrived just as the cannon-fire announced that *namaz*, the morning prayers, were over and the Vali was ready to receive. In the great hall, I was ushered past the crowd waiting for an audience and brought to the Vali's private quarters. He was seated at a low table finishing his morning meal.

'Stippet, my friend,' he said. '*Selamın Aleyküm.*'

'*Aleyküm Selam.*'

'Did I send for you? I did not think I sent for you. My new tooth is good. See.'

We discussed his new denture, which I had fitted on my last visit, before I mentioned that I was looking for a favour. He wagged his finger at me. 'Stippet, you are looking to build again.'

I told him I had come about another matter and described the events of Vardan's wedding day. At first, I thought I was imagining it, but then I realised there was a subtle but definite dimming in the brilliance of the Vali's smile. 'Aykanian is old and feeble,' I said, begging for clemency, 'just an ordinary farmer.'

But the Vali didn't appear to be listening. He was playing with the ring on his hand, as though he had never noticed it there before. 'If the gendarmes found rifles in his barn, then why should I think he is innocent?' he asked.

'Because I can vouch for him.'

'Your word means much in Trebizond, my friend, but there are favours even I cannot grant.'

In all my time in the Empire I had never been refused before, so I decided to try a change of tactics. I told the Vali I knew he had the ear of the Sultan and wondered if there was another avenue of appeal I could pursue?

He regarded me coldly, then rearranged his expression into one of sorrowful regret. 'Stippet, my friend, in certain cases where the Jendarma and the army are concerned I cannot interfere. Their orders come directly from Constantinople. Not from the Sultan but from the CUP. Now if this man was a Turk or caught stealing chickens perhaps I could do more.'

I should have guessed that the old Armenian question was at the bottom of this. The smallest whiff of sedition and Aykanian will be in real trouble. Of course, I have no way of knowing what the old man and his son are really involved in. The villagers are tribal and who knows where their allegiance lies?

The Vali pushed back his chair and his servant opened the door behind him.

'Come back, my friend, when you are building your new wing.'

Anyush

Anyush arrived long before the captain. Sitting inside the ruin, she had shelter from the wind and a view of the entire beach. In the days since the wedding nothing had been heard about old man Aykanian, and Parzik and Vardan were distraught. Dr Stewart and Meraijan Assadourian had approached the gendarmes for news of the old man's whereabouts but had been told nothing. Nobody seemed to have anything to say about Mislav Aykanian.

Deep in thought, Anyush hadn't noticed the captain standing in the doorway. At the sight of him her mouth went dry.

'I have news,' he said, coming inside. 'But not what you'd like to hear.'

In the dim light of the old ruin, Anyush felt cornered, cut off from the brightness outside. The ruin was too remote and she wished she had not gone so far in.

'They've taken him to Trebizond. To the city jail. It seems someone has spoken against him.'

'An informer?'

'Someone from the village. The gendarmes were acting on a tip-off. They were told to look for rifles and ammunition, and they found them under the floor of the hay barn.'

'The only weapon Aykanian possesses is a sharp tongue.'

'Well, it has made him enemies.'

'No one in the village would betray him. Someone must have put those rifles there.'

'What about his son ... the groom? Who's to say he's not working for the Russians?'

'Vardan only works at the shine on his boots.'

The captain laughed, the sound unnaturally loud in the circular space. He leaned against the wall, catching her glance towards the doorway.

'So the groom's a peacock then?'

'He's a farmer.'

'The perfect cover.'

'It wasn't Vardan. He didn't put rifles in the barn.'

In the silence that followed, the captain's eyes never left Anyush's face. They took liberties, those eyes, and she felt vulnerable and afraid. How had she thought it was safe to come here? To be alone with a Turkish officer? Deciding to bolt for the door, she took a quick step towards it.

'Not so fast!' He blocked her with his arm. 'How do you know my name?'

'You were talking to the lieutenant,' she said. 'I overheard you. He called you Captain Orfalea.'

'Jahan. My name is Jahan.'

The sun had dipped in the sky, and there was now very little light inside the church. Only the soldier's outline was visible in the halo of light behind him.

'You haven't been to the beach,' he said. 'I haven't seen you there.'

'Am I being watched?'

'Of course not, but I was concerned. That I had made life difficult for you.'

'No more difficult than dancing with a Turkish soldier.'

He threw back his head and laughed. 'That *did* make you squirm but it was worth it to see the look on your face.'

'In our village everything follows tradition, captain. There is no tradition I know of where soldiers flirt with village girls in full view of the elders. Especially one who dances as badly as you do.'

He smiled apologetically. 'Mademoiselle ... Anyush ... if I ever have the honour of dancing with you again, I promise you will see a noticeable improvement.'

He dropped his arm and let her pass outside.

Dr Charles Stewart

Mushar

Trebizond

April 30th, 1915

Mr Henry Morgenthau

US Ambassador to the Ottoman Empire

Constantinople

Dear Henry,

I am very grateful to you for sending on Hetty's parcels from Constantinople. It was with some disappointment we discovered, on opening them, that the ladies of the Illinois Mothers' Circle have seen fit to send mufflers and mittens in this the hottest spring since our arrival. I would have been happier with seeds, or the smallest amount of filthy lucre, but no doubt next winter we'll be glad of the woollens.

In answer to your enquiry regarding Hetty's health, the hot dry weather has worked its seasonal cure on her bronchitis, and she is looking much the better for it. Her school is doing well and she has children attending from age six to fifteen of both sexes. A Turkish mudir has been recently appointed to oversee the running of the school and Hetty takes classes with him sitting silently at the back. He is obviously concerned that the children will be much *too* educated because he has removed most of the older boys to work on the railway and road gangs. Their poor mothers come to me hoping I can intervene, but my appeals have fallen on deaf ears. We are at war, I am told, and everybody has to play their part.

Your news of the arrest of prominent Armenians in Constantinople is disturbing, but I understand that city Armenians have become very politicised in recent years. This insurrection in Van is not helping their cause and a show of solidarity with the Empire would do much to improve the situation. I cannot help but think that

Armenians have brought this on themselves, especially when everyone needs to concentrate on the war effort. Which leads to my reason for writing. Mislav Ayka-nian, an old farmer and native of the village, was recently arrested and taken to the jail in Trebizond. The gendarmes raided his farm and discovered rifles and a few rounds of ammunition. Treason is the charge, but a less likely insurgent you would be hard pressed to find. His son is young, and who knows what he may be involved in, but the old man is simply not capable of it. The authorities refused to say what they're planning to do with him, though I have the impression the Vali knows more than he's saying. There is no hope of influencing the authorities here to release him, so I wondered if you could do something from your end of things? Any effort on his behalf would be appreciated by the family who are extremely concerned. As always Hetty and I are grateful for your kindness in this, as in so many matters.

While on the subject of disturbances, I appreciate your concerns regarding our safety if, and indeed when, America joins the Allies, but there is no question of quitting the Empire. You understand, Henry, that there is too much at stake here. I am grateful that you have kept us abreast of developments, but Hetty and I are resolved to sit it out. In any event, I am certain that with America's involvement the war will be concluded swiftly.

Next time we correspond, Henry, I hope the subject matter will be of a more pleasant nature.

Please extend our kind regards to Josephine and the children.

Yours sincerely,

Charles Stewart

Anyush

The house was silent as Anyush came down the loft stairs. Above her head the joists creaked and grumbled in the morning sunshine, but the room below was quiet and still. Tiptoeing past her grandmother, she looked over at Khandut's door. It was firmly shut. She let herself out to the garden and crossed the narrow road that led to the village. Turning away from the town, she passed the wood and walked in the direction of the coast. There was no mist in the fields or the hollows of the road, and the sun shone brilliantly on a sleepy-looking sea.

Beneath the headscarf her hair was warm from the sun, and Anyush tilted her face for a moment towards it. This was the perfect time of day, before the heat silenced the birds and blurred the line of dark green pines. She tried to think only of the morning air and the smell of the sea but found herself thinking about the captain, Jahan. In her mind's eye, she was dancing the tamzara with him, his arm curled around her waist. She could recall the smell of his cologne, a mixture of pine-needles and wood-smoke. She remembered his eyes, dark with long lashes like a girl's. And she couldn't forget how it felt to be imprisoned by him and the way he had of looking at her. A hungry look that reminded her of Husik.

She reached the track to the shoreline and climbed down onto the old wadi bed, making her way along the stony bottom. The wadi eventually joined the long beach where she took the Stewart children, but a narrower course leading eastward from it cut down onto a smaller cove. The stones slipped under her feet as the trail fell steeply to sea level, and she scrabbled on all fours until she reached the pebbly shale dividing the sand from the land mass.

From where she was crouched, halfway down, she could see the entire length of the bay stretching away to the sandy dunes on the western end and the bulk of the cliff wall to the east. The tide had gone out, and the wet, tobacco-coloured sand was smooth and undisturbed. Anyush made her way to the water's edge, where aside from the fly-strewn ribbons of kelp and the twiggy, criss-crossed pattern of gulls' feet, nothing moved but the waves.

A light breeze flapped the tip of her scarf noisily as she walked along the shoreline to the stone steps in the cliff-face. The little hilltop circular church was as deserted as the beach below, and her footsteps echoed in the musty space. She inhaled deeply. There was nothing in the air except the smell of salt and damp.

Outside, past the leaning headstones at the edge of the cliff, the sea lay empty and green. Not so much as a fishing boat interrupted the skyline. She sat there for a time watching the sun cast its glittering net across the surface of the sea and the young seal which broke through the swell at the base of the cliff.

Her attention wandered. The same thoughts came back to her from the day of Parzik's wedding. She pressed her palms against the hot skin of her cheeks and got to her feet. Gathering her skirts she left the clifftop and made her way down the steps and across the beach. The sand had begun to dry and filled her boots, so that she had to sit on a rock and empty them. Once they were laced again and the stray hairs tidied beneath her scarf, she started the steep climb along the river bed. She didn't realise that one of her laces had come undone until she tripped and fell heavily onto her knees. A tear appeared in the fabric of her skirt and in the chemise underneath. Annoyed, she flung the offending rock all the way down to the beach below.

'Are you in the habit of throwing things, or is it just for my benefit?'

Jahan

The captain could see that she was halfway down the track and appeared to be in some distress.

'I fell,' she said, by way of an explanation.

Slithering sideways to where she was crouched, Jahan extended his hand and helped her to her feet. A strand of hair was stuck to her forehead and the skin of her face was flushed. A long tear gaped in the fabric of her skirt, and the captain saw blood oozing through it from where she had cut her knee.

'Are you all right? Can you walk?'

She nodded.

'Were you climbing up or down? You look as though you could do with some air.'

Before she answered, he guided her back down towards the beach. At the bottom of the scree, he tried to take her arm, but she pulled away and walked to the water's edge.

'You might want to clean that,' he said, nodding to where the blood was drying on her skirt.

'It's nothing.'

'In this heat it's unwise to leave it.'

She was heading for the far cliff, her face turned towards it and her fingers curled into her palms. Her thin blouse flapped around the bones of her shoulders and the wet, sand-encrusted hem of her skirt left swirling tracks on the beach as she marched purposefully ahead of him. Since their last encounter, the captain had been thinking of Anyush Charcoudian more than he might have expected. Despite rumours of an Azeri army gathering in Baku and talk of being moved south-east to bolster the Fifth Army at Van, he had found himself distracted by thoughts of her. It took courage to meet him in the old ruin, but he hadn't expected her to be frightened of him. She hid it well, only two spots of high colour in her cheeks, but she was uneasy all the same. It was not what he had intended.

'This is a beautiful beach,' he said. 'And nobody seems to come here.'

Walking was painful for her, but she didn't slow her pace or turn to look at him.

'Tell me, why do you come here?'

'Because it is my refuge.'

'And, aside from myself, who are you seeking refuge from?'

She stopped abruptly and turned towards the ocean. With her back to the captain, she lifted her skirt and splashed water on her cut knee. He turned away, facing towards the wadi, until he felt her draw level with him again.

'My mother,' she said. 'I disappoint her and she likes to complain. She also hates men.'

'Thank you for the warning.'

'Turkish men in particular.'

'So,' he smiled, 'you come here to get away from your mother.'

'From everyone. And to swim.'

Jahan already knew she swam on a nearby beach. It was the beach visible from the hill at the top of the village and more easily accessible than the one they were walking on. He had seen her bring the American children there one day, when she had divested herself of everything but her underclothes and dived into the waves beside them. What had struck him most was not that she was an accomplished swimmer or that she seemed so unselfconscious in the children's company, but that the person who emerged from the water in the wet, clinging underclothes had the shape and figure of a woman – thin but shapely legs, a slim waist and pert breasts, tantalisingly visible behind the wet chemise. It was a revelation to him, and, from where he had been hiding at the top of the wadi, he hadn't been able to take his eyes from her.

'Not on this beach,' she was saying. 'The currents are too dangerous, but I swim on the main beach sometimes.'

'It's rather exposed,' he said. 'I've swum there myself but not that often.'

'There are other places. Beaches that are hidden.'

'I haven't seen any others.'

'There is a cove,' she said hesitatingly, 'a hidden cove at the bottom of the cliff, but it's difficult to get to.'

'More difficult than here?'

'Much more.'

'Could you show it to me?'

'No.' She looked away.

'Why not?'

'Because it's not safe.'

'You swim there.'

'I've been swimming since I was very young.'

'As have I.'

But she would not change her mind.

'Tell me where it is then, and I'll go by myself.'

'You'd never find it.'

'So bring me there.'

She was looking towards the cliff, and he followed her gaze along the line of rock out into the white water churning at its base. It didn't seem possible to swim anywhere near it.

'There's a very long drop to the bottom,' she said. 'This is not the place to go if you have a fear of heights.'

'That settles it then,' he smiled. 'I have no fear whatsoever.'

Anyush

'Anyush and the captain were crouched near the edge of the clifftop, looking at the tiny pebbly cove below. It was completely screened from the beach to the west by the side of the cliff that extended like a rocky arm out into the ocean and by the rank of low cliffs to the east.

'Nothing except a bird could manage to get down there.'

'I do.'

'Then you're braver than I am. That's a sheer drop.'

'There's a track just there.'

'For rabbits maybe.'

'And footholds.'

He got up from his knees. 'You're making fun of me. I'll plunge to my death.'

'It was your idea to come,' she said. 'I don't care if you climb down or not.'

He stood looking doubtfully at the drop, his black hair blowing around his face.

'Well ...' he said, glancing at her long skirt, 'I suppose if you can do it ...'

Reversing over the edge of the cliff, Anyush climbed backwards down the track. It was not difficult for her but by the time the captain reached

the bottom his palms were scratched and cut and covered in bird droppings from the gulls' nests he dislodged on the way down. His dusty,
chalk-stained uniform was a sight and his face was red and shining with
sweat. Anyush smiled, but the smile quickly faded when she thought
about where she had brought him. They were completely hidden, tucked
into the cliff like babes in arms. Should anything happen, there would be
no one to call on, no one to come to her aid. She could swim out to sea
around the headland and leave him make his own way back up the cliff,
but she hoped she wouldn't have to. He stood for a moment to catch
his breath, watching the low sun play on the water. Beyond the cliffs the
waves rolled and broke into plumes of spray, but within the small bay the
water was calm and still.

'This place is Paradise,' he said quietly. 'No wonder you keep it to
yourself.'

Like a lake of fallen stars, the late afternoon sun sparkled across the
blue-green surface.

'Can you see the cove from above?'

'No.'

'What about the fishermen?' he said, scanning along the horizon.
'Don't they come here?'

'They have to stay far out to avoid the rocks.'

The heat of the day had almost gone, leaving only a gentle warmth in
the pebbles beneath their feet. In the evening sky above them the colour
was shifting from the palest yellow to rose gold along the horizon. He
sat on the pebbles and began to pull off his boots and jacket. The wide
plane of his shoulders shrugged out of his shirt, revealing a narrow waist.
Each time he bent to remove a sock or boot, muscle rippled over bone
beneath the surface of his skin. Anyush had never seen a man's naked
body before, nothing more exposed than an arm or a face. Her own
self was known to her only in the shivering lengths glimpsed when she

93

undressed in the loft or in the reflection of a window pane. The thought of seeing her mother or grandmother without clothes was unimaginable, and men's nakedness was completely unfamiliar to her. A man's body was for ploughing and building and for imposing itself on the body of a woman. Every girl knew she should look at a man as if he had no body at all, but seeing Jahan undress on the pebbles before her, Anyush couldn't look away. His skin was startlingly white, the smooth surface of his chest broken by a triangle of silky black hair that dipped into the hollow of his navel and out again before disappearing beneath the band of his trousers. Anyush pulled her scarf over her ears and tightened the lace on her shoe. Getting to his feet the captain waded into the sea, pulling up his shoulders against the chill. He dived beneath the water and surfaced again, swimming with easy, unhurried strokes towards the reef. Watching him, Anyush felt strange, heavy-limbed and loose, as though a part of her had come unglued, and her heart pumped somewhere it shouldn't. She closed her eyes and dug her feet into the pebbles, kicking against the smooth stones. When she looked up again he was swimming towards the mouth of the bay.

'Stay in the middle!' she shouted. 'The rocks are dangerous. Don't swim too close to the cliff.'

The waters of the bay were deceiving. There were dangerous rips and tides along the base of the cliff and spit and beneath the smooth surface of the water. But he kept swimming, his bare, broad shoulders dipping easily in and out of the waves. He was very close now to the mouth of the bay. Approaching the line of breaking waves, he turned and swam slowly back towards the shore. Anyush sat with her arms pulled tightly around her knees.

'Come in,' he called. 'It's perfect.'

She shook her head.

'Heavenly. Not cold at all.'

He eased himself back into the water and swam towards the open sea. She watched him turn and float on his back, the light catching the outline of his face and toes where they broke the surface. There was no sound except the gentle splash of his limbs and the distant breaking waves. His movements were graceful in the water, more practised than her own. She dropped her head onto her arms, closing her eyes against the sight of him. When she looked up again, he was nowhere to be seen. She got to her feet and walked along the shoreline, shading her eyes against the low sun. The flat calm sea appeared undisturbed, but a movement in the dark water at the base of the spit caught her eye.

He was over near the rocks on the western side of the cove, swimming against the breaking tide. Although the evening was still and the water calm, the waves broke with surprising heft over the promontory. He was very close now to where the sea frothed on the dark stone, and she realised he was in the grip of an undercurrent pulling him onto it. Again and again, he attempted to swim towards the centre of the bay, but the undertow was too strong and he was washed back every time.

'Don't fight the current!' Anyush shouted. 'Go with it!'

He didn't seem to hear and kept thrashing about in the waves. She could see he was tiring and swallowing water. Pulling off her skirt, blouse and boots she dived into the sea and swam as close to him as she dared, but it wasn't close enough. She had to stay away from the pull along the base of the spit.

'Listen to me ... Captain Orfalea ... Jahan, listen. Pull up your knees. Can you hear me?'

Turning as best he could, he nodded.

'Watch what I'm doing. You must do the same ... you understand? Keep your legs away from the rocks. Let the tide carry you onto them.'

His eyes widened, and she knew what she was asking him to do sounded dangerous, but he was too tired to break away from the current, and his only hope was letting the force of the waves carry him in. She had managed this herself once before, but it had been a high tide and there was less chance of hitting the higher rocks. It was a risk, but he had no other option. Taking a deep breath, she let herself drift into the current. The pull sucked her along by the rock face and she swam parallel to it so that she could get herself into the best position facing the spit.

'Watch the waves!' she shouted. 'Wait for a big one!'

Out to sea a huge roller came thundering towards the bay and then broke on the reef into a smaller swell. It moved at speed towards her. Drawing up her knees, she took a deep breath and turned her back to it. Lifted suddenly aloft, she had a brief and terrifying view over the entire cove before falling towards the spar of barnacled granite. Pushing down on her heels, she landed forcefully but intact as the water rushed back between her ankles. Grabbing a finger-hold in the rock, she managed to cling on at the outward pull and crawl onto the higher rocks before the next wave broke over her. At her back she saw Jahan turn towards the incoming waves. One smaller than the other drifted inwards until, finally, another huge roller gathered in the bay. He was in a bad position from the start and then misjudged the timing so that he was pulled back into the water only to be thrown up again. Anyush's heart beat like a bird's as she realised the rocks would cut him to ribbons. Tiring and swallowing water, he struck out again for the spot she had launched from. In position just as another big wave hit, he turned his back to it and was carried onto the rock. This time he clung on when the water washed out, gripping hard with both hands. Coming as close as she dared, Anyush reached out and pulled him onto the dry rocks beside her.

They collapsed onto the pebbles, both trying to catch their breath.

'That was very brave,' he said.

Anyush couldn't speak. She should have been angry that he had ignored her warning and put their lives in danger, but all she felt was relief. 'You're bleeding,' she said. 'And your trousers are torn.'

He looked down and saw that one side of his chest was grazed, and watery blood trickled through his ripped trousers along his right shin. 'I look like I've been in the wars.'

She tried to smile, but her teeth chattered and her lips were stiff with cold.

'Here ...' He fetched his tunic and placed it around her shoulders. She was suddenly conscious that she had nothing on but a chemise. Despite the cold, blood rushed to her face. Gently he teased away the wet hair from her cheek. She was trembling, and cold had nothing to do with it Heavy with seawater, her plait dripped onto her shoulder, and he moved it away, resting his hand on her collarbone. Her breath quickened as he traced the drop of saltwater to the low neckline of her chemise and she closed her eyes. In some part of her she knew she should run, get away as fast as she could, but her feet wouldn't move and her legs wouldn't carry her. His hand lingered at her breast, pushing against the nipple behind the wet fabric. She wasn't thinking any more, only that she didn't want him to stop.

'Anyush,' he whispered, tilting her face to his, 'look at me.'

She looked at him. Hope, reason and any good sense she might once have had deserted her.

'Anyush ... you need never be afraid of me.'

Turning abruptly, he walked to where his shirt and boots lay discarded on the stones. 'You should get dressed,' he said. 'I have to get back.'

Jahan

Jahan sat against the wall of the ruin, just inside the doorway. Below him the line of white sand swept a majestic curve around the headland, past the rocky promontory, and merged in the far distance into the grey sea. The beach was deserted. She wasn't coming.

Since the day in the cove he had not been to the ruin. He had stopped keeping track of Anyush's movements and tried to put her from his thoughts, but being saved from drowning does strange things to the mind. Her courage in the service of a man, whose motives were, at best, questionable, had a profound effect on him. She had risked her life without a moment's hesitation, and it was the most selfless act any other human being had ever undertaken on his behalf.

He felt ashamed. He had decided to seduce Anyush, and, watching her shivering and half naked on the stones, he knew she was his for the taking. A bit of harmless fun to stave off the boredom of being banished to the back end of the Empire. But it didn't seem so harmless any more.

A year previously Jahan had been in Paris finishing his officer's training at the French Military Academy. Enver Pasha, the commanding officer of the Turkish army, was determined to rid the ranks of the older *alaylı*, those officers who had been appointed without going to military school, and replace them with the *mektepli*, young, eager graduates of the Military Academy such as Jahan. Like other cadets sent to Berlin, Vienna, Rome, London and St Petersburg, Jahan's head was full of the modern advances he would bring home with him. He was determined to establish the first Ottoman aviation corps, and an armoured vehicle squadron, and his superiors were suitably impressed. But the outbreak of war put an end to all Jahan's dreams. The cadets were recalled to Constantinople to bolster a decimated Ottoman army. The military had never recovered from the disastrous Balkan War which had destroyed it as an effective fighting force. As the events of 1914 lumbered towards the inevitable, the Ottoman army found itself understaffed, ill-equipped and totally unprepared for another war.

Not every aspect of the war was unfavourable for the Orfalea family. Jahan's father, a leading figure in the Ottoman military, had substantially increased his fortune during the Balkan War and since the advent of the Great War. The family tannery in Constantinople had become the biggest army supplier of saddles, bandoliers and boots, and, being the only son and heir of his father's business, Jahan ought to have been grateful for an armed conflict.

In reality, he was disenchanted with all things military and disturbed by the nationalistic fervour spreading throughout the country like fire. 'Armenian,' he thought, looking up at the darkening sky, had become a dirty word.

Over the course of a few restless nights, Jahan had decided never to see Anyush again. His company was moving to the Russian front in a couple of days, and it would be his parting gift to her, a sincere thank you for saving his life. So sincere in fact, that he had come to the ruin in the hope of saying it in person.

A stiff breeze blew up. The sky and sea merged in a heaving mass of grey and the first drops of rain hit against his face, presaging the storm to come. Pushing his cap firmly onto his head, he stepped into the wind to walk back to the base.

Anyush

'**S**hort, Anyush,' Bayan Stewart said. 'Keep a little length on top but cut the rest short.'

'I don't need a woman to cut my hair,' Robert complained. 'I like it long.'

'Sit still, Master Robert,' Anyush said, holding the scissors away from him.

'Nobody complains about Mahmoud Agha's hair. Nobody makes *him* cut it off.'

'Mahmoud is a Kurd,' his mother said. 'Cut it like you did Thomas's, Anyush dear.'

'Think how much cooler it will be,' Anyush said, snipping off a lock. 'Short hair is easier in the heat.'

'That's what hats are for,' Robert muttered.

'Told you you'd have to cut it,' Eleanor smirked.

Her brother made a face.

'Charles ... I was wondering when we'd see you.' Bayan Stewart rose to greet her husband who seemed a little distracted.

'*Barev*, Dr Stewart.'

'*Barev dyzez*, Anyush. You're here today? I expected you at the clinic.'

'Clinic tomorrow, *Doktor*.'

'Oh ... yes, that's right.'

'Robert is having his hair cut,' Bayan Stewart smiled. 'Samson shorn by Delilah.'

'Not before time,' Dr Stewart said, lowering himself into a chair.

Taking the comb, Anyush began to pull the tangles from Robert's hair.

Since the evening at the cove she had not been to the beach. She never walked that way and kept busy from early morning until she fell onto her bed at night. But sleep didn't hold her for long. In the early hours she would find herself awake and thinking of Jahan. Telling herself that nothing had happened and knowing that everything had changed. What she had felt sitting on the pebbles that day did not go away but lingered like a sickness in her veins. She thought of him constantly. She tried to imagine what might have happened if he hadn't behaved as he did. She wanted to know what that would have been like. The warmth of his hand against her breast left her aching to be touched again. In her bed at night she touched herself, but in the cold light of morning she was ashamed. Days went by and she struggled through them – ordinary days, where only the thought of him gave her any pleasure. You need never be afraid of me, he had said, but, in fact, she was more afraid of herself.

'What was the commotion on the square this morning?' Bayan Stewart asked.

'Soldiers. Some sort of manoeuvres. They're packing up apparently.'

'Leaving?'

'Yes, and good riddance. They're a damn nuisance.'

'Where are they going?' Thomas asked.

'The Russian border. There won't be a soldier left in Trebizond by nightfall.'

'Oww! My ear!'

'I'm sorry ...'

The scissors fell from Anyush's hand as Robert pressed his bleeding ear to the side of his head.

'I'm very sorry, Master Robert ...'

'It's only nicked,' Dr Stewart said, prising away the boy's fingers. 'Let me see, Robert. Take away your hand. A tiny cut, that's all. Keep it compressed. Anyush, he's fine. You're terribly pale. You're not going to faint, I hope.'

She shook her head.

'I knew I shouldn't have had my hair cut,' the boy whined.

'Are you certain you're not feeling weak?' Bayan Stewart asked. 'You really do look pale.'

'I think I need some air.'

'Go home, dear. We can do our lesson another day. The weather is about to change for the worse anyway and your mother will be concerned.'

When she was no longer visible from the Stewarts' house, Anyush started to run. Taking the shorter path through the wood, she followed the river until she came to the stony track along the old river bed. The wind pushed hard against her when she reached the beach but she didn't stop. It was raining now, slanting into her face and streaming down her neck. The sky was so dark and the rain so heavy that it was hard to make out the landmarks, but her feet brought her to the cliff and the steps leading to the ruin. Her lips were blue from the cold, but she whispered the same words over and over.

'Let him be there ... please, please let him be there.'

Soaked to the skin, she climbed upwards, stumbling once on the slippery stone. At the top the wind roared in her ears, buffeting her across the little graveyard. From what she could see, the place was deserted. Nothing moved except gusts of wind threatening to blow her over the cliff. The church doorway was in darkness, but it was darker still and noisier inside.

Currents of air whipped around the circular interior giving voice to the whistling winds. She was too late. He wasn't there. Battered by the rain, she stood gripping the crumbling lintel until she saw something move in the darkness ahead of her.

'Anyush ...'

It was the light reflected in his eyes that she saw coming towards her, and the outline of his uniform. His hands caught her as she fell against him. Combing her fingers through his hair, she pulled his head towards her, searching for his lips. They found each other, and her mouth opened to his, but she felt him hesitate.

'I can't.' He drew away. 'This is wrong.'

But she already knew what he wanted. She began to open the buttons of her blouse, her fingers trembling as the fabric fell to the floor and the cold air touched her skin.

'No, Anyush.'

His eyes dropped to where her breasts pushed against the drawstrings of her chemise. Until that moment it might have been possible to put an end to it. To be themselves again, the soldier and the girl they once were. But she couldn't stop what had been started and she didn't want to. She needed to go beyond the point of return – to put an end to everything childish and all that marked them as different. She wanted to be seduced. Used by him. Opening the last button, she took off her blouse and stood in her chemise. They looked at each other while the storm blew outside and her clothes dripped pools of water by her feet. He came towards her and picked up her wet blouse. Draping it carefully around her shoulders, he stepped away. But she reached for his hand and placed it against her breast. She pressed his fingers hard against her nipple like he had done that day in the cove. Suddenly his lips were on hers and he pushed her against the wall, pulling away her blouse and the straps of her chemise. The stone pressed into the bones of her back, cold against the heat of her skin. Cupping her breasts in his hands, he bent and took a nipple in his mouth. A shudder passed through her, long waves of pleasure that grew stronger as he worked his tongue. She heard a sound, an animal noise that seemed to be coming from herself. An intense feeling was building at the base of her spine, spreading to her belly and limbs and changing the rhythm of her breath. His lips had moved to the base of her throat, kissing the hollow between the bones, licking the angle of her jaw. He took the lobe of her ear between his teeth.

'Is this what you want, Anyush?' he whispered. 'Tell me. Say it to me.'

With his free hand he bundled up her skirts and tugged down her drawers. They felt wet where they brushed against the skin of her thighs. His fingers moved inside her and her head fell back against the wall as though the muscles and sinews of her neck were no longer strong enough to support it. She had the feeling of being borne upwards, higher and higher while the air rushed from her lungs.

'Say it, Anyush.'

'I ...'

'Say it.'

'... please.'

He moved her away from the wall and they stumbled to the floor. Pushing her clothes to her waist, he pulled her drawers below her knees and tugged them off. She was barely aware of the cold stone beneath her and her nakedness. She felt no shame only an unbearable desire to have him inside her. Of their own will her legs parted and his hand caressed the inside of her thighs and the mound between. She began to sigh, incapable of anything like words. His eyes were fixed on hers when he released himself from his trousers. Stiff and swollen his flesh stood rigidly from him and her body opened to receive him. She closed her eyes, all feelings of fear and hesitation gone. This was not what she had been told to expect, the whisperings and half-truths among the village women, giving no hope of pleasure or joy only pain and humiliation. A flash of anger shot through her at the unfairness of it, the trickery of her own sex. But she was distracted by Jahan's tongue moving across her belly, her breasts and nipples, and then, shockingly, inside her until she could think of nothing but their two bodies coming together and an urgency she couldn't contain.

'Now Jahan ...'

Her breath was coming too fast.

'Please ... now.'

She felt him enter her and then a sharp, penetrating pain. He hesitated when she cried out, but she put her hands on his hips and guided him back inside her. Barely there at first and then deeper, faster, swelling so that they moved almost as one. Just when she thought she could endure it no longer, a wave of pleasure such as she had never imagined broke over her, flooding though her body again and again as she arched her back beneath him. Distantly, she heard him call her name, but she was gone from him, cast adrift on a warm and welcoming sea.

Jahan

Sometimes Jahan thought he had failed Anyush. That if he had acted in her best interests, he would have said his goodbyes or not come to the church at all. But the fates had conspired to bring them together, and he was glad of it. Had he not taken shelter from the storm, she would have found the church empty, and had the army not rescinded orders to join the Fifth Army on the Eastern Front, he might never have seen her again. But they had found each other that night, and oh what a sight she had been! His lieutenant had said that Armenian women were different, and Anyush certainly was. Jahan had expected her to be shy, hesitant and self-conscious, but when they had made love that first time she was none of those things. In the same way she had thrown herself into the water to save his neck, she had come to him wholeheartedly, and he delighted in every second of it. He hadn't been able to look at her long enough. Her skin was so pale it seemed to be a source of light in itself, a soft radiance glowing against the dark granite stone.

After they had made love, he had undressed her fully, letting his eyes linger slowly over her, from the upward tilt of her small breasts, to the depression above the jutting edge of her hip bone. His fingers had run along the protuberances of her spine to the rising mounds below, across her taut belly and into the hollows between her ribs. Just below her left nipple he had discovered a small brown birthmark, a smudge or thumb-print left by her creator's hand.

Did he regret what happened? Not for a moment. As they had walked home their separate ways, he had only been able to think of when he might see her again.

Anyush

Anyush didn't sleep that night. In the early hours when a faint glow lit the horizon she stood outside the cottage listening to the waves tumbling on the shore. It was a peaceful sound and she closed her eyes. She might have expected to feel troubled by what she had done, but all she felt was a quiet calm. She prayed for the day to come quickly so that she could be with him all over again. Every part of her hummed like a wire in the wind. She was drunk from his touch, his smell, the way he had looked at her as if he had never seen a woman before. Being with Jahan was the only form of happiness she desired. And she *was* happy. She fell asleep finally as the sun came up and an hour later rose from her bed, the happiest girl in the Ottoman Empire. But others were not so lucky.

Ṳ Ṳ Ṳ

'I need to see Dr Stewart,' Parzik said.

Anyush found her friend slumped on the clinic steps and brought her inside.

'*Inch' skhal*? Tell me, what's wrong?'

'They're going to hang Vardan's father. They're going to do it in a few days.'

Anyush stared at her. She had to be mistaken. Aykanian was innocent. Everybody knew he was.

'Who said this? It's only gossip. Rumour ...'

'They told Vardan. The gendarmes. They're going to make him watch.' Parzik hung her head, tears dripping into her lap.

'Dr Stewart will know what to do,' Anyush said. 'He'll put a stop to it.'

But Dr Stewart had bad news of his own. 'There is nothing I can do.'

'*Doktor, efendim*, you could talk to them. Tell them he's innocent.'

'Believe me, I have exhausted every avenue on Mislav's behalf.'

'It is not too late, *Doktor*. I beg of you ...' Parzik knelt at his feet, touching her forehead to his boots. 'Please, *Doktor* ... you are the only one who can help him.'

'I'm sorry. Really I am.'

Ü Ü Ü

On the day of the hanging the entire village gathered in the square. A platform was set up at one end where the wedding party had been, and a scaffold erected. Bayan Stewart told the children to remain in the house, but Thomas and Robert climbed out a window and slipped into the crowd behind where their father and the priest stood next to Vardan. Sosi and Anyush stood either side of Parzik, and nearby her mother and Gohar linked arms. The sun rose and began to sink towards the west, but still the heat beat relentlessly down. People retreated beneath the lemon trees or leaned against the platform, looking every now and then towards the southern end of the square. Husik was standing at the back of the scaffold, his eyes roaming over the rope and gibbet, and his father, a little behind, waited to catch the first glimpse of the prisoner. The day wore on and still there was no sign of Aykanian. Anyush's arm ached where

Parzik's fingers gripped through the fabric of her sleeve. Vardan's new wife was pale and drawn, and had hardly spoken. Every few seconds she glanced over to where Vardan stood by the scaffold.

Finally, a lone gendarme walked into the far end of the square, followed by ten or twelve more. Vardan's father shuffled along in the middle of them. Aykanian had always been thin, but the stooped, stumbling old man trying to walk with bound ankles drew a collective breath from the crowd. Every bone and sinew in his body was visible, his thin skin straining to hold them together. He was muttering to himself, mumbling with his eyes fixed on his feet as though unaware of others around him. A sob escaped Vardan's lips, and Parzik's trembling fingers covered her mouth. Some of the older women began to keen and others counted off what time was left to the old man on their prayer beads. At the steps to the scaffold Aykanian hadn't the strength to climb but was pushed and prodded so that he stumbled and fell. His face hit the wooden step with a sickening thud, and before anyone could stop him Vardan ran over to where his father lay bleeding at the foot of the platform.

'Get back ... move away,' a gendarme shouted, but Vardan remained crouched beside the old man.

'Papa ... *hayrik*,' he whispered, wiping blood from his father's face. 'I'm here ... it's me, Vardan.'

Aykanian looked at him with a mixture of confusion and fear. He shook his head and turned away.

'I said move back.' Using his boot, the gendarme kicked Vardan into the dust.

'Give them a moment,' Dr Stewart said. 'It's Aykanian's son ... his boy ... he only wants to say goodbye.'

'I know who he is,' the gendarme said contemptuously. 'Now get him away or I'll hang him alongside the old man.'

Father Gregory helped Aykanian to his feet as Dr Stewart led a weeping

Vardan back to the crowd. The priest finally got the old man up the steps to the scaffold.

'*Hayrik … hayrik …*' Vardan cried as the noose was put around his father's neck. Parzik buried her head in Anyush's shoulder and Gohar made the sign of the cross. The old man was still talking to himself, a torrent of words spilling from his mouth as if he knew he hadn't long more to say them. He shook his head from side to side as the rope burned against the loose skin of his neck. At a signal from the commanding officer, the rope was pulled taut so that Aykanian teetered for a few seconds on the tips of his toes. With a bang the trapdoor flew open and Vardan's father fell into the void. There was complete silence. No one uttered a sound as the old man's legs kicked, and his mouth opened, and his lips swelled and turned blue. It was only when the body had become completely still that a long and terrible cry welled up from his son.

For three weeks following the hanging the Jendarma refused to allow Vardan to take down his father's body. The decaying remains would serve as a warning, they said, to other Russian sympathisers. Finally, through the intervention of Dr Stewart and Father Gregory, permission was given to bury Aykanian and he was laid to rest in the Armenian cemetery adjoining the church.

A new admission caused a stir on the men's ward today. I was glad of the distraction because the mood in the hospital has been gloomy ever since the hanging. Nobody speaks openly of Aykanian but I am constantly hearing snatches of whispered conversation and bitter words. Perhaps I'm imagining it, but some of this vitriol appears to be directed at myself. Nobody can stomach the unpleasant truth that guns and rifles *were* found on the Aykanian farm. There was no denying the evidence, a fact people seem happy to overlook.

Late this morning Anyush informed me we had a new patient in one of the private rooms on the male side. I walked in to see guns, cartridge belts, powder horns, swords and daggers decorating the walls, and sitting on the bed like the Sultan himself was the outlaw, Murzabey. He's a powerfully built man in his middle years with the weathered features of a bandit and a deceptively brilliant smile. For as long as I can remember he's been the leader of the renegade Shota tribe, but unlike Mahmoud Agha and the hill tribes around Trebizond, he is a violent man and is wanted throughout the province for various crimes. Hetty has treated one of his wives for puerperal fever and I saw him once years ago when he lost his right hand in a pitched battle against the local gendarmes. He is not a man you would easily forget. The stories circulating about his cruelty are legion. He keeps tight and extortionate control of the lands to the south and west of Trebizond and brutally dispatches any man threatening his position. The landowners throughout the province live in fear of him and even Mahmoud Agha makes him annual 'gifts' of sheep and horses to remain in his favour. In the real sense of the word, he is legendary, so why he should have installed himself in my hospital I couldn't imagine.

Entering the room, I saw Manon finish dressing Murzabey's leg, as six of his men trained their rifles on her. In fluent Kurmanji she told them to drop the rifles or they would have to dress the leg themselves. Murzabey was scowling at her when he saw me in the doorway.

'*Selamın Aleyküm*, Doktor Stippet,' he said. 'You come just in time. I want you to look at my leg.'

Manon informed me that he had a leg ulcer and that she'd already treated it and bandaged it accordingly. I assured Murzabey there was no need for me to look at it again.

'The *kuledoken* is not you, Dr Stewart. You will decide what is wrong with it.'

I was about to tell him that I had every faith in Manon and that she had treated his leg as I would myself but decided to humour him. I unwound the perfectly applied bandages as my nurse swept imperiously from the room. The wound was friable and smelled of rotting flesh, but had been expertly debrided by Manon and treated with zinc paste. There was nothing further to be done. I told him he needed to have the wound dressed daily and gave him an appointment for the clinic.

'You will not find me at any clinic, *Doktor*,' he said. 'As you can see my men are eager to be gone.'

He then reminded me that, although he had lost his hand all those years ago, I had saved his arm and he was quite sure I could fix his leg into the bargain.

'It is not for nothing you are called "Big Doktor Stippet".'

'Then take this doctor's advice,' I told him. 'If you do not look after the leg, it will become gangrenous and you'll lose it. Then there is nothing that I or any doctor can do for you.'

For the first time since entering the room Murzabey was silent, staring at me out of those remarkable green eyes. The men standing around the bed moved in close as though braced for the order to slit my throat, but, to my relief, Murzabey smiled.

'Very well, *Doktor,* I will do as you say, and you will fix my leg like new. Send the *kuledoken* back to do up my bandages. Tell her the rifles will point only at the door.'

His laughter rang in my ears as I left the room.

Anyush

The hanging of old man Aykanian marked the start of everything that was to come. While the year wore on and events beyond the village were already casting a long shadow, Anyush thought only of Jahan. In the weeks after the hanging, they met whenever they could at the ruin, but more gendarmes had been drafted in from Trebizond and it was difficult for her to go out alone. Everyone was being watched and people were suspicious of each other. Two weeks went by when she saw nothing of Jahan at all. Her mother and grandmother kept a close eye and it was often impossible to get away. One afternoon Jahan came to the clinic to buy quassia for mosquito bites. Anyush was so happy to see him that it was hard to concentrate on what she was doing. The clinic was full that day and she had to behave as if he was just another patient in a long line of the sick and the hungry. Jahan watched her whenever she came and went into the room so that she was sure someone would notice, but Dr Stewart was busy with a patient, and the nurses were working elsewhere. She handed Jahan the brown glass bottle of quassia and he whispered that she should meet him that evening at the ruin.

ṳ ṳ ṳ

The day had been unusually hot and still, and, although the sun had almost set, heat rose in waves from the headstones in the graveyard like a silent and deadening tune. Jahan was waiting in the doorway, and, without speaking, they pulled their clothes from each other, impatient with buttons and laces and ties. The cold stone was deliciously cool beneath her as she lay shamelessly, her body arching in need of him and her breath broken for the want of him. But he would not give in so easily. Pinning her arms to the floor, he stroked himself along her thighs and belly until she called out for him. Then barely entering her he withdrew again, repeating it over and over so that, in the bliss of this torment, she felt herself drawn to the very edge of what she could bear. He suddenly stood up.

'Don't stop ...' she begged, but he had already pulled her to her feet.

Turning her away from him, he pressed her towards the wall and pushed her feet apart with his boots.

'Now ...' he said, his breath hot in her ear as she felt him enter her from behind and heard her own voice cry out.

He hesitated as if to prolong the moment and then surged inside her, touching off long shuddering waves that threatened to break her apart. She closed her eyes, abandoning herself to the joy of it.

Afterwards, they lay together, bathed in the light from the setting sun. She could feel his eyes on her as she watched the evening sky outside.

'You know you're extraordinary,' he said, kissing the skin of her neck. 'Not like any woman I've ever known.'

'Don't.'

Confused, he sat up to look at her.

'Don't make me feel any more shameful than I do already.'

Something darkened in his face, but she reached up and lightly touched the corner of his mouth.

'It's not that I'm sorry for what we've done. I'm not. But I'm ashamed of the way I behave when I'm with you. At the things I'm willing to do.'

'I thought you wanted this.'

'I do,' she said, stroking the dark skin at his jaw. 'I can't help myself.'

He pulled her into his arms again and they lay curled into one another, looking through the door at the headstones. For the first time unwelcome thoughts crept into Anyush's mind. What would become of her if she was caught? How would she keep this from Sosi and Parzik? After what had happened to Kevork, Sosi would never forgive her, and Parzik would be unable to keep it to herself.

She felt Jahan's lips graze her cheek.

'Don't think too much, Anyush. Talk to me. Tell me about this place. What kind of church was it?'

'Armenian,' she said, looking up at the dome above their heads. 'It was burned when my mother was a child.'

'Does she remember it?'

'She was very young, but she tells me she does. She said there were gold paintings on the walls and on the dome.'

Flaking plaster and the cone-shaped mounds of swallows' nests were all there was left to see on the crumbling ceiling above them.

'The weather must have destroyed everything the fire didn't,' he said, looking above him.

'I'm glad the paintings are gone.'

'You prefer that it's home to bats and birds?'

'I'm glad no one's watching.'

'You mean the Heavenly Host?' he laughed.

'Don't mock. And don't make fun of me.'

'I would never make fun of you.' He sat up and gripped her by the shoulders. 'I love you, Anyush. I can't remember what life was like before I met you.'

Unexpected tears stung her eyes.

'I didn't have the first idea what I was doing in Trebizond but now I do. I was meant to find you. Something wonderful came from that terrible day in the farmyard. You have become my world, Anyush. Tell me you feel the same.'

She nodded, and he took her in his arms, kissing her more tenderly than before. Lying back on the cold stone floor, they put from their minds all that was happening beyond the little church, beyond the borders of the village, beyond the boundaries of birthright and war. All that was sensible and prudent in his nature and hers was pushed aside. With the selfishness of lovers they thought only of each other. She loved the way he looked at her, the way he said unspeakable things with his eyes and clever things with his mouth. He loved the wildness in her and her disregard for convention. They were the limits of each other's existence, citizens of a country all their own. They were in love, and because it was forbidden and endlessly precious, they risked everything for it.

Anyush

'**Y**ou're dripping water all over the place,' Khandut said. 'Get the mop and clean it up.'

Anyush skirted around the puddle and went to climb the ladder to the loft.

'Kazbek's laundry is not going to wash itself and your grandmother has conveniently fallen asleep again.'

Gohar was dozing on the day bed under the stairs.

'I'm going to the village with the eggs. Make sure those clothes are ready by the time I get back.'

She wrapped a scarf around her head and slammed the door behind her.

'Is she gone?' Gohar asked, opening her eyes.

'Yes.'

'Good because we need to talk.'

Something in her grandmother's tone gave Anyush pause.

'Sit down. I can't talk to you when you look as if you're about to flee.'

Anyush pulled out a chair and sat at the table facing her.

'I've seen you. With the soldier.'

Water was dripping from Anyush's hair, falling in drops by the leg of the chair. She watched it darkening the wooden floor.

'I went to the beach looking for you. You're lucky it was me and not your mother. I take it by the look of him he's Turkish?'

Anyush nodded and the old woman closed her eyes.

'I thought ... I hoped you would know certain things but it's clear to me that you do not.'

'I know what I'm doing.'

'You know nothing! How could you when I've brought you up that way? I've tried to shield you from the terrible things I've lived through and it seems I've succeeded.'

She sighed. 'You have eyes and ears, Anyush. You are well aware of the way we live. How could you do that to yourself? And with a Turk?'

'Jahan is my friend.'

'No Turk is a friend to Armenians! Why do you think Armenians cannot buy land, only work it for some Turkish landlord until we're too old or too broken to be of any use any more? Oh our men are good enough as war fodder, or for the labour gangs, but for nothing else! We're mules to them, Anyush. Less valuable than the dogs on the street.'

The loose-rimmed lids beneath Gohar's eyes were swollen and red as though she had been crying. Anyush had never seen her grandmother cry.

'There hasn't been a single generation of Armenians who weren't burned or tortured or had their women raped by the Turks,' Gohar continued. 'I hoped you would escape. You are educated and clever so I thought you would know better. But now ... Anyush, what have you done?!'

'*Tatik* ...' Anyush got up from the chair and crouched at her grandmother's feet. The old woman looked at her as though she had stolen the blood from her veins. Anyush couldn't bear it. She laid her head in Gohar's lap and the old woman began to stroke her hair.

'Who owns this house, Anyush?' her grandmother asked.

'Kazbek,' the girl murmured.

'And who built this house, the house you've grown up in?'

'Kazbek I suppose.'

Gohar moved her hand away. 'Sit up, Anyush. There are things you need to hear.'

They sat opposite each other at the table as Gohar told her granddaughter the story of the house. It had been built by Anyush's grandfather, Aram, on his own land, family land for generations. When Anyush's father was nine years old, the Turks issued an order declaring that Armenian taxes were to be doubled. Twice what the Turkish farmers were expected to pay and twice what the family could afford. Gohar's husband worked hard to raise the money but it was never enough. The land and the house were taken and sold to Kazbek for a fraction of its value. For the rest of his life Aram lived with the shame of paying a man he hated for something that was in fact his.

'It killed him,' Gohar said.

'But Kazbek is Armenian. How could that be?'

'Kazbek has a pact with the Devil and the Devil looks after his own!' Gohar looked behind her as though he was listening beneath the loft stairs. 'The story I told you about my mother and sister,' she continued, 'that they were killed in a fire ... it's not the whole truth.'

She sighed, looking through the window in the direction of the sea.

'My sister Haroun was unmarried and lived with my mother in Andok, near Sassoun. From the moment of her birth she was never normal. She didn't look different from anybody else, but her mind never developed beyond that of a six-year-old child so she lived with my parents into her middle age. I was married by then, living here with your grandfather and my two sons. As I've often told you, Andok is a very beautiful place, tucked into the foothills on the slopes of Mount Gebin with a small forest between the mountain and the town. The story I'm about to tell you happened in 1894 and I remember the year well because one of my sons, your father Koryun, had just become betrothed to your mother. It was the month of August. There hadn't been rain for weeks and the heat was terrible. The Sultan, Hamid the Bloody as he was called, had just dissolved the parliament in Constantinople and suspended the Armenian National Constitution. Of course in Sassoun and here in Trebizond people took little interest in what the Sultan was doing. That was the pity of it. Like now, all the Armenian men were gone. Some had been conscripted into the army, but most were in hiding because of the massacre earlier that year in Gelie-Guzan. One day, Turkish soldiers arrived in Sassoun. They rounded up all the women and children and chased them into the forest. The villagers thought they were safe there, and they didn't try to run or climb onto the mountain – not until the soldiers set the forest alight and shot everyone who wasn't burned alive. My father had died in his sleep two years before, but my mother and sister weren't so lucky.'

Anyush knelt at her grandmother's feet not knowing what to say. She wasn't sure she believed the story. What if it was only a tale, a fable to warn Armenian children against the evil of the Turk? It had never been mentioned before and Khandut never spoke of it.

'You need to know this, Anyush. You need to realise what you're doing.'

'I know what I'm doing. Jahan is not like that.'

'He's a Turk and capable of things you couldn't begin to imagine.'

'If you knew him as I do—'

'I pray to God,' the old woman said, closing her eyes, 'that I never will.'

Today for the first time since she was hired, Manon failed to show up for work. Or to be more accurate, she came and left mid-morning, which is equally alarming. I have never known her to leave early because of illness, or for any other reason, and I was concerned. It was a relief to discover that she had sprained her ankle when she tripped over a mop, and that, aside from losing her temper with my student nurse Patil, who had left it on the floor, she was otherwise well. Leaving Bedros and Grigor to attend to the last few patients, I went to pay Manon a call. It was the first time I had been to her quarters, a couple of rooms at the back of the dispensary building which was originally built as the caretaker's lodge. I knocked, but the reception was not what you might call warm. A voice instructed me in no uncertain terms to go away.

'*Allez-vous en!*'

Ignoring this, I announced myself which elicited a long silence. Finally, I was instructed to open the door and let myself in. The small space was difficult to navigate because the drapes were drawn and the room was in darkness. As my eyes adjusted, I could see Manon sitting on a divan in the corner, her foot resting on a low stool. She commanded me to open the curtains before inviting me to sit. In the light coming through the dusty glass I could see that the room was neat and tidy, as I might have expected, but otherwise quite bare. There was little by way of furniture in the room, just two armchairs, a stool, a drop-leaf table against one wall and a single chair next to it. A large Isfahan rug covered the middle of the floor lending the room a splash of colour, but it was what was on the wall behind Manon that drew my attention. Every inch was covered with souvenirs: a collection of prayer beads made from semi-precious stones; burqas in various styles, including one that looked like steel but was actually made from burnished leather; macramé bowls lined up alongside incense burners on one shelf, and brass and copper coffee pots on another; baby-shakers from the gold souk, prayer rugs from the carpet souk and miniature icons which I suspected were the most valuable items in the room. Hanging from silk thread, so that they appeared as if they were suspended in mid-air, was a selection of silver khanjars – short, curved knives sheathed in elaborately wrought scabbards. The objects and the way she had displayed them took me by surprise. I never thought her the type to take an interest in such things, but it seemed there were sides to Manon I had never guessed at.

'*Mes enfants*,' she said, casting her eyes over the display.

I asked about her sprained ankle, and, after dismissing it as a 'slight twist', she granted me permission to examine it. It was swollen and turning a bruised blue-green colour and must have been causing her some pain. I advised her to keep it in a bucket of cold water and that I would come back later to strap it for her.

'It has already been put in water and I will do the bandage myself,' she said dismissively.

'Well, if there's anything you want—'

'No more bandaging. *Halas*!'

It took me a moment to realise she was poking fun.

'Murzabey!' I said. 'You still haven't forgiven me.'

'I have not.'

'Then accept my apologies and my congratulations on a successful outcome.'

'*Accepté.*'

I made to leave but she insisted I have a glass of grape juice. She nodded to where a curtain screened off a corner of the room and behind it I found a sink, a row of shelves with crockery, and one small cupboard and drawer. Taking two glasses and a carafe of juice, I filled them and brought one to her. We discussed her collection for a while, particularly the khanjars, which I said Murzabey would have been envious of. But Manon's face darkened at the mention of his name.

'He is a murderer and a thief,' she said. 'He should not be permitted in the hospital.'

'Everyone is allowed in the hospital,' I protested. 'And I'd rather not be the man to refuse him.'

From the way Manon was watching me, I knew there was something on her mind. She asked how I had come to know Murzabey and I told her that years before I had amputated his hand after his thumb and four fingers had been blown off. I had been given little choice in the matter when two of his men had engaged me at gunpoint and had taken me blindfolded to his camp in the hills. At that time Murzabey moved from place to place and nobody was allowed know where he was hiding. Luckily for me, we both lived to tell the tale.

'Is it not strange that he comes here? To the hospital?' Manon asked.

It actually is a little strange, but the times are strange and there is no accounting for any of it. Manon was not convinced. She wanted to know why, as an outlaw, he was coming with impunity to the hospital and setting up camp in a room next to the prefect of the local Jendarma.

Before I could reply, there was a loud rapping on the door and Paul Trowbridge let himself in. He looked flushed and dishevelled, as if he had ridden to the village at great speed. He wouldn't sit or take off his coat but said he had come looking for me. The Vali had paid him a visit and had asked him to draw up a list of all the Armenians working at the Municipal Hospital, including the medical staff.

'What for?' I asked.

'They haven't said but it's not good. Similar lists have been drawn up in Ordu and Sivas.'

'Nobody has asked me for any list, but if they do, I've a pretty good idea why. Your staff are being conscripted, Paul.'

He looked at me as if I hadn't the first idea what I was talking about. All those on the list, he said then, were Armenian or Greek. This seemed perfectly reasonable to me, given that the hospital was run almost exclusively by them, but he also said that half those on the list were women.

'We're at war,' I said. 'Who do you think is nursing the wounded at the front? It certainly isn't the Vali.'

'Armenians,' Paul said. 'They're taking only Armenians and liberating known criminals from prison. Explain that to me, Charles.'

'*Murzabey est un criminel,*' Manon said.

At the mention of the bandit's name Paul became even more agitated. He wanted to know what Murzabey had to do with anything, and before I could stop her Manon had told him about the Kurd's stay at the hospital.

'A reward of two hundred lira was offered on Murzabey's head only a year ago, Charles. Why has that suddenly changed?'

I couldn't answer, but I wasn't about to get embroiled in one of his theories about a Turkish conspiracy, so I decided to go back to work.

'You need to warn your staff,' Paul said as I got up to leave. 'You need to prepare them. Sorry about your leg, Manon, but I have to get back to Trebizond.'

Paul and I walked across the yard to the stable block together, and I had the impression that I'd been tested in some way and found wanting. He climbed into the saddle, insisting he couldn't stay or come to dinner. As a peace offering, I told him I would speak to the Vali and find out what, if anything, was going on, but this did not seem to impress him.

'With all due respect, Charles, you're wasting your time. Give Hetty my best.'

Jahan

The lieutenant and Captain Orfalea rode side by side, letting their horses pick their way at a leisurely pace along the narrow coast road towards Trebizond. Past the shade of the treeline and emerging into the sunlight, Jahan looked down on the sea below. It sparkled a dazzling blue and reflected his happy mood. He and Anyush had spent a number of evenings together and he was quietly planning when he would see her again. Slackening his grip on the reins, he leaned back in the saddle, scanning the distant line of the horizon.

'All quiet, lieutenant.'

'As ever, *bayim*.'

'Would you rather we'd moved out with the infantry?'

'I'd rather spend my time fighting the Russians, sir. Provisioning is women's work.'

'"Theirs not to reason why; Theirs but to do and die."'

His lieutenant looked blankly at him.

'Lord Alfred Tennyson. An Englishman who wrote about the Crimean War.'

'Don't hold much with reading, *bayim*. Never learned.'

'Didn't you go to school?'

'I did but there were too many books. Too many words.'

'You should have stuck with it, lieutenant. Everyone should know how to read.'

'Wish I could now, *bayim*. I see you reading your books and think it must be a good distraction from all this.'

'It is.'

'Though you don't read as much as you used to. Not with all your other amusements.'

'Amusements?'

Jahan looked at the lieutenant.

'The girl.'

They had come to a stop at a bend in the road with a sheer drop on the seaward side of them.

'The men are talking, *bayim*.'

'Really. And what are they saying?'

'That she's Armenian. And other things you don't want to hear.'

Jahan looked at the sea spread out below him.

'These men are hard won, Captain. It's easy to lose their respect.'

'I have no respect for men who string up young boys for amusement.'

'You cannot hand-pick them, *bayim*. They're soldiers, good and bad, but all you've got.' The lieutenant took off his cap and wiped his brow with his sleeve. 'I'm only saying, sir, for your own sake.'

'Is she in danger?'

The lieutenant shrugged. 'This is war, *bayim*. No woman is safe.'

They made their way down the track, without speaking of it again.

Anyush

Anyush hated going to Kazbek's house. Delivering the laundry to that grim cottage loomed like a black hole in every week. It sat in a hidden corner of the wood, and Gohar maintained that Kazbek built it there so he could carry out his nefarious deeds, away from the prying eyes of man and God. Approaching the cottage, Anyush watched for Husik. He had a knack of sneaking up on her, without making a sound, no matter how often she changed the time of her coming.

'*Inch' skhal*, Anyush?'

'Husik! Don't sneak up on me like that!'

'Bet you thought I wasn't coming. Bet you would've been disappointed.'

He walked backwards, his mud-coloured eyes fixed on her face. There was something new in his expression, something bold and sly. She shifted the sack of linen to carry it at her waist.

'Where are you going?'

'You know where I'm going, Husik.'

'Come with me. There's a place I want to show you.'

'Not today.'

'Come on. You know you want to.'

He was leering at her with an unpractised attempt at a smile, and it made her uneasy. Kazbek's house was nearer now, but not close enough. She picked up pace as he fell into step beside her.

'It's a secret place, Anyush. Could be our secret.' His breath was hot and moist on the side of her cheek. 'Aren't you curious? Don't you want to know?'

'Husik, I can't see.'

She moved off the main path onto a narrow track that ran parallel to the treeline. Instantly he followed her.

'Do you know the thing about boys, Anyush? Other boys? I'm not like them. I'm better than all of them.' One of his hands was clutching at the front of his trousers. 'I know what you like, Anyush. I know more about you than you think.'

'You're in my way, Husik.'

'I could put a lot more in your way.'

His full, girlish lips hung open and his eyes shone with a menacing light. This is just Husik, she told herself. Stupid, brainless Husik. But she was frightened and he sensed it. He pushed up against her and she could feel his erection through the fabric of her skirts.

'Come on, Anyush …'

'Get off me!' She thrust the sack into his belly and knocked him backwards to the ground.

'Husik!'

Kazbek was standing at the door of the house, watching them.

'Get up here.'

The boy grinned, his hand still playing at the front of his trousers. Getting to his feet, he disappeared round the back of the cottage to avoid his father's cuffing.

Anyush's face burned. She stepped onto the porch and handed Husik's father the sack of clean clothes. Prayer beads clicked at Kazbek's wrist as he took the laundry and made to go inside.

'There is the matter of payment, *efendim*,' she called.

Kazbek turned around. He was a big man with the long body and wide sloping shoulders of a pickaxe. Unlike his son's opaque eyes, Kazbek's were clear as glass and shone with a yellow-grey light. Father and son had the same head of hair, a faded mink-brown, more pelt than human, but whereas Husik's stood up from his scalp like wiry porcupine quills, Kazbek's was oiled back from his face except for a few lank strands that hung in front of his ears.

'Payment? Maybe we should discuss the three months' payment your mother owes me in rent!' He smiled, his teeth a darker colour than the skin of his face. 'I'm tired of her promises. Tell her I want to see my money. Tell her my patience is wearing thin.'

Anyush stepped down from the porch and turned away. At the bend in the path where the house disappeared behind the trees, she picked up her feet and ran.

Ü Ü Ü

The smell of pilaff from the koghov only made Anyush more hungry. The meal her mother had cooked was watery and thin, rice with mushrooms and onions finely chopped, to make it go further. It had been difficult not to clear her plate of every last bit, but she had promised Sosi and Havat that she would keep some for them and a little for their mother. Walking up the lane to the Talanian farm, she wondered what it would be like to get up from the table feeling full, to know she couldn't eat another bite. Before the famine she had always had enough, but like most people in the village she had been hungry for so long that she couldn't remember what full felt like. It would be good not to dream of food all the time but it didn't really matter. So long as she had Jahan she didn't want for anything. She tried not to think beyond their next meeting, their next kiss, but the future was never very far from her mind. The war was coming to claim Jahan and nothing was going to change that. What would she do without him? She couldn't go back to the way things were. She wished her life would stay just as it was at this moment, a dreamed-of life, one that was completely happy. Her only concern was that she would not conceive a child, but Jahan promised he would take care of it. He knew about these things, he said. She could trust him. Anyush laughed the first time she'd seen him put on his 'device', tying it at one end with pieces of string. It had reminded her of the goat-hair bags the village women used for curds and cheese. Jahan had also instructed her in the practice of douching with alum and quinine. In all Anyush's life she had never stolen so much as a fistful of flour, but she wasn't about to risk becoming pregnant, so she'd started taking small quantities of both from the dispensary after Malik had gone home. Her mother would have said that her daughter had become a thief as well as a whore, and her grandmother for once would have agreed with her.

Approaching the Talanian farmhouse, Anyush saw a number of people gathered in the yard and milling around the outbuildings. Sosi stood in the middle of them with Doctor Stewart on one side and Bayan Talanian, still in her night attire, next to him. The Talanians' neighbours, the Hisars, and Bayan Egoyan, a young widow who lived on the other side, were talking to the doctor's sons, Thomas and Robert Stewart. Something was wrong.

'Havi's missing,' said Sosi, her face white and tear-stained. 'She's been gone all day. Nobody's seen her.'

'I saw her at the gate this morning,' Anyush said. 'On my way to the clinic.'

'She went out early to check the hens and we thought she had wandered down the lane as usual, but when she hadn't come in for breakfast, I went to look for her and couldn't find her. Something's happened Anyush ... I know it has.'

'She'll be found. She probably wandered off and lost her way.'

But there was a growing sense of unease among the people gathered in the Talanians' yard. Havat never went beyond the house without Sosi and never missed a meal.

'We're going to form a search party,' Dr Stewart said. 'Sosi, you and your mother stay in the house in case Havat returns. Anyush, you should stay with them.'

'I want to help in the search, *Doktor*. I know some of the places Havi goes with Sosi. I can bring you there.'

'Very well. We'll start with the road to the village.'

I've been wondering if I should perhaps not write about the events I witnessed today, as I have no wish to relive them, but what happened was of such a pitiful and barbaric nature, that it cannot be ignored.

Havat Talanian, a young mongoloid Armenian girl who lives on the outskirts of the village, went missing from her home this morning. I had dropped in to the house on a routine call to see her mother who suffers from chronic depression, only to find the woman in a highly anxious state and claiming that her younger daughter had been abducted. It is another in a long line of misfortunes for the Talanians, who are more or less destitute and depend largely on the charity of others. The older of the two Talanian girls, Sosi, told me how her sister had not come in for breakfast after going out to feed the hens and that some of their neighbours had come to help look for her. I was reasonably confident that Havat had simply wandered off and lost her way and that we would find her unharmed. We had decided to split into a number of groups when two mounted Turkish soldiers advanced on us from the coast road. I recognised Captain Orfalea and his lieutenant. The captain asked what was going on and I told him about the missing girl. The lieutenant insisted that we were an 'unauthorised gathering' and had to disperse immediately, but, to my surprise, the captain volunteered to help in the search. He sent the lieutenant with half our group in the direction of the village, and the rest would search the coast road. An arrangement had been made that whoever found Havat would send a runner to the second party to call off the search, but by late afternoon there was still no trace of her. Anyush had looked along the shoreline and the headland but had no luck. On the chance that the two soldiers had missed Havat earlier, the captain rode halfway to Trebizond and back but didn't find her either. The remains of

134

our group walked the main pathways around the wood in the direction of the town but, despite thorough searching, the Talanian girl appeared to have vanished. As the light began to fade, we were deciding to call off the search for the night when the captain saw something moving at the edge of the wood.

'There,' he said, 'among the trees.'

It took me a moment to realise what Captain Orfalea was looking at, and before I could say anything he had drawn his pistol. Anyush shouted as Husik, the trapper, emerged slowly into the dim light. The captain ordered him to stand in the road, and I told the boy to come out, that it was perfectly safe. I explained to the captain that Husik works for me and that he's a trapper and knows these woods better than anyone. But Orfalea wouldn't lower his pistol, and Husik's hand remained on the knife at his hip. He was peculiarly agitated, his eyes shifting from one face to another.

'You're looking in the wrong place,' he said. 'You'll never find her.'

I asked if he'd seen the missing girl, but he seemed more interested in Anyush. He stared at her with open hostility.

'Husik,' I said again, 'if you know where the girl is then please say so.'

'I'm not telling *him*,' Husik said, looking at the captain.

I reasoned with the boy but he refused to say anything more. It was clear the captain thought Husik was in some way responsible for the girl's disappearance and kept asking what he had done with her. At this point, Anyush begged the trapper to help find Havat, but he only laughed in a strangely insolent manner.

'There's so much I *do* know,' he said. 'So much I *could* say.'

'Answer the question,' the captain snapped. 'What have you done with her?'

'With *her*? What have *you* done?'

'Enough!' I said, stepping between them. 'For once and for all Husik have you seen the girl or not?'

The boy half turned towards the wood, cocking his ear as though listening for something.

'I didn't say I saw her,' he said. 'I heard noises. That's all.'

'What kind of noises?'

'Screaming. Like an animal in a trap. Only it wasn't an animal.'

Anyush turned pale, and the captain was clearly sceptical, but I knew the boy wouldn't lie to me.

'Whereabouts?' I asked.

'I might not remember.'

'Please ...' Anyush begged. 'We can't leave her out here.'

The trapper clammed up again, and I was getting weary of the exchange. I took off my hat and wiped my brow. It was still very hot and the mosquitoes were out in force.

'Look, Husik,' I said finally, 'if we don't find Havat, she will almost certainly die. She doesn't have the wit to survive in the wild as you do. You are the only one who can help her.'

I still wasn't sure what he would decide, but he turned abruptly and disappeared into the trees. The captain, Anyush and I hurried to catch up with him.

Beneath the canopy the path was barely visible, but Husik's step never faltered. Turning abruptly east, he left the track and made his way through scrub, low-hanging boughs and fallen trees. We had to move quickly not to lose sight of him, stumbling and lacerating hands and faces. Gradually the darkness seemed a little less intense and what initially appeared to be a clearing proved to be a wide path-way following a linear course through the wood. It was overgrown with moss and spindly trees reaching for the light, but it was clear that it had once been an avenue or thoroughfare of some description. Husik moved along it, following its south-ward course, constantly looking to right and left as though expecting company. Abruptly he came to a halt and waited for us.

'There,' he said pointing, 'that's where I heard it.'

At the end of the avenue, hemmed in by trees on all sides, was a two-storey wooden house or what had once been a house but which was now collapsing in on itself. The roof sagged so badly that broken joists and wooden roof tiles lay in a jumble on the the floor below. Only one set of shutters hung from a rusty hinge.

The glassless window frames had warped and buckled and thick ropes of ivy twined around and through them. And everywhere, from every niche and crack, greenery grew abundantly.

Anyush, the captain and I walked to where the door had once been, but Husik hung back as though this human habitation in his dominion was repugnant to him. Inside, it took my eyes some time to adjust to the darkness. The ground floor was more or less intact, and although the ceiling had crumbled in places and some of the dividing walls to the other rooms were mere wooden laths, it retained the shape and feel of a house. A rank house, which smelled of animal droppings and vegetation. Of mildew and mould and something else.

'Cigarette ends,' the captain said. 'A dozen or more over here near the door. Ugh! What the Devil?!'

I turned to see him trying to shake something from the sole of his boot. He kicked it away as I looked around, unable to rid myself of the feeling that this house was overpoweringly sinister. The trees, the dark, the sickening smell of decay. And then I heard it. The first pitiful sound, weak and forlorn like a wounded animal.

'Over there,' the captain said, pointing to a spot near what remained of the stairs. I was closest and got there first.

'Dear God!'

Someone moved behind me and I thrust out my arm to block their way. 'Stay back,' I said. 'Don't come any closer.'

It was Anyush, standing at my shoulder, her eyes staring and her face ghostly in the green half-light. Havat lay on her back, partially clothed but naked from the waist down and her breasts exposed. Her legs were still spread as though she was unable to move them, and one lay at an unnatural angle to the floor. The clothes beneath her hips were soaked with dark clotted blood, and pools of paler liquid congealed on her stomach, thighs and naked breasts. Her arms had been tied behind her back with one of the laces from her shoes, and her other shoe, laced tightly by her sister that morning, was still in place on her foot. She was lying in her own excrement, the smell of faeces and urine growing stronger by the minute. Suddenly the house was filled with a terrible noise. Havat's eyes stretched wide and terrified sounds issued from her throat. She bucked and flailed, her useless leg flapping against the floor, and a raspy, gurgling scream came from the depths of her chest. Husik was standing looking at her, but it was the captain she was staring at in terror.

'Get out!' I ordered him. 'It's your uniform. Move outside, Captain!'

But the captain was unable to look away. His eyes were staring at Havat's face and chin which were covered with dark, black blood.

'Allah be merciful!' he whispered. 'Her tongue ... they cut out her tongue!'

'Captain ... outside. Now!'

He stumbled across the room and lurched towards a window. Clutching the thick wooden frame, he threw up his last meal against the rotten shingle. It was now abundantly clear what had stuck to the underside of his boot. Anyush had recovered a little and was kneeling at Havat's side, gently stroking her matted hair. The screaming quietened to a low sobbing as Havat recognised her friend. As gently as I could, I attempted to move the damaged leg, but the girl moaned loudly in pain.

'The hip is dislocated,' I said. 'They must have used terrible force.'

From my coat pocket I took the bottle of laudanum I always carry and pulled out the stopper.

'This is for the pain,' I said to Havat. 'I'm going to pour a few drops into your mouth. It's a little bitter, but it will help.'

She grimaced as the tincture hit the back of her throat, and her hand reached out for Anyush. After a few moments she became quiet.

The old door to the house was lying near the back wall and between us we managed to lift Havat onto it. Using his knife, Husik hacked two holes in the wood and lashed his rope through them, so that he and I could pull the door along the ground like a sled. Havat didn't make a sound. Her eyes were open and fixed on Anyush as though she were afraid her angel of mercy might disappear.

Anyush

Water closed over Anyush's head as she slipped beneath the swell. In the heaving silence she swam through the silty green until she had to come up for air.

She was alone in the cove because Jahan was unable to get away, and although he had warned her not to go anywhere without him, she needed the comfort of the sea.

Whenever she passed the wood she saw Havat again, her body lying in filth and the smell of her tormentors rising from her. The violence of what had happened frightened Anyush. The cruelty of it. She closed her eyes and dived again.

Word had spread quickly about the assault on Havat Talanian. Aside from the girl herself, the effect of it was most apparent on Sosi. Anyush's friend was like a shadow of herself, tormented and silent as though it was she, and not Havat, who could no longer speak. She blamed herself for what had happened and nobody could persuade her otherwise.

Sosi's mother was like a woman possessed. Bayan Talanian abandoned her bedroom and nursed Havat to a form of recovery. It was she who held her to the bed when Dr Stewart put her hip back in place. She who taught her how to walk again and fed her soups and broths until the swelling in the stump of her tongue died down. But nobody, neither Havat's mother nor her sister nor indeed any living person, could persuade her to leave the house or the protection of its old and crumbling walls.

Havat Talanian's ordeal occupies everybody's mind. People talk and talk as if they might talk it out of being. For all our sakes, I wish it were that simple.

I've managed to relocate Havat's hip and it has healed reasonably well, but her psychological state is fragile. She has become incontinent and screams uncontrollably whenever she's left alone. I haven't told Hetty any of the more distressing details and find myself becoming more circumspect generally. Paul's stories of death lists and Armenian pogroms has upset her. As it happened, she learned of the assault for herself because it is talked of everywhere, and everybody has an opinion as to who is responsible. The streets are deserted at night. Families lock their doors and some of the children have been taken out of school. Our own children are forbidden to wander beyond the house, giving them the perfect excuse to idle for hours indoors, but at least we know they're safe. Hetty's arranged for the remaining schoolchildren to be escorted to and from the schoolhouse, and she herself is accompanied by Mahmoud Agha whenever she visits her patients outside the village. I am as fearful for my own wife as anybody else and cannot understand the mind of a man who would do such a thing. Arshen Nalbandian claims he saw a group of soldiers near the wood that morning, but Captain Orfalea assured me his company had spent the day at the barracks digging latrines. Could I take the captain at his word? From his reaction when we discovered Havat, I certainly believe that if his men were responsible, he at least knew nothing about it. Which begs the question, what other soldiers were involved? It has put me in mind of the invitation we received last week.

Another high-ranking Turkish officer, Captain Ozhan, invited Hetty and I to dine at his home in Trebizond. The captain's second wife was attending Hetty for obstetric care in the run-up to the birth of her first child, and I had met Ozhan once or twice at the Vali's mansion. He is a small, fair-haired man with deep pockets and big ambitions. His phaeton collected us at the outskirts of the city, along with a groom to bring our horses to his stable yard. The house was large and impressive, surrounded by a great garden containing fruit trees, vegetables and flowers. A conservatory, a pond with goldfish and even a flock of doves added a distinctly Victorian touch. Wearing a dark evening suit and stiff collar, he met us in the salon and offered me an expensive imported whiskey, although he didn't partake himself. The older of his two wives, a shy, small woman, wearing a hijab and plain black dress, had set the table for dinner and called Hetty aside to ask if it was done properly. The younger, pregnant wife also wore a hijab but her skirt was more European in cut and a brightly coloured pair of shoes peeped out from underneath. The women got on well and Hetty spent most of her time with them, while Ozhan insisted on showing me around the estate. Most of the land had been inherited from his father, but he had enlarged it, buying the adjoining plots and tilling it for grapes, olives and hazelnuts as well as keeping cattle and sheep. On the Ozhan farm there didn't appear to be any problem keeping livestock fed or crops watered, and farmhands were very much in evidence despite conscription for the war.

Overall, Ozhan and I got on well enough. He was educated and showed a keen interest in modern medicine, but I did not like the man. There was an arrogance about him, a casual cruelty in the manner he adopted with his servants and wives. The following day, when we made to leave, Ozhan did not hide his annoyance that we would not stay longer. He had made arrangements, he said, that he and I would hunt for partridge in the hills. I thanked him but made the excuse of pressing commitments at the hospital and we left immediately. It was Hetty who overheard him castigating his older wife with a resounding slap for failing in her duty to impress.

Jahan

'**I** want to know who they are.'

'Captain, sir ...'

'I want you to find out if the men who did this are in my company.'

'It could have been the Jendarma, *bayim*. You have no proof they were soldiers.'

'They were men in uniform, that's all I know. If they were soldiers, I want the name and rank of every one. Every man who had a part in this.'

Lieutenant Kadri closed his mouth.

'If you have no success, then I want you to find someone the men will talk to. Someone they trust. Use your contacts in the Jendarma if you have to. And check again where Corporal Hanim was that day.'

'You saw him here yourself, *bayim*.'

'Do it anyway. You are to report back to me. Everything you learn, understand? As soon as you hear, I want to know.'

'Captain ... whoever did this will not like being informed on by one of their own.'

'You need to be discreet, but you have my word your name will not be mentioned.'

'It's not just that, *bayim* ... there are similar stories coming out of

Trebizond, and beyond. This is not the only incident of this kind.'

'They attacked a simpleton, Lieutenant. A halfwit. We are soldiers of the Empire not animals in the field. I would expect my men to behave accordingly.'

'With respect, *bayim*, you will never stop this. Do you punish some and not others? Whether you like it or not the men are being encouraged in it.'

'To behave like beasts?'

'Armenians are viewed as a threat, sir. The fewer the government have to worry about the better.'

The captain regarded his lieutenant coldly.

'I am only repeating what the men are saying, sir. What they're being told.'

'Lieutenant, I'm trusting that you understand me when I say I have my reasons for wanting those names. I'm not particularly concerned how you get them, but I want them. Every last one.'

Ü Ü Ü

Jahan sat at his desk in the room he used as an office. It was cool and pleasant to sit in, both because of the thickness of the stone walls and the fact that it faced north-east, away from the midday sun. It was empty of furniture, except for a rickety table and chair, a wooden chest containing various documents and a series of nails hammered into the wall, on which he hung his tunic. Situated on the outskirts of the village, it had once been a mill house and grain store but was now used as a billet and storehouse for the provisions the company had been gathering since their arrival. Most of what they had accumulated, and it wasn't much, would be sent to the Third Army in Van, north of the Persian border.

Pushing away the page in front of him, Jahan abandoned his attempt to write a letter home. It seemed futile writing letters when he never received any and had no way of knowing if his ever arrived. Anyway, his concentration was gone. When he had stood on that girl's tongue, it was as if she robbed him of his peace of mind. The memory of her in that awful place would not leave him, her broken body, her nakedness and shame. It could have been any girl, or one in particular.

A knock on the door interrupted his thoughts and Lieutenant Kadri, let himself in. His expression was grim.

'You have news?'

'Names. All the men involved were soldiers but not from our company.'

'Allah be praised! Where are they stationed?'

'Trebizond.'

'And their commanding officer?'

'Captain Nazim Ozhan.'

'General Ozhan's son? His father is adviser to the German attaché. Thank you, Ahmet. I will write to him. On second thoughts, I will see him in person.'

The lieutenant remained standing before him.

'Is there something else?'

'This visit to Captain Ozhan, sir. You can make it if you wish but you'll be wasting your time.'

'I presume you're going to tell me why.'

'Because Ozhan was one of them.'

On two occasions this week I made visits away from the hospital, and I have to admit I remain more than a little disturbed by the second.

Firstly, I went to see the Vali. Paul's talk of an Armenian blacklist is gaining momentum in certain circles, and Hetty is beginning to credit these stories herself. She believes we have to exert our influence with the authorities to safeguard the hospital and the Armenians in the village, even though she knows my feelings on the matter of Paul's 'theories'. However, for my own peace of mind and hers, I agreed to talk to the Vali.

The Vali was more sombre than usual, but he vigorously denied there was substance to the rumours. The attack on the girl was being investigated, and the Armenian list was merely a formality, he said, a step towards taking a census of the country as a whole. I was relieved. Easier in my mind than I had been for months. Paul had overreacted as he was prone to do. It now became imperative that I talk to him and set this straight. Unusually, we had not had a visit from Paul in weeks, so I travelled to Trebizond to see him. At the hospital I was told he had been operating through the night and was resting in his quarters. Like Manon, Paul lived on the complex but in a single, sparsely furnished room on the top floor. I found him sitting on his bed fully clothed, unshaven and only just awake. I apologised for intruding and told him to stay where he was. In contrast to Manon's apartment, there was nothing comfortable or welcoming about the room. Nothing of a personal nature, no pictures or ornaments, only the smell of an unwashed body and stale cigarettes. Paul was looking distractedly around him, searching the floor and patting down his pockets. He found his cigarette case in his white coat, and he lit up. I was shocked to see how thin he had become. His unwashed hair stuck to his

146

head and he had the pallor of a coal miner. I mentioned that we were wondering why we hadn't seen him for so long, and he said to tell Thomas he hadn't forgotten his birthday and would make it up to him. I suggested he tell him himself, but Paul insisted he couldn't get away.

'The others can cover for you,' I said. 'Take a few days off. You're always advising me to take things easier.'

Tilting his head back, he directed a long plume of smoke towards the ceiling before lying flat against the pillows.

'They're gone, Charles,' he said.

He told me then that all the physicians and surgeons in the hospital had been taken, with the sole exception of Professor Levonian, who's allowed stay only because he's looking after one of the Vali's wives. This made absolutely no sense. The Municipal Hospital has five times the number of beds I have, as well as three operating theatres, an orthopaedic clinic and a TB sanatorium. It is not possible to run it on a reduced staff, never mind two doctors working alone. I asked him what exactly he meant by 'taken'?

'The list,' he said. 'All their names were on the list.'

Now I began to understand. As usual, he had misinterpreted the facts completely. It was clear to me what was happening, and I told him as much. 'They've been conscripted,' I said. 'Exactly as I thought.'

I asked him if the nurses were still working, and he said that yes they were, which tied up my argument neatly. I then told him about my visit to the Vali and how his officials were gathering statistics for the census. Paul didn't react to this. He kept staring at the brown water stain on the ceiling above his bed.

'There has never been a census in the Empire, Charles,' he said. 'What makes you think the government would embark on one now?'

I told him that I didn't know, that I would guess it had something to do with troop numbers and statistics, but Paul said that the Empire didn't have the resources or the manpower. That no one in their right mind would take on a census in war-time. I had to laugh.

'This is Turkey, Paul,' I said. 'Whoever said there had to be a logical explanation?'

He sat up suddenly, swinging his legs over the side of the bed and looking directly at me. A look so fierce that I thought he was going to hit me.

'That's a much loved saying of yours, isn't it, Charles? "This is Turkey."'

I didn't like his tone and I didn't like what it implied, but I reminded myself that he was overworked and exhausted.

As if to confirm it, he wandered off on a tangent so obscure that I hadn't the first idea where the conversation was leading. He talked about the declaration of martial law, and the bank refusing to pay depositors, and the non-existent postal service. 'But then we all know the postal service is something of a joke,' he smiled. 'This is after all Turkey.'

At that point, I was tempted to get up and leave, but he wasn't finished. He reached for the glass on the cabinet beside his bed and threw his cigarette into it. 'Everything going on around you, Charles, is what happens in wartime. Normal in a very abnormal way. But this ...' he pulled a sheet of paper from under the glass and waved it at me '... this list of Armenian names drawn up by a Turkish member of my staff and meant for the governor has nothing to do with war. This is a death list.'

I must have looked at him disbelievingly because he crushed the paper in his fist and got to his feet.

'You *know* what's been happening in Constantinople.'

'That's very different—'

'It's history repeating itself! The war is just what the Turks have been waiting for. The perfect opportunity to wipe out an entire race.'

'That's ridiculous!'

'It's already happening, Charles. Even in the village.'

I couldn't think of anything to say. I was dumbfounded. What had happened to the man? The only reasonable explanation was that he wasn't well. My anger left me and I asked him, pleaded with him, to come stay with us.

'Levonian will manage on his own for a few days,' I said. 'Hetty and the children would really like to see you.'

He reached for his white coat and put it on. Without another word, he went to the door and opened it. I thought he would turn back. I was certain he wouldn't leave things like that, but he only nodded and left me staring after him.

Captain Jahan Orfalea

Mushar

Trebizond

June 24th, 1915

Enver Pasha

Minister of War

The War Ministry

Constantinople

Sir,

I am writing in the hope of securing your attention for a crime committed here in the Tre-bizond area within the past two weeks. This outrage perpetrated by soldiers of the Empire was such that it sullies the name of every man who proudly wears the Turkish uniform.

Their victim was a simple Armenian girl whom they abducted and took turns in assaulting. When they tired of torturing her, they cut out her tongue and left her in an abandoned house where she was eventually found. I will spare you the details of her pitiful state, except to say that it would have been a mercy had she died. The villagers, with whom my corps had developed a certain trust, are terrified and less likely to cooperate in the procurement of provisions in the future.

As someone who took the oath of allegiance in good faith and who is proud to serve my country, I could not let this go unheeded. Because these men have dis-graced the uniform and dishonoured their compatriots, I know you would wish to be appraised of their cowardly and terrible act.

I have enclosed the names of those involved, including their commanding officer who was one of them.

I remain yours faithfully,

Captain Jahan Orfalea

Captain Jahan Orfalea

Mushar

Trebizond

June 30th, 1915

Enver Pasha

Minister of War

The War Ministry

Constantinople

Sir,

Having failed to secure a response to my last letter regarding an incident in Trebizond, I understand that it may not as yet have come to your attention. I feel certain it is an issue you would want to be made aware of and so have enclosed again the particulars of this terrible crime.

Yours faithfully,

Captain Jahan Orfalea

Jahan

Jahan and Anyush were lying in each other's arms in the old church. It was almost completely dark outside but the breeze that blew across the cliff was warm and redolent of the sea. From inside the ruin they could see the last vestiges of the disappearing light.

'I don't like the way he looks at you.'

'How does he look at me?' she teased.

'You know what I mean.'

'It's only Husik. He thinks he's protecting me.'

'He's obsessed with you and *I* should be protecting you.'

'You are,' she said, leaning in to kiss him.

His mood that evening was sombre and irritable. Events of the past weeks were still fresh in his mind and the dangers Anyush faced daily troubled him. It was madness bringing her to the ruin, but the thought of not seeing her at all was worse. What they were doing was wrong on so many levels that he couldn't think clearly. There had to be a better way to manage the situation, but if there was it eluded him. In light of what had happened, he couldn't expect her to keep coming, as he couldn't live with himself if anyone should harm her. There had to be a way around it, a solution that would keep her safe and both of them together. Out of the blue, the perfect answer came to him.

'Marry me.'

She sat up, blood rushing to her cheeks.

'You don't need anyone else to protect you. Marry me.'

He couldn't read her expression. She seemed shocked at first, but then pressed her lips together and drew away from him.

'You want to marry me because you're jealous of Husik?'

'No. Well, yes but that's not—'

'A trapper?'

'He's Armenian and has more claim to you than I'll ever have!'

She sighed. 'We can't change who we are, Jahan.'

'Why not? Why does an ignorant peasant have more right to you than I do? You want to know why I'm jealous? I'm jealous of your family who see you every day. I'm jealous of the bed you sleep in and the food you eat and the damn air you breathe!'

He got to his feet, unnerved by his sudden temper. He looked out at the sea, almost invisible now but murmuring quietly in the distance. Night had fallen and only a greenish glow lit the sky above the horizon. The gravestones leaned into the darkness, black shapes cut from the evening sky. 'Don't you get tired of it?'

'Of what?'

'This place. A filthy ruin. Having to hide like criminals. I'm tired of it, Anyush. I'm tired of pretending I don't know you because I'm not supposed to. Or feeling that what we're doing is wrong. I want to make it right. Anyush, marry me.'

The moonlight threw his outline in a long black shadow towards her as she sat there in the dark.

'You make it sound so simple.'

'It is simple! Anyush, it *is* if we make it so.'

He went to her and took her hand. 'Don't you want to marry me?'

'How can it be possible, Jahan? It would never be allowed.'

'I'm not asking anyone's permission. Only yours.'

'You know how things are in the village —'

'I know how things could be. I never said it would be easy.'

Anyush looked at him and he saw the cold light of fear in her eyes, the first time he had ever seen it there. But he felt strong enough for both of them. He was young, and certain of his decision. He gripped her hand firmly in his.

'If you don't feel anything for me, then I will accept that. Really I'll try. You can marry Husik, or anyone you like, and I'll not say a word against you. But if you feel about me as I think you do ... if you love me, Anyush, then I'm asking you to be brave. Trust me. I will make you happy. I know I can.'

'Jahan, what we've done —'

'We've done nothing to be ashamed of. We love each other ... is that wrong? Are you ashamed of me?'

'No,' she said, laying her hand against his cheek.

He shifted his weight so that he was kneeling properly, one knee resting on the stone floor. 'I can't imagine life without you, Anyush. I'm miserable when I'm not with you and there's nobody that makes me this happy. I love you, Anyush Charcoudian. So please ... I'm asking you again ... will you marry me?'

Her eyes, grave and dark, looked into his. He knew that it was not a simple proposal of marriage he was offering. Anyush would have to deny her Armenian upbringing, her religion, family and friends. As a Turkish wife she would be expected to convert to Islam or to practise her own faith in secret. His parents would oppose the marriage for any number of reasons and might never accept her. Many would consider the sacrifice too great. But then she smiled, slowly at first, spreading to her eyes and bringing a rush of colour to her cheeks. It was too dark to see her

154

blush, but he could feel it. The heat warmed his hands when he laid them against her face and even the lobes of her ears were tingling. He began to laugh and she laughed with him.

'Yes,' she said, 'I will marry you.'

'Say it again.'

'I will marry you. I love you, Jahan.'

He leaned in to kiss her, but just at that moment there was a shuffling, scraping noise over their heads. They looked up to see a bat flying crazily above them, darting in all directions and beating its wings frantically against the walls before escaping outside into the evening sky. Anyush started violently in his arms and that was the memory of her that stayed with him: her pale face looking upwards at the broken dome as though the heavenly host was sitting in judgement above them.

Anyush

'I hate Turks,' Parzik said, brushing away angry tears. 'I curse their entire miserable race.'

On the other side of the treatment room door, Dr Stewart was putting stitches in Vardan's face. He had come home from Trebizond swollen and bruised, his ribs broken and unable to see out of his left eye.

'He did nothing. Nothing that deserved this. How could he be working too slowly? He was plastering same as usual.'

Twisting the thin gold band around her finger, Parzik glanced at the door to the treatment room. Like everyone in the village, Anyush knew that Vardan had been trying to make the job last in an effort to avoid conscription now that Parzik was pregnant. She took her friend's hand and held it.

That morning Anyush had come to work thinking only of Jahan's proposal. Nothing could spoil this day. She was to be married to Jahan, the man she loved, the man she scarcely believed wanted her for his own. Her name would no longer be Anyush Charcoudian, village girl, but Bayan Orfalea, army officer's wife.

All through the wood she had whispered her name to the leaves, Anyush Orfalea. Bayan Anyush Charcoudian Orfalea. There was a rhythm to the names together, a perfect fit. She had wanted to shout it at the treetops and at the waves breaking on the shore. Near the end of the path Husik had appeared.

'*Barev*, Husik,' she'd said, smiling.

He had stared at her, his mouth hanging open. Her greeting had taken him by surprise, but she'd said nothing more, holding her secret close.

Anyush had told no one of her news but longed to tell Sosi and Parzik. It was not so long ago that the thought of stepping into Parzik's shoes seemed laughable, but now she could think of little else. Would there be enough money to buy a calf for her shordzevk? Would Sosi decorate the church as she had done for Parzik? And the dress ... what should she wear? Bayan Stewart's dress. And who could she ask to give her away? Dr Stewart maybe, if Father Gregory would allow it.

But finding a badly beaten Vardan on the clinic steps changed everything. As she listened to Parzik rage against the Turkish race, the reality of what she had been planning struck her. Did she really believe her friends would be happy for her? That Parzik would welcome the news of her marriage to a people who had hanged her father-in-law and beaten her husband? Or that Sosi would feel anything but horror after what had happened to Kevork and Havat? As well as the fact that her mother would disown her or throw her down the well. And what would she tell her grandmother? Sitting in the waiting room, holding her friend's hand, Anyush tried to swallow her fear. If she married Jahan, she would lose the right to call herself Armenian. Living in the village would not be possible and she would leave it an orphan. She could, of course, call herself Bayan Orfalea, but everyone she cared about would call her something far worse. And yet she knew that she *would* marry Jahan. Losing everything only proved how much she loved him. Gripping Parzik's hand, she whispered a prayer that God might intercede for all of them.

Jahan

The lieutenant followed behind his captain, their horses walking the path in single file and treading carefully over the loose stones. On the landward side, the treeline rose along the foothills, throwing the riders into deep shade, while on the seaward side the ground crumbled away steeply towards the ocean and the rocks below. They had climbed up through the hills to the lookout, the highest point overlooking the Black Sea, and were making their way back down to the base. In the distance, the water met the sky in an uninterrupted blue line.

'No Russians today, lieutenant.'

'No, *bayim*.'

'Time for breakfast. An empty sea does wonders for the appetite.'

'Yes, *bayim*.'

The captain looked at his second-in-command. 'Something on your mind, Lieutenant?'

'Word has got out, sir. About your letters.'

'Go on.'

'Our own men are not too concerned. They're mostly loyal to you. But Ozhan's company are not pleased.'

'Their well-being is not my concern.'

'Captain Ozhan is well connected, *bayim*. He's not a man who likes to be threatened.'

'Ozhan is a rapist and a brute. He deserves to be flogged.'

'Word is out that he's been making contact with important people. It worries me, *bayim*.'

'Stop worrying, Ahmet. I have connections of my own and I'm not afraid of a man like that.'

They rode slowly along the trail, descending gradually down the steep incline. Where the track joined the coast road, they had a view of the village below and the grain store on its northern side. Drawing nearer, they could see mounted soldiers assembled in the yard and others moving in and out of the building. These were not his men. As Jahan watched from the top of the hill, he realised that Ahmet's concerns were well founded. The arrival of these soldiers could mean many things but none of them good.

'Lieutenant, I need you to do something for me.'

Reining in his horse he took the small volume of poetry he carried with him in his pocket and tore out the fly-leaf. Writing out his father's name and family address in Constantinople, he handed it to Ahmet.

'Bring this to Anyush Charcoudian. You know who she is. I'm not going to pretend that you don't. Wait for her at the clinic or at Dr Stewart's house. Give this into her hand, not to anyone else. Tell her to write to my parents. They'll know where I am.'

Jahan and his lieutenant had been spotted at a distance of a half mile, so that when they entered the yard it was full of waiting soldiers.

'Captain Orfalea?'

The man standing in the doorway was roughly the same height as the captain but had light brown hair that might once have been fair and a thin ginger moustache.

'I believe you know who I am, Captain. Well, of course you do. You've been writing about me.'

'Ozhan.'

'Captain Ozhan. I have been given the pleasure … the honour … of escorting you to Trebizond.'

'You wouldn't know the meaning of the word.'

'No indeed. I am a savage and a barbarian after all. *The* barbarian who was chosen to relieve you of your command.'

'By whose authority?'

'By the authority of Colonel Abdul-Khan. Now, Captain, if you turn about, my men will accompany you to Trebizond.'

'I have to get my belongings.'

'We already have your belongings and papers. Very meticulous they are too. Oh and don't worry about the villagers. I understand you are something of a champion for Armenians around here, but I will take good care of them. Rest assured, I will give them my particular attention.'

Anyush

'Please wait, Anyush. Dr Stewart will be back in a moment and he'll escort you home.'

'I'm going to Parzik's house, Bayan Stewart. Her uncle will bring me.'

'Really, Anyush, we promised your mother. I would prefer if you waited.'

'It's very close. Just over there.'

'Well ...'

'*Bari yereko*, Bayan Stewart. I will see you tomorrow.'

The doctor's wife stood watching until Anyush had turned the corner at the end of the lane. Lying to Bayan Stewart did not come easily to Anyush, but it was the only way to see Jahan. Once she was close to Parzik's house, she would double back through the wood and meet him at the beach. She hadn't gone very far when she heard a sound behind her. Footsteps. She thought it might have been one of the Stewart boys coming to escort her, but when she looked over her shoulder, she froze. A soldier was giving chase and fast bearing down on her. Taking off in the direction of the village, she ran towards Parzik's house. Anyush risked a glance behind her. The gap was closing, and the soldier shouted something she couldn't catch. Taking a left into the churchyard, she ran down the lane, skirting round the vestry at the back. This was not a safe place, dark and overhung with trees, but if she could make it out the other side, it would take only seconds to get to Parzik's house. She was almost there. She could see the window of Parzik's old room with a wedding braid still hanging from the shutter, when a hand clamped roughly over her mouth. She bit down hard.

'*Khoz*! Do that again and you'll feel my fist.'

Anyush recognised the voice. It was Jahan's lieutenant. His arm was across her chest, lifting her bodily off the ground. She kicked at his shins with her heel.

'*Kakhard*! Be still you, witch. I have a message from Captain Orfalea.'

The fight drained out of her. Something was wrong. The lieutenant put her down and took a paper from his pocket. He handed it to her, telling her about the events of that morning.

'The captain has been relieved of his command. He'll be sent back to Constantinople and then ... who knows? Probably the front. He wants you to write to this address.'

Anyush stared at the paper.

'Do you understand what I'm telling you? Captain Orfalea is being punished for something he should never have become involved in.'

The soldier talked on, but all Anyush knew was that Jahan was gone. Really gone.

'He's not coming back. You know that, don't you? Better for everyone if you do.'

'He'll come back,' she whispered. 'He will.'

She looked into the lieutenant's face and, whatever she thought she might find there, she did not expect his pity.

My dearest Jahan,

I have just learned that they have taken you away from me. The lieutenant says you are to be sent to Constantinople and I hope this letter will reach you there. My heart is broken, Jahan. The village already seems so different without you. Everything is changed. Everything is wrong. I went to the ruin, even though a storm was blowing and the noise inside was deafening. The rain and the wind comforted me, Jahan, because no one could hear me weep. I said a prayer that they have not hurt you and that you will be with me again very soon. My only consolation is that you thought of me as they took you away. I will write to you every day, Jahan. I will think of you every second until we are together again.

Let me know that this letter has reached you and that you are safe.

Yours always,

Anyush

̈U ̈U ̈U

'I was afraid when he finished plastering that they'd send him away, but he's re-roofing the barracks now and it's the answer to our prayers.'

Parzik and Anyush were sitting by the edge of the pool, the laundry at their feet. Parzik's old uncle Stepan was dozing in the shade and the washing-pool was otherwise empty. Since the attack on Havat, fewer women were coming there, and those that did came in large groups or with male relatives.

'He hates the work and hates the gendarmes, but it's a job,' Parzik said, her voice carrying across the water.

She paused to shift her position and rest her hand on her belly. 'At least I know where he is so I don't worry so much. Anyush ... are you listening to me?'

'Sorry, yes. That's good.'

Parzik looked at her friend closely. 'You don't look well. Is something the matter?'

Anyush could have told Parzik then. About the prayers she was saying twice, three times a day that her monthly bleed would come. She could have said she had blasphemed in the house of the Lord and that He was punishing her. That she would carry a bastard child with no one to console her. Khandut would banish her from the house, and she couldn't bear to think what it would do to her grandmother.

'I haven't been sleeping,' she said. 'Because of Havat.'

'Poor Havat. What will become of her?'

Parzik picked up a pair of trousers and held them to the light. 'There's a new captain in the village. From Trebizond. I wonder what happened to the other one?'

Anyush remembered the day in Sosi's yard. The first time she had seen

Jahan. She closed her eyes, thinking of the last time.

'There was something strange about that captain ... you know ... at the wedding? The way he danced with you?'

A shrill, piercing whistle rang out across the water. Near the treeline Husik was standing on the bank, gesturing to them. 'Soldiers!'

The girls ran to the shore, picking up clothes as they went.

'Leave them!' Husik shouted. 'This way. Quickly ... hurry.'

Parzik shook old Stepan awake and led him after Husik into the trees. They could hear the sound of the soldiers' boots on the high shore and a lone voice telling the others to be quiet. Husik moved without making a sound, bringing them further into the wood, but Stepan, half blind in the darkness and disorientated from his sudden wakening, was crashing through the undergrowth, hitting off low branches and stumbling over roots. Husik went to him and signalled everyone to be still. They had been climbing upwards along the hillside and could see through the trees down to the river below. Standing around the water's edge, the soldiers were looking at the deserted pool. A man in a uniform, just like Jahan's, kicked over the abandoned clothes basket. He turned slowly, surveying the land around him, before looking upwards at the exact spot where they were hiding. Stepan was out of breath, breathing far too loudly. If the soldiers entered the wood, they would have to keep climbing, but Stepan would not get far. Parzik's lips moved in silent prayer and her arm curled around her belly. Only Husik looked out from behind his tree, one hand raised to keep the others quiet. For what seemed an age, they stayed hidden in the trees before another sound reached them. Anyush risked a look. The soldiers had gone back onto the road and were leaving, the sound of the horses' hooves dying away.

My dearest Jahan,

With every day that passes, I pray it will be the day I hear from you. The lieutenant told me you were to board a ship in Trebizond, so you must surely have reached Constantinople by now. I worry that you have been arrested or are unwell, because I know if it was possible to write to me you would have done so.

Life here in the village grows more dangerous every day. The captain who replaced you is feared by everyone and even the Jendarma are said to stay out of his way. A few days ago another girl was assaulted like Havat Talanian and people are saying Captain Ozhan and his men are to blame. Everyone is afraid to leave their homes but even there they are not safe. Arshen Nalbandian was dragged from his house and beaten. Nobody knows what his crime was, but it seems these men do not need a reason. Our village begins to look like a ghost town. The Armenian houses are empty, the contents stolen and the doors kicked in. The few animals left have been taken or butchered, so that even the air itself seems to reek of blood. And those who still have homes are being evicted from them. Parzik and Vardan watched Ozhan's men burn their farmhouse to the ground. Poor Vardan. It is as if he has been twice bereaved.

As for myself, Jahan, every day seems as long as a lifetime. I wait and hope and pray to hear from you.

Yours always,

Anyush

Another member of staff was missing today. Anyush Charcoudian's reliability is second only to Manon's, and when she didn't show up at the clinic this morning everybody was concerned. The mystery was resolved when I found the girl's grandmother, Gohar Charcoudian, waiting in our garden to see me. The old woman is thinner than when I last saw her, and seems a little unsteady on her feet. Her arthritis has come back with a vengeance, and there are bruised-looking pouches beneath her eyes. She has all the appearance of an anxious, frightened, old woman, but then everyone in the village looks the same. Since the arrival of Nazim Ozhan, attacks on women have become commonplace. Everything I suspected about the man has been borne out. He is a bully and a thug who takes the law into his own hands and delights in the suffering of others.

The old woman asked if she could speak with me, and I invited her to come inside. Hetty sat her at the table and put a bowl of soup before her, which she took in both hands and ate as though she hadn't tasted a hot meal in quite some time.

'*Teşekkür*,' she said, when she'd finished, and asked if she could have a word privately.

'Thomas, go help Robert in the stables,' I said, 'and tell the others they can watch Arnak shoeing the mare.'

My eldest son sloped reluctantly from the room as a creaking noise came from the bassinet in the corner. Lottie's tousled head peered out from under the canopy, and two thin arms reached for her mother. My youngest daughter is small for her age and slight, with purple shadows like pewter half-moons beneath her eyes. An ill omen, the chekeji would say, an indication that she is under the influence of the evil eye. Lottie's poor colour and small size have more to do with a weakness of the kidneys and a tendency to infection and fever than any misbegotten hex. She sat on Hetty's lap, her little blonde head ducking like a sparrow's beneath her mother's chin, while Gohar Charcoudian told us that her granddaughter was ill with inflammation of the stomach.

'I'm sorry to hear it,' I said. 'Would you like me to see her?'

'That will not be necessary, *Doktor*. She has eaten mussels she should have thrown away and her stomach has been complaining ever since.'

I assured her she wouldn't be the first, and Hetty insisted that Anyush should stay in bed for a few days' rest.

'*Teşekkür ederim*, Bayan Stewart, Dr Stewart.'

The old woman stood up from the table and looked for a moment at my daughter. Gohar Charcoudian is an arresting sight, tall with deformed, arthritic hands and clothed from head to toe in sepulchral black. She is a woman who is full of common sense and is mostly responsible for the charming girl her granddaughter turned out to be, but on first sighting she is intimidating. Lottie, however, liked her instantly and smiled happily at her.

'God bless you and your baby,' the old woman said.

I couldn't be certain afterwards, but as I escorted her to the door I thought I saw tears in her eyes.

Anyush

'Enough for this evening, Anyush. We can continue this tomorrow.'

Anyush closed the book of French grammar and was startled to feel Bayan Stewart's hand on her arm.

'I'm concerned about you. Are you fully recovered? You don't seem well.'

'I am better, Bayan Stewart. Just a little tired.'

'Forgive me but I know what it is to feel tired. Is that really what troubles you?'

Tears filled the girl's eyes so that she had to turn away.

'Anyush ... my dear! You know how fond Dr Stewart and I are of you. You are like one of the family. I think of you as a friend. Are we not friends?'

Anyush nodded miserably.

'Then can you not tell me what is the matter?'

With all her heart she wanted to. If anyone would listen and not judge her too harshly it was this woman. She didn't want to imagine what Dr Stewart would think of her carrying a bastard child, but she knew Bayan Stewart would not turn her away. Her good opinion was more important to Anyush than that of any other living person, the very reason she said nothing.

'I'm sorry, Bayan Stewart. What happened to Havat has upset me. I just need to go home.'

Mushar

Trebizond

July 15th, 1915

Dear Jahan,

If you receive this and if it is within your power to do so, I beg you to write to me. Rumours about the war are on everyone's lips, and there is talk of terrible losses suffered by our troops. I have been dreaming the same dream of you lying injured on the battlefield. In my dream I can see you from the top of a hill but I cannot get to you. The nightmare is no worse than my waking one. I am utterly lost. There is so much I need to tell you. Your silence frightens me.

Anyush

Today I came as close as I've ever been to dismissing Manon. What stopped me is the knowledge that I cannot run the hospital without her, and the fact that she is only partly responsible for what happened.

I arrived at the hospital late, having done an early morning call to Father Gregory who looks to be in the early stages of TB. By the time I got to the hospital I was already concerned that we were running behind with the surgical list and was further disconcerted to discover that the operating theatre was empty. No nurses, no prepared trolleys, no patients. I went to look for Manon, who was in the treatment room removing a cast from an old man's arm. Outside on the corridor, I asked her where everybody was, specifically the two student nurses, Mari and Patil, whose job it is to prepare the operating theatre. All Manon would say was that the list had been rescheduled for Friday.

'What do you mean Friday?' I asked. 'Why can't it be done today?'

'It is better Friday when Anyush is here.'

I reminded her that Anyush was not a nurse, and that I was depending on Mari and Patil, but she would only repeat that they were away. I couldn't get her to reveal where they were, or why they had gone, until I told her I was going to write to the director of nursing services at the Municipal Hospital to complain.

'Please, you must not do that.'

'You leave me very little choice.'

With a look of weary resignation, she informed me that both girls had left the night before for Batum.

'Batum? In Georgia?'

'Please do not shout, Dr Stewart. Yes, Georgia.'

I asked her why, and, taking me by the arm, she marched me through a rear door out to the back of the clinic. Once we were out of earshot, she told me that the girls had been smuggled in a fishing boat across the border to Georgia. The skipper was a friend of Paul's and he had hidden them in the hold with a consignment of fish.

'Stop right there,' I said, a knot of anger unravelling in my stomach. 'What has this got to do with Paul Trowbridge?'

'I must ask you again to be quiet, please, Dr Stewart.'

In no uncertain terms, I told her that this hospital was not run by Paul Trow-bridge and that I wouldn't have his paranoia coming between me and my work.

'He is not paranoid.'

'What exactly would you call stealing my nurses away in the middle of the night?'

'I have told you,' Manon said, regarding me coldly, 'but you will not listen. Ozhan came to the clinic last week.'

At the back of my mind I vaguely remembered her saying something about Ozhan appearing on some pretext or other, but the details eluded me. Manon said he had talked to the staff, asked them many questions and written down their details. What their name was. Where they were from. Who was Turkish and who was not. She said he spoke to the Armenians most of all, especially Mari and Patil.'

'Manon,' I said, trying to control my temper, 'Ozhan likes to know about every-one. It is typical of the man but no reason to send the staff away.'

'He does not proposition everyone.'

'What do you mean?'

'He told Patil she must come to the barracks. If she does not come, she will have the same fate as Havat Talanian.'

I assured Manon that although Ozhan was a bully and liked to intimidate people, there was an understanding between us and he wouldn't dare harm any of my staff. I knew the man and understood how he operated, but my reasoning appeared not to have the slightest effect on her.

'There was no need for this,' I said. 'How am I to run a hospital without nurses? Why didn't you come to me first?'

'I did not consult you, Dr Stewart, because I already knew what you would say.'

 Jahan

Constantinople, 26 July 1915

Jahan was escorted to Trebizond by Ozhan's soldiers and put on a naval frigate returning to Constantinople. On board ship he spent restless days cursing his own stupidity and worrying about Anyush. He couldn't bear to think of what Ozhan might do, and felt utterly helpless to protect her. Dr Stewart afforded her some measure of safety, but it was not nearly enough. A man like Ozhan would not let a foreign giaour come between him and his depraved distractions. Jahan had to get back to the village or find a way to bring Anyush to Constantinople. Every fibre of his being itched to be with her, but as Trebizond receded into the distance, his thoughts began to turn towards home.

Late one sunny afternoon, the ship docked in Constantinople and Jahan felt a rush of joy at returning to the city of his birth. Stepping onto the quayside and seeing Galata Tower looming over Beyoğlu on the far side of the Golden Horn, his spirits rose. But at Army Headquarters nobody seemed to have the first idea what to do with him. He spent an hour waiting to see Enver Pasha, only to be told the War Minister wasn't in the building. His secretary then directed Jahan up three flights of stairs to where a sullen German colonel presented him with a new command. The men awaited him at Scutari barracks in Üsküdar, a motley corps of injured veterans who looked as though they would put a knife in his belly sooner than return to the front. Most of them were twice his age, or appeared to be, hardened men whose only certainty was that they would not survive another campaign. Disillusioned and distracted by events in Trebizond, Jahan made his way to his parents' home in Galata.

The house on the Grande Rue de Pera was surrounded by embassies, schools and churches of Constantinople's non-Muslim population. In this part of the city, and for the more progressive Turks, French was the common language. Jahan's family spoke it fluently along with Turkish, English, German and Greek. A facility with languages was a mark of breeding and education, and in Constantinople it was a necessary skill. There was nothing unusual in the fact that every sign and every official document was printed in four languages and sometimes in as many as six. During his stay in Paris, Jahan had been surprised at the uniformity of the city, the genteel absence of mélange. It was this, Constantinople's teeming variance, that he loved the most.

Jahan paid the toll to cross Galata bridge and strolled into the Grande Rue past the Bon Marché store. Ladies in elaborate hats were gossiping in the shade of the arches and Jahan tipped his cap at them. On this street the Turkish men were distinguishable from the Europeans only by the wearing of the fez, still more popular than the bowler.

Seven-year-old Tansu, the youngest of Jahan's sisters, came running into his arms when Azize opened the door.

'You're home! He's home! Jahan's home!' she said, squeezing him hard around the neck. 'Are you back for good? Did you bring me something?'

'Don't squeeze so hard and maybe I can tell you. How are you, Azize? Cross as ever I hope.'

His old nanny smiled and patted him on the arm.

'Jahan … this is a surprise!' In a rustle of silk his mother advanced on them with a wide smile. Madame Orfalea was a head shorter than her son and, although she bore herself with style and grace, she inspired awe rather than familiarity. Jahan kissed her on both cheeks while Tansu nuzzled in against him.

'Tansu, *arrête-toi*. Run and tell your sisters your brother is home. *Va-t'en.*'

'Maman has a surprise for you,' Tansu said, dropping to the floor. 'We've been having a visitor while you were away. A very special visitor.'

'Bring her upstairs, Azize.'

'She's a teacher, a teacher, a teacher,' his sister sang, skipping around his legs.

Azize took her arm but Tansu slipped out of her grasp.

'And she's very pretty. And *très gentille*.'

'Tansu!'

She ran up the stairs two at a time and disappeared into the nursery while Azize climbed slowly after her.

'A surprise?' Jahan asked, but his mother was already walking into the salon.

For the next hour or so he was taken up with his sisters and everything that had happened in his absence. Dilar, six years younger than himself, had become engaged to Armand, the son of the French Ambassador. Armand was a childhood friend of Jahan's and also a captain in the French army. The wedding was to take place in a year, or whenever the end of the war allowed.

'Marie-Françoise was to be my bridesmaid but she became engaged herself last month and will be in Paris by then.'

The corners of Dilar's pretty mouth drooped.

'Maman says I'll have to content myself with Tansu and Melike, but nobody is really married with only two bridesmaids.'

'Especially when they're your sisters!' Jahan said, winking at the others. 'And what about you, Melike? What have you been doing while I was gone?'

His second sister smiled shyly. Too old to pull onto his lap like Tansu and too young for the society of Dilar, Melike was awkward and reserved and spent her time with books and painting. She wasn't pretty or charming like the other girls but claimed a special place in his heart for all that.

'Thank you for all the letters, Melike,' he said. 'I only received a few of them but it was a great comfort to know you were writing to me.'

As a boy Jahan's favourite place was on the roof. In the dark evenings he would signal with a lamp to his friends in the houses across the street with a system of flashes they had worked out between them. No one else knew the code or how to decipher it, except for Melike. She used to spy on him from the top of the stairs, where she had eventually been discovered. Jahan let her stay on the condition that she didn't talk too much and kept the secret to herself. As they grew older they often went to the roof together, sitting by the wind tower as Jahan blew smoke rings with the cigarettes he had stolen from his father.

'For you,' Jahan said, handing her a small volume from his valise.

She took the book, turning the pages slowly. Inside were coloured drawings of plants and flowers in beautiful delicate detail.

'They're by an English artist called Mrs Delaney. They remind me a little of your paintings.'

'They're beautiful,' Melike said, kissing him on both cheeks.

'What did you bring me?' Tansu asked, nudging her sister out of the way.

'Nothing.'

'Really? You didn't bring me anything?'

'Not a thing.'

But she had already spotted the bulge in his breast pocket.

'Oh that's for another little girl.'

'Show me, show me, show me!'

'You have to say "*s'il te plait*".'

'Please, please, please, Jahan.'

'Was she a good girl, Maman, while I was away?'

Madame Orfalea raised an eyebrow.

'I will take that as a yes,' he said, and took the gift from his pocket.

It was a tiny filigree silver box with a little gold monkey crouched on the lid and a key underneath, that Jahan had bought from a silversmith in Trebizond. Tansu wound the key and the monkey turned in time to a tinkling tune. She squealed with delight and ran off to play with it in the nursery.

Some time later when all the presents had been given out and his sisters had gone to their rooms, Jahan took the opportunity to talk to his mother alone.

'How is Papa? He's at the factory?'

She shook her head. 'He's not well. He insists on going to the Ministry in the mornings and the factory after *déjeuner*, but it exhausts him. The factories could run themselves.'

'What do the doctors say? Is he having treatment?'

'*Non.*' She attempted a smile. 'There's nothing they can do for him. You'll notice quite a change. He can hardly walk without becoming breathless and of course he's still smoking.'

'He'll never give it up, Maman. Even if he wanted to. By the way ... what was Tansu talking about earlier? The visitor she mentioned?'

His mother took a moment to rearrange herself on the *fauteuil*.

'I was going to bring it up later, but ... well, as you know, Dilar will be married shortly to Armand. And, as you are a good deal older and should be married by now, your father and I have been making introductions on your behalf.'

'Introductions?'

'We were making enquiries. Suitable girls don't just happen, and of course we wouldn't make any decisions without your approval.'

'You mean ... a wife?'

'A prospective wife, yes.'

Jahan hadn't meant to broach the subject of Anyush so soon, but it seemed his hand was being forced. But before he could say anything further, the front door opened and he heard footsteps walking across the marble hall. Slower footsteps than a year previously.

'Jahan ...'

His father stood in the doorway, bundled into his outdoor coat.

'Melike told me you had returned and here I find you with your mother as usual.'

'Papa.'

Rising to shake his hand, Jahan tried to hide his shock. This was not the father he remembered. He was leaning on the doorknob like a man twice his age and had lost both height and weight. Everything hung loosely about him, his coat, his skin, his wispy hair. His eyes were sunken in a face deeply scored with lines and tinged an unhealthy yellow colour.

'*Viens*, come sit with me while your mother dresses for dinner.'

Jahan followed his father onto the balcony off his parents' suite of rooms, catching a hint of the smell he had always associated with him. A mixture of lime, woad and urine used to cure the skins in large open vats at the tannery. It was the biggest tanning enterprise in Constantinople, the main factory taking up three hectares in Beykoz on the Anatolian side of the city, and a leather goods factory on the Stamboul side of the Bosphorus. The business had been founded by Jahan's great-grandfather, an illiterate from Adabazar who started out as a skinner and dung gatherer. He built Orfalea Tanneries into the leading manufacturer of gloves, saddles, footwear, bandoliers and cartridge belts, and sold across the Empire and to Greece, America, Persia and Egypt. It thrived for two generations and there were great expectations of the third, but his father chose a very different career. Olcay Orfalea joined the army and rose through the ranks with impressive speed. He seemed destined for great things, but ill-health was to be his undoing. Chronic congestion of the lungs left him breathless and invalided, and his career slowly ground to a halt. Little by little, he found himself sidelined or assigned to lesser duties in the domestic sphere. Madame Orfalea consoled her husband that he had the tannery to fall back on and could safeguard the family interests, but although Jahan's father was an able businessman, his heart was never in it.

'You look different,' his father said, once they were seated.

He opened the cigar box on the table beside his chair and lit one of the thin cheroots to which he was partial. 'Older. I'm sure your mother remarked on it.'

'She thinks I'm thinner.'

'If that's possible. I at least have an excuse.'

His father coughed, his shoulders jerking violently and smoke spilling from his nose and mouth. The spasm passed and he left the cheroot burning between his fingers.

'I've been hearing about you. Some trouble you got yourself involved in.'

In the building across the street a woman with dark hair pushed back the window shutters to let cool air into the rooms beyond.

'*Désolé*, Papa ... you said something?'

'I said you've not endeared yourself to your superiors.'

'They didn't particularly impress me either.'

'Don't play games, Jahan. This is a serious matter.'

'I was trying to bring their attention to something I witnessed. Something I felt strongly about.'

'Then keep your feelings to yourself. There's a war on. One which is going badly for the Empire. The Ministry has more pressing matters to deal with than some Armenian feud.'

'It wasn't a feud. It was a savage attack on a young girl.'

'You think that's the worst that could happen in wartime? Thousands of men are dying and you're worried about some girl?'

'They cut out her tongue!'

'They could carve her into a thousand pieces and it's not your concern. You're a soldier Jahan. A captain. Your job is to lead your men and follow orders, not whine like a woman. How you acquit yourself in this war will affect your entire career.'

'I'm not a career soldier, Papa. I never wanted to be.'

'What you want and what you need are two different things.'

'You mean what *you* want!'

Olcay Orfalea's breath wheezed noisily in and out through his mouth as he turned to look at his son. Jahan was repelled by him. The disease which was slowly destroying his lungs had squeezed his humanity dry, toughened him like one of his own hides.

So Jahan ... you would prefer to work at the tannery, then?'

'Of course not.'

'I'm sure you would make a fine cobbler.'

'Papa ...'

'The army needs boots. What better way to help the war effort?!'

Same old argument, same old harangue. Across the street the woman had gone, the shutters open and bolted in place. Shadows moved to and fro in the room beyond and he could hear the faint sound of the pianoforte. It was coming from below them, Dilar or Melike practising a tune.

'Armenians are a misfortunate people,' his father was saying. 'They deserve our pity and our charity, but they are not a breed to become involved with.'

'Ah, but there lies my problem,' Jahan said, turning to him with a smile. 'I am already involved, Papa. In fact, I'm going to be married to an Armenian girl as soon as I can get leave or temporary discharge.'

'What nonsense is this?'

'You are about to have one of the unfortunate breed for a daughter-in-law.'

'Is this your idea of a joke?'

'I'm getting married, Papa. Nothing could be simpler.'

'You are throwing away your career—'

'It has nothing to do with my career.'

'... on an Armenian peasant!'

'It might be kinder, especially in front of Maman, not to speak about my future wife in that way.' Jahan got to his feet and looked down at his father. His face was suffused unevenly with colour and his lips were pale and tight. 'I feel sorry for you, Papa. Really I do.'

'Sit down, Jahan!'

'Tell Maman I'm not staying for dinner.'

'Jahan ...'

Captain Orfalea stopped in the doorway and looked back to where his father was sitting.

'You have been very fortunate in life. You have parents who care about you and three sisters who are devoted to you. But should you think of doing anything rash, it would be wise to remember that this city is not kind to orphans.'

Colonel Olcay Orfalea

Jahan's father stood at the balcony and watched his son disappear into the evening crowd. After a while, he became conscious of the wind blowing up from the river and the chill settling across his shoulders. He closed the balcony doors and went inside, taking a seat at the bureau opposite the window. When he had decided what he wanted to say, he took a pen and ink and wrote a letter to Colonel Kamil Abdul-Khan, requesting a transfer for Jahan. Sealing it into an envelope, he put the name and address in Sivas on the front. The second letter was more straightforward and required little or no forethought. It was addressed to the barracks' postmaster and instructed him that all post sent or received by Captain Jahan Orfalea was to be redirected, unopened, to himself, Colonel Olcay Orfalea, at the above address on Grand Rue de Pera. Before sealing it, he put a substantial bundle of kuruş into the envelope and left both letters on the salver in the hallway for posting in the morning.

Jahan

The boy was stripped to the waist and sweating profusely as he dug. His hands were blistered from the quicklime as well as the spade, and it would be a few days before he would grip a gunstock without wincing. Unblocking the barracks latrines was a job for the hamals, but the back-breaking, foul-smelling work was also useful as a punishment detail. Jahan watched him dig for a time, before turning away from the nauseating stench and the swarm of black flies hovering over the pit. He was sorry he had lost his temper with the boy. Jahan was usually not so concerned with minor breaches in regulation, but the punishment had more to do with his irritable humour and the argument with his father. His bravado of the previous day had deserted him, as Olcay Orfalea knew it would. They understood each other too well. Jahan was fully aware of the lengths to which his father would go, because the colonel did not make threats lightly. It would be unthinkable to be turned away from his home, from the company of his mother and sisters, but what was the alternative? Never to see Anyush again? Losing his family would cause him infinite sadness, but if he had to chose, there was only one decision he could make.

'Captain Orfalea. Sir ...' His aide beckoned from a safe distance.

'You have a visitor, Captain.'

'Who?'

'A lady.'

Madame Orfalea was sitting drinking tea in the barracks parlour.

'You need to bathe,' she said, drawing away as he kissed her. 'As a matter of urgency.'

'Give me a few minutes,' Jahan said, and went to his quarters to wash.

When he returned, it was to see the aide peering through the open door at his mother.

'Thank you Refik. That will be all. What are you doing here, Maman?'

'I was out for a stroll and was hoping you might escort me home.'

They left the barracks and walked arm in arm through Üsküdar and into the residential district of Stamboul, past Seraglio Point, which marked the border of the Muslim Quarter with the City of the Infidel, and into Galata beyond. The two German warships, the *Goeben* and the *Breslau* were berthed on the southern side of the bridge, dwarfing the shipping agencies and banks that bordered that part of the Golden Horn. Fleeing from a British naval vessel, the ships had been given safe harbour by the Empire and were responsible for closing the Dardanelles and bringing Turkey into the war. Jahan counted many Germans amongst his friends, and his father had been instrumental in setting up the German Military Mission, but he deeply resented the Empire's participation in a war not of its own making. As well as the termination of training projects and the channelling of all resources away from new developments, he had seen a return to the pre-Balkan arbitrary promotion of untrained officers and the drafting in of young inexperienced German officers on fat salaries, while Ottoman foot soldiers subsisted on low wages paid once every five or six months.

'It's so easy to forget we are at war,' his mother said as they crossed into Galata. 'I've heard rumours that there are British submarines in the waters off the Dardanelles, waiting to pick off our ships.'

'The war will be decided in the Dardanelles. Every able-bodied soldier will be drafted there in the next few weeks.'

Madame Orfalea shivered and hugged her son's arm tightly. They continued on through the familiar streets of Galata, past the theatres, patisseries, bars and the opera house. But as they approached the Grand Rue Madame Orfalea insisted they keep walking, climbing up through the narrow streets of Pera onto Taksim Square towards Galata Tower. At the very top they stopped to look at the view below.

'The sun is hot. Let's sit in the shade for a moment.'

They took a seat in a small café where they could watch the city and the ships plying their trade along the Bosphorus.

'Your sister was in something of a state this morning.'

'Which one?'

'Dilar of course. She's worried that France is about to declare against Turkey.'

'Armand?'

'Yes, poor Armand. It is one thing to fight for your country but quite another to fight against the homeland of your future wife.'

'Does she want to postpone the wedding?'

'On the contrary, she wants to bring it forward. They plan to move to Paris as soon as they get their travel permits.'

A waiter came and placed two tiny cups of coffee and a stand of pastries on the table before them.

'Your father is upset. It bothers him that he cannot fight.'

Jahan sipped his coffee, aware of his mother's eyes on him.

'He told me of your conversation.'

'Did he?'

'He mentioned your ... friend.'

A strong breeze blew up from the harbour, lifting the corners of the

cloth covering the small table and knocking the sugar basin. They waited
while the waiter rushed over with clips for the cloth and a fresh basin of
sugar.

'This girl,' his mother began, 'your father said she is ...?'

'Armenian.'

'And you've brought her here? To Constantinople?'

'She's still in Trebizond.'

'But you intend bringing her?'

'Yes. As soon as I can arrange it.'

A ship's horn blew in the distance and the parasol of a woman at a
nearby table sailed past. With a snap, Madame Orfalea closed her own
parasol and put it by her feet. Jahan watched, knowing there was more
to come.

'Jahan,' she said, leaning across the table to put her hand on his arm,
'*écoutes*. Your father is the kind of man for whom pride is everything.
Pride in his country most of all. When you threatened ... when you spoke
of leaving the army to marry this girl, it flew in the face of everything
he believes in. Everything he has worked so hard for. This war will not last
for ever. By the end of the year, two at most, it will all be over. I know ...
I understand how things are. You fell in love. It is natural at your age. I
know that right now nothing seems more important, but I'm asking you
... begging you, for my sake, Jahan, not to do anything for the moment.
If you provoke your father, he is capable of things he would regret but
never undo. And with his health as it is ...' She shook her head, her eyes
unnaturally bright. 'You have my word, Jahan, when the time is right I
will talk to him. I know how to get around him. *Je t'en pris*, Jahan. I'm
asking that you do this for me.'

Jahan looked down the hill over the jumble of tiled roofs and flat roofs,
past the clutter of masts and rigging on the water to the huge iron bulk
of the German warships. Across the Horn to the mosques and minarets

and wind-towers on the Stamboul side. His mother was watching him, expecting an answer, but how could he wait? How could he abandon Anyush to chance? But if he *did* do as his mother asked, he would have an ally in the battle with his father, the one person capable of interceding with him. Jahan would have to hope that the Stewarts were influential enough to keep Anyush safe and that the demands of war would keep Ozhan distracted.

'Very well, Maman,' he said. 'I will do as you ask. But don't expect me to wait too long.'

Anyush

Mushar, Trebizond, 30 July 1915

Before Anyush could make her journey to the village, she had to leave the laundry at Kazbek's cottage. Husik had not appeared and only his father stood on the porch steps, prayer beads swinging at his wrist. She walked quickly on towards the town, touching the letter in her skirt pocket. It was the last letter she would send, her final hope that Jahan would write. She had written everything she wanted to say, offering her love, her prayers for him and for the child she was carrying. Nothing was left unsaid.

Anyush stayed on the path skirting the wood, careful to keep beneath the trees. She took the letter from her pocket again and looked at the address. Grande Rue de Pera. It seemed so foreign, so far away. She slid her hand over her belly and felt it strain a little against the folds of her skirt. For a thin girl, it was becoming difficult to hide. Unwed mothers were dealt with severely in the village, and the only hope for her baby and herself lay in marrying Jahan. She had to find him and tell him what he could not know. What he would want to know.

'Anyush.'

Husik sprang out from behind a tree.

'Don't do that!'

'Did I frighten you?'

His eye fell on the letter in her hand and he snatched it from her fingers.

'Who are you writing to, Anyush?'

'Give it to me.'

'Nobody has ever written to me. Can't I have this one?'

'Husik, give me the letter.'

She tried to take it from him, but he held it just out of reach.

'I wonder what's written inside. Maybe I'll have a look.'

'Don't you open it! Don't you dare!'

'You'd better have it, then. But you'll have to catch me first.'

He took off, and she had no choice but to follow. Rounding the bend and coming on to the long straight stretch of road, she could see nothing only the dark silent wood on either side and the church spire in the distance.

'Husik ...?'

A flock of crows shook out their wings, calling forlornly in the canopy above her.

'Husik, I'm not in the humour for this.'

A volley of shots rang out, sending the birds shrieking into the afternoon sky.

'Over here.'

He was standing on the path, listening, her letter forgotten. She snatched it from his hand.

'You shouldn't be out here,' he said. 'I'll bring you home.'

'I'm going to the village.'

'The village isn't safe. I'll post your letter for you.'

'No!'

'Don't you trust me?'

His pale face looked into hers. She did trust him. She would have trusted Husik with her life but not with this letter. Pushing it into her pocket, she turned in the direction of the town.

Ü Ü Ü

The post office was a flat-roofed, ramshackle building on the corner of the square, leaning at an angle up against the Tufenkians' shop and doubling as the town hall. Until recently, it had been run by Dikkran Gulakian, an uncle of Sosi's, but her uncle had been conscripted and the post office was now run by Bekir Hisar. The Hisars were neighbours to the Charcoudians, helpful at harvest time and the main buyer of any surplus vegetables from Gohar's small plot. Hisar greeted Anyush warily as she came through the door.

'You shouldn't be here,' he said, barely glancing at the letter. 'The village is swarming with gendarmes.'

He franked the letter and put it in a bag on the floor.

'Go!' he hissed, nodding to where a group of uniformed guards had gathered on the street outside. 'If they find you here ...'

He beckoned her behind the counter to a back door. 'Hurry!'

But the men were already on the threshold.

'Allah, help us!' Hisar whispered.

The gendarmes crowded inside, six or seven of them spreading like bees in the cramped space. They were young, somewhere in their early twenties.

'Well, look what we have here! Told you I spotted one. And all on her own too.'

The gendarme turned to Hisar. 'She doesn't belong to you, does she?'

Bekir shook his head, his eyes cast to the floor.

'Didn't think so. No decent Turkish girl would parade herself through the town.'

He moved closer to Anyush, near enough that she could see drops of sweat in the tufts of hair on his upper lip. 'You're Armenian, aren't you?'

There was no way past him and no access to the rear door. The circle closed around her.

'What did you say? I didn't hear you!' He grabbed her by the arm. 'Don't you think she looks Armenian?'

They laughed, pushing her over and back between them from one pair of hands to another.

'Someone must have cut out her tongue because I didn't hear an answer. Are you Armenian, whore?'

Her voice had deserted her. She felt as though she were falling, weightless and helpless at their feet.

'I asked you a question. Are ... you ... Armenian?'

'Yes.'

'Ah ... we have an answer! Now what do we do with Armenian whores? Any ideas?'

Suddenly there was a tremendous burst of glass as the small shop window exploded in a thousand shards. The gendarmes fell to their knees and hunkered down around the walls and in front of the counter.

'What's happening?'

'Somebody's shooting!'

'It's a revolt!'

'Armenian rebels!'

'There's one of them!'

They crowded through the door as a stocky, dark-haired figure ran across the square and disappeared into the maze of alleyways. Just as Anyush thought her knees would give way, Hisar's bony fingers grabbed her by the arm. He pushed up the counter and led her to the lane outside.

'Go to Dr Stewart's house. They're moving in the opposite direction, so if they don't catch that poor bastard you'll have enough time. Go now. Run!'

Although moments before she could hardly stand, she ran as fast as her legs would carry her, praying over and again that Husik would not get caught.

ʊ̈ ʊ̈ ʊ̈

The following morning, Anyush waited by the river where Husik brought the cows to drink. She had spent a restless night, not knowing if he had escaped the gendarmes.

The first of the cattle ambled down the track, shuffling and raising dried mud into the morning air. The cow's dusty hide was stretched over her frame, and the bones of her pelvis thrust upwards from her rump. There were fewer of them than before, less than half a dozen. Some had been taken by the army and others had died of starvation so that Kazbek's herd had been reduced to a few hollow-eyed beasts. Anyush tried to see past the animals to the back of the line, but to her horror she saw Kazbek flicking and prodding at them with a stick. He peered at her from his glassy eyes.

'*Selam, efendim*,' she said, falling into step beside him.

He flicked the switch over and back, the sound cutting through the cow's lowing and the clodding fall of their feet.

'I was wondering, *efendim* ... about Husik?'

'Husik is none of your concern.'

'Yesterday ... in the village ...'

'Nothing happened yesterday.'

'But, *efendim*, he —'

'Did you hear what I said? Nothing!'

She hung back, wary of the stick's whip and flick.

'Tell him I'm grateful,' she called.

Kazbek stopped and turned around. He looked at her coldly, spitting on the ground by her feet. 'I'll give him no messages from you. Mad like your mother! You're nothing but trouble. Stay away from him, you hear?'

He flicked his switch at the beast nearest him and followed after it, disappearing into the rising cloud of dust.

Ü Ü Ü

Gohar Charcoudian sat on a chair in her nightgown as Anyush took down the brush from the mantlepiece. With the passing of years more of the old woman's scalp was visible through the strands of her thinning hair. Anyush brushed from the hairline to the nape of her grandmother's neck with the firm strokes the old woman loved.

Gohar was quiet, her swollen fingers lying in her lap and her misshapen knees poking through the fabric of her nightdress. Her arthritis was bad again, and although she never complained she was in constant pain. A gust of wind rose, rattling the small window. Gohar closed her eyes, and just as Anyush thought she was nodding off she reached up and caught her granddaughter by the hand.

'When were you going to tell me?'

The door to the cottage flew open, and Anyush's mother came into the room. A strong wind whistled into the corners and blew Gohar's nightdress up over her knees.

'I need to speak to you, Anyush,' Khandut said, pulling the scarf from her head. 'To both of you.'

Gohar struggled to cover herself, and Anyush caught the unmistakable stench of their landlord.

'I've been to negotiate the rent. I don't have to tell you we have no

193

money and no way of paying, but Kazbek and I have struck a deal. He's willing to write off the debt and drop the rent on the top field.'

'We'll owe him nothing?' Anyush asked.

'Nothing.'

'But that's … that's wonderful,' Anyush said. 'Isn't that good news, *Tatik*?'

Beneath her granddaughter's touch, Gohar had tensed like a spring. 'What were his terms?' the old woman asked. 'What did you offer him in return?'

Khandut was looking at the empty grate. Soot had fallen onto the hearth and she tipped at it with the toe of her boot. 'He wants a wife.'

'You're going to marry him?' Gohar whispered. 'You're going to live there? In *that* house?'

'I never said anything about marrying him.'

'So what did you agree? Are we to understand … Oh dear God, no!'

'What's the matter?' Anyush asked.

'Tell me you didn't.'

'There was no other way.'

'You sold her? To him? To that monster?'

'I had no choice.'

'*Me*?' Anyush said. 'You're talking about *me*?' The hairbrush fell from her hand.

'It is the answer to our problems. We'll never have to worry about rent again.'

'Marry Kazbek?' She looked in horror from her mother to her grand-mother.

'You don't mean it. Tell me you don't.'

'You can't send her to live in that house.'

'If you have a better idea, then let me hear it.'

'For the love of God she's your daughter! You know what happened to his first wife.'

194

'And who else will marry her, eh? Tell me, who? What man will marry a woman who is bewitched by the sea? You know what they say about her in the village? That any man who marries her will drown. And their children too.'

'That's just village talk. Khandut, I beg of you, put this from your mind.'

'I won't marry him! Never!'

'Would you prefer to walk the roads when he evicts us?' her mother snapped. 'With your grandmother a cripple who can hardly turn to look at me? If you marry him, we'll have food in our bellies and a roof over our heads.'

'Food?' Gohar said, struggling to her feet. 'When he beats her like his last wife, will you think of food then? When he kicks her like a dog? You who has blamed me all your life for your own unhappy marriage! No. Anyush stays here. With us.'

'You're just a stupid old woman, Gohar. I was used! Forced into a marriage I didn't want just so you could get your hands on some useless piece of land. *This* marriage will do good. It will save our lives.'

'Good! You talk of good? There is only evil in that house!'

'Wait ...' Anyush stood between them. 'There are ways ... other ways. He wouldn't throw an old woman out on the roads.'

'You'd better believe he would,' Khandut said bitterly. 'In a minute.'

'The Stewarts will help.'

'The Stewarts can hardly feed themselves.'

'Please ...' Anyush's voice broke, words coming apart in her mouth. 'I can't ... I beg you ... not that man ... please don't ask me.'

'You won't marry Kazbek,' Gohar said quietly. 'Will you tell her or will I?'

'Tell me what?'

'Go on. She has to know.'

'What do I have to know?'

Anyush's grandmother nodded. The moment had come. She couldn't put it off any longer.

'I'm carrying a child.'

Khandut's knuckle made contact with Anyush's cheekbone and she fell backwards onto a chair.

'For the love of God, woman …'

'Who is he? Who's the father?'

Khandut hit her daughter again, so that she tumbled sideways to the floor.

'Leave her alone.'

'Who-is-the-father-of-the-child?'

Trying to protect her belly, Anyush inched away from her towards the wall.

'Is it the American? Is it Dr Stewart?'

'No!'

'One of the men at the hospital then? It's that Bedros, isn't it? Nothing to say? Maybe your grandmother would like to tell me.'

Picking up the brush from the floor, Khandut brought it down hard on Gohar's shoulder, and the old woman whimpered in pain.

'A soldier! He's a soldier. Don't hit her again!'

Khandut dropped the brush and sat heavily into a chair. The wind roared down the chimney, blowing a thin veil of soot around the room.

'Did he force you?'

'No.'

'Where is he, then?'

'He's gone.'

'So,' she said, looking at her daughter crouched on the floor, 'we'll just have to get rid of it.'

'No! This baby is mine.'

'This baby will have you stoned! You think you're the first woman to dispose of a soldier's brat?'

'You can't touch it. I'll marry Kazbek.'

'Kazbek wants a virgin, not some whore carrying another man's child. Unless ...' She glanced at her daughter's waist. 'How far gone are you? How many months?'

'I don't know.'

'You must have an idea.'

Anyush looked at her grandmother.

'Three months, by the looks of things,' Gohar said 'Maybe less.'

'Then it might just be possible.'

'What are you talking about?'

'We have to convince Kazbek that Anyush is carrying Husik's child.'

'*Husik?*'

'The boy makes no secret of his feelings for her. All she has to do is persuade him that the child is his.'

'No!' Gohar's fingers gripped the chair. 'If Kazbek ever found out, he'd kill her. It's too dangerous.'

'Not Husik,' Anyush whispered.

'You think you have a choice?' Khandut rounded on her. 'You think I did?'

The wind dropped and the room was suddenly quiet.

'It was your father who wanted you, Anyush. He had a weakness for children, but children are a burden. You'll learn that the hard way. If your grandmother means as much to you as you'd have me believe, then your choice is already made.'

Ü Ü Ü

Anyush went to the only place she could find comfort. Running across the beach, she almost didn't see the footprints in the wet sand. On the promontory at the western end she saw Husik sitting as though he was carved from the rock. He was staring out to sea, and it struck her as strange to see him so absolutely still and exposed to the wind and the air. He turned his head and looked at her. Neither of them moved. They were like figures in a painting, both the observer and the observed. Stray hairs from her plait blew across her face, but she didn't try to brush them away. It felt as if she was standing on the edge, on the brink of something there was no going back from. If she married Husik there would be a future for her baby and her family but a lifetime of misery for herself. No happiness or hope or joy and, like her mother before her, married to a man she didn't love. Because of the child in her belly it was what she had to do. What she would do. But she was weak. Closing her eyes, she prayed for a miracle. She saw Jahan walking on the sand, his arms open and his voice calling to her. Saying this was just a dream, a nightmare he had come to waken her from. But only the gulls moved across the bay, wheeling in great circles above her. She started towards the figure on the rock, praying for the courage to do what had to be done. Raising her hand, she waved at Husik, knowing she had changed her life for ever.

Henry Morgenthau

US Ambassador to the Ottoman Empire

Constantinople

July 31st, 1915

Dr Charles Stewart

Mushar

Trebizond

Dear Charles,

I am writing as your friend and ambassador to keep you abreast of recent developments in the capital and further afield. What I am about to relate may change
your thinking on a possible return to America, and although I would not presume
to influence any decision you might make I urge you to give serious consideration
to the following.

Although America has not yet declared against the Empire, you are probably
aware that the United States joining the Allies is inevitable. Following the April
24th assassination of high-ranking Armenians, which I mentioned in my last letter,
all remaining Armenians have been systematically rounded up and taken from the
city. The arrests were initially confined to men who had reached the age of major-
ity, but in recent weeks have included women, children and the elderly. The official statement from the Government claims that they are to be interned in camps in
the interior and at Deir al-Zor in Syria, but I am hearing accounts from our consuls
countrywide that many of them are dying of starvation and exposure on the roads.

Of immediate concern to yourself, Charles, is the extension of these marches
across the Empire and into eastern territories. As you are aware, I had attempted to
intervene with the Government, but to no avail, and have redirected my energies
into publicising the story in the American papers. I had hoped that international

opprobrium might shame the powers that be into more humane treatment of the Armenians, but thus far without success. The dissemination of the story in the *New York Times* and other broadsheets has resulted in an avalanche of donations, and I have established a relief fund which I hope will help ameliorate conditions in the camps. Should there be camps established in Trebizond, I will make funds available for you to disburse in any way you see fit. While I am humbled, Charles, by the largesse of the American people, I fear that what little we can do will not nearly be enough.

Forgive the gloomy tone of this letter, Charles, but it reflects in no small way my fears and misgivings on the Armenian question and life in Turkey generally. I sometimes wonder about the wisdom of raising a family here. I would urge you to give what I have written due consideration, and if you do decide to return to America let me know if I can be of help with travel arrangements, etc.

Please give my fond regards to Hetty and the family,

I am, as always, your friend,

Henry Morgenthau

One of the calls I have always enjoyed making is to the Armenian Children's Orphanage at the top of the hill on the southern side of the village. The children are well, by and large, and if it wasn't for the Matron, who talks too much, I would happily visit more often. Today I was calling because the orphanage was commemorating its 15th year in the village and Matron had decided to celebrate the occasion.

As I rode up the hill, I wasn't thinking of the orphans but mulling over Henry Morgenthau's latest letter. The news was disturbing, but there is no question of leaving Trebizond. War hysteria is the order of the day. If there is a bias against Armenians it is because of old alliances with the Russians, just as there is an anti-Turkish bias in the Caucasus. Added to which, the country cannot survive without its Armenian population as most of the hospitals are staffed by Armenian doctors and nurses. What government would cripple its emergency services in wartime?

By the time I got to the orphanage I was late. I rang the bell and the twins Adom and Aleksander opened the gate and took my horse to the stable yard. Inside, Manon and most of the hospital staff were already seated as well as the orphanage patrons and some of the local dignitaries. Hetty threw me a look as I took my seat between Matron and Meraijan Assadourian. At a signal from Matron, the side door to the hall opened, and all the children filed into the room. They stood before us, boys to the right, girls to the left, smallest children sitting cross-legged at their feet. On cue they started to sing. Armenian songs, Greek songs, Turkish songs, even a Russian lullaby. For a finish they belted out the 'Star Spangled Banner' and had all the ladies in tears. Afterwards, Matron gave a little speech about my work at the orphanage and announced that the children had made me a gift. She clapped her hands and Aleksander and Adom marched in, carrying a rolled-up rug between them. Unrolling it, they stood back to watch my reaction. It was a colourful Turkey rug in shades of reds, blues and yellows, much sought after in the salons of New York. As the twins pointed out the patterns woven by the various groups of children, I thought to myself that a rug like this would raise a pretty penny for our much-needed hospital funds.

Thanking the children and the matron, I assured all those assembled that the monies from the sale of the rug would go directly towards the TB sanatorium. The gathering broke up quickly after that, and people drifted to the refectory for tea. Hetty was waiting for me by the door. She wanted to know why I had said I was going to sell the rug when the children had been working on it for months. I explained that I appreciated the children's efforts but that it was worth a lot of money and would be turned into some badly needed cash. Hetty then suggested I hold on to it for a time, for a couple of months at least, which made no sense because I would only become attached to it. I urged her to think of all the good the money would do, but she was not in the frame of mind to hear it.

'One rug is not going to fund an entire unit!' she said sharply and turned on her heel.

Before I had time to digest this, my nurse came marching across the hall and praised my '*discours magnifique*'. I ignored the caustic tone and asked if there was any news of Mari and Patil.

'Do not talk so loudly,' she said, looking around her. 'They are on the boat. That is all I know.'

I told her then that I had spoken with Ozhan. This business with Patil was all a misunderstanding, and Ozhan had merely wanted to check her papers. In the coming weeks, he told me, all citizens' papers would be checked systematically, including my own. The man had been convincing. Everybody, he claimed, had to present papers and Armenians were no exception.

'He knows the nurses are gone,' I continued. 'I told him they went back to Trebizond to finish their training, but I think he knew I was lying. I *did* make it clear that there is to be no further interference with my staff.'

Manon did not react. It was as if she hadn't heard a single word.

'As you are talking of staff,' she said instead, 'I must discuss with you about Anyush.'

Just then a latecomer arrived.

'Is everything over?' Paul asked. 'My horse threw a shoe and I had to walk the last four miles.'

'If you had come last night as I told you there would be no walking,' Manon said irritably but she was obviously glad to see him.

I was happy to see Paul myself, and relieved. He hadn't been to the village since our last meeting and I knew I was somehow to blame. He was my oldest friend in this country, and it pained me to think that our regard for each other might have changed. Still, he had made an effort to be there and that was something in itself.

'Paul,' Hetty said, kissing him on both cheeks. 'I'm so glad you made it. I'm on my way back to the house. Why don't you join us for supper? You too, Manon.'

Manon said she had a few things to attend to at the hospital and would join us shortly. Hetty went on ahead and Paul and I walked with the horses together. Our conversation was stiff and awkward, inevitably turning to the one subject we should have avoided. I asked how things were at the hospital, and he told me they hadn't changed. There was just himself and Professor Levonian.

'What about the others?' I asked. 'The nurses?'

'Gone. Almost all of them.'

'Gone?'

'Yes, Charles. I told them to leave.'

'Like Mari and Patil?'

To my surprise, Paul smiled. 'You shouldn't complain, Charles. You still have Manon. And Anyush of course.'

'Unless you arrange for *her* to leave also.'

'I was rather hoping you might do that yourself.'

It took a considerable effort to control my temper, so I said nothing and we walked on in silence. At the house Arnak came out of the stable yard to take our horses, and Robert and Milly came running down the path.

'Papa!' Robert burst out. 'There's a wedding at the church.'

'We saw it, Papa,' Milly said. 'We were there.'

Hetty came out of the house with a pitcher of lemonade and asked the children what exactly they meant.

'The church door was open,' Robert said. 'Milly and I looked inside and Father Gregory was at the top with a man and a woman.'

I reminded them of the Aykanian wedding where the whole village was present. It couldn't be a wedding, I assured them, if nobody knew about it.

'It *was*, Papa,' Milly insisted. 'I saw them doing that thing with the string.'

'Are you sure?' Hetty asked doubtfully. 'Was the woman dressed like a bride?'

'No.'

'What about the groom? How was he dressed?'

'You know him, Papa,' Robert said. 'It was Husik.'

'Husik? The trapper?'

'You don't mean Husik Tashjian?' Paul asked, a cigarette halfway to his mouth. 'Who was the girl?'

'Well ...' Robert glanced at his sister, '... we think it was Anyush.'

Paul's hand froze.

'Now listen to me,' he said, bending down to the children. 'Think carefully. This is very important. Are you sure it was Anyush?'

'It was,' Milly said belligerently. 'I know it was.'

'But if she was wearing a scarf, how can you be certain?'

'Because I saw her plait. It was Anyush's hair.'

'Lots of girls have plaited hair. You might think you saw her but it could have been someone else.'

'It was Anyush,' Milly said and started to cry.

I'd had enough. 'For God's sake, Paul, you're frightening her.'

'Don't you understand anything?' He rounded on me. 'Didn't you hear what they said? Anyush is marrying Husik Tashjian.'

It was a little strange but not unheard of. I told him that the girl may marry whomsoever she chooses, but Paul was beside himself. He insisted I put a stop to it and that I had no idea who she was marrying. Naturally I refused.

'Look, Paul, I don't know what you've got against him, but Husik is not the worst.'

'It's not Husik I'm concerned about.'

'Then who?' Hetty asked.

'His father!'

The garden was suddenly quiet. The birds, the dog that had been barking in the yard and even the creaking boughs above our heads seemed moved to silence.

'Oh my God!' Hetty whispered. 'Jane!'

The children's confused faces looked from one adult to another. What Paul was telling me didn't seem possible. Anyush Charcoudian, my assistant nurse, the little girl who had taken her first American cookie from my hand, would be living in the same house as a sadistic rapist. Paul grabbed my arm. 'We still have time. We can put a stop to this.'

'You're too late.' Walking beneath the fig trees, Manon came slowly along the path. 'It is over. The marriage is done.'

Anyush

One year later

The baby had fallen asleep at Anyush's breast and her head lay heavy in the crook of her mother's arm. Her tiny, perfect lips were parted, making small sucking noises in her sleep. On the skin of her chest, just visible under the loose cotton shift, was her birthmark. Anyush touched it with her finger. It was in the shape of a tulip, rose pink and perfectly formed. Gohar had frowned when she had seen it, pinning on the *atchka ooloonk* to ward off the evil eye. Anyush loved the mark, as she loved everything about her baby daughter. Jahan was stamped all over her, from the long lashes and brown eyes to the silky-fine black hair. It hurt they were so alike. She tried not to think of Jahan, but every time she looked at her daughter he was there. Anyush bent her head to kiss the baby and put her in the crib she had been given by the Stewarts.

The pregnancy had been a long and frightening time. So many changes, so many lies. That day on the beach she had taken Husik by the hand and led him to the wood. What happened after was something she tried to forget, but weeks later when she told him she was pregnant he took the news calmly. Telling his father had been a different matter. He called Anyush every devil's name and damned her to Hell, but some days later he had a change of heart and agreed she could marry his son.

Others took the news badly. Sosi burst into tears and Parzik refused to believe it. It was to settle the debt her family owed Kazbek, Anyush told them, and to protect her mother and grandmother. Parzik knew she was lying, but Anyush could not tell her that she'd had a Turkish lover and that the father of her child was an Ottoman soldier.

Throughout those long months dark thoughts troubled Anyush. What if she didn't love this child? What if she had no feelings for the baby as Khandut had none for her? She worried that her mother's strangeness was buried inside her all along, but the moment the midwife put Lale into her arms she felt nothing but love for her child. Her friends came to bless the baby and celebrate the arrival. Sosi made infant clothes, and Parzik, who had lost her first pregnancy and was with child again, held her and said how lucky Anyush was. Havat came with her mother and bestowed one of her rare and heartbreaking smiles. The three friends saw a lot of each other during Anyush's lying-in, but when she moved back to Kazbek's house after the birth, it came to an abrupt end.

Anyush's father-in-law was a man who liked his clothes clean and his shoes polished but whose house was stiffening into its own filth. He swung his beads like a jailer and shouted his prayers like an assault, but was too strong, too fleshy to give himself to any power greater than his own. There was little in his manner that spoke of a fear of God, only a will to instil it in others. Because she was afraid of him, and partly in an effort to please, Anyush tried to win his favour. She washed and scrubbed the house until it shone. She convinced Husik to repair the window sashes so that they opened again and let in air to blow away the smell of male sweat. With Gohar's help, she planted a small vegetable garden at the back of the house and put back the potato drills that had been there in Husik's mother's time. Kazbek complained constantly. Nothing was done to his satisfaction and the harder she tried the more bad-tempered he became. He liked to drop to his knees praying aloud that she might be forgiven for her laziness and sinfulness, and forced her to kneel beside him on the newly cleaned floor.

Then there was Husik. Her husband was as strange as his father but without the same malice. Anyush tried not to compare him to Jahan, but it took all her strength not to recoil from him. She thought he would consume her in the close confines of their bed, his eyes pinning her to the mattress and his rough hands exploring her body like a blind man. He baited her into the bedroom they shared with the baby, heedless of Lale's cry or his father on the other side of the wall or anything else that might distract him from his needs. He was a man obsessed, and yet she couldn't bring herself to hate him. She was touched whenever he held Lale, a name he had suggested and which meant 'tulip'. After the birth, Anyush had cried bitter tears when she saw the mark on her baby's chest, but it was Husik who persuaded her that it was beautiful. She was thankful to him then, and grateful for the kindness he showed her grandmother. It was this she kept in mind when his thick fingers pulled impatiently at the ties of her dress, and when he squeezed her breasts painfully as he reached the peak of his excitement, and when he lay spent beside her as she battled with tears and shame.

Beyond the house other battles were being fought. Raids on farms and shootings became common. Every other week someone was hanged in the square like Mislav Aykanian. The villagers hid away their women, but there was no protection from Ozhan and his men. Armenian girls were theirs for the taking and any girl would do. It was a relief whenever Ozhan disappeared to the city and a torment when he returned. The Stewarts were doing their best for the villagers, but the soup kitchen was no longer enough. People took to the roads to beg and some tried their luck in the city, where they fared no better. The Talanians and the Setians, who now had Parzik and Vardan living with them, were barely eking out an existence.

After Lale's birth, the Stewart family paid Anyush a visit, bringing Lottie's old crib as a gift. Millie touched Lale's birthmark and said that having a tulip mark on her skin meant that she would always be a very lucky baby indeed. Bayan Stewart and nurse Manon had visited often during her confinement and Anyush had lived for those visits. Kazbek did not like the women calling and became difficult and rude in their presence. He never moved from his chair in the corner so that Anyush couldn't talk freely and neither could anyone else. Finally he forbade her to have visitors altogether. At first, Bayan Stewart ignored him, but Kazbek frightened the doctor's wife with his long body and yellow eyes. Nurse Manon continued to come as far as the wood and whistled for Anyush to come outside. It was better than seeing nobody, but everything changed for the worse after Dr Trowbridge called. She watched from the window as he approached along the path, getting off his horse and walking to where Kazbek was driving the cattle back from the river. They talked quietly at first, but soon Kazbek was shouting and waving his stick at the doctor.

'You don't know who you're threatening!' he said.

Life became more difficult after that. Kazbek accused Anyush of sleeping with the Englishman and told Husik his wife was a whore. Again, she was forced to kneel on the floor while her husband looked the other way. One day Dr Stewart called, and to Anyush's surprise Kazbek allowed him inside. The doctor examined the baby and offered Anyush her old position at the hospital.

'Bring Lale with you,' he said. 'You should remain on the staff and we would happily have you both.'

But Kazbek would not hear of it, and nothing Dr Stewart could say would change his mind.

Ŭ   Ŭ   Ŭ

The baby was soundly asleep when Anyush got to her feet. Her stomach was rumbling. There was wild garlic growing in the wood, and with a few potatoes and some rice she could make a jermag pilaff. Picking garlic reminded her of her grandmother's khash, a meaty beef broth served with garlic and lavash. It was the most delicious food imaginable, but nobody had meat to make it any more.

Tiptoeing out the door, she slipped under cover of the trees, picking her way carefully over the spongy forest floor. A narrow track leading past bunches of hyssop led to where the garlic grew. The canopy was dense, shutting off the bright sunlight, but she spotted the white flowers just ahead in the clearing. A twig cracked and then another followed by voices. Looking around for somewhere to hide, she pressed herself against the trunk of two trees that had fallen onto each other.

'What do you mean, nothing?' a wheezy voice was saying. 'What are we paying you for?'

'People are nervous,' a second voice said. A voice Anyush knew only too well.

'They're being careful. Nobody's saying anything. Especially since Aykanian and all the others have been hanged.'

'Aykanian was hoisted thanks to you.'

'I didn't think you'd hang him. Just rough him up a bit.'

'Listen to me, you worthless shit, you knew very well the minute you gave us his name that he was finished. So save your crocodile tears for the priest.'

Kazbek laughed nervously. 'No, no, of course. He had it coming. It's just that it makes people wary.'

There was a loud crack of a match against flint and the sound of smoke drawn deep into lungs. Anyush risked a look. The gendarme had his back to her.

'So they should be. There's going to be a lot of changes around here.'

'What do you mean? What kind of changes, *efendim?*'

'You'll find out soon enough.'

Grinding his match under the toe of his boot, the gendarme pointed a finger at Kazbek. 'You'd better have something for me next time. Unless you want to swing like the old man.'

Ü Ü Ü

The heat had built up to an almost unbearable intensity. Anyush opened every window, but the house felt as if it was holding its breath. Lale seemed to sense the change in the weather. She had been uneasy all day, crying in her mother's arms and finally falling asleep from exhaustion. Since the evening in the forest Anyush jumped whenever Kazbek entered the room. His eyes followed her and his jet beads flicked through his fingers as though counting down to her last breath. Anyush tried to stay out of his way, to make herself invisible, but there was nowhere to hide from Kazbek. Husik seemed unaware of the atmosphere in the house. He spent his days with his traps in the wood and laughed when his wife suggested she go with him.

'No, Anyushi bai. Not there.'

The lavash bread she had taken from the tandoor in the yard was cooling on the table. It was too hot to tear with her fingers so she fetched the knife to slice it. At her mother's cottage Gohar had made the lavash every morning, flattening the dough by throwing it in the air between her spread fingers. The force of its own weight gradually made the dough thinner and thinner, turning it into a large fine sheet ready for the oven. Anyush loved to watch Gohar make the bread and missed the rhythm and comfort of it. Her mother also made lavash but with impatient slaps of dough against the kitchen table. Khandut had been to visit only once since Lale's birth. She had held her granddaughter with such tenderness

211

that Anyush had to look away. Gohar hadn't said a word. She had gone outside and dug the vegetable garden until it was time to leave. Khandut had never come again.

Anyush put the bread knife on the table. Through the window she could see the long path leading through the wood and she thought she saw her grandmother walking with her slow, shuffling gait. But there was no one there, only the branches of the trees moving in the wind. The Stewarts had asked Gohar to work for them as Lottie was not well and Bayan Stewart was nursing the child. If nothing else, Anyush thought, it was time away from Khandut.

Undoing the top buttons of her chemise, she fanned herself with a handkerchief. Her hair was pinned up and bound in a scarf, but still she felt as though she would melt. Sweat trickled down her breastbone and into the cleft between her breasts. Pressing her hand to the back of her neck, she had a sudden sense of the room darkening. Kazbek was standing in the doorway, watching her. His face was in shadow and the bright daylight pressed like a halo around him. Without taking his eyes from her, he pushed the door shut, his beads making small tapping noises on the wood.

'Are you looking for, Husik?' Her voice sounded weak and thin in the airless room. 'He should be back soon.'

'I'm not looking for Husik,' Kazbek said, slipping his beads into his pocket. 'I sent him to the village. On an errand.'

He stood in the middle of the room staring out the small side window. 'Cover yourself.'

The buttons of her dress seemed too large for the holes she tried to push them through. Milky stains seeped into the fabric around the thin cotton yoke.

'Do you think you fool me, Anyush? Do you think I don't know what you're doing when you expose yourself to me like this?'

'No … no, Kazbek I was feeding Lale.'

'I don't see the child.'

'She's in her crib, asleep.'

'Lust is a sin, Anyush.'

In the cool room Lale cried out and then fell silent. She cried again more urgently, and Anyush went to go to her, but Kazbek caught her by the arm. His fingers pressed into her flesh. 'Did I say you could leave?'

'Lale's crying.'

'Let her cry.'

'She needs me.'

'You'd know all about need, wouldn't you?' he said, his voice dropping to a whisper.

She could see his dusky grey gums and felt her stomach rise as he pushed her towards the table. It hit the bone in the small of her back.

'What do you imagine is going through my head, Anyush, when I have to listen to you and my son in the next room? Do you think I'm saying my prayers? Is that what you think?'

She was almost lying flat now, curved backwards over the lip of the table and fighting the urge to turn her head away from his hot fishy breath.

'Well you'd be wrong. I've been sinning, Anyush. Pleasuring myself. And who could blame me?'

A sour gush of fear filled her stomach. She tried to twist away, but he was strong and held her where she was.

'I've been driven to it. By you, Anyush. There's only one way to deal with sinfulness like yours. Fire with fire.' His hand was fumbling at his trousers. 'Fire with fire and sword with sword.'

'No!' She lashed out with her nails at his face and arms.

'Whore!'

The force of his hand banged her head against the table and everything darkened for a moment. When she could see again, he was directly over her and she was finding it difficult to breathe. His arm was pressing with his full weight across her throat.

'Why did you think I let Husik marry you? So I could keep my son happy? Is that what you thought?'

Blood was pooling in her lips and her vision began to swim.

'I let him marry you so I could do this!'

'Husik!'

'Husik?' Kazbek laughed, pushing his trousers down with his free hand. 'Husik is miles away. Now,' he leaned heavier and spots danced before her eyes, 'unless you want that child of yours to end up mother-less, open your legs.'

The pressure eased and she found her breath, but she couldn't fight him. She hadn't the strength. Tears trickled down her face and into her ears. Her arms fell limply beside her head and something cold knocked off her hand. The knife. She grabbed it and struck Kazbek in the shoul-der. A wild roar bellowed from deep within him and his weight slid off her. Anyush's legs were unsteady when she stood, but she inched away from him holding the knife with both hands.

'Don't come near me! Stay back or I'll kill you.'

Edging around the crouched, bleeding figure, she risked a glance at the door and hesitated. She couldn't leave without Lale, but Kazbek was on his feet again, lurching towards her.

'Stay away! I mean it.'

'Should have stuck it in my eye, Anyush.' Blood seeped through his fingers where they grasped the wound. 'Should have done the job prop-erly, like I'm going to do.'

He lunged at her, but she sidestepped him to find herself in front of the table again. He was staggering like a drunk but moving purposely towards her.

'Stay back!' she jabbed the knife at him. 'Stay back or I'll tell everyone you're an informer.'

Kazbek became perfectly still as if he had been struck with something of greater mass than himself.

'That's right. I know your secret. Your dirty dealings.' Her voice was shaking, but the fear in his eyes gave her courage. 'How many people would like to know the name of the man who betrays his own to the Turks? How many Armenians in our village? Vardan Aykanian maybe?'

In the cool room Lale started to cry.

'It would give me nothing but pleasure to tell them, Kazbek, and I swear to you if you ever come near me or mine, every man, woman and child in the village will know what you are!'

They stood watching each other, heaving air into their lungs. From the look on his face she thought he would kill her anyway. But he moved away, pulled open the door and was gone.

Ü Ü Ü

From the shoreline Anyush walked the short distance to the start of the hazel wood. The trees followed the path of the river and linked up after a mile and a half with Kazbek's wood and house. Along the road was easier, but there was less shade that way and it was no longer safe. Lale stirred in the sling, her cheek snug against her mother's breast.

Since the attack, a week before, Anyush had spent as much time as she could outside. Some days Kazbek stayed away, disappearing in the early morning or locking himself behind his bedroom door. To Husik he was as cruel as ever, taunting him or putting him to the most menial of tasks, but to Anyush he spoke not one word. She started going further from the house again, visiting her grandmother and friends, as far as the Stewarts'. Nothing was said. No barriers were put in her way. Life was never easy within Kazbek's four walls, but it was a little better.

Anyush seldom went to the village and most people avoided it. Vardan Aykanian had never returned from Trebizond, where he had been working on the police barracks. The Jendarma claimed to know nothing, and Dr Stewart learned little from them when he called to make enquiries. Vardan wouldn't have gone away without telling his pregnant wife, but soldiers were trawling the towns, picking up unlisted men and taking them to the front. Turks as well as Armenians, old as well as young. It was of little comfort to Parzik, but it could have been worse. How was it, Anyush wondered, that Husik had managed to avoid conscription? He wasn't clever, but he was healthy and strong. Kazbek had something to do with it. Secretive, brooding Kazbek, whose land remained untouched and who always had plenty on his table. The Devil rewards his own, Gohar had said. Perhaps Kazbek's house was the best place for them after all.

Something brushed off her face. She pushed it away and was surprised to feel that it was smooth and solid. Anyush looked up. A body swayed and twisted from its impact with her head. Kazbek's shiny black shoes were just visible under the trousers bunched around his ankles, and streams of brown-red blood had dried into the black hair on his legs. At his groin pubic hair, and torn skin and blood were congealed where his genitals had been, and more blood spattered onto his shirt which was torn open. Black-jet prayer beads bit into the skin of his wrists, tied behind his back, and, above the noose, his face had a mottled, liverish hue. His penis hung between swollen lips, where his tongue should have been, and Anyush noticed there was a word carved into the skin of his chest. The crude letters were distorted with blood so that it took a while to decipher them. A single word. 'Informer'.

In my career as a doctor I have never had to step into the shoes of a priest until today. Kazbek Tashjian was found hanging in the wood close to his house, and Mahmoud Agha and I were the first on the scene. It was a grisly sight, enough to turn the stomach of most men, but my first concern was breaking the news to Husik, his son. It took some time to find the boy. He often disappears for days at a time, even when he's supposed to be keeping order at the clinic. I put the word around that if anyone saw him they were to contact me immediately. Husik turned up at the hospital with a brace of rabbits for Manon. I brought him to my office and told him what had happened, but before I had finished he fled from the room and ran to the wood where Mahmoud Agha had taken the body down from the tree. Husik began to wail like an animal, pulling at his hair and digging his fingers into the skin of his face. The sounds he made were unnatural, almost inhuman. After a while he composed himself and went back to the house to begin making a coffin. All afternoon he hammered and sawed, carving Kazbek's name painstakingly onto the lid. The boy's devotion impressed me, but like most people in the village I did not mourn his father's passing. Kazbek Tashjian was a dangerous man and had been the cause of serious discord between Hetty and me.

It was shortly after Anyush's marriage to Husik. Manon was told by Khandut Charcoudian that the girl had moved to the Tashjian house and would no longer be coming to the hospital to work. This did not surprise me. Armenian girls usually stay within the home. But Hetty decided this was a further calamity, and she and Manon set up a vigil for our assistant nurse – a cordon of watchfulness beyond whose boundaries Kazbek would not dare trespass. I thought it madness and none of our affair and I told her as much. Hetty accused me of being indifferent and asked how I would feel if Anyush was *my* daughter. This offended me deeply. I care for the girl as much as Hetty, but the law is the law. The only person who has any say in Anyush's welfare is her husband and if he cannot protect her then nobody can. I pleaded with Hetty to drop the idea, to stay away from the Tashjian farm as it wasn't safe.

'No safer than it is for Anyush,' she said.

I promised her I would do whatever was within my powers as a doctor to do but that I could not interfere with what happens behind closed doors.

'Cannot or will not?'

When I said nothing, Hetty turned her back to me. 'Turkey has changed you,' she said.

Her words stung. They rankled with me for days. If Hetty had not been so influenced by Paul and Manon, she would agree with me that this is how the world is made. A woman is subject to her husband no matter what the country of her birth or our own personal opinions. Had my wife's sound judgement not been so trenchantly cast aside, she would recognise that I have already done much for the women of Trebizond, and Anyush in particular. I have endeavoured to put the needs of others before myself from the day I swore the Hippocratic oath, but I will not break the law of the land. If there is any truth to Hetty's words, it is surely that Turkey has changed all of us. These were my thoughts as I looked at the mutilated corpse of Kazbek Tashjian.

Because of the heat and the fact that the body had been hanging for some days, I advised Husik to bury the corpse immediately. People in the village did not have the means to buy a coffin and put their dead directly into the ground wrapped in a sheet, but Husik wouldn't hear of it. Two evenings ago, on his insistence, the coffin was placed on the table in the house and the soul of Kazbek prayed for throughout the night. Husik stood dry-eyed as Gohar Charcoudian recited the prayers, oblivious to the heat and the smell permeating the room. Towards midnight Arnak called with the news that the priest could not be found.

'My father cannot be buried without a priest,' Husik said. 'There has to be a priest.'

I knew that in certain religions it is permitted for someone to take the priest's place, and I told Husik that I would be happy to officiate. He reluctantly agreed.

At first light we loaded the coffin onto the cart and brought it to the village, the women following on foot. By the gates of the Armenian cemetery a small group of old men had gathered. My chemist Malik Zornakian, a close friend of Vardan Aykanian, stood at the head of them.

'I am here to bury my father,' Husik said when the body of men blocked the entrance.

They refused to move, throwing menacing looks at Husik and his father's casket.

'The man has to be buried,' I said. 'And soon.'

Nayiri Karapetyan, whose son had disappeared and whose tobacco stall had been burnt by the Jendarma, stepped forward and said that Kazbek Tashjian would never be buried in the village cemetery.

'My father is dead,' Husik said. 'Every man deserves a decent burial.'

But the men would not give way. Husik's face changed, taking on a mean and belligerent look. He clipped the reins on the horse's neck and the mare shied, her hooves coming dangerously close to the men at the gate. They scattered, and only Malik stood his ground. He grabbed the bridle.

'Now listen to me, Doctor Stewart,' he said, 'I'm sorry you had to be involved in this but thanks to the scum in that box Mislav Aykanian is buried with noose marks around his neck. That bastard's bones will never defile holy ground.'

With that he drew back his head and spat at the coffin. Husik dived at his legs and the two rolled to the ground. Nayiri and I eventually managed to pull them apart but the way remained blocked. I persuaded Husik to bring the body to our house and that we could decide what to do from there.

Hetty was fixing her hat on with a pin when we pulled into the stable yard. She offered Husik her condolences but he seemed incapable of a reply. He stood in the yard beside the coffin as I recounted the morning's events. It was Hetty, finally, who came up with a solution. Kazbek would be buried in a secluded corner of our garden under an ancient fig tree, with a distant view of the graveyard.

The sky overhead threatened to drench us as we stood around the spot chosen for Kazbek's grave. Purple cloud gathered above us and presaged a break in the unrelenting heat. The breeze was strengthening with a salt tang and I knew the rain would come sooner rather than later. The only prayer I could remember was the Lord's Prayer, which I recited in English and asked the Almighty to have mercy on the deceased. It must have sounded odd to the mourners when I could have been calling on the flights of angels or damning Kazbek to Hell. Not that it mattered. Only to Husik maybe. I thought Gohar Charcoudian might have been praying but she was looking over to where Anyush stood with Lale in her arms. The girl had her head bowed, murmuring softly into the dark mass of her baby's hair. Hetty and Khandut Charcoudian were standing together, while Husik stared silently at the casket. The mountains disappeared as the sky darkened to a dull pewter. Taking a shovel and a pickaxe, Husik and I attacked the hard ground, heavy drops of rain falling into the split earth.

Jahan

Sivas 1916

Some eight months after leaving Trebizond Jahan found himself in Sivas, the capital of Sivas Province in East-Central Anatolia. The order to leave Constantinople had come unexpectedly when he was woken at first light one morning and told there was a ship leaving for Terme and that his passage had been booked. After five days at sea, he disembarked at Samsun and began the long mosquito-ridden trek over the mountains to Sivas. The town lay in the broad valley of the Kızılırmak river and was built at the crossroads of the main trading routes to Mesopotamia and Persia. By the summer of 1916 it was overrun with Germans looking to link the town with the advancing Baghdad Railway. Jahan was puzzled to find himself there, when all anyone could talk about was fighting in the Dardanelles. He had received nothing in writing and was given no time to say goodbye to his family or his men. He clung to the thought that he was now, geographically at least, closer to Anyush, even though all his letters had gone unanswered. The mail service was unreliable, but one letter at least would surely have reached her. He wondered if Ahmet had never given her the note and then discounted the possibility. The lieutenant would not disobey him, no matter what he thought of the affair. Something else lay behind her silence. Something less easily explained. Did

221

she still love him? Did she still think about him as he constantly thought of her? Could she ever be with another man the way she was with him? Jahan didn't believe it. If he hadn't heard from her, it was for a good reason, or possibly the worst of reasons. So long as Nazim Ozhan was in the area Anyush would never be safe. In this gloomy frame of mind he arrived in Sivas, and the town only worsened his mood. The people seemed wary, the streets mean and the climate too extreme. Another backwater with none of Trebizond's charms. One piece of good news was that Lieutenant Kadri and his old company were stationed there. Jahan questioned the lieutenant closely about events in the village since he had left, but the news was grim. More assaults, seizure of property, unexplained arrests. Only Dr Stewart's employees had been left alone and the hospital seemed busier than ever. Why then did Anyush not write? The captain's certainties wavered. He began to think she had forgotten him, that she didn't care what happened to him. He fell into a state of apathy, passing his time playing cards or composing angry letters to Anyush which he never posted. He became unreasonable with the men and demanding of the lieutenant. After two weeks of this, the lieutenant decided the captain needed distraction. A trip away from town and an introduction to a new friend.

Armin Wegner held the rank of second lieutenant in the retinue of Field Marshal von der Goltz who was overseeing the building of the Baghdad Railway. The field marshal was in Sivas to explore the feasibility of a spur-line around the feet of the Taurus Mountains and had brought a number of German engineers with him, along with Wegner as the company photographer. Von der Goltz had come down with malaria and Wegner had taken the opportunity to explore the region, hiring Lieutenant Kadri as his guide.

They were to travel first by boat and then on foot to the Monastery of the Holy Virgin, a deserted ruin on the mountainside outside the town.

The lieutenant and Jahan arrived at the dock in the early morning, stowing their supplies into the bottom of the boat.

'Where is he?' Jahan asked irritably. 'I thought Germans were supposed to be punctual.'

Ahmet pointed to the figure approaching from the direction of the town. He was a full head taller than Jahan, broad across the shoulders and long in the legs. In each hand he carried a wooden box. Wegner was dressed in the German army uniform but wore an Arabic ghutrah and agal on his head. Although his face was half in shadow, Jahan could make out large dark eyes, high cheekbones and a long aristocratic nose. The German didn't smile when Ahmet introduced them and took Jahan's hand half-heartedly.

'Careful with those boxes,' he said when Jahan stowed them beneath the seat. 'There's very valuable equipment in there.'

He checked the boxes again and seated himself next to them. By the time they pushed off, Jahan already disliked him.

The boat moved at a snail's pace along the Kızılırmak river and in a short time Ahmet was grunting with the effort of rowing in the heat. They had set out while the sun was low, but it was a windless day and already very hot. Sliding past the broad, treeless valley, the slopes of the Kuzey Anadolu Dağlari advanced on them from the hazy distance.

'There's nothing to photograph in this place,' Jahan said. 'Only miles of the same.'

'I'm not interested in this,' Wegner said dismissively.

Jahan fell back to his contemplation of the water. Every now and then he glanced at the lieutenant whose face was red and whose beard glistened with sweat. They would get eaten alive or burned raw, Jahan thought irritably, and all for a disagreeable German. After a time, Ahmet stopped rowing and pulled the oars into the row locks. Balancing them on the gunwales, he let the boat drift with the current while he took off his tunic and stowed it under the seat.

'Better,' he said, opening his collar and rolling up his shirtsleeves. He took the oars again and manoeuvred the boat straight, keeping it parallel with the riverbank.

'I would keep my skin covered if I were you,' Wegner said in perfect English. He nodded at the swarm of mosquitoes hovering above the surface of the water.

'Not a problem for me,' Ahmet said, pulling more easily on the oars. 'Mosquitoes like only the infidels.'

The boat made slow progress along the valley, splitting the water like oil. There was no sound, no birdsong leavening the heat, only the splashing of oars and the constant scratching of cicadas. The mountains inched closer, falling from the sky in stark relief. Jahan watched the German who seemed untroubled by the heat or the flies.

'How did you come to be taking photographs?' he asked. 'Are you a photographer by profession?'

Wegner looked at him as though he had forgotten who he was. 'I'm with the Sanitary Corps. Photography is just an interest.'

'You're a doctor?'

'A nurse.'

The large French woman who ran Dr Stewart's mission hospital came into Jahan's mind.

'Something amuses you?' Wegner asked.

'No. Not at all.'

'I am a *field* nurse,' Wegner said. 'My job is to bring in the wounded.'

'I see.'

'Do you?' Wegner looked as if he would say more but turned back to the water and the hills.

'Move over Ahmet,' the captain said to the lieutenant.

They changed places and Jahan sat between the oars. It wasn't as easy as Ahmet made it look and he kept pulling the boat diagonally across the river.

'Pull more with your right, *bayim*. And sit straight in the seat.'

Eventually he got the hang of it and the oars rose and fell with an even rhythm, pushing the boat smoothly along the valley. The sun was almost at its highest, and the horizon disappeared behind a shimmering wall of heat. Jahan's hands were slipping and he found it hard to maintain Ahmet's pace. Just when he thought he could row no more, the lieutenant told him to bring the boat to the left bank. They pulled up at a jetty that was mostly rotten and choked with river-grass and reeds. Ahmet held the boat steady as Jahan disembarked and Wegner retrieved his boxes.

'The path to the monastery is behind us,' he said, heaving the boat onto the riverbank. 'Up the side of that mountain.' He pointed to a barely visible track disappearing into the scree at the base of the hill. 'It's further than it looks and stony. Watch your footing.'

The Monastery of the Holy Virgin clung to a rocky outcrop close to the top of the mountain and had once been the size of a small village, but what came into view as they climbed was little more than a crumbling ruin. The monastery had almost vanished, reclaimed by the mountain that had given life to it. Stone arches over the windows of the church were still intact as was the main doorway, but some of the walls had collapsed or were starting to buckle. Fine dust whipped into their eyes as they walked around outside, and it was a relief to go into the roofed interior out of the sun and the wind.

It took a moment for their eyes to adjust. Frescoes of the Virgin in faded shades of azure blue and gold covered the surviving wall. Wegner walked slowly around the interior, examining the crumbling colours of brick red and cerulean blue. On one wall, a downcast virgin carried her child and his solemn benediction. On another a crush of halos above a host of saints was pressed like gold coins into the plaster.

'There might be enough light.'

Wegner retrieved his equipment from where he had left it inside the door and mounted it on the stand. By the time he had finished, a light mist had snaked around the foothills, the sun had settled in the west and the air on the mountain had grown cold.

Wegner emerged from the church looking pleased. 'Stand over there,' he said to the others. 'I will take a photograph of you before the light disappears.'

Ahmet buttoned his jacket to the collar and set his cap straight on his head. Jahan stood at his shoulder, two Turkish soldiers looking solemnly into the lens.

'I've been sending the plates back to Germany,' Wegner said, as they made their way down the track. 'This one I will develop myself. I've set up a photographic laboratory in the cellar under my landlady's kitchen. If it turns out properly you can have the photograph.'

It was the longest speech the German had made since they left Sivas and as they drew near the boat he fell silent again. He loaded his boxes on board and just as they were preparing to push off Jahan spotted something white in the water nearby. He went to have a look.

'Captain,' Ahmet called after him, 'we have to get back before dark.'

The white object Jahan had seen was a body floating face down in the reeds. Taking off his boots, he waded in and turned the corpse over. The blue-white face of a young man looked up at him. A boy with filmy eyes and a deep cut riven from one side of his neck to the other. Grabbing him under his arms, Jahan pulled him onto the bank.

'I've seen that boy in the square,' Wegner said. 'Outside Colonel Abdul-Khan's office.'

'Armenian,' Ahmet said. 'His father used to work in my family's carpet factory.'

A cold wind blew along the river as the men looked at the body. It frilled the surface of the water, bending the reeds towards the shore.

'We have to bury him,' Jahan said. 'We can't leave him here.'

'Not possible,' the lieutenant insisted, thumping his heel against the hard-baked earth. 'The ground is like stone.'

'There must be something on the boat? A shovel or a pick?'

'We have two oars, captain, nothing more. Throw him back in the water. He's beyond caring.'

Jahan looked at the body. Only a boy. Maybe a few years younger than himself. He looked up at the path to the monastery, partly hidden by the darkening mountain.

'Plenty of stones up there.'

Catching the corpse under the arms, he began to pull him backwards along the ground.

'You'll never get him up there. Captain, this is madness. We have to get back on the boat.'

Jahan's feet began to slip on the shingle as he struggled with the corpse, but suddenly the weight lightened. Wegner had taken hold of the boy's legs, and between them they began to carry the body up the track.

'Stop!'

The lieutenant put his arm around the boy's waist and slung him easily over his shoulder. With the others following behind, he carried the boy towards the monastery.

Ü Ü Ü

The night markets were closed and the patrons in the coffee houses long gone by the time the three men reached Sivas. Ahmet, Wegner and Jahan moored the boat and took out their belongings. Very little had been said on the homeward journey, but as they disembarked at the dock, the

German held out his hand and gripped Jahan's.

In the weeks that followed, Jahan came to know Armin Wegner better. It was Ahmet who discovered that the German had been awarded the Iron Cross, but Armin would never talk about his experiences on the battlefield. Instead, he spoke of his poetry and his idea for a novel, and how he hoped to write seriously after the war. Jahan was impressed, and surprised by the German's sensitivity. The photographs he took were not of Turkish palaces and landscapes, but of orphaned children, and street beggars, and buildings collapsing under the weight of those who lived in them. He sought out the marginalised and the ruined, and saw things Jahan would not ordinarily see. Armin captured pictures that at times made the captain uncomfortable and occasionally ashamed. It was easier to look at Armin's photographs of the partly built Baghdad Railway, or Field Marshal von der Goltz and Enver Pasha on the steps of the Topkapi Palace, or the formal portrait of Colonel Kamil Abdul-Khan. Shortly after seeing this picture, Jahan was called to a meeting with the man himself.

He had been instructed to present himself at the headquarters of the National Guard. The three-storey stone building was located in the central square, its main axis running the length of one side, with two further wings taking up the adjoining sides. A centrally placed campanile towered over the arched doorway in the middle block, and rows of classical windows flanked it. At the rear of the building well tended gardens extended to the banks of the Kazil river, lending the structure the appearance of a chateau in France rather than a soldiers' barracks. In the anteroom where Jahan was asked to wait, the ceiling was decorated with ornate plasterwork and religious pictures. Jahan looked at them closely. Not Ottoman or Islamic. Christian probably. There was something about this place that nagged him, something he couldn't remember.

Jahan took a seat and thought about the conversation he'd had the previous day with Armin. A rumour was circulating around the German barracks that Armenians were being deported to Syria. Whole villages, Armin claimed, were being emptied of their Armenian population and moved to the desert near Deir al-Zor. Jahan listened with growing unease. In Constantinople he had seen for himself the empty Armenian premises, windows broken and shopfronts defaced. Newspapers rife with nationalistic fervour and anti-Armenian propaganda, and at every street corner talk of how the Nationalists were going to restore Turkey to its glory days with no place for Armenians or Greeks. Jahan decided then that he had to find Anyush. Whatever her reason for not writing, he had to know she was safe. As soon as he could get leave he would make his way to Trebizond.

Muffled laughter could be heard on the other side of the panelled doorway. From what Jahan knew of Abdul-Khan, not many people laughed in his company. Before Olcay Orfalea had been invalided out of the army, Abdul-Khan had served under him for a number of years. The colonel had been to the Orfalea house on Grande Rue a number of times, and Jahan could remember his mother's uncharacteristic dislike of this pale, stocky man with a look in his eye that was subordinate to no one. Whatever the reason for coming to the great man's attention, the captain understood that it did not augur well.

The door to the colonel's office opened and a group of men in the costume of the Shota militia strode across the room and disappeared through the door. The Shota, a band of renegade highlanders, were considered the most dangerous criminals in the region and had been outlawed across the Empire. There was a price on their chief's head in every small town and province. Before Jahan could wonder what they were doing at the National Guard headquarters, an aide put his head round the door and told the captain to go in.

The colonel was seated behind a desk that seemed too small for him.

On the wall at his back hung a large framed portrait of the three Pashas who ruled the Empire through the Committee of Union and Progress. Abdul-Khan was not short in stature but his girth made him seem as round as he was tall. The buttons of his tunic strained at his belly and a fold of skin spilled over a damp-looking collar. Black hairs from a sparsely grown beard stuck out like porcupine quills and sprang in wiry tufts from his nose. Only his moustache grew luxuriantly down either side of his mouth and mirrored the bushy eyebrows that gave his face a deceptively hang-dog look.

'Well, well! Olcay Orfalea's boy. Your mother's son to look at and I gather your father's in every other respect. Sit.'

Jahan pulled out a chair and sat opposite him.

'So how do you like Sivas?'

'Well enough, sir.'

'Not Constantinople of course but it has its charms. You look pale, Orfalea. Is there something the matter with you?'

'No, sir.'

'You sure? I wouldn't want it said we weren't looking after the colonel's son and heir.'

'Lack of sleep, sir.'

'For all the wrong reasons I'll bet!' The colonel laughed. 'Take yourself off to Mother Yazgan's place behind the bazaar. She'll fix you up with a nice little virgin. Tell her I sent you.'

The colonel leaned back in his chair and extended a well nourished leg beyond the corner of his desk. 'You've been stationed in Trebizond, I hear. Are you familiar with the area?'

'We were in a small village just outside Trebizond, sir. But yes, I know it.'

'Good. I have an assignment for you. A chance to demonstrate some of your father's mettle. You've heard of the Armenian resettlement plan?'

'Rumour only, sir.'

'It's no rumour. The Armenian population is being moved to the interior and you will escort the Trebizond Armenians to Erzincan. You will be relieved of the convoy there and return here to Sivas.'

'You mean ... only Armenians, sir?'

'You heard right the first time.'

Abdul-Khan picked up a pen and started writing on a document in front of him.

'But, sir ... *efendim* ... when you talk of Armenians ... you mean the military population?'

'I mean the lot of them. Every last one. When you leave Trebizond, there will be no Armenians in it.' He signed his name at the bottom of the page and put the pen down. 'Is that clear Orfalea?'

'I ... yes, sir ... but women and children? Is it necessary to—?'

'All of them!' the colonel said, banging his fist on the desk.

A pewter cup toppled over and dropped to the floor, coming to rest near Jahan's foot. Bending down, he picked it up and placed it on the desk beside Abdul-Khan.

'This is war,' the colonel said, looking directly at him. 'Armenians across the Empire are deserting to the Russians. We will remove traitors from our borders in any way we can. Every man, woman and child of them. Do you understand?'

'Yes, sir.'

'Speak up. I didn't hear you.'

'Yes, sir. But sir ... I've been relieved of my command. I have no rank.'

Abdul-Khan smiled and handed him the document he had signed. 'Congratulations, Captain. You've just been reinstated.'

Ü Ü Ü

The covered market was hot and crowded and smelt of sweating bodies, henna and overripe fruit. The captain and the lieutenant were moving in single file through the main thoroughfare, standing aside for the veiled women at the fruit and vegetable stalls. Propped against a pillar in the spice market, a beggar held up his stump as they passed by.

'Why does he choose me? Someone who's been disgraced?'

'That's just the way of it, *bayim*.'

'Not with Abdul-Khan.'

A dog raced between the stalls, a large fish in its mouth.

'And why the Trebizond Armenians? There are other companies closer than we are.'

Small cupolas in the roof filtered pools of light into the teeming, sunless space. At the end of the main walkway they turned left and entered the gold souk. Reflections from the jewellery and brass weighing scales cast a yellow glow on the whitewashed barrel-vaulted ceiling and along the walls. On both sides, dealers set out their trays of gold, and groups of black-clad women fingered the goods and haggled. A bracelet studded with lapis lazuli caught Ahmet's eye and the stall-owner materialised in front of him. 'Very beautiful. Perfect for your mother, *efendim*. Or your wife.'

Ahmet threw it back, but Jahan picked it up again. The stones were the colour of the sea at Trebizond. 'How much?'

'Persian lapis,' the gold-seller said, wiping the disappointment from his face. 'Very good quality.'

'Your best price?'

They haggled for a while before finally agreeing on half.

'I saw Shota in there,' Jahan said, putting the bracelet into his pocket. 'In the colonel's office.'

'Couldn't be Shota, *bayim*.'

'I'm telling you they were. I was as near to them as you are to me. One of them had no right hand.'

'Murzabey?'

'Yes, and by the looks of things he wasn't about to be arrested either.'

Leaving the gold souk, they walked beneath the twin columns of the Northern Gate into the sunlight. Pushing past the shoppers, they headed towards the Gök Medrese.

'Let me buy you a coffee, *bayim.*'

The coffee house faced the immense stone pillars of the Northern Gate and the twin minarets of the Gök Medrese, the city's thirteenth-century religious school. The tables were empty except for two old men sitting in a far corner. Jahan and Ahmet took a seat at a table near the pavement and the lieutenant ordered. Over by the souk veiled women in brightly coloured skirts passed through the main gateway. The waiter arrived with two cups of coffee and a dish of figs.

'Maybe this isn't as bad as I thought,' the captain said. 'Maybe the Armenians are better off this way.'

'*Bayim?*'

'They'll be out of Ozhan's reach. If they leave, I mean. I can't see Ozhan moving to Syria, can you?'

Ahmet stirred his coffee.

'You know there are Armenian settlements in Syria? Whole towns of them. If fighting breaks out along the Georgian border, the Armenians will have to move anyway. Better to go with us than wait for the Russians.'

'*Bayim,*' the lieutenant said, placing his coffee spoon on the table, 'there are things you should know. This is not—'

'Hey, Jahan!' A tall, uniformed figure in a ghutrah and agal waved over from the shadow of the Northern Gate. He was carrying his wooden boxes, and a troupe of small boys fanned out behind him like a peacock's tail.

'Lieutenant Wegner,' Ahmet said, getting to his feet.

The men shook hands and the waiter brought more coffee. Behind them the boys stood guard over Armin's boxes.

'I was at the Medrese,' Armin said. 'Trying to photograph the interior and I picked up some onlookers.'

'*Gitmek!*' the lieutenant shouted.

'Leave them. They're not bothering me.'

The boys retreated a little, keeping one eye on Ahmet and another on Armin.

'I was in the bazaar earlier, trying to set up a shot of the gold souk, but I got ushered out. Thrown out actually.'

The boys seemed to understand and smiled.

'What is it? Did I do something wrong?' asked Armin.

'You must never steal a photograph of another man's wife,' Jahan explained.

'What do you mean?'

'Women. It is forbidden to photograph them.'

The old men in the corner stared as the boys laughed louder, covering their mouths like girls.

'But they were veiled. You couldn't see anything.'

'No photographs of women. Veiled or not.'

'I see.' Armin's pale face coloured.

'The Seljuk Keykavus is near here,' Ahmet volunteered. 'I show you today.'

'Well, if you don't have previous commitments.'

'Seljuk is old hospital. Very old. You will like it.'

'Ahmet is forgetting that we will be gone in a few days,' Jahan said.

'You're leaving?'

'For Trebizond.'

'I'm joining von der Goltz there in a week's time,' Armin said. 'Do you know the town?'

'I was stationed near there for a year.'

234

'Good. I will travel with you, then.'

They finished their coffee and Armin announced that he was finished for the day. 'See you here tomorrow?'

'Outside the souk.'

Armin left, walking through the crowds with long strides as the boys ran after him.

'Captain,' Ahmet said when Armin was out of earshot, 'you should not have agreed to bring Wegner to Trebizond.'

'Why not? He's going there anyway.'

'This evacuation, *bayim*. It is not what you think.'

'What do you mean?'

'My cousin Naim was involved in relocations in Bitlis and Diyarbekir. They were told to bring Armenians to camps in the interior as you were, but the idea is not to bring them anywhere.'

'That doesn't make sense. They have to go somewhere.'

'Not if they die on the way. They are marched without food or water until they collapse from starvation and exhaustion. Those that survive are handed over to the Shota.'

'Shota?'

'They're tipped off in advance and the soldiers turn a blind eye. That's what Murzabey was doing in Abdul-Khan's office. There's an arrangement. They take the younger women and ...' he shrugged. 'You know the rest.'

'Are you telling me ... are you saying I will be marching these people to their deaths?'

'I'm saying, *bayim*, that because of the way this is organised it couldn't be otherwise.'

Jahan felt cold. The crowds on the street were too close, and the press of bodies threatened to smother him. He walked away from the coffee house, elbowing passersby out of his way.

'Captain!'

Jahan kept moving. He had no idea where he was going, only that he couldn't stop. People scattered right and left to avoid him. He tripped on something hard and immovable and fell against a tobacco stall, scattering the ground with cigarettes and broken matches. Someone swore and a crowd gathered. The tobacco seller's face pressed up close, cursing and calling for the Jendarma.

'Here, *hacı*,' Ahmet said, pressing a note into his hand. 'For the damage.'

He took the Jahan by the arm and steered him down a side alley away from the crowd.

'My father,' Jahan said. 'This is my father's doing.'

'With respect, Captain, this is Abdul-Khan's doing.'

'You don't understand. I know he did this.'

'You said it yourself, *bayim*: Abdul-Khan answers to no man.'

'I can't do it, Ahmet. I can't do this.'

'You have no choice.'

'I have to get to Trebizond. I have to find Anyush.'

'Forget about her.'

'How can I forget her when she's going to be my wife? Am I supposed to march her to her death or present her as a gift to the Shota?'

The lieutenant looked away from him, up along the alley to where the dome of the mosque gleamed like a half-moon above the streets below. The figure of the muezzin was just visible on the balcony, preparing to sing the words of the Tekbir.

'*Bayim*,' the lieutenant said, 'this evacuation will go ahead with or without you. If you don't carry out the order, Ozhan will, and you know what will happen to the girl then. She would not last beyond the borders of the village. You call her your wife and perhaps she is that to you, but if there's any hope of her surviving, and it is only a faint hope, it is with you leading that convoy.'

Anyush

Anyush made her way to the washing-pool. Nothing had been laundered for two weeks since she was forbidden by Husik to go out alone, but she couldn't bear being imprisoned in the house any longer. Her life should have been easier with Kazbek gone but it was as if he never left. He was there in the breath that lifted the hairs on her neck and the shadows that followed her from room to room. He watched from his chair in the corner and settled with the heat and dust blowing in under the door. She wasn't the only one haunted by him. Husik was drinking heavily and staying up nights, reciting poems for his father or singing love songs to his wife until he passed out at the table. Other times, he forced Anyush to her knees, shouting drunkenly the badly remembered words of his father's prayers. Piece by piece, a little more with each passing day, Husik took on his father's shape. He wore his father's clothes and squeezed his feet into the old man's shoes. Dressed in this way, he would disappear into the wood and go missing for days – long days Anyush spent alone with Kazbek's ghost and the threat of what lay in the wood beyond.

She walked on, keeping to the shade beneath the trees. On her hip, curled up amongst the clothes in the basket, Lale lay asleep. Every few steps she stopped to listen. She knew why the gendarmes hadn't bothered the Tashjians and understood also that this protection was gone. There seemed to be more and more of them, making impossible demands and imposing new taxes on Armenian families. Turkish neighbours, the Hisars and many others Anyush had known all her life, turned away. They locked themselves behind a wall of fear so that they saw nothing and heard nothing and pulled their children indoors so they would hear nothing either. It felt as if the ties that bound her to Trebizond had already been cut. The cups on the shelf, the distant sea, the unyielding earth in the potato drills had all turned faithless against her.

Lale stirred in her sleep, her little mouth widening into a smile.

'Please God look after Lale,' Anyush prayed. 'Please God look after us all.'

When she looked up again, Jahan was standing on the path before her.

Jahan

Anyush had changed. Something was gone from her, an innocence perhaps, and yet she was more beautiful than Jahan remembered. He would have liked to take her in his arms, to press his lips against hers, but something in her face prevented him.

'How are you, Anyush? You are well?'

'Yes,' she said, putting the basket of laundry at her feet.

'And your mother and grandmother, they are in good health?'

'They are well also.'

'I've thought of you often, Anyush. I've been to the church on the cliff—'

'You've been away a long time, Jahan.'

The wind shook the leaves, throwing them for an instant into shade. She shivered and hugged her arms around her.

'Are you cold?'

'No.'

Nothing about this moment was as Jahan had imagined it. Many times he had rehearsed what he would say but now he couldn't find the words. The wind veered around to the east, bringing with it the acrid smell of burning. Behind the wood in the direction of the village, Jahan could see dense black smoke rising into the blue sky. 'Trebizond has changed.'

'Everything has changed, Jahan. This is not the place you knew.'

There was a wariness about her. She seemed distant and guarded with him.

'I passed Dr Stewart in the village. With his friend ... the Kurd.'

'Mahmoud Agha.'

'Yes. The hospital is still running then?'

'It is.'

'Good. That's good.'

A small sound like an animal's cry came from somewhere near them and Anyush's eyes flicked to the basket at her feet. It was moving slightly and a baby's hand waved for an instant above it. A bar of sunlight glanced off the gold ring on Anyush's finger.

'You ... you're married?'

'Yes.'

'When?'

'Does it matter?'

The infant began to cry lustily.

'The child is yours?'

'Yes.'

Jahan looked at her, his face stiff as stone.

'Why did you come back, Jahan?'

'I've been ordered to come. The Black Sea coast is vulnerable and people are being moved to the interior.'

'People?'

'Armenians.'

'I'm Armenian, Jahan. Do you mean to take me?'

'It's for your own good. For security reasons.'

'Security?' A bitter little laugh. 'What about my Turkish neighbours? Are they not a threat to your security?'

240

'I can offer you my protection,' he said stiffly. 'No harm will come to you.'

She shook away the words as though they were insects biting at her ears. Bending down, she picked up the basket at her feet.

'My child,' she said, holding it out to him, 'will you offer her your protection too? And my husband?'

When he didn't answer, she turned to leave.

'Anyush ... Anyush wait! If you won't come with me, go east. Take the coast road to Batum. Leave immediately. Today.'

They stood for a moment as if something could still be reclaimed between them. She turned her head and the sun caught the weave of her plait hanging below her scarf. It touched the blade of her shoulder where it pressed against the thin fabric of her blouse. Jahan closed his eyes, and when he opened them again she had gone.

Anyush

Lale had fallen asleep by the time Anyush reached the house, and she put her in the cool room at the back. In the bedroom she emptied one drawer after another and crammed the contents into a sack. In the kitchen she opened doors and cupboards, throwing objects at random onto the table. The pair of silver serving spoons Gohar had given her as a wedding present, still wrapped in their blue cloth. A gourd of water filled from the barrel. A side of salted pork wrapped in muslin. A knife. Bread. Some rice. A fistful of Gohar's seeds. A shaving blade that had belonged to her father. A lock of Lale's hair. Every inch of the table was covered as tears dripped onto the growing pile.

The soldier she had met under the trees was not Jahan. He was a stranger, an instrument of the Government and an officious Turk. Wiping her eyes, she went to the door of Kazbek's bedroom and opened it. It was dark and close and still smelled strongly of him. The outlines of the bed, table and chair were barely visible in the light creeping around the shutter slats. She pushed up the iron bar, sending motes of dust drifting in the sunlight to the floor. Old blackened ash spilled from the small fireplace, but otherwise everything was neat and tidy. Her stomach rose at the smell of him, stronger here than anywhere else. Facing the door, the huge oak headboard rose like a gravestone halfway up the wall. She had noticed on the few occasions he told her to clean the room that the bed was sometimes moved slightly to one side, enough to leave scrape marks on the wooden floor. She pushed the side rails with both hands but the bed wouldn't move. The headboard was too heavy. Crouching down, she put her back to it and pushed again. This time it moved a couple of inches. She tried once more and the wooden feet scraped along the floor. It was enough to allow her crawl in behind it. On her knees she looked at the wall. The wooden planks were fixed with pairs of nails and seemed even and undisturbed. Only the plank behind the top of the headboard showed any sign of wear and it was fixed solidly to the wall. She must have been mistaken. She had been so sure. With her fingertips she felt along the bottom of the wall where the shingles met the floor. Something scratchy touched her skin and she recoiled. She felt for it again and pulled it out into the light. Horsehair. Used to fill the gap between the inside and outside walls. It had to be coming from somewhere. Running her hand along the bottom slat, she stopped suddenly. She could feel a thumb-sized hollow on the underside of the last board. It came away easily and, in the space behind, she found what she had been looking for. A leather drawstring pouch containing Kazbek's blood money.

'What are you doing?'

Anyush jumped.

'I told you never to come in here.'

'Husik … you frightened me.'

'Where did you get that? Give it to me.' He snatched the pouch from her hand. 'So this is where he kept it! I should have asked you sooner.' He looked around at his father's room. 'Close those shutters.'

Anyush dropped the bar across the slats, plunging the room into darkness.

'We have to leave, Husik,' she said, following him outside. 'All of us.'

He pulled out a chair and sat at the table. His eyes roamed over the pile in front of him and settled on the side of pork. Picking it up, he unwound it slowly from its muslin wrapping. With his skinning knife, he began to carve off paper-thin slices.

'People are being taken from their homes, Husik. Armenians. We have to leave. If we can get to Batum we can stay with Gohar's relatives. We'll be safe there.'

He chewed slowly, his eyes moving over her in the way they did when he surprised her in the bedroom or the stable or the wood.

'You have to listen to me … we don't have much time. I heard from … from a soldier that they're evacuating Armenians in the village. We have to leave, Husik. Now.'

'Would that be the soldier you whored for in the old church by any chance?' The floor timbers groaned as he sat back in his chair. 'You really thought I didn't know? About you and the Turk-man? There's nothing I don't know about you, Anyushi.' He speared some meat onto the tip of his knife and offered it to her. 'No? It's good,' he said, eating it himself. 'Sit down, you look pale.'

She gripped the back of the chair nearest her.

'I was probably there every time you fucked him. I even know the sounds you made. Only someone very stupid would take on another man's whore and his child, but it pays to be stupid sometimes, Anyush. I got what I wanted in the end. I got you.'

He pushed the pork away, wiping his hands across his thighs. 'You never make those noises with me, Anyush. Maybe we should try now, eh?'

He stood up and came towards her. 'What do you say? See if you'll scream for me.'

'Please, Husik,' she said, placing a hand against his chest. 'I know what you must think of me but—'

He laughed and the baby whimpered somewhere in the back room.

'We have to leave, Husik. There's no time for this now.'

'Where were you really going, Anyush? Running off with your captain?'

'No! It isn't like that.'

'Really? What's this on the table then? And this?' With a sweep of the knife, he tipped the leather pouch onto the floor. 'What's he ever done for you, Anyush, aside from putting a child in your belly and running away? He was never there for you. Never protected you the way I have.' The marks on her neck had almost disappeared, and Husik traced their faint outline with his finger. 'I know what my father tried to do. He was a dangerous man, Anyush. Greedy. He wanted you for himself; I've always known that. He killed my mother when I was seven. Beat her so badly I didn't recognise her. Kicked her in the belly until she lost the child she was carrying and locked me in the room with her so I couldn't go for help. The same room where you so cleverly found his money. I sat in a corner and watched my mother die. He told everyone she bled to death when she lost the baby, but she died because of him. Not you though. He was never going to touch you, Anyushi.'

'No,' she said, backing away.

'You should thank me for all those things I did to him. Didn't you dream of doing them yourself?'

'No, Husik ... not your own father—'

'He killed my mother!' Husik roared, plunging the knife into the table. 'He deserved to die. He would have killed you too.'

'No—'

'Don't walk away from me.' He grabbed her by the arm and pulled her towards him. 'You're mine, Anyush. Understand?'

The trapdoor to the potato cellar was just inside the front door, and he dragged her over to it, pulling the iron ring and opening it wide.

'No, Husik, please! Not in there I beg you.'

'In you go, Anyushi-bai. Plenty of time to think in there.'

'Husik ... no!'

He dragged her over to the opening and kicked the back of her knees so that her legs folded beneath her. With a final push, she fell into the hole. The potatoes were stacked almost to the opening and the drop wasn't far, but she landed on her ribs and rolled down towards the dried mud floor. Over her head Husik's face grinned down at her. 'Say some poetry, Anyush. Helps pass the time.'

The trapdoor slammed shut, sealing her into the darkness with the dust and potato mould. Panic took hold. She scrabbled up the mound, slipping and clawing her way to where a frame of light backlit the trap-door. But the potatoes rolled from under her and she lost her footing, tumbling helplessly onto the mud below.

'Husik!' Her voice was no more than a whisper. She couldn't catch her breath. Rolling onto her knees, she tried to fill her lungs but the air seemed too heavy and her heart beat like a bird's. She was going to suffocate. Locked in under the ground while her child called out above. Lale. She held the image in her mind. Behind her, she could pick out tiny slits in the dark, vents cut into the underside of the porch steps to prevent potato rot. She crawled on her belly towards them and pushed her face against the slices of air.

'Husik!' she shouted. 'Let me out, Husik. Please.'

Above her, the sound of distant laughter. With an effort, she steadied her breathing and crawled again to the top of the potato mound until her head was just under the trapdoor. Digging in her feet for purchase, she raised her hands until they were flat on the underside of the hatch. She pushed upwards and the door gave slightly before falling heavily shut. Again she pushed hard and this time the door lifted so that shafts of light poured into the hole blinding her.

'Oh no you don't!'

Husik stamped the trapdoor shut again, sending shock waves down her arms.

'Husik, please,' she sobbed. 'Lale needs me.'

246

A shadow moved over the frame of light and she heard a chair being scraped across the boards. It creaked on the trapdoor when he sat on it. 'No place like home, Anyush.'

Showers of dust fell onto her face as he thumped his feet in time to a song. She pressed her hands over her ears.

'How are you doing in there, Anyushi?' he asked after a while. 'You've gone very quiet. One of the things I always liked about you, your quietness.'

His words were coming thick and slow and she realised he was drunk. After a while he fell silent. Something like an empty bottle rolled across the wooden floor and came to a stop. Shifting position to ease the stiffness in her limbs, Anyush fell into a waking doze.

Loud knocking woke her with a start. She was confused. How long she had been shut in? The chair over her head creaked as Husik got up to open the door. A single gunshot rang out, then a thud as something heavy fell across the trapdoor. Warm drops dripped onto her shoulder and face.

'Looks like this one had planned on going somewhere,' a voice said.

'Not any more,' a second voice laughed. 'Look what I found. The bastard was throwing his money around.'

'Piece of shit like his father. Take those spoons. And the meat. Check if anyone's hiding in the back.'

Don't cry, Lale. Please please don't cry.

'Bedroom's in a mess. Someone left in a hurry.'

'What's at the back?'

'Cool room probably.'

'Take the food.'

Dear God, dear God, dear God …

'On second thoughts, forget about it. It won't last in this heat. Come on. We're finished here.'

The footsteps moved over her head and went outside. She stayed huddled in a ball under the floor as minutes went by, hours maybe. She lost track of time. She could feel Husik's blood caking on her skin. Then into the dark, tugging gently at her consciousness, came the sound of Lale's lonely cry.

She had the weight of Husik and the door to contend with and neither would budge. Again and again she tried, slipping helplessly down the potatoes each time. Husik's body blocked the light so completely that she was becoming disorientated. She focused on the slits of air at the base of the mound, lighting her prison like candles in the dark. Lale's crying was more urgent now, loud enough for anyone passing outside to hear. She crawled to the space under the trapdoor once more and dug her feet to the ankles in the potatoes. Taking a deep breath, she pushed and kept pushing. The trapdoor lifted enough for Husik to roll a little to one side and give her room to squeeze her head and chest out. With the remaining strength left to her, she pushed her husband's body off the hatch and pulled herself clear. Dizzy and disorientated, she sat on the floor for a moment, her energy spent. Husik lay beside her, his mouth open and a blank look on his face. Her dead husband. The man who knew she had deceived him and wanted her anyway. Leaning across, she touched his cheek. It was already cold. She wanted to feel something for him. Sorrow or gratitude. Pity even, but she was numb. She felt nothing only a great emptiness and a wish to be gone.

The past weeks have been hellish. It started when Manon called to the house visibly upset, to say that Paul had been arrested. Spying and assisting fugitives was the charge, along with others the Jendarma were unwilling to discuss. I went from the Vali's mansion to the City Prefect and every other influential official I could think of. I called in every debt, every favour until the Jendarma agreed to release Paul into my custody. It was conditional on him remaining in the village under my supervision and not returning to the hospital in Trebizond. An informer had told police that Paul paid the captain of a coaling ship a large sum to smuggle Professor Levonian to Batum In Georgia. Since then the Municipal Hospital has been closed and the remaining staff suspended with the result that the only medical facility for miles is ours.

I collected Paul at the Trebizond jail and we rode to the village in silence. Exhaustion and anger put paid to any conversation we might have had. We were almost at the village when Hetty came running on the road towards us.

'Charles!' she said. 'They've taken them! They're gone!'

'Who are gone?' I asked, dismounting.

'The schoolchildren. They've taken them all. Even the little ones.'

'Who took them?' Paul asked.

That morning in school the mudir had barged into Hetty's classroom accompanied by Trebizond gendarmes. He said they were taking the children, and when she asked where, he wouldn't answer. She stood in front of the door and refused to move until he told her. They were being brought to another town, the mudir said, where their mothers were waiting for them. The children began to cry, pushing up against Hetty's skirts and clinging to her, but the gendarmes took them away.

I gripped my wife's cold hands and asked which road they had taken.

'They wouldn't tell me. I said I would see them safely into their mothers' care but I was not allowed. They were … most insistent.'

'Did they hurt you? If they so much—'

'No, no, Charles, I'm fine but I followed at a distance. They took the road south. To Gümüşhane.'

Paul made to remount his horse but I grabbed the bridle.

'Stay where you are,' I said. 'You're in enough trouble already. Where are our own children, Hetty?'

She said that Gohar hadn't come that morning as arranged, so she had sent the children to the stable loft to look out for her.

'Bring them into the house,' I told her. 'Keep them there until I return.'

Moments after I left, the first woman arrived. Her baby was three months old, perhaps four, and she told Paul that she wanted to give her child into the care of the khanum. Hetty was dumbfounded, but, moved by the girl's distress, she took the child. The next woman came shortly after with a newborn, and the floodgates opened after that. By the time I returned, the house was full of crying babies while soldiers stood in the garden waiting to seize the mothers at the first opportunity. Paul was talking to a young recruit not much older than Thomas. I saw the boy shrug indifferently and follow the line of weeping women to the village.

Inside the house, Milly was dragging a pair of drawers across the flagged kitchen floor and Robert followed with a bundle of linen in his arms. Hetty was standing in the middle of them nursing a baby and issuing orders. 'Put them over there, Milly, beside the others. Thomas, help Robert fold the sheets into those drawers and when you're done bring in milk from the cold room.'

I wiped my bleeding lip, trying to hide it from her.

'Dear God what happened to you, Charles?'

She handed the baby she was carrying to Eleanor and went to fetch some iodine. Paul came in from the garden looking agitated. 'We have to do something,' he said. 'They're marching all the Armenians out of the village.'

I stared into the bowl in Hetty's hand, blood from my lip discolouring the water. I couldn't argue with him.

Ü Ü Ü

On every road from the village I had witnessed people being herded like cattle: women and children, old people who should have been in their beds, the sick and the frail marching without provisions or water. Many had been walking in bare feet with no protection from the sun.

Ozhan's men had been prodding and lashing out at them, and when one had started to beat one of the Zornakian twins with the butt of his rifle I had tried to intervene. Grabbing the muzzle I'd shouted at him to stop but two more had descended on me and a hail of blows had rained down on my head. Someone had called them off and I'd looked up to see Nazim Ozhan standing over me.

'Go back to your hospital Dr Stewart,' he'd said.

'You have no right to take these people. No right. It's inhumane.'

'On the contrary, I have every right. This is my country and I will not be dictated to by interfering foreigners. Government business is none of your concern. Take my advice Dr Stewart, stick to what you know best. Dr Trowbridge has already caused enough trouble for giaours like you.'

Ü Ü Ü

'Why are the babies here?' I asked Hetty, looking at them lying in baskets and drawers and on sheets on the floor.

'The infants can be left behind if someone is willing to take them,' she said dabbing at my lip. 'But we need wet nurses. And help with feeding the older ones.'

There was still no sign of Gohar and nobody had any news of Anyush. I stood up and reached for my hat.

'Where are you going?' Paul asked.

'To get help.'

'You're wasting your time. The Vali will do nothing.'

I told him that Abdul-Khan's brother was a patient of mine and I intended going over the Vali's head and approaching the colonel directly. Paul insisted on coming with me.

'You're not going anywhere.'

'I'm not sitting around while Ozhan and his butchers wipe out the entire village.'

'You're under house arrest. Unless you want to go back to prison, you *will* stay here.'

'And do nothing? Like you've been doing for God knows how long?'

We faced each other in that small room, hurt and anger unspoken. It dawned on me then that I knew nothing of this country. I should never have come to this god-forsaken place. But if there was any hope of redeeming myself, it was with Abdul-Khan. If I rode hard and luck was with me then I might persuade him to see reason.

'You're right,' I said. 'I did nothing. I was wrong about everything.'

Paul shook his head.

'But I'm going to see Abdul-Khan. I'm going to ask him for a letter of protection for the villagers and as many of those in Trebizond as I can get.'

'It's too late for letters, Charles. Don't you understand?'

'I'm going anyway and I want you to stay here. As a friend I'm asking you. If you leave the village, they'll arrest you, and Hetty and the children will be left alone. Please, Paul, stay in the house with them. You're the only person I trust. I'm asking you ... begging you ... stay here and keep them safe.'

 Anyush

In the open door of Khandut's cottage, Anyush stood with the baby slung in a shawl at her breast. A single chair was knocked over in the middle of the room, but Gohar's bed under the ladder was neatly made and everything else in its usual place. To her right, the door of Khandut's room was open, and Anyush walked inside. The bed was at an angle to the wall, as though it had been pushed off centre. The covers were crumpled and stained. On the floor a small pile of clothing was half-hidden under a pillow. She picked up Khandut's underclothes. One of her stockings was just visible in the darkness under the bed and something black and solid a little further in. She bent to see what it was. A shoe. Just one. Gohar's shoe.

The Stewart House

'**M**ummy.'

'Not now Milly. Go and have a look through the window for Paul. Any sign of Manon? Thomas, is that child still crying? Did you try spooning in the milk?'

'I did, but he won't take it.'

'If he's hungry enough, he will. Try again. Eleanor, one of those babies needs changing. Did you finish cutting up those sheets? We're going to need a lot more diapers judging by the smell in here.'

'Mummy!'

'I said not now, Milly. Go find Charlotte.'

'It's a funny colour.'

'What is, Eleanor?'

'The stuff in the baby's diaper. And it smells bad.'

'Darling, all baby's diapers smell bad. Thomas, put that child down and go help Leyla with the rice. Bring it into the cool room as soon as it's sieved.'

254

'It's red.'

'Red? In the diaper? Which baby?'

Eleanor brought Hetty to see one of the children lying listlessly on a pile of folded sheets. They were assaulted by a putrid smell. The baby, a girl of about six months, had a waxy yellow complexion and her brow was cold and clammy to the touch. Every now and then she arched her back and emitted a high-pitched, pitiful scream. Hetty pulled down the cloth around her legs to reveal a mess of bloody diarrhoea.

'Poor child!'

Between spasms the baby's thin body lay limp, her eyes closed to everything going on around her.

'Has this baby taken any milk?'

'No, nothing.'

'Go fetch some warm water and a clean cloth. Robert ... has any of that water cooled yet?'

'Just about.'

'Put some in a bottle for me.' Hetty wiped her forehead with her sleeve. 'And Milly, keep that door open or we'll all pass out from the heat.'

'Mummy!'

'What *is* it, Milly dear?'

'There's a man outside.'

A few feet from the back door Captain Jahan Orfalea waited, cap in hand.

Jahan

'**I**'m looking for Anyush Charcoudian, Bayan Stewart.'

The doctor's wife folded her arms. Jahan had met Dr Stewart on a few occasions but never his wife. She wouldn't easily trust a Turkish soldier asking for a pretty Armenian girl.

Ü Ü Ü

A couple of days previously Jahan had learned that a second company, under the command of Captain Ozhan, was to assist in the Trebizond evacuation. The soldiers had already carried out a similar clearance in Erzurum, with predictable results. Rape, torture and murder. That morning, as Jahan had walked through the village with Armin, a girl's cry had drawn them to a spot behind the market. Some of the stalls had been set on fire and had fallen down, and the network of alleyways linking the main square had been empty except for a few hungry dogs. A turbaned old man sweeping the dusty tiles of his coffee house had eyed them suspiciously, oblivious to the screams coming from the alley behind his shop.

Three soldiers had been crouching at the end of the lane taking turns with a young woman. Jahan had grabbed the man kneeling over her and had pulled him off. Fists had been raised and insults hurled, but the men had become subdued when they'd spotted the insignia on his sleeve.

'Armenian women are there for the taking,' the man had said. 'By the authority of Captain Ozhan and the colonel himself.'

A second soldier, who had been holding the girl's arms, had risen to his feet. Short and heavy-set, his fingers had played with the buckle on his belt. 'Any woman we like. That's what they said.'

The girl had whimpered.

'If you touch her, I'll have you arrested for refusing to obey an officer.'

But the soldier had not been deterred. He'd smiled, his lardy cheeks compressing his eyes to little slits. 'Which officer would that be, sir? You or Colonel Abdul-Khan?'

Unhurriedly he'd opened his fly buttons and dropped his trousers. Laughing, his friends had looked over to gauge the captain's reaction.

'Excellent. This I will photograph. *Sehr gut.*' Armin had taken his camera from its box and had proceeded to assemble it onto its stand. He'd placed it so that he'd had a sidelong view of the half-naked soldier and the girl cowering beneath him. The soldiers had stared at the German.

'*Fahren Sie* ... continue please ... *gut, gut.* The German army is interested in this, *ja.*'

Everyone had watched as he'd steadied the camera on the stand. Like a predatory spider it had sat on the spindly wooden legs, facing the soldier's capacious bare bottom.

'As you were, *bitte.*' Nodding reassuringly at them, Armin had disappeared under the black cloth. Only his disembodied hand could be seen, and it had urged them to continue. The men had looked at each other, less sure of themselves now. The figure below the cloth might have been complimenting them or insulting them. They'd decided the latter. Pulling up his trousers, the fat soldier had followed the others out of the laneway, spitting on the ground by Armin's feet.

Jahan had helped the girl up and realised she was familiar. Her name was Sosi, one of Anyush's friends. The two men had brought her to the convoy of people assembled in the square where she'd found her sister and mother. At the back of the line the lieutenant had been walking rest-lessly up and down, waiting for word to pull out.

'Which route is Ozhan's company taking?' the captain had asked.

'Half are moving south to Gümüşhane. There's a second group headed north-east. They're drag-netting as far as the Russian border.'

The hair had stood up on Jahan's scalp. 'By what road?'

'Coast road. To Batum.'

Running from the square, the captain had circled round the village towards the other side of town.

Ü Ü Ü

On the doorstep of the doctor's house, Bayan Stewart assured the young captain that Anyush hadn't worked there for some time.

'Would you know where I might find her?'

'I have no idea.'

'I am a friend, Bayan Stewart.'

'Then try her family home. She's probably with her mother and grandmother.'

'I called to her mother's house. It was empty.'

The light in the doctor's wife's grey eyes changed as she looked at him. 'You know she's married? To Husik Tashjian.'

'Yes, I know.'

Jahan had been to Kazbek's house, stumbled on it from Anyush's mother's cottage nearby, where he had seen Husik's body. It was the trap-per, the boy who liked to spy on them. Poor bastard! There was a time Jahan had envied him. Near the body a trapdoor lay open. Jahan looked inside, but the cellar was empty except for a pile of mouldering potatoes. He kicked the door shut and a cloud of dust rose, heavy with the smell of blood and rotting meat.

'If she contacts you, Bayan Stewart, you should know that she's not safe here.' He glanced in the direction of the square where Ahmet and the others were waiting. 'I cannot guarantee she will be safe with me, but I am her best hope.'

Anyush

Anyush's plan was to stay under cover of the trees until she reached the village. If she could make it to the Stewarts' house, Dr Stewart would know what to do. Lale was hungry and eagerly took the breast as Anyush picked her way through the scrub. Husik had shown her little-known tracks through the wood and she moved now into the darkest part of it. Her progress was slow as the light was blocked by the tightly woven greenery overhead. Where had the path disappeared to? Behind her was as dark now as in front. She stopped to look around, panic rising within her.

'Which way, Lale?'

What was it Husik had said about getting lost? Something to do with the river? Listen for it. But she could only hear the crows and her heart pulsing in her ears. She closed her eyes and imagined herself in the branches of a tree, right at the very top, away from the humid murmuring of the forest below. And there it was, the faint sound of water flowing over stones. The trees began to thin as she moved towards it and weak sunshine threw her surroundings into a gloomy twilight. She could see the river now, laced like a silver ribbon around the wood. Changing direction, she kept it on her left and stayed well inside the treeline. The village wasn't far away and there was more light here and she had to be careful. Lale looked up at her when she stopped suddenly. Voices. On the near side of the river and moving closer. She ducked behind a fallen tree, slipping her nipple into Lale's mouth.

Heavy footsteps and the sound of breaking twigs came close to their hiding place. 'Hold on there a minute. I need a piss.' There was fumbling on the other side of the trunk and then urine sprinkling on leaves. Drops fell on Anyush's clothes and face. On and on it went, longer than seemed humanly possible. It slowed finally and came to a stop. She could hear him fixing himself and the sound of his boots breaking the leaves. It was only then she realised Lale had come off the breast. The tiny chest moved against her own and she saw her daughter's mouth widen into a cry. She pushed her finger between Lale's lips, but not before a small sound escaped her. The footsteps halted.

'Come on. What's keeping you?'

'I heard something.'

'What?'

'A noise. Around here somewhere.'

'Too many onions. You'll kill off the wildlife.'

They laughed as Anyush pressed herself into the trunk. He had stopped just in front of them. She could see the side of his face and beard as he looked around, straining to listen.

Please God, please God, please God.

Muscles like tree roots stood out on the back of his neck and his hand hovered over the knife at his belt.

'What're you doing in there? Come on. We're going.'

A gust of wind shook the leaves and whined in the branches overhead. He took one last look into the greenery and walked away.

The Stewart House

Paul returned to the house with a small woman who frowned at the scene that met her in the kitchen.

'I think you know Bayan Efendi,' he said to Hetty. 'She's going to help with the babies.'

Bayan Efendi was someone Hetty had met many times before. Small and thin, she was a midwife, healer and herb woman. Despite the heat she wore many grubby layers of black and her headscarf was worn low on her forehead in the local manner. Her pale face was wrinkled and coarse, and nobody knew her age exactly but she had presided over the births in the village for as long as anyone could remember. A pungent mixture of smells emanated from her, wood-smoke, henna and something altogether less agreeable.

'Where are the other women?' Thomas asked, holding a crying baby in his arms. 'The wet-nurses?'

'Bayan Efendi has excellent nursing skills,' his mother said.

'But how are we to feed the babies?' Eleanor asked.

'We'll have to feed them ourselves.'

The midwife began speaking in Kurmanji, her eyes darting from face to face.

'She is saying she's not afraid,' Paul translated. 'She has brought many of the soldiers into the world and will see them out.'

Five dirty fingernails waved dismissively in the air.

'She says Captain Ozhan's wife will start her confinement shortly and there are no other midwives. She says she's not afraid of him.'

Every face turned to look at the unsmiling, odoriferous, unprepossessing little woman.

'We are grateful, Bayan Efendi,' Hetty said. 'And honoured.'

On the midwife's instructions the cow's milk being fed to the babies was replaced with goat's milk and the older children fed a mixture of puréed rice and water. In what seemed a relatively short time an order of sorts was established. The sour smell of Bayan Efendi seeped into every room and seemed to be to the infants' liking. They cried less and slept in their drawers and baskets or dozed in the older children's arms. Only Millie wrinkled her nose and complained about the awful whiff.

'Manners, Milly,' Hetty said with a smile.

Paul found less to smile about. On examining the baby with diarrhoea, he agreed with Hetty that this was a case of cholera. In such close proximity to the other children and in the awful heat, it could spread swiftly through the house with catastrophic results.

'We have to isolate her,' he said. 'Has anybody else handled this baby?'

Everybody shook their heads, except Eleanor.

'Go scrub your hands thoroughly. Only one person should care for the child.'

'Let me look after her,' Hetty said. 'I've been trying to give her water but she hasn't taken much.'

'Keep trying. I'll burn the soiled diapers outside.'

Anyush

Anyush could see Dr Stewart's house from her hiding place behind the trees. There were soldiers standing in the front and back gardens waiting for the women coming and going through the door. Most of the mothers were crying. They went in with their babies and came out alone.

Earlier on, she had skirted around the village under the cover of the wood, to where the roads divided west to Trebizond and east towards Batum. Hundreds of women and children, young and old, had been walking westward, a long line stretching as far as the eye could see. Some had been pushing carts loaded with bits of furniture, but most had been on foot, blindly following those in front. A couple of soldiers had walked at the back, lashing out with whips at the stragglers. The eerie quiet had been broken by a child's crying and the pitiful keening of an old man. Anyush had watched as the line passed, looking for Gohar and Khandut. The people she'd recognised were from north of the village and her mother and grandmother had not been among them. Slipping into the cover of the wood again, she had made her way back to the Stewarts'.

Ṳ Ṳ Ṳ

From her hiding place Anyush saw three soldiers knock loudly on the Stewarts' front door. Leyla, the Stewarts' maid, opened it.

'Call the *doktor*,' one of the men said.

The girl disappeared, returning moments later with Dr Trowbridge.

'*Merhaba*,' the Englishman said. 'Can I help you?'

'*Merhaba, doktor sahip*,' the soldier bowed. 'We have come to search the house.'

'For what reason?'

'We are looking for Armenians, *Doktor*. The resettlement convoy is leaving and we want to be sure no one is left behind.'

Two of the three men on the doorstep were young, not much older than Anyush, and the third was somewhere in his middle years. He salaamed to the giaour in the traditional manner, but his voice betrayed an ill-concealed dislike.

'Where are you bringing these people?' Dr Trowbridge asked.

'Gümüşhane, *sahip*. And Bayburt.'

'What for?'

'I am only a poor soldier, *Doktor*. They say "bring people here", I bring. They say "look in the *doktor*'s house", I look.'

'Dr Stewart is away. I cannot give permission in his absence.'

The soldier pulled his lips into a smile as his eyes swept over Eleanor and Milly who were watching from the hallway. 'That is a shame, *Doktor*, because we have been told by Captain Ozhan that the house is to be searched. It would be most unfortunate if we had to break windows and doors.'

Dr Trowbridge looked at the men, then dropped his hand from the doorframe and stood aside. 'Go where you want. There is no one here of any interest to you. But I should warn you that there is a case of cholera in the house.'

'Cholera?'

The soldier stood down from the step.

'Yes. One of the infants has contracted it. It has spread, but most of the adults are still on their feet. I was just about to burn these.' He held up a pail of soiled cloths, and the soldiers jumped as though it contained poisonous snakes and the dreaded disease was seeping through every window and door.

'It will not be necessary, *Doktor*. I will take you at your word. *Teşekkür ederim*.'

Ü Ü Ü

'Clever, clever Dr Trowbridge!' Anyush whispered. 'No one will enter a cholera house. I wonder who he's hiding?' She could think of only one person and hoped fervently it might be her. 'Gohar! Of course it is.'

There were no more soldiers in the garden and any minute now she would leave the tree cover and make a run for it. Dr Trowbridge was still outside, and he made a fire and stoked it with wood until the flames rose high. He emptied the contents of the pail onto the fire.

Anyush slipped back beneath the trees. If what he had told the soldiers was a trick, then surely the babies' clothes would be washed not burned?

A small woman in black emerged from the house and joined him. It was the midwife who had delivered Lale.

'Another baby has the sickness, *Doktor*.'

'Same symptoms?'

The woman nodded.

'Put it with the baby from this morning. How is that child faring?'

'Not well,' the midwife said, following Dr Trowbridge into the house.

Anyush slid along the trunk of the tree until she was hunkered down with Lale hidden in the valley between her stomach and knees. He hadn't lied. There *was* cholera in the house. Bending her head, she touched her forehead to her daughter's. 'What are we to do, Lale?'

The baby's dark lashes fluttered away her mother's tears as the birds grew quiet and the midday sun beat down.

Jahan

J ahan watched Armin ride to the head of the line with the lieutenant, his camera boxes swaddled in blankets and tied to his saddle. The
German was accompanying them, as arranged, and he too was heading in the direction of Gümüşhane. He had been taking photographs
earlier before the chaos erupted. Some onlookers had thrown stones at
the people gathered in the square and tensions ran high. Jahan's soldiers
moved along the line, breaking up fights and keeping the two sides apart.
Screaming and crying and rearing horses added to the confusion. Children wandered everywhere. Some ran dangerously close to cartwheels
and horses' legs, desperately trying to find their mothers. Old people
wept. Young women struggled to carry bundles on their heads and hold
onto the children at their sides. As the last of the refugees left the village their faces changed. Grim determination took hold as though they
would kill or be killed. A heavily pregnant woman sat wearily on the
edge of a cart only for another to shove her roughly off. A skinny old
man pushed hunks of bread down his throat watched by a starving child.
Jahan looked on with a growing sense of unease. He had been so hope-
ful of finding Anyush when he discovered her mother and grandmother
in Ozhan's convoy. Bribing one of the guards, he had them released to

his convoy, but they had no news of her. Now he had to leave. It wasn't possible to delay any longer. A sudden squall sprang up and blew the cap from his head into the dust. He turned to retrieve it and saw a figure walking towards him. A slender woman with braided hair holding a baby in her arms.

Anyush

The old woman wept as she embraced her granddaughter. Gohar and Khandut had been searching for Anyush among the people in the square, and when they hadn't found her they assumed the worst. It was Khandut now who was missing. She had gone to look for Sosi and Parzik, hoping for news of Anyush, and had never returned. Past the back of a wagon Anyush saw the line stretch ahead of her like a snake with its head buried in the hills. A lone figure on horseback broke away from it. As he drew closer Anyush could see it was Jahan, and she stepped back into the line beside her grandmother.

He tried to talk to her, to engage her in conversation. He spoke as if nothing had changed, as if he was not a soldier nor she his prisoner. Did he really believe their situation could be redeemed with a few meaningless words? His need for forgiveness was contemptible to her and she turned away. She had nothing to say to him any more.

Gohar was tired and thirsty but insisted on carrying Lale, pressing her like a relic to her breast. Further up the line, bread and goatskins of water were being handed out on the captain's orders. Gohar insisted Anyush join the queue, but she refused. She would rather starve. Some time later Jahan rode past and dropped bread and a canteen of water at her feet.

'Take it,' Gohar said. 'For the child's sake.'

Anyush picked it up and broke the bread in half, giving some to her grandmother and taking a little herself. The rest she put in her skirt pocket. Only for Lale, she told herself, feeling that the bread would choke her with every bite.

They had walked a while when Anyush noticed her grandmother's bare foot poking out beneath her skirt.

'Here,' she handed her one of her own shoes. 'Put this on.'

'I don't need it. My feet are as hard as leather.'

'You carry my daughter, *Tatik*, you wear two shoes.'

Gohar's old face broke into a smile.

'Your mother eh, Lale? Just like her father.'

She kissed her great-granddaughter's head, as Anyush bent to tie the shoe onto her foot.

'You there!' A soldier, the Ferret, was watching then.

'You,' he pointed his whip at Anyush. 'What were you doing?'

'Nothing. I gave her my shoe.'

'What's in your shoe, old woman? She put money in your shoe?'

'No, *efendim*. A little comfort for the road, that's all.'

'Take it off.'

Gohar levered her foot out of the shoe and the soldier peered inside. Picking it up with his whip, he raised it to eye level then flung it into the scrub behind him.

'What else have you hidden under there?'

The tip of his whip was pointing at Anyush's skirt.

'No money or silver allowed,' he said, his eyes creeping over her.

'I have nothing.'

'Give me the ring.'

Anyush pulled her wedding band from her finger.

'Hand over the rest of it. Now or I'll have to look for myself.'

'I swear, *efendim*, I'm carrying nothing.'

'Lift your skirt.'

Gohar closed her eyes.

'Lift it!'

Anyush hitched her skirts to her knees.

'Higher.'

'*Efendim*, she was only—'

'Shut your mouth, old woman. Lift it. To your waist.'

Others were listening, their faces turned away so as not to draw attention to themselves. Anyush did as he asked. The Ferret moved closer and placed the tip of his whip against her drawers.

'Take them off.'

'*Efendim* ... please ...'

'Pull them down.'

'Hanim!'

Jahan and a foreign-looking man trotted down the line towards them, and Anyush dropped her skirts.

'What were you doing?'

'These women are carrying weapons, *bayim*. I saw her trying to hide something under her clothes.'

'Get back to the line.'

'But, Captain—'

'Do as I say.'

'We were told—'

'One more word and I'll charge you with insubordination. Now find Düzgünoğlu and look for somewhere to set up camp.'

Ŭ Ŭ Ŭ

That first night on the march the sky was clear, and stars and a crescent moon lit the faces of the people lying or sitting on either side of the road. Exhaustion had quietened the children's cries and a hush settled over the camp. Here and there the red tips of soldiers' cigarettes flared near the supply wagons.

At the base of a stony mound Gohar and Anyush sat close to where the horses were tethered. They were exhausted, and, although Anyush had alternated her shoe from one foot to the other, her feet were cut and blistered. Gohar was lying back in the sedge while Lale suckled at her mother's empty breast.

'You alright, *Tatik*?'

'Better since the water.'

She passed Anyush the goatskin and the half loaf of black bread.

'I was at the house,' Anyush said. 'In the bedroom.'

The horses' hooves knocked off the hard ground and their bridles jangled as they nodded and whinnied into the warm night

'You need to find your mother,' Gohar said. 'It was bad for her.'

Ü Ü Ü

Early the following morning Anyush pushed past the line for water at the supply wagon. The old and the very young were still lying or sitting by the road, while the more able were gathering what belongings they had. Mothers rubbed mud on their children's faces as protection from the sun and on their daughters' faces as protection of another kind. The foreign soldier Anyush had seen with Jahan was perched on a low hill looking down on the caravan below.

Further along, she spotted Sosi huddled with her mother and Havat by the side of one of the wagons. She ran over. Sosi raised her head, catching the sun full on her face. Her left eye was closed and her nose swollen into a bruised, misshapen mess.

'Sosi,' Anyush whispered, unable to take her eyes from her, 'Did you ... have you seen Khandut?'

Her friend shook her head and turned her face towards her mother's shoulder. Beside them Havat rocked to and fro, clutching her knees in dumb silence. Bayan Talanian's eyes were closed, tears running silently down her cheeks. Nearby, a young woman Anyush knew from Bayan Stewart's sewing group sat in the road like a stone thrown by a wheel. A pitifully thin child lay across her lap. The woman seemed unaware of her surroundings or the people moving in ever-widening circles around her.

'Don't go near.' Jahan caught her by the arm. 'The child has cholera.'

Anyush shook herself free.

'Go back to your grandmother,' he said. 'We're moving on.'

Ü Ü Ü

The second day was much like the first and all those that followed, though longer, hotter and more difficult. Food ran out. Children took to thievery and adults followed suit. Fights were common as the mood in the camp swung from aggression to exhaustion. No quarter was given to the pregnant, the sick, the young or the old. There were many miles to be covered in a day and everyone had to walk them.

In the last stages of pregnancy, Parzik went into labour one hot afternoon. She walked and laboured, and walked again, and her cries could be heard the length of the caravan. Parzik's mother and the twins had been taken in Ozhan's convoy, so there was only her sister, Seranoush, and Anyush to soothe her in her distress. Jahan took the decision to set up camp early, and Gohar delivered a male child as the sun set behind Kızıldağ. Parzik wept that Vardan would never know he had a son. Because of her weakness following the birth, the captain allowed her to ride in a wagon on the following day's march where she lay in a pool of her own blood calling for her mother. Following behind like a sleep-walker, Seranoush carried her new nephew for a number of days, but exhausted and too weak to hold him, Parzik's sister finally abandoned the baby by the side of the road.

Ṳ Ṳ Ṳ

'Did you find her?'

'No.'

Anyush took Lale from Gohar's arms and sat down to feed.

'Did you look at the front? Behind where the soldiers are?'

'Yes.'

'We have to find her. You have to keep searching.'

'Why?'

'What do you mean why?'

'Why do we have to keep looking?'

'Oh ... Anyush!'

'Don't pretend, *Tatik*. She made your life as miserable as she made mine. She hated me, her own daughter. If she had her way, I would be married to Kazbek. Why should I worry about her?'

'She didn't hate you, Anyush.'

'You have another name for it? I will never treat my daughter that way. Never! If I hadn't had you, *Tatik*—'

'If you hadn't had me, you might have known her better. How much she cares about you.' The old woman gripped Anyush's arm. 'I'm a stupid old woman, Anyush. Stupid and selfish. When your father died somehow I blamed Khandut because it was easy to blame a woman I never liked. She didn't want to marry your father but I was one of those who insisted on it. The marriage was to settle a land dispute between our two families

275

and it suited both sides. Everyone except Khandut. She was always different. A little strange because of what happened to her as a child. She was attacked in Kazbek's wood at nine years of age and it left its mark. As time went on she became more peculiar. She never liked the company of men and found herself forced to marry one. It was an unbearable situation for her. But your father did love her. That was the tragedy of it. He saw a different side to her, a gentler side. He believed she would change. That she would come to have feelings for him.'

Anyush wasn't paying attention. The past was a place that didn't concern her any more, only the present.

'Anyush, listen to me. When your father died and you were born you looked so like him I felt I had my child again. I wasn't about to lose him a second time. Nobody was going to take you from me, not even your own mother. There were times she tried to get close to you. Many times, but she found it hard. She didn't trust easily and I made sure she got none from you. I came between you.'

Lale had finished feeding and Anyush held the baby against her shoulder, but Gohar wasn't done.

'When the soldiers came and took her into the bedroom, I could see what I had never seen before. That she was only a child herself. A girl who never had a chance. But it was too late. There was nothing I could do for her. God forgive me, it was too late.' Gohar shook Anyush's arm. 'You have to find her. Promise me, Anyush.'

'*Tatik*—'

'Promise. You must promise.'

'Yes ... yes, I will find her. I promise.'

Ṳ Ṳ Ṳ

As darkness fell on the sixth day the convoy stopped for the night just short of a mountain pass. They were now in bandit country where the Shota tribes held sway. Rather than enter the defile as night approached, the captain decided that the caravan would pass through at first light while the sun was still low in the sky. Gohar's progress had noticeably slowed by this time and she collapsed onto the roadway when the caravan halted. With very little water in the goatskin, Anyush had barely wet her lips all day so that her grandmother might have more. She had also been carefully rationing the bread and had almost lost it to the pilfering hands of an old man sleeping near them. What little was left she kept hidden in a fold of her skirt. Between stops she made her way to the wagon where Parzik lay in a fever. She no longer recognised Anyush or Seranoush, but called in a weakening voice for her child. Her two thin arms reached out for Lale, nestled in the sling at her mother's breast. Anyush laid her daughter beside her friend, and Parzik smiled, kissing the baby until they both closed their eyes.

Over the past few days Lale had become quiet, so still that Anyush could scarcely feel her breathe. Every now and then, Anyush would stop walking, pressing Lale tightly against her until she felt the small chest move against her own.

In the evenings, at Gohar's urging, she searched for her mother. Looking at the faces she passed, the dead as well as the living, she could find no trace of her. Khandut seemed to have vanished. Cholera and dysentery were spreading rapidly through the camp and on that sixth evening it claimed Parzik's godfather, Meraijan Assadourian. His body was left at the side of the road when the convoy marched into the gorge the following day.

Ṳ Ṳ Ṳ

The five-mile ravine was almost in full shade in the early morning, but by noon the sun was directly overhead and burned through headscarves and clothes. People cried out for water, but there would be no stopping. The captain announced that the convoy had to be fully through the gorge by nightfall. With Lale slung across her back, Anyush linked her grandmother's arm and urged her to keep walking. Some time in the afternoon Gohar whispered that she needed to relieve herself urgently. Squatting down by the side of the road, the old woman clutched onto her granddaughter for support as evil-smelling diarrhoea splashed onto her legs and feet. Anyush struggled to keep them upright, watching the old woman clutch at her belly in pain.

'Please God,' Anyush prayed, cleaning her grandmother as best she could with a piece of her own skirt. 'Please God, may it not be cholera.'

The old woman's legs were shaking as she tried to stand, and Anyush tipped the last dregs of water into her mouth.

'I have to sit down. Just for a minute.'

Gohar's breath was coming unevenly, and Anyush lowered her gently to the ground.

'You. Get up.' The Ferret walked over, whip in hand. 'Captain says no stopping. Get up, I said.'

His hateful, animal face leered down at them. Anyush wanted to shout at him, to scream that her grandmother was old and hungry and sick, but she bit her tongue and whispered in Gohar's ear. 'Come on, *Tatik*. Let's get this rat off our backs. Up you get. Lean on my arm, that's it.'

The Ferret covered his nose with his sleeve. 'Wallowing in your own shit! Armenian sow!'

Spitting on the ground at their feet, he backed away.

The caravan struggled on and they clung to the base of the defile where shade was starting to creep across the valley floor. Jahan, the lieutenant and the German soldier rode up and down the line, scanning the slopes either side and shouting at the marchers to keep moving. For a time Jahan rode at the back where Anyush was walking with Gohar, holding her by the arm and urging her to walk just a little further. Something fell on the ground near her feet. A piece of salted meat wrapped in oilcloth and a water bottle. Anyush dived for them.

Jahan

A progress of sorts had been made. Despite the diminishing water and food supplies and the outbreak of cholera, the convoy had marched enough miles that reaching their destination began to seem possible. If Jahan could maintain this pace for four or five days more, they stood a good chance of reaching Gümüşhane. It would take another six days to get to Erzincan, and at a terrible cost. For every mile marched there was a slew of bodies in their wake. Disease and hunger, exposure and dehydration would claim many more. The number of marchers falling ill grew daily but there could be no stopping. He had to keep them moving. In open countryside they were an obvious target.

Jahan hadn't spoken to Anyush since leaving the village but watched from afar as she tried to keep her grandmother on her feet. They were separated now by a new reality, hunger, fear and desperation. All they had was this unending present where time existed only in miles. He watched her become frail and thin, weakening like the others. It was only in her eyes that he recognised something of her. Her eyes gave him hope.

The broad expanse of plain was tantalisingly visible beyond the valley walls when he spotted the first of the Shota at the mouth of the gorge. A second group closed in behind where Anyush and her grandmother brought up the rear. The convoy was surrounded. A wall of mounted bandits was strung across the valley, shaded by the mountain behind them. Jahan scanned the long line of faces. To look at, these men might have been musicians or entertainers who trawled the bazaars and marketplaces in the towns. They wore colourful waistcoats, wide-sashed breeches and blue caps, which lent them an almost comical air. In contrast to their style of dress they carried belts of bullets across their chests and rifles at their sides. Far and wide these men had a reputation for rape and murder. Jahan and his sisters had been reared on cautionary tales of their brutality, and even the dogs on the street lived in fear of them. Word spread quickly down the line. Women stifled screams and those children who had mothers clung to them.

Two men, one older and broader than the others, broke away from the Shota line and rode towards the caravan. Ahmet and Jahan moved out to meet them. The older man greeted the captain in Kurmanji.

'*Merhaba*,' Jahan replied, noticing the bandit was missing his right hand.

Murzabey smiled, revealing even white teeth. 'You are travelling with quite a following, young captain. Where are you making for?'

'I was about to ask you the same question.'

Murzabey threw back his head and laughed. 'This ...' he gestured to the flat expanse beyond the valley, 'is my country. I cross it at will.'

'On the contrary, this land belongs to the Ottoman Empire of which we the soldiers of the 23rd Regiment are a part.'

The Shota's smile never faltered as his eye travelled over the line of women and children at the captain's back.

'The convoy is going to Gümüşhane and then Erzincan, by order of Colonel Abdul-Khan,' Jahan said.

'Then the colonel is an expedient man. You are carrying very little provision for such a journey.'

'We have enough.'

'I hear Gümüşhane is not a very welcoming place. It would be too bad if you were turned away on empty bellies. My friend the colonel tells me it's a rough town.' A ripple of laughter spread through his ranks. 'But I will tell you, my friend, what I will do. I will relieve you of your charges. Take your men and ride on to Gümüşhane, and my men …' Murzabey paused as more Shota appeared along either side of the valley walls and bolstered his rear. 'My men will give you safe passage.'

Jahan's horse pawed the ground nervously and, out of the corner of his eye, he could see Armin watching. The German's camera would be of no use this time.

'If the colonel is your friend, then you will already know about this convoy.'

'What if I do?' Murzabey said guardedly.

'Then you know of the convoy coming two days after us.'

'I know nothing of a second convoy.'

'Presumably the colonel has taken you into his confidence about the final destination of this one?'

'You've already told me you're going to Erzincan.'

'Is that what he told you?' Jahan laughed. 'You know Mother Yazgan's brothel? Her Erzincan establishment?'

'I know the old whore,' Murzabey said. 'What of it?'

'The colonel has, shall we say, an interest in the place. A business interest. But as his friend you already know this.'

'What are you talking about?'

'I shouldn't have said. I spoke out of turn.'

'What does Yazgan have to do with this?'

'I'd rather not say.'

'You will speak of it or I will rip your throat out.'

The Shota's voice echoed around the valley walls and the marchers cried out in fear. Jahan looked at his lieutenant. Ahmet had no idea what the captain was talking about but took his cue and nodded.

'Yazgan pays the colonel for every serviceable woman or child he delivers and a percentage of the profits. On condition that she hand-pick the best herself.'

Murzabey looked unconvinced.

'If the colonel promised you spoils, then it's from the convoy behind us.'

'How do I know you're telling the truth?'

'You don't. But if you know the colonel, you will think long and hard before crossing him.'

Murzabey took time to consider. Either side of him Shota eyes counted the marchers, eager for the reckoning. 'Very well. Bring the colonel his women. I will congratulate him on his talent for business next time we meet.'

The Shota leader spurred his horse closer, coming to within whispering distance. 'But if I find you have lied to me, be assured you will beg for mercy and I am not a merciful man.'

With that he turned about and, as suddenly as they had come, Murzabey and the Shota disappeared.

Ü Ü Ü

'I hope you know what you're doing,' Armin said.

'We have to reach Gümüşhane before Murzabey talks to the colonel. Is it possible Ahmet? Can we get there in two days?'

'Two days!' the lieutenant shook his head. 'Even if we had enough food and water to go around and if everybody was healthy and well, the best we could hope for is three and more likely four.'

Jahan looked at what remained of the convoy. Most of them couldn't walk another mile and those still on their feet would not last much longer. His eyes landed on Anyush sitting near the end of the line.

'We'll just have to try.'

Anyush

Gümüşhane might have been on the other side of the world to the marchers who struggled towards it. Young and old had been taken by cholera, starvation and exhaustion. Food had run out and people were drinking whatever water they could find. Anyush went to check on Parzik, only to see her corpse tipped from the wagon into a culvert by the side of the road.

Anyush saw Jahan looking into the ravine where the German had set up his camera and was taking photographs of Parzik's body. A little to one side, the Ferret was holding the captain's mare by the reins. His closed hand slid beneath the saddle blanket and the horse gruntled and pulled away from him. Looking furtively around him, the Ferret withdrew his hand and led the mare over to the captain.

Ü Ü Ü

In her more lucid moments Gohar still asked about Khandut, but Anyush didn't tell her that she had stopped searching. A new purpose occupied her: Lale, Gohar, herself. The hunger, dizziness and weariness that threatened to defeat her time and again was set aside whenever she looked at her daughter or coaxed her grandmother to walk one more mile. For their survival, and her own, she did the unthinkable. From the corpse of a young woman she took a pair of shoes for herself and from a dying older woman a pair for Gohar. Without opening the laces she pulled them roughly off and the woman groaned in the throes of her lonely struggle to die. It was Elsapet, Meraijan's wife. Anyush took the shoes anyway. At night-time, when the long-tailed desert rats came hopping across the scree, she pounced on them and tried to force Gohar to eat some of the raw meat, but Gohar was vomiting constantly and it was becoming difficult to get her to drink. Anyush realised too, as the milk in her breasts dried up and Lale became more silent, that her baby was slipping away from her.

'Please God, please God, please God,' she prayed, mile after mile after mile.

Jahan

Leading his horse by the reins, Jahan walked to the head of the column. Two of his men had died of cholera and three more were clutching their bellies in one of the covered wagons. It was spreading like plague and would take more before they reached Gümüşhane. He couldn't bury them, couldn't bring them with him. Along with the others, they lay at the bottom of the ravine, carrion for the wild animals and the crows. Anyush was still on her feet. a walking ghost but alive. Her grandmother was a different matter.

The mare pulled the reins through his hands and pawed the ground uneasily. She was fidgety and nervous.

'Easy. Easy there girl.' Jahan clapped his horse on the flank, but she jerked her head around and pulled hard again. Throwing the reins over her neck, he put his boot in the stirrup and grabbed the pommel, but the mare danced away from him so that he had to hop on one foot after her.

'Whoa there. What's the matter? Hold up.' Swinging his leg over her back, he let his weight fall into the saddle.

The mare screeched and whinnied and reared up on her hind legs. Grabbing her by the mane, Jahan held on as she bucked and kicked and finally threw him off. Before he hit the ground, his leg knocked off the corner of one of the wagons, the bones snapping in two and pushing out through his skin.

Ü Ü Ü

'Don't move him,' Armin said.

The captain lay at an awkward angle, his face white with shock. A group of soldiers were staring at him when the lieutenant elbowed them out of the way.

'What happened?'

'Give me your rifle and your belt,' the German said, splitting Jahan's trouser leg to above the knee. The leg was already swelling and he cleaned the broken skin as best he could. Opening the breech of the lieutenant's rifle, he shook out the bullets and splinted the captain's leg to the gun barrel.

'It's a bad break, but the real enemy out here is the heat. Is there a hospital in Gümüşhane?'

'No. Sivas is closest,' Ahmet said.

'We need a wagon and a driver.'

The lieutenant disappeared as word spread that the captain had been injured.

Jahan tried to sit, convulsed by a sudden urge to vomit, but collapsed back, spent.

'You'll be OK,' Armin said when it had passed. 'Keep drinking. It seems I will have to teach you the German way to ride a horse.'

'This wasn't an accident,' Jahan said through gritted teeth. 'My horse has never so much as whinnied at me before.'

A wave of pain washed over him and he retched again.

'Don't talk. Drink some more.'

'Ahmet will have to take over. He's the only one capable of it.'

The lieutenant appeared with something wrapped in a tarpaulin and a blanket to cover his leg. 'It will keep the flies off,' he said, tucking it in at the sides. 'There's food and water under there.'

Jahan grabbed him by the sleeve. 'I want to speak to Anyush. Get her for me.'

'*Bayim*, there is no—'

'Get her, now.'

Anyush

Anyush held Gohar's hand tightly in hers. The old woman was lying flat on the side of the road, a stolen shawl folded beneath her head. Her breathing was uneven and her mouth hung open, as though her teeth had outgrown her face and could not be contained by her lips. It was what her grandmother had become, a body of teeth and sinew and bone. Anyush looked down at her fingers. The knotted joints had more of Gohar in them than her wasted face. Her fingertips were discoloured a blue-black colour, as though someone had dipped them in indigo ink. The vomiting and diarrhoea had passed, but from Anyush's days working with Dr Stewart, she understood what the discolouration meant. She thought for a moment about the Stewarts. About the hospital and the village and her home. It belonged to another time.

The convoy had grown quiet. Some sort of commotion had drawn the soldiers to the front of the line and Anyush thought the Shota had returned, but there was nothing to be seen across the plain or on the hills behind her. Everybody else took the chance to sit or lie by the roadside and rest for a while. Anyush bent her head and kissed Gohar's cold hand.

'You there.' The lieutenant was watching. 'Come with me.'

Jahan was lying in the back of a wagon, his face slick with sweat and drained of colour. A shading of blue darkened the wings of his nose and the outline of his lips. From the clenching of his teeth, Anyush could see he was in great pain. The German pulled back the blanket covering him to reveal a bloodied mess of skin and bone. Jahan looked at her, his eyes a reflection of his daughter's.

'Anyush,' he said, 'I want you to come with me.'

'*Bayim*—' the lieutenant interrupted.

'Ride with me in the wagon. I can hide you under the blanket.'

'Not in broad daylight,' the lieutenant said.

'We'll wait until nightfall, leave under cover of darkness.'

'You can't wait that long,' the German said.

'And you'll both be shot if you're caught.'

'Get me a driver, Ahmet. Someone I can trust.'

'You wouldn't get two miles—'

'She can hide under a tarpaulin then.'

They argued back and forth while Anyush stood by the wagon holding Lale.

'I'm not asking you, lieutenant, I'm telling you.'

'You want me to send both of you to your deaths?'

'Just do as I say.'

'I'm not going.'

The three men turned to look at her.

'I won't go.'

Jahan pushed himself onto his elbows. 'Anyush, you have to come.'

'I won't leave my grandmother.'

'She's dying. She's not going to make it ... for pity's sake, I'm offering you a way out.'

The horse hitched to the wagon grew restless, pawing the ground and pulling against the traces. Jahan winced in pain.

'Anyush,' he said, 'please listen to me ... this is your only chance. You

290

have to come. If you won't do it for my sake, then do it for the child.'

Anyush looked at Lale, the small silent bundle in her arms. She was all that was left to her, everything that was precious and good. Gohar would not survive for much longer, she already knew as much. Anyush wanted her to die. She prayed for it as she had begun to wish it for herself. It was only because of Lale that she chose to go on. She looked at Jahan. Pain had dulled the light in his eyes, but she remembered their brilliance and how she had lost herself in them.

'Take her,' she said, holding Lale over the wagon. 'Take her, Jahan. She is my only hope.'

Anyush laid the baby beside him and whispered in his ear. He turned towards her, his eyes clinging to hers. He was speaking, saying something she couldn't hear. His mouth was open and his eyes were full but Anyush walked away from him. She knew if she went with them they would be discovered. Her feet moved faster and faster, trying to distance herself from what she had done. Trying to forget the sight of Lale lying on the filthy floor of the wagon. Trying not to feel she had abandoned her, and knowing she would go to her grave believing it.

Jahan

Armin took out a silver brandy flask from his pocket. 'For you, when the pain gets bad. And for her.'

Pouring a little into the cap, he trickled some into Lale's mouth and it dribbled onto her chin. She made hungry sucking noises, opening her mouth wide as though wanting more, before the alcohol hit and the tiny face puckered in a grimace.

'It will keep her asleep,' Armin said. 'Top it up from time to time.'

Jahan tilted the small face to look at her. His child. Anyush's child. His daughter had the same colour hair as he did, but he couldn't see her eyes, which were closed. She seemed lifeless, her tiny chest barely moving and her head too heavy for her fragile neck. How would he care for her? What hope did she have with him?

'I'm not leaving without Anyush.'

The German screwed the cap onto the flask and put it into his hand.

'I won't go without her, Armin.'

'You can't force her.'

'She'll die if she stays with the convoy.'

'I think you must respect her wishes.'

'Why doesn't anybody respect mine?!'

Armin put his hand on his shoulder before arranging the blanket to cover Lale, so that only her nose and the top of her head were visible.

'I have a favour to ask of you,' he said, pulling a stack of photographic plates from under his coat. He tucked them beneath the blanket at Jahan's feet.

'If word reaches the colonel about my photographs, they'll be destroyed. There's a division of the German Sanitary Corps stationed in Sivas. A friend of mine by the name of Günther Stoll will take these from you. Don't give them to anybody else and don't let the Field Marshal get his hands on them.'

Ahmet and one of the young privates appeared carrying a water barrel between them. They dropped it into the wagon with a sickening jolt.

'Muslu is taking you to Gümüşhane,' the lieutenant said, handing Jahan a filled goatskin. 'You can trust him. He'll organise fresh horses and bring you on to Sivas.'

'Ahmet ... listen to me ... I want you to find Anyush. And something to cover her. One of the big tarpaulins.'

The lieutenant glanced at the German.

'It doesn't matter what she says. Take her by force if you have to.'

Private Muslu climbed onto the buckboard and took the reins in his hands.

'She'll be with the old woman somewhere at the back of the line.'

But Ahmet was looking at where Muslu sat waiting for the order to leave. The lieutenant nodded and the boy cracked the reins over the horse's rump.

'What are you doing? Stop! Ahmet, tell him to stop!'

Clouds of dust rose as the wheels turned and the wagon began to move.

'Muslu turn around! That's an order!'

The boy ignored him, whipping the horse furiously, as Armin and the lieutenant watched. The figures grew faint behind the sunlit haze and Jahan craned his neck to see behind him. They were still there, less substantial now, like ghosts fading into the day. Jahan's eye followed the line of marchers until he saw her. She was behind the others, head bent over the recumbent figure of her grandmother.

'Anyush! Anyush!'

But the dust cloud swallowed her and there was no answer, only the sound of the wheels turning beneath him.

The Stewart House

'Leyla? Has anyone seen Leyla? Where is that girl?'

The cook had gone to the village and had not been seen since.

'Paul, have you seen Leyla? If the children are not fed shortly they'll fall down.'

Bayan Efendi murmured something in Kurmanji.

'Gone? Did she say Leyla's gone?'

Paul nodded.

'Not another one!'

That morning Arnak also had left without a word.

'People are afraid, Hetty. They don't want to be associated with Armenians.'

'They're children, for heaven's sake. Infants.'

'Mother!' Thomas came running through the door from the garden. 'There are army vehicles outside the house. And soldiers. Lots of them.'

'Where are the other children?' Paul asked.

'They're in the stables,' Hetty said. 'I sent them to look for Arnak's old shirts. We were going to cut them up to make diapers.'

'Bring everybody into the house and lock the doors.'

The family crowded around the window, watching Paul approach the soldiers who were climbing down from a high-sided cart. One man, a captain, was pointing to the house and shaking his head determinedly. Hetty recognised him.

'What do they want, Mama?'

'I don't know, Eleanor.'

'Why is Uncle Paul arguing with that man?' Robert asked.

'I don't know that either.'

'They want to search the house again,' Thomas said, his face pressed to the glass.

One side of the cart was let down and the soldiers moved into the garden.

'Mama ...' Millie said, tugging the sleeve of Hetty's dress.

'Hush, darling. I can't hear what they're saying.'

Millie looked back into the kitchen where she had found Lottie, seemingly asleep under the table. 'But, Mama …'

'Not now, Millie.'

Paul stood with his head bowed as soldier after soldier pushed past him into the stable yard and the outhouses.

'They've come for the babies,' he said when Hetty let him in.

'Dear God, no!'

'I told them about the cholera, but it made no difference. They say there has been an orphanage set up in Erzincan and the children will be reunited with their mothers there.'

'But there is no one to care for them. Who will care for them on the journey? And the babies in the cool room are too ill to travel. They have to be left here.'

Loud hammering on the door echoed around the small space.

'Open up!'

Hetty shook her head, her eyes pleading with Paul's.

'Open the door.'

The children crowded around, glancing fearfully towards the garden.

'Uncle Paul,' Milly whispered.

Before she could finish, the hall window smashed in a burst of broken glass and the butt of a rifle knocked the remaining shards to the ground. Paul pulled back the bolt and let the soldiers inside.

'Search the house,' Ozhan said.

They paired off, turning out the ground-floor rooms and climbing the stairs to search the bedrooms on the top floor.

'You have no right,' Paul said, as they filed past him. 'This is a private house. You have no permission to enter it.'

'Dr Trowbridge, I presume?' the captain said. 'We haven't had the pleasure.'

'That's not a word I would use.'

'Oh but I know all about you, Doctor. I know you were responsible for Professor Levonian's untimely death. And of course you smuggled those two unfortunate girls to Georgia. Now, why, I ask myself, would you do something like that? But then I've been hearing stories about you. That one of those poor girls was pregnant with your child. The one you had to get rid of.'

'That's a lie!'

'Is it? Interfering with young women is a very serious offence in this country. If it wasn't for my friend, Charles Stewart, you would be rotting in a Trebizond jail right now.'

'Charles is no friend of yours.'

'On the contrary, he and his charming wife have been guests at my home. Is that not so, Bayan Stewart?'

Hetty's eyes dropped to the floor.

'You might like to know, by the way, that I met your husband. At a meeting with the colonel, no less! Well, I hope his efforts are successful, but perhaps it's just as well he's not here when we close the hospital.'

'Close the hospital? What do you mean?'

'The Armenian doctors have been taken with the resettlement convoy, Bayan Stewart. There is no medical staff to run it, and, as your husband is away ... well. Nurse Girardeau cannot manage on her own.'

'But the hospital is full. Every bed is occupied. Dr Levonian and Dr Bezjian are the only ones capable of looking after it.'

'Fully occupied, no. As I said, the Armenian patients have gone with the rest of the convoy.'

'You bloody bastards!' Paul spat. 'Some of those people are dying.'

'The Turkish patients,' Ozhan continued, 'are being moved to Trebizond. Now, if you will stand aside, Dr Trowbridge, we have work to do.'

The soldiers picked up babies from baskets and drawers, and the sound of the infants' crying filled the house.

'You can't let them,' Thomas said, his eyes darting from one soldier to another. 'Uncle Paul ... do something!'

A soldier carrying one of the cholera babies from the cool room passed through the hallway. He held the child away from him, his face a picture of disgust. Before anyone could stop him, Thomas grabbed the baby and ran with her to the kitchen, but the captain stepped behind Robert and put his gun to the boy's temple. Hetty screamed as the safety catch snapped off.

'Yeter!' Bayan Efendi got to her feet, clicking her tongue and shaking her head. Ozhan dropped his gun as the old woman gestured to Thomas to hand her the baby. The child was listless and pale, insensible to everything that was happening around her. Bayan Efendi took her in her arms and smiled at the little face. Taking off her headscarf, she wrapped the child in it and walked with her outside. Very gently she laid her on the dirty floor of the cart. Moments later, Hetty followed with a baby nestled against her and settled him on a pair of Arnak's old trousers. The children came after, each carrying a child like a prayer. Only Thomas and Paul remained inside, standing mutely by the doorway.

The soldiers stopped tramping through the house, stopped turning out wardrobes and stopped pulling apart the hay in the stables. Through windows and doorways and from where they waited in the garden or by the boundary wall, they stood and watched. Everyone present would remember the moment. Some as old men repenting on their deathbeds, others despairing of their belief in God, and others still vaunting the power of the victor over the vanquished. But they would all remember it.

How do I write of the things I have witnessed? How to make sense of events that defy reason, compassion and justice? Do I pass judgement when my understanding of morality does not apply?

Mahmoud Agha and I made it to Sivas in four days of uninterrupted journeying. It was easier to keep moving, not to look at the growing numbers of starving and dying on the roads. I knew many of them. Some held out their arms to me and others wept as I rode by. I kept my eyes on the way ahead and my hopes on the man I was about to meet.

Colonel Abdul-Khan extended us a courteous welcome. He insisted Mahmoud Agha and I dine with him in his quarters after we had washed and refreshed ourselves. Everything about the man seemed sensible and reasonable and I began to believe there was hope.

After the meal I brought the conversation round to matters in the village. I told the colonel about the importance of the hospital and that it could not be run without my Armenian staff. I described the mission farm and how we were feeding most of the villagers from that one small enterprise. I begged immunity for Trebizond's Armenians, even as I felt helpless to protect all the others.

The colonel gave me a full hearing, nodding sympathetically from time to time. When I had finished he leaned back in his chair and called for an aide. Taking a pen and paper, Abdul-Khan wrote a letter of immunity and stamped it with the official letterhead of the National Guard. My relief was immense. I thanked him sincerely, suppressing the urge to snatch the paper and run. But before I could leave, the colonel had a favour to ask in return. Both surgeons at the local hospital had been conscripted and the patients were being looked after by student doctors and nurses, he told me. He would greatly appreciate if I were to give them the benefit of my experience before I left for home. Railing inwardly against this delay, I smiled and said it would be a pleasure.

Three days, six operations and four clinics later, Mahmoud Agha and I were finally on our way. Arriving back in the village seven days after we left, it was to the realisation that it was all too late. Only the sound of our horses' hooves broke the silence as we rode through the streets. Every Armenian house was empty, looted or burned. Broken glass, discarded furniture and children's clothes littered the cobbles. We stopped at the Armenian church and went inside. The doors had been wrenched from their hinges and the interior gutted. The pews in the choir had been piled one on top of the other and set on fire. Smoke still rose from the embers, illuminated by light coming through a hole in the roof. There, amongst the ruins, I was overcome by a terrible fear. My family. Leaving Mahmoud standing in what remained of the church, I ran through the backstreets to our home.

They were all gathered in the kitchen, the silence in the room echoing the stillness of the streets outside. Eleanor ran over and wrapped her arms around me, sobbing disconsolately. The other children stood motionless around the walls saying nothing. It was so quiet, unnaturally quiet. Only then did I notice that the babies were gone and that Hetty was nursing Lottie in her arms. The colour had drained from my wife's face, and her eyes, when they looked into mine, were rimmed with fear.

Lottie's illness took our minds temporarily from the loss of our charges. After the soldiers had left, and Paul had gone to the hospital to find Manon, Millie finally succeeded in catching Hetty's attention. She took her by the hand and pointed to where Lottie lay in a fever under the kitchen table. Shortly after came the first tell-tale bout of diarrhoea and stomach cramps. We moved her to the cool room where the other cholera babies had been, wrapping her in cold, wet towels to bring down the fever as she asked in her weakening voice for water. Our youngest daughter was never out of her mother's arms and Hetty put her down only when I suggested she would be cooler and easier away from the heat of her mother's body. At intervals we dipped her in a pail of cold water, but the fever raged unabated. Lottie's refusal to take watered goat's milk was a worry, but my worst fears were realised when she refused any liquids whatsoever. By this time she had lost so much fluid through her bowel that she didn't have the strength to lift her head.

'I'm going to the hospital,' I told Hetty. 'We need to set up a Murphy drip.'

Coming across the yard I saw that the door to the room I used as a laboratory was open. I stepped inside and heard glass crack beneath my shoes. Every slide was smashed on the floor, every shelf emptied of files. My microscope lay broken beneath the window, and the notebooks I kept of my trachoma research were shredded in a sea of paper around me. I bent to pick up a page near the door. It bore the name of Mahmoud Agha's youngest son, Biktash, my first trachoma patient. It fell from my hands – the work of a lifetime in ruins.

Next door, the dispensary was in a similar state, and as I looked in from the doorway I began to fear the worst. Turning left into the hospital proper, I walked the long corridor of the women's and men's wards. Either side of me I saw overturned beds, glass on the floor, something dripping on metal close by. The sound was unnaturally loud, amplified by the emptiness of the rooms. On a chair to my right an arm cast lay shattered in powder and plaster pieces. A curtain flapped at a broken window. Slashed mattresses spilled their contents onto the floor. All except one. In the last bed near the end of the corridor somebody lay beneath a blanket. My nurse was sitting on a chair beside him.

'Manon?'

Above the covers the patient's face stared at the ceiling. It was old man Tufenkian, father of the Tufenkian sisters who ran the shop in the village, who had come to the hospital a month before with liver disease.

'He died before they came,' she said.

Tufenkian's lips were lightly closed and his eyes turned to the ceiling. I looked from the old man to my nurse. Her hair had come undone and blood stained her uniform. She appeared strangely calm.

302

'Where are the others? The staff?'

'Gone.'

'But ... where's Paul?'

'They took him.'

'Who did?'

'Gendarmes.'

'They can't do that. He's been released to me. Into my custody.'

Manon reached out and closed Tufenkian's eyes.

'He was arrested for the murder of Kazbek Tashjian.'

'That's impossible!'

Pulling the sheet over the old man's face, Manon stood up and smoothed down the bedcovers. She ran her fingers through her hair and straightened her skirt as though expecting the family of the deceased at any moment. A glass bottle hit against her shoe and I remembered why I had come.

'I need you to help me, Manon. Lottie has cholera. I'm going to give her a Murphy drip and I need you to mix the solution for me.'

I thought she hadn't heard because she seemed to be looking for something among the debris and shards of glass on the floor.

'Broken ... everything is broken.'

'Manon, please.'

My nurse turned to me as though she had only just come to realise I was there.

'We have to find an infusion set,' she said. 'You must help me look.'

Between us we administered the infusion to Lottie, watching the salty water flow out of her little body as soon as it went in. But I wouldn't give up. Between the infusions Hetty and I slept little, taking turns to watch over our daughter while Bayan Efendi and Manon took on the role of nanny and cook for our other children.

'Go rest, Hetty,' I said. 'Lottie's settled for the moment.'

But Hetty was exhausted. So tired she couldn't sleep.

'I'm going to the beach, Charles. I have to get away.'

'You can't go alone. It's not safe.'

'I have to get out of here.'

'Then go into the garden.'

'I need to walk, Charles. By the sea.'

'I will stay with Lottie,' Manon said. 'Go with her, Dr Stewart.'

A strong onshore wind pushed against us, as though the sea and its dreadful secrets didn't want us there. Hetty indicated that she wished to walk as far as the cliff and that she would prefer to walk alone.

Leaving her at the shoreline, I went over to the nearby promontory of rocks where I could sit in its lee out of the wind. The imprint of my boots sank into the wet sand and the turning tide threw seaweed and stones at my feet. I didn't blame Hetty for being angry. Or Paul or Manon or any of them. I should never have gone to Sivas. Never left my family alone. Abdul-Khan had been very devious and I had been blind to his manipulations. I lifted my gaze to the horizon where the sea met the sky in a thin, grey line. Out of that line, they said, the Russians would come, bringing war and devastation and horror, but some sort of inversion had taken place. The horror was happening on land behind me and out to sea was silence and simplicity.

In the shallows Hetty was walking with her boots on, head bent as though she were praying. The breeze blew her hair around her shoulders and flapped against the silky fabric of her blouse. Something knocked against her boot, a hessian cloth or sack moving over and back with every wave. She bent down to investigate, and I noticed there were more of them dotted along the high-tide line and one or two washed up between the rocks. I got to my feet and started towards her. The loose sand pulled at my shoes as though trying to hold me there, and a terrible feeling of dread came over me. I could see one of the objects clearly now, a weighted sack tied with crude bits of string. A bag with heavy, rounded shapes bulging against the sides.

Dear God! Sweet Jesus, no!

I began to run, but Hetty's raw red fingers had prised the wet ties apart.

'Hetty! Hetty, no!'

I watched her bend and look inside the sack, and for a moment it felt as though the wind had stopped blowing and the waves refused to break on the sand. Her head snapped back on her neck and she opened her mouth to the sky but no sound came.

Hetty had no words to speak when I managed to get her back to the house. No words when, by sunset the following day, Thomas and I had buried all the babies' bodies in the graveyard of the ruined church. And no words when our youngest daughter, Charlotte Emily Stewart, was buried next to them.

Dr Charles Stewart

Mushar

Trebizond

July 22nd, 1916

Mr Henry Morgenthau

US Ambassador to the Ottoman Empire

Constantinople

Dear Henry,

I am writing this letter in the fervent hope that you have not yet departed Constantinople. Since I last wrote you, events have overtaken us and I find it is imperative to bring my family back to America and out of this godforsaken country. As well as the unforgivable treatment of the Armenians in our village, Hetty and I witnessed a horror of such magnitude that I cannot bring myself to tell you of it. And if I imagined that the living nightmare we find ourselves in could get no worse I was sorely mistaken.

Our beloved daughter Lottie succumbed to cholera only a few days ago. It leaves me heartsick to bury her under the accursed soil of this place, but my every waking thought has turned to bringing Hetty and the family home.

You offered in a previous letter to arrange passage for us on a ship to Athens under the protection of the Consulate, and it is my ardent hope that it is still within your remit to do so.

Before we leave, I have one final request to ask of you. Paul Trowbridge was arrested by Turkish soldiers the day of the Armenian exodus from the village. He was accused of murdering a local man, which is easily disproved as he was working in Trebizond at the time. I have written to the authorities but so far have heard nothing. Given that he is a British subject and there are no grounds for his arrest, I am hoping that you or your British counterpart might be able to secure his release.

Do not reply to this letter as we are leaving for Constantinople immediately.

I pray that a safe repatriation, yours and ours, will be granted us.

Your friend,

Charles Stewart

Anyush

'W'e're moving out. You have to get her up.'

Anyush looked at the lieutenant. Around her, all those who remained of the convoy were once again struggling to their feet.

'Up now or she'll be left behind.'

Anyush had been thinking of Lale. The strength of her five-fingered grip and the way the baby held her thumb as though she knew that some day her mother would let her go.

'Are you listening to me? Get her up.'

He stared at the old woman, and then turned away. Gohar's lips were closed, her fingers laced at her breast and two small pebbles covered her eyes.

'We're moving out,' he said.

Ŭ Ŭ Ŭ

The Harşit river rises in the peaks dominating the town of Gümüşhane and follows the old Silk Road to the sea. Ten miles outside the town the river bends away to the west and it was here the caravan stopped to refill the empty water barrels. The marchers collapsed by the side of the road while the soldiers plunged headlong into the cool waters of the river.

'Fill up those barrels. Get a move on,' the lieutenant shouted.

Three men lined the barrels up at the water's edge and held each one under the surface until it was full and the lid hammered back into place. Another soldier pushed them up the steep incline onto the road and over to the supply wagons. Anyush sat on the riverbank a little away from the others. The sun beat down on her back and shoulders but she didn't try to find shade. She would have liked to get into the water, to feel the comfort of it close around her but she hadn't the strength. She looked at her hands, brown and burned by the sun. There was still a faint mark on her finger where her wedding band had been. Something moved through the wall of heat at Anyush's back. The Ferret hovered near the empty barrels and while the others were distracted he kicked one into the water. It was caught by the current and floated slowly towards the middle of the river.

'Hey,' the lieutenant shouted to a soldier swimming nearby. 'Catch that barrel.'

The soldier swam to it and put his arm over the wood, but the greasy staves slipped out of his grasp and floated away. A faster-moving current in the middle of the river caught it and pulled it further downstream.

'Are there only women in the Ottoman army?!' Pulling off his jacket and boots, the lieutenant sprinted down the bank and waded into the water. He swam hard, passing the barrel in a few strokes and placing himself in its path so that it bumped off his chest and bobbed between his outstretched arms.

'Get up.' The Ferret was standing behind Anyush. 'I said get up.'

He kicked her hard with the toe of his boot and she tried to move away from him, struggling to get to her feet. She was shaky and dizzy from lack of water, and when he pulled her back along the road behind a group of spindly acacia trees she didn't cry out. Nobody noticed when he ripped open the top of her dress and pushed her to the ground.

'Don't make me use this.'

Pulling a pistol from his pocket, he pointed it at her head and pushed down his trousers with his other hand. Anyush lay like a corpse beneath him as he positioned himself between her legs. His face loomed above her so that she was looking into his animal eyes, one brown and one blue.

'No!' She lashed out at him and kicked with her legs. Like a wild animal she bucked and twisted until the cold click of his pistol sounded in her ear.

'If I have to screw your dead corpse, I will.'

Drops of his sweat fell on her face and she became still like a broken bird. He grabbed her chin when she turned away and wrenched her head around. 'Look at me. You're going to remember this.'

Straightening his back, he pushed her legs apart with his knees. 'Have a good look. I want you to know how it feels to be fucked by a man like me.'

His mouth widened into a smile, and a trace of that smile still played about his lips in the instant before he collapsed on top of her. Above him, Khandut stood like the ghost of someone Anyush had once known. Throwing the rock to one side, she grabbed the soldier's legs and dragged him off. Anyush got to her feet. The two women looked at each other. Khandut was hardly recognisable. She was wasted and ill, and tufts of her hair were missing so that large patches of her scalp were bare. At the side of her head a bloodied ear hung by a band of skin. Anyush heard a keening sound and realised it was coming from herself. Tears she had not shed at the surrender of her child or the death of her grandmother. Khandut took her in her arms and held her. They stood together as if they had spent a lifetime holding each other just so.

On the ground, the Ferret had started to twitch. A low moaning sound came from him, as he began to crawl towards the road. In one quick movement Khandut picked up the rock and brought it down again and again on the back of his head. Bits of bone and hair flew into her face and blood spattered her dress. Anyush watched in silence. As the life's breath was beaten out of him, she wished only that he would be still. When the rock finally slid from her mother's hands, very little remained of the Ferret's head. Khandut crouched beside the body and rolled him onto his back. Wiping the sweat from her brow, she began to undo the buttons of his tunic.

'Quickly.' She glanced at Anyush. 'Get your clothes off.'

Ü Ü Ü

Anyush sensed the lieutenant approaching before she saw him. Keeping her eyes down, she made as if to empty a stone from one of her boots. Relief flooded through her when he walked away, and panic took hold when he came back again. The Ferret's cap was pulled well down over her eyes and the uniform fitted reasonably well, but up close she wouldn't fool anyone. A bead of sweat trickled from her hairline. Khandut was walking ahead and sensed something was wrong. She stopped and turned around. The lieutenant was now less than two feet in front of Anyush and she had no choice but to look at him. He stared directly into her face. A look she recognised. One she had seen on other soldiers' faces when they distanced themselves from what they were about to do. He pulled the cap from her head so that her plait uncoiled onto her shoulder. Grabbing her by the hair, he jerked her head back, exposing the skin of her neck. She could hear the whisper of the blade pulled from its sheath and winced as the sunlight reflected off the metal into her eyes. This was it. This was how it would end. Very soon it would all be over. Please God, let it be quick.

Then, the strangest sensation. Pleasant almost. Made her feel sleepy.

Her head swung free, dipping towards her chest before righting itself again. The lieutenant's knife was clenched in one hand and her plait in the other. He retrieved the cap from the dirt and handed it to her. Throwing her hair into the scrub, he left her staring after him.

Ü   Ü   Ü

As the sun was beginning to dip in the western sky, the Shota reappeared. Once again, they surrounded the convoy, lining up along the opposite bank of the river and the near side of the valley. Murzabey was at the head of them. Anyush slipped around the back of the crowd and positioned herself so she could hear.

'That was quite a story your captain spun at our last meeting,' Murzabey said to the lieutenant. 'I was going to teach him a lesson, but it seems his horse has taught him a very painful one on my behalf.' He laughed. 'Don't worry, I let him go. Not many men lie to me and survive, but the colonel tells me he is not to be touched.'

'What do you want?' the lieutenant asked.

'I want what is mine.' The bandit nodded at the convoy. 'Abdul-Khan made me a promise. You and your men ride to Gümüşhane, and I will take the Armenians.'

All eyes turned to the lieutenant. The captain had saved them from the Shota before and they prayed for redemption again. One of the women began to keen and an old man wept shamelessly. Lips moved in silent prayer and still the lieutenant would not speak. From the cholera wagon the German looked on, his camera forgotten. All around them, on every side, the bandits were ranged like bars in a cage. They had cut off all routes of escape and any hope of help. Two hundred Shota faces watched from the crest of the hill, eager for the reckoning. The lieutenant stood before them, his head bowed. Murzabey was smiling. He knew what the lieutenant would decide. He had been counting on it. When the soldier nodded, a terrible cry rose from the Armenians at his back.

Ü   Ü   Ü

Anyush found Khandut where she had left her at the end of the line. Khandut looked at her daughter and nodded. 'You have something I want,' she said.

Hidden in a pocket of the tunic was the Ferret's pistol. Anyush's fingers closed around it but she didn't draw it out.

'Don't prolong this, Anyush. No man is ever going to touch me again.' Khandut held out her hand. 'Give it to me.'

Anyush pulled it from the jacket and laid it in her mother's palm. The sound from the convoy behind them was growing louder: keening and crying and the gathering words of a prayer. Khandut slipped the gun into her pocket, and, without speaking to her daughter again, she pressed herself into the crowd.

No words, no keepsakes, no memories. More lonely in that moment than she had felt in her life before, Anyush looked into the space where her mother had been.

'You. Follow me.' The lieutenant appeared out of nowhere. 'Stay at my back. Don't speak to anyone and don't go anywhere without my say-so.'

He walked over to where the other soldiers were already mounting their horses and packing the wagons, but Anyush couldn't move. Her legs were weighted to the ground as though she were tethered. Around her people clung to each other; they prayed, some stood in silence. Children pressed their hands to their eyes and mothers wept for them. Everyone watched the soldiers prepare to ride away. The lieutenant saddled his horse and was about to mount when he realised the girl hadn't followed. He looked back to where she was standing and their eyes met. Anyush understood what the look meant. That she could stay if she wanted. That she could die here with the rest of them because there was nothing more he could do for her. Anyush wanted to stay. She wanted to be with her mother and the people of her village, but her legs began to move. She advanced on him slowly as though trying to walk through stone. The covered wagon carrying the cholera soldiers had already moved out, and the rest of the company were mounted and waiting for the signal to leave. Handing her the reins of the Ferret's mare, the lieutenant mounted his own horse and led the cavalcade away. Anyush climbed unsteadily into the saddle and fell into step behind them.

The screams reached them when they had covered less than a mile. The air was suddenly thick with them. The horses' ears flattened along their necks and their eyes bulged. The men of the 23rd rode as if their lives depended on it and didn't look back. Not once. Not even at the first gunshot scattering flocks of roosting birds into the evening sky.

 Jahan

He remembered the early part of the journey clearly. Each stone, each hole and rut in the road jolted him into pain-wracked consciousness. Lying beneath the sun in his sweat-soaked clothes, he could feel the blanket sticking to his leg where blood oozed from the wound. Muslu had rigged a canvas bivouac over him for shade, but with the heat and choking dust the air beneath was almost unbreathable. At times reality eluded him. He felt himself drifting into a daze, a dream-like state where he was floating on the sea, struggling to keep himself above the waves. Then he was awake, staring at the canvas above him and jolted into consciousness by the agony in his leg. Tiny movements at his side reminded him of his daughter. He reached beneath the blanket and felt for her chest, less than the span of his hand and barely moving.

After the first couple of hours Muslu stopped so they could drink and water the horses. Jahan had to force Lale's mouth open with his finger so that she might take some. Armin's alcohol was having an effect, but her shallow breathing was a worry. Watching the captain's efforts, Muslu whistled mournfully between his teeth.

'Her spirit is fading, Captain. She will not last long.'

On the road, he lashed the horses with his whip and drove hard without slackening the pace. If they lasted at the speed he was driving them and if the water supply held, then he believed they stood a chance. But that chance faded as a line of Shota appeared on a bluff rising in front of them. Muslu reined in the horses and Jahan pushed Lale further beneath the blanket.

'We meet again,' Murzabey said, looking down on the captain from his horse. 'In much changed circumstances.' He smiled. 'Colonel Abdul-Khan and I had a most interesting conversation. Between friends, you understand. You are a convincing liar, Captain. You disobeyed the colonel's orders, which didn't please him. Not in the slightest.'

'I was protecting Turkish citizens. I would do it again.'

'Fortunately for both of us you are unlikely to get the chance. But you must remember that you are guilty of a far more serious crime. Of lying to me. I did warn you that I would have my retribution.'

The bandit dismounted and walked over to the wagon, holding his rifle in his good hand. Using the muzzle, he lifted the blanket from Jahan's leg. The weight of the captain's arm held it down on Lale's side.

'Nasty injury, young captain. You must be in a lot of pain, and yet you bear your suffering well. I have a strange reaction to seeing someone in pain ... I want to prolong it or end it. Which do you think I should do, Captain? Choose.'

The captain looked into the bandit's eyes. They shone in anticipation. Death at Murzabey's hands would not come with a bullet to the heart.

'Let my driver go,' Jahan pleaded. 'He had no part in this. Let him drive on to Gümüşhane.'

'A man of honour! I wonder if the colonel knows of such admirable qualities?'

Murzabey signalled to two of his men who unstrapped a water barrel from a pack horse and rolled it towards him. Taking the empty barrel from the wagon they replaced it with their full one.

'The colonel has his reasons for wanting you alive, and I will honour them,' Murzabey said. 'Unlike you, Captain, I keep my promises.'

Rolling the empty barrel up the incline, his men strapped it to the pack horse. Tentatively Muslu picked up the reins. Jahan felt a tiny movement at his side and willed the child to be still. Murzabey was looking into the wagon again. Something had drawn his attention.

'Oh I almost forgot. There was one other thing. About that retribution ...' In one quick movement Murzabey swung his rifle by the muzzle over his head and brought it down with all his strength on Jahan's broken bones.

Anyush

Darkness was falling when they arrived in Gümüşhane. The lieutenant, the German and Anyush lagged behind the others by a couple of miles and were the last to arrive. In the course of the journey the German discovered their companion was not a soldier. Anyush had slipped from the saddle and lost her cap, revealing her identity to him. Armin stared at the Armenian and the lieutenant looked nervously at him. Nobody said anything. Anyush lay on the ground thinking of the pictures the German would take of her, like the ones he had taken of Parzik. Getting off his horse, Armin approached. He put his hand inside his tunic and she flinched.

'Drink?' he asked, handing her his goatskin. 'You should have some.'

Taking the canteen from him she emptied it to the last drop.

'Can you ride?'

She nodded.

He helped her into the saddle and guided her horse back onto the road. With a nod to the lieutenant, they travelled the last few miles to Gümüşhane.

Ŭ Ŭ Ŭ

The main gateway to the town was just visible in the darkness when a group of gendarmes stepped into the road. The soldiers were ordered to dismount.

'Stay on the horse,' Armin whispered. 'Don't talk.'

He and the lieutenant got down.

'Armin Wegner?' one of the gendarmes said in English. 'You are under arrest.'

'What am I accused of?'

'Where is your camera?'

The German indicated the wooden boxes on the pack horse, and two policemen unstrapped them and placed them on the ground.

'What's this about?'

The boxes were opened and the gendarme peered inside.

'Your equipment is being impounded by order of Colonel Abdul-Khan and Field Marshal von der Goltz.'

He nodded and the lids were put back in place.

'You have upset two very important men, Lieutenant Wegner.'

His eye travelled over the German and the lieutenant before coming to rest on Anyush.

'You. Get down off that horse.'

'A word of caution ...' Armin said. 'If that soldier gets down you will not get him up again.'

'That is not my concern. Dismount at once!'

Cold fingers of fear crept along Anyush's spine. She tried to move but couldn't.

The gendarme strode over, his arm raised to pull her off.

'Don't touch him!' Armin shouted. 'He is highly infectious.'

'What's wrong with him?'

'Cholera.'

'A number of our men contracted it on the march,' the lieutenant said.

'We buried three along the road.'

'Then get him out of here,' the gendarme said, stepping away. 'Bring him wherever you were going! You, Lieutenant Wegner, will come with me.'

With a last look at his companions, the German followed the gendarmes into town.

Jahan

Everything was confused. Day became night and night day. Muslu pushed the horses hard, keeping one eye out for Shota and another on the captain. At times he was delirious and at other times lucid, reaching for his daughter lying beside him. Early on a bright, clear morning, Muslu drove the wagon through the old walls of Gümüşhane. There was no hospital in the town but there was a medic attached to the barracks and that was where he was headed. Jahan came to, as houses and buildings swam into focus above him.

'Where are you going? Stay away from the barracks. Muslu, listen to me. Look for a boarding house.'

'Captain, *bayim*, the barracks will have a doctor. You are in no fit state to go anywhere else.'

'Not the barracks ... understand? The *ev sahibi* at the boarding house will help but no soldiers.'

Reluctantly, Muslu did as he was told and turned off the main street. Manoeuvring the wagon carefully, he drove down a narrow cobbled lane in the direction of the river.

The *ev sahibi*, the landlady, was small and thin with startling blue eyes and wrinkled skin. She was wearing the traditional costume of the nomadic desert tribes and a burnished leather burqa over the lower half of her face. Her house stood in a street barely wide enough to accommodate the wagon, but it had a gated archway leading to a yard which was hidden behind a high wall. Muslu offered her a substantial *bahşiş*, which she took without a second glance. If she thought it odd that a wounded soldier should wish to hide in her house rather than return to the barracks, she kept her opinions to herself. Children began to cluster around, but she shooed them away and bolted the gate shut behind them. Once inside, she pulled back the blanket covering the captain's leg. She clicked her tongue and shook her head, sniffing loudly at what she saw. Jahan made an effort to sit up. The smell of rotting flesh was overpowering and the leg had turned dark purple in colour.

'No doctor in Gümüşhane,' the old woman said. 'Old Doctor Kemal died of cholera and young Doctor Kemal moved to Sivas.'

'There must be someone ... a bone-setter or *chekeji*?' Muslu insisted.

'No *chekeji*'s going to fix that.' She turned her pale eyes on the captain. 'Deserter?'

He shook his head. On impulse, he lifted the blanket to reveal the tiny figure lying beside him. Lale was on her back, limbs splayed and head rolled to one side. Her mouth hung open and her eyes were tightly closed.

'Ayeiiaa!' The landlady poked a finger at the child. Lale shifted slightly but her eyes remained closed. 'Very far gone,' she said softly. 'She will go first.'

'Can't you do something?' the captain begged. 'Feed her.'

'Do I look like a woman who can nurse? Even if I gushed like a fountain, Allah be praised, it would do no good. The child is too weak.' She hit the wagon with the back of her hand.

'Leave my house. A dead baby will draw the evil eye.'

'*Matmazel ... efendi ...* the captain won't make it to Sivas,' Muslu said.

'We have nowhere else to go.'

At that moment an intruder jumped down into the yard.

'Eh ... you ... *oğlan!*'

The *ev sahibi* marched over to where a boy of nine or ten had jumped down from the wall and was desperately trying to get back up again. She grabbed him by the trousers and yanked him to the ground, pulling him up by the ear. 'What were you doing? Spying were you?'

'No, Bayan Fatima,' the boy whimpered, 'I only wanted to see.'

'See what? What did you see?'

'Nothing ... I saw nothing ... you're hurting me, Bayan Fatima! I saw the soldier. The one in the wagon.'

'And what else? The truth now or I'll pull your ear off.'

'Nothing ... only the child ... I saw the child.'

'And what did you hear? Tell me now. Quick, before I take the broom to you.'

'Bayan Fatima, let go. I know a doctor who can help.'

'What doctor?' Muslu asked.

The *ev sahibi* released the boy and gave his other ear a sharp tug for good measure. 'He's lying. There aren't any other doctors.'

'My aunt keeps lodgers,' the boy said, pressing his hand to the side of his head. 'She has giaours staying in the house. Americans. The man of the family, he's a doctor. My aunt said he was. She said his name is Dr Stewart.'

Anyush

The lieutenant and Anyush walked along the main thoroughfare in Gümüşhane. The street was full of evening shoppers and men heading towards the mosque, but the town made little impression on Anyush. She didn't notice the tall thin houses with their steeply pitched roofs and heavily studded doors of dark wood. The ancient Süleymaniye mosque cast its shadow over her and Abdal Musa, the highest of the Gavur mountains, loomed above her, but she may as well have been walking in the desert. She followed the lieutenant with no thought of where she was going or what lay ahead. Somewhere in her mind she had an idea of herself, a woman dressed as a man and walking, always walking.

'Keep up,' the lieutenant hissed.

A strong smell drifted by every now and then, and she realised it was coming from herself. People were stepping off the path, and a number of them crossed to the other side of the street.

'What am I supposed to do with you?' the lieutenant muttered. 'A stinking, half-dead Armenian? Who in all the Ottoman Empire would be stupid enough to take you?'

They turned into a square set out as a souk and spice market.

'Stay here,' he told her, pointing to a covered alleyway.

When the lieutenant had gone, she dropped to her haunches and laid her head on her knees. She wanted to close her eyes, to sleep, but someone came running down the lane.

'*Merhaba*,' the boy said.

His small dog sniffed around her feet. It barked once and sat on the ground beside her.

'Come here!' the boy called, reversing out the way he had come. 'Come on, Kapi.'

'Watch where you're going!'

The lieutenant grabbed the boy by the shoulder and spun him round. 'Your mother never tell you to respect your elders? Hey ... I know you. You're Hasan's son!'

The terrified boy wriggled out of the lieutenant's grasp and darted down the street, his dog chasing at his heels.

'Wait ... come back!'

But the boy had disappeared into the crowd milling around the souk. The lieutenant turned to Anyush and looked thoughtfully at her.

'Put these on,' he said, handing her an abaya and burqa. 'I know just the man who will take you.'

We have been on the road now for almost four weeks and this gruelling journey is taking its toll. Heat and dust have exacerbated Hetty's bronchitis to such a degree that I have decided to stay another two days in Gümüşhane. Her physical vulnerability concerns me, but her mental distress worries me more. The children too are not themselves. They have become watchful and silent, disturbed by the terrible sights we encounter as we travel across country: lines of walking skeletons, abandoned and dead-eyed children, bodies left to rot by the roadside. Thomas has avoided me since leaving Trebizond. He disappears like a shadow whenever I enter a room, and speaks in monosyllables if at all.

This evening I stood at the window of our lodgings watching the crowd milling in the street. Hetty lay resting on the bed behind me while the children were eating with the landlady downstairs. I was thinking of America and how it has become an unknown country to me, when I realised Hetty had spoken.

'Did you say something?'

'How do you do it? How can you bear being amongst them or touched by them?'

She was lying against the bolster, her hair hanging loosely around her shoulders and her eyes bruised from lack of sleep.

'Savages and child murderers.' She pushed herself into a sitting position, her gaze ranging over the meagre furnishings and patched bedlinen in the small room. 'Everything is evil. Corrupted. Even the damn food.' With a sweep of her hand, she pitched the tray on the bedside cabinet to the floor.

'Hetty!'

'I wish I was back in Springfield. I wish I could wake up in my old room and hear my mother playing the piano downstairs.' She began to weep. 'I wish the last year had never happened and that I might wake up with Lottie in my arms.'

I went and held her to me. I have never desired anything so much as to give her what she wanted but she pulled away from me and lay down again, turning her face towards the wall. The bed was small but she took up very little of it. I reached out to touch her hair and it was soft between my fingers. A young woman's hair. There was not a trace of grey. I wanted to bury my face in it. To feel her wrapped around me like a cocoon. I wanted to make love to her in a way I hadn't done for years, but she kept her back to me, pulling her shoulders around her like a shield.

'Father ...' Robert put his head round the door. 'Somebody wants to speak to you downstairs.'

A diminutive old woman stood in the doorway, covered from head to toe in a black abaya and burqa. Gripped in both hands was a large covered basket such as the vendors use in the market. She was speaking to the maid in the dialect of the Jenaibi nomads and I understood very little of it.

'Thank you. Nothing today,' I said, closing over the door.

But the woman placed herself solidly in the door frame and lifted the heavy basket towards me. Just as suddenly she dropped it again and made to hide it behind her skirts. The landlady had materialised in the hallway and was listening.

'*Teşekkür ederim*,' I said, 'I will deal with this.'

Reluctantly the landlady took herself off down the passageway while I turned my attention to the visitor. The children crowded around, staring curiously at the caller. Nothing was visible of the woman except two darting blue eyes and small wrinkled brown hands. She spoke too quickly for me to pick up more than a word here and there, and she kept glancing behind her and pointing to the pannier on her arm.

'I don't understand,' I said. 'You want me to buy something from you?'

'Perhaps she needs a doctor,' Thomas suggested. '*Doktor*?'

'*Hayır*!' the woman said, shaking her head.

'Then I'm afraid I can't help you.'

I made to close the door, but the woman planted her foot on the threshold and stabbed a finger at the basket, muttering something none of us understood.

'Why doesn't she just show us?' asked Milly, reaching out to lift the lid, but the woman slapped her hand away.

'Maybe there are snakes in there,' Eleanor whispered.

'Don't be stupid,' Robert said. 'There are no women snake-charmers.'

I had understood she'd said something about being thrown in prison and began to suspect she was selling black market goods, something she clearly thought we would want.

'I'll ask the landlady to translate,' I offered.

'*Hayır*! *Hayır*!' Thrusting the basket into my arms, the woman turned on her heel and disappeared.

'No,' I said, as the children made to look inside.

The landlady was watching from the kitchen doorway.

'Upstairs.'

Everyone thundered up the steps to our bedroom where Hetty was sitting upright, her eyes wide with alarm.

'Nothing to worry about,' I said. 'Just a pedlar making a delivery.'

She relaxed and made to lie back on the bed, but something about the basket caught her eye. 'Bring it here.'

I put it on the coverlet beside her and took off the lid. The children crowded around to see. Inside, an almost naked baby lay curled up asleep. Small, emaciated and smelling strongly of alcohol, the baby tried to open its eyes and closed them again, mewling softly like a kitten. Milly and Robert reached in, their mouths round with wonder, but Hetty shooed them away and lifted the little girl into her arms. 'She weighs almost nothing.'

The child's head turned towards her breast and everyone grew silent.

'There's a letter,' Thomas said, taking a folded paper from the bottom of the basket.

'Read it.'

'It's just an address,' he said, looking at it closely. 'In Constantinople.'

'Bring me that ewer and basin,' Hetty instructed Eleanor. She took the cloth from around the baby's legs and started to wash her.

'Look,' Millie said, 'it's a tulip!' Her finger traced the shape of a flower just below the baby's left nipple. 'This is Anyush's baby!'

All eyes looked at the tiny creature nestled in Hetty's arms. The street below grew quiet, and somewhere in the distance the muezzin called the faithful to prayer.

'*Allāhu Akbar.*'

In the room beneath us the landlady stopped arguing with the maid and we heard the soft thud of a prayer mat unrolled onto the stone floor. The people of Gümüşhane bowed their heads, prostrating themselves before their God.

'*Allāhu Akbar.*'

Allah is great. Allah is good.

'Milly,' Hetty said, 'fetch me Lottie's baby clothes from the trunk.'

Jahan

'The room smells,' his mother said, drawing back the drapes and opening the shutters to let in the morning light.

Jahan kept his eyes closed, hoping that if he didn't answer she would leave and let him back to sleep. Every day since his return to his parents' home in Constantinople, he lay awake through the night, listening to the house groan and the wind whistle down the lane that separated the Orfaleas from their neighbours. He kept his eyes on the shadowy patterns of the Chinese wallpaper while the room grew dark and then lightened again towards dawn. He counted the number of figures in every square foot. He knew the shape of the low-branched spreading trees drooping elegantly over water. He could tell that all the birds were flying east and the turtles sitting on the rocks looked to the west. The clock in the hall counted out the hours as he waited to hear the call at dawn to morning prayer. Then he would sleep, deeply and dreamlessly.

He woke in the late morning to sunlight crashing through the windows and gusts of girlish laughter drifting up the stairs. His sisters came to see him, looking wonderingly at the cripple in their brother's bed.

Madame Orfalea's skirts rustled as she busied herself about the room. She threw open the window, letting in the sound of a carpet being beaten in the yard below.

'*Lèves-toi*, Jahan,' she said, coming over to the bed. 'Madeline is here to change the linen.'

'I want to sleep.'

'You've been doing nothing but sleeping, and Madeline has plenty of better things to do.'

'Tell her to come back later.'

'Jahan, do me the courtesy of looking at me when I'm speaking to you.'

He turned onto his back to see his mother holding out his crutches and the maid standing with a stack of sheets in her arms. Reluctantly, he threw off the covers and sat up. Madame Orfalea's eyes turned to his stump. The oozing had stopped and the bandages were dry. With a satisfied nod, she left his crutches by the bed.

'Your clothes are on the chair,' she said. 'And your father's barber is here. Ring the bell when you're dressed.'

'I am perfectly capable of shaving myself.'

'As you wish.' She paused at the door. 'Your father is a little better today. He's asking to see you.'

'I have no desire to see him.'

'Jahan ... please ...'

'I will breakfast in my room.'

After his mother and Madeline had gone, he collapsed back on the bed and closed his eyes. He was beginning to remember the last weeks in Sivas before he returned to Constantinople: the smell of the hospital, the filth, the overcrowding, soldiers calling for their mothers and hamals bickering over their belongings before they were even dead. Jahan could see Muslu's face peering anxiously into his own and he had an idea that Armin was there, telling him they were going to cut off his leg. Or maybe it was a dream. Like the dream he had about Murzabey. The bandit was standing beside his bed, holding a huge scimitar. It hung on the end of his good arm, the tip of the blade buried in the dirt and old bloodstains tarnishing the hilt. In the dream Jahan prayed it might be too heavy for him or broken, but Murzabey lifted it over his head and the metal flashed in the sunlight, and there was something warm on Jahan's face and he heard someone scream and remembered no more.

Sitting up, he took his crutches from the chair and swung away from the bed. Time to go outside. The wandering started as a means of getting away from the family because his moods frightened them and their offers of help were met with storms of bad temper. Getting downstairs wasn't easy, but as he grew stronger he managed it without sliding on his backside. The cobbled streets were difficult to negotiate with crutches, and the skin of his arms erupted in sores from chaffing against the wood, but he wouldn't give up. Nobody looked twice at the one-legged soldier. By 1916 the citizens of Constantinople were used to the sight of the maimed and wounded on their streets. At first, he got as far as the squares close to Grande Rue, hobbling past the cafés and embassies, but as his strength grew he travelled further, reaching the quayside or crossing over Galata Bridge into Stamboul. He spent the day wandering the streets, taking refuge in coffee houses and with the raki sellers until it was time to go home. Because there was no gasoline to light the street lamps he often walked back in almost complete darkness, and on one such evening he stumbled near Galata Bridge.

'Captain Orfalea!' the soldier said.

'Muslu!'

'Sir … are you hurt?'

'No, no, I'm fine. It's good to see you, Muslu.'

'You too, sir.'

'I never got the chance to write to you. I wanted to thank you.'

'Wouldn't have got it anyway, *bayim*. I've been in the Mediterranean.

Our company will be back there in two days. Whole army is being sent out if you ask me.'

The corporal was trying not to stare at the captain's amputated limb.

'Let me buy you a coffee,' Jahan said. 'The Brioche is still open.'

They took a seat inside, out of the wind blowing up from the river, and ordered coffee and pastries.

'You look well, sir.'

'You too, Muslu. Where were you in the Mediterranean?'

'Gallipoli. It was terrible. They say the Anzacs and the Allies lost thirty-two thousand troops but our losses were nearly as bad. The Fifth Army has been decimated.'

'I know. I heard.'

Muslu tucked into a slice of baklava.

'What about the others?' Jahan asked. 'Were they in Gallipoli with you?'

'Only Düzgünoğlu and Lieutenant Kadri.'

'Ahmet! I've been wondering where he ended up. How is he?'

Muslu looked at the captain. Flakes of pastry clung to his moustache.

'The lieutenant is dead, sir.'

'Oh ...'

'Took a sniper's bullet.'

'I'm sorry. I hadn't heard.'

'How could you, *bayim*? With troubles of your own ...' His eyes flicked to Jahan's leg and quickly away again. A cat crept under the table and Muslu kicked it with his foot. Beside them, a waiter began to sweep the floor, getting ready to close for the evening.

'Sir,' Muslu said, 'the child in the wagon, the one you hid ... I always wondered did you ever hear anything of her?'

'No. Nothing.'

What happened in Gümüşhane was only dimly present in Jahan's memory, but he did remember the old woman and that she had brought

Lale to the Stewarts. Every day Jahan checked the post arriving in Grande Rue, and every day he was disappointed.

'You will hear, *inşallah.*'

'*Inşallah.*'

'Düzgünoğlu is here, sir. In Constantinople. He's at the hospital, with a stomach wound, but they say he'll recover. He was asking for you.'

They talked for a while longer about the company and what had happened in the past months. When they finished, Muslu stretched out his long limbs and wiped his hand across his mouth. 'Not many left now, *bayim.*'

'No. Tell me,' Jahan said, 'when you met Lieutenant Kadri at Gallipoli … did he say what became of the convoy?'

'He never discussed it. But the Shota came back. You knew that, sir?'

'No. I had hoped …'

'Düzgünoğlu told me. They came after they stopped us.'

'What about the convoy? The Armenians … did any of them …?'

'No, *bayim.* None.'

Refusing Muslu's offer of assistance, Jahan got to his feet and bade him goodbye. In almost complete darkness, he walked to the house on Grande Rue and lowered himself onto the front steps. The night had grown cold and the granite beneath him radiated a tomb-like chill. He sat there while the lamps in the windows went out and dense black cloud gathered above him, obliterating the stars and the night sky.

One of our last days in this country and it has proved to be a difficult one. We have been staying with Henry Morgenthau and Josephine while waiting for a steamer to take us to Athens. One final obligation remained to be resolved, which I had put off until today.

This afternoon we went to the home of Colonel Olcay Orfalea, a man who is known to Henry through diplomatic circles. The house is a large pale stone building with balustraded steps leading to the front door and wrought-iron clad balconies on the second and third floors. It is the home of a man with ideas of status, and I was curious to meet him. A maid showed us into the salon where Madame Orfalea, a small, dark-haired woman, waited to receive us. She apologised for her husband, saying he's an invalid and permanently incapacitated, and that she was deputised to entertain us on his behalf. Henry made the introductions and we sat in awkward silence while the maid brought in the tea things and set them on the low table before us. Lale sat quietly on Hetty's knee, and Madame Orfalea complimented us on our beautiful child. I drank my tea, wishing with all my heart that this were over.

'Forgive me, Madame Orfalea, for not writing in more detail,' Henry said. 'But discretion was essential. This is a matter of some delicacy and I think it would be better if you heard it directly from Dr Stewart.'

I put down my cup and related our story. How we had come to be the guardians of Anyush's child, the details of the baby's anonymous delivery to our lodgings and the note instructing us to bring Lale to the address on Grande Rue. I told her finally that Anyush's whereabouts were unknown.

'Why should this woman's child concern my family?' Madame Orfalea asked. 'There are institutions for such children. I would be happy to recommend one.'

I explained that although we did not know who wrote the note, the child was brought to us in Gümüşhane where we believe her son, Captain Orfalea, was at the time.

'What are you saying, Dr Stewart?' Madame Orfalea asked.

'We are as mystified by all this as yourself,' Henry cut in. 'But the note was quite explicit. The child was to be brought here.'

'Let me see it.'

I took the letter from my pocket and gave it to her. She studied it intently before handing it back to me.

'I do not know what you are suggesting, Dr Stewart, but this is not my son's writing and the address is vague in the extreme. It could be any one of the houses on Grande Rue.'

'Begging your pardon, Madame, but is that not your name on the bottom?'

'This house is not a welfare institution, Dr Stewart. I cannot be expected to take in Armenian orphans simply because my son has a misguided sense of charity. Do you know the penalty for harbouring Armenians? I would not put you or your family in such a position and I am offended that you would ask it of mine.'

'It is *because* this child is so threatened that we hoped you would feel sympathy for her,' I said, my dislike of the woman increasing with every word.

'Madame Orfalea,' Hetty interrupted, 'my husband and I are more than happy to keep the baby. Lale has been with us for some time and we have grown very fond of her. If you have no objection ... that is, if there is no one in your household who has any ... we will bring her with us to America. Henry has assured us he can arrange the papers.'

'You do not require my permission. I have no claim on the child.' Madame Orfalea smiled brightly. 'You will hear no objection from me.'

'Objection to what, Maman?' Captain Jahan Orfalea, the young man I had last seen in his office at the old mill, was standing in the doorway.

'Jahan, I didn't hear you come in. You know Ambassador Morgenthau, of course and these are —'

336

'Bayan Stewart! Dr Stewart! You are most welcome.'

The young captain was much changed. He was thinner and his face was scored with lines either side of his mouth. His hair was unwashed and his clothes hung indifferently on his frame. He had become a cripple since our last meeting, but a short leg and a pair of crutches were not what altered him. He came across the room to stand beside Hetty's chair, his attention on the small bundle in her arms. 'Is this who I think it is?'

Hetty looked down at Lale sitting in her lap. She held her for a moment before getting to her feet and indicating that the captain should take her place. Gently, she placed Lale in his arms. Despite the restrictions of the bonnet, Lale's eyes were wide open and curious. She blinked a couple of times at this new and unfamiliar face.

'She is ... she looks so healthy,' the captain said. 'You have performed a miracle.'

I told him that Lale was severely dehydrated and malnourished when she came to us but that she hadn't contracted any disease and was otherwise healthy.

'And she's stubborn,' I added.

Lale chose this moment to vent her displeasure at being handed to a stranger. Her lips puckered and her chest heaved, and she opened her mouth and bawled.

'Hey, hey ... little one,' the captain soothed, jogging her up and down on his knee.

Lale looked at him and cried louder, the white bonnet flopping around her wet, red face. She reached out to Hetty who stood with her arms pinned to her sides as though she had been turned to stone.

'We will take our leave,' Henry said. 'Thank you for your hospitality, Madame Orfalea.'

Our hostess nodded curtly and rang for the maid. Lale was crying louder, straining to reach Hetty whose lips trembled and whose eyes shone with tears.

'Hetty,' I said, taking her gently by the shoulders, 'it's time to go.'

Jahan

It was Madame Orfalea who decided what friends and family would be told. She put it about that her son had married secretly in the east and his wife had borne him a daughter but had not herself survived the birth. The story caused a ripple of gossip in Constantinople's drawing rooms for a week or two but was soon forgotten. For the family and Jahan, Lale's arrival marked the beginning of a new phase in their lives. His sisters adored Lale, spoiling her and fighting over her, while Azize, the old nurse, was delighted to have a baby in her care once again. Jahan wrote to Dilar, who was now living with Armand in Paris, telling her about his baby daughter. She replied at length, bombarding him with questions and announcing her own imminent motherhood in the spring.

Jahan never tired of seeing Lale or of counting her small victories: her first tooth, her attempts to crawl, her shy smile so reminiscent of Anyush's. What surprised him most of all was his mother's reaction to her grandchild. Everybody agreed that Lale was an exact copy of her father, and it was this likeness that enabled Madame Orfalea to overlook her Armenian pedigree. Despite her protestations to the Stewarts, she took to his daughter in a way he did not remember her bonding with his sisters or himself. By the time Lale had started to creep along the floor, she invariably made her way not to her two adoring aunts but to her grandmother's outstretched arms.

Another person who took a great interest in Jahan's daughter was Mademoiselle Hanife Bey. She had replaced his sisters' tutor when old Monsieur Grandjean fled the country after France joined the war. Hanife was the daughter of Jevdet Bey, a brother-in-law of Enver Pasha and one of the leaders of the CUP. She was intelligent and handsome, and when she began to join Jahan regularly for afternoon tea his mother was more than pleased. Madame Orfalea would drop in to take Lale upstairs or for a nap or a walk in the park, leaving Hanife and Jahan to talk alone.

Jahan was not sure what his father had been told. Because of his illness Colonel Orfalea was confined to his room and had not encountered his grandchild, but Jahan would not have brought her to him anyway. He couldn't forgive him for what he had done and, despite his mother's pleas, father and son remained apart.

The years 1916 and 1917 would be a bloody for the Allies, the Germans and the other Central Powers alike. Two of the most important battles of the war took place during this time, the Battle of Verdun and the Battle of the Somme. In the Middle Eastern theatre the war was being fought along the Mesopotamian front mostly against the British with varying degrees of success. It was a year that saw the first use of armoured tanks and the Germans' highly efficient 'Fokker Scourge' aircraft. As an engineer it should have been a time for Jahan to prove his worth, but he had little interest in any of it. Because of his amputation he had not been recalled to active service nor had he been offered any of the desk jobs many of the injured officers were given at the War Ministry. Neither did he look for one.

His world had contracted to the vicinity of his parents' home, and what had at first seemed like a prison was now his refuge since Lale's arrival. He could sometimes forget what had happened beyond its walls, beyond the boundaries of the city, beyond the limits of his waking day. As the old year drew to a close and the New Year brought no signs of victory for the Ottoman Empire and the Central Powers, the household of one crippled soldier and his family had found an unexpected tranquillity.

 Anyush

The lieutenant left Anyush in the care of his widowed uncle, Hasan Kadrı, a wealthy merchant in the town of Gümüşhane. Kadri was about to leave for his summer home in İskenderun and agreed to take the Armenian, disguised as a Muslim servant.

In the Kadri household she had been taken under the wing of Nevra, the cook, who fed her, deloused her and asked no difficult questions. The other servants were not friendly but mostly they left her alone. Once in İskenderun, Kadri arranged passage for her on a boat leaving for Beyrouth, and after procuring the necessary travel permits and her ticket, he left her at the dock.

She waited by the booking office where she could see the boats coming and going into Iskenderun sound. Dressed in her abaya and burqa, she looked no different to other Muslim woman and sat near a family group who were waiting for the same boat. In a small bag at her feet was a change of clothes, a small sum of money and her ticket. She sat looking at the water, watching the surface lapping greasily against the dock wall, when a shadow fell across her.

'We were never properly introduced,' the man said. 'My name is Armin Wegner.' He removed his hat and the sun shone on his cropped hair and pale face. The German soldier looked different somehow, his uniform hanging loosely on him and his skin stretched tight over his cheekbones. He seemed diminished, as if the people in his photographs had claimed part of him for themselves.

'I am in your debt, Armin Wegner,' she said. 'How did you know it was me?'

'The man who bought your ticket at the booking office ... he called you Anyush. I wasn't sure but I hoped it might be you.'

'What are you doing here?'

'I'm working at the cholera hospital. At least I was.'

'I thought you had been arrested in Gümüşhane.'

'For a time, yes. They found out about my pictures and I would have been court-martialled if Von der Goltz hadn't intervened. I was sent to work at the fever hospital in Sivas and then the cholera hospital here. I've been ill so they're sending me home.'

Behind him, stevedores were unloading crates from a cargo ship when one fell and broke open, strewing the quayside with bananas. The family next to them rushed over.

'My train leaves tomorrow for Berlin,' Armin said. 'I was killing time wandering around the port when I heard that man mention your name. It's an unusual name.'

Shouts and curses from the crowd gathered around the broken crate carried to them on the wind, and small boats tugged at their moorings like dogs chained to the harbour wall. Rigging clattered and clanged in the breeze blowing off the sea, and a ship sounded its bell as it passed the breakwater and reversed its engines to berth.

'Do you know what happened to the others?' Anyush asked. 'To Captain Orfalea?'

'I've seen him. He was operated on in Sivas. They did the best they could, but he lost the leg. He's been sent back to Constantinople.'

'He's a cripple?'

'Yes.'

Turning towards the water, Anyush could see the outline of a ship on the horizon. It appeared to hang between the sea and sky while the sun shone in bright flashes around it.

'Did he mention Lale to you? My daughter?'

'He spoke about her. He said she was given into the care of an American couple. A Dr Stewart and his wife.'

'Dr Stewart? Are you sure?'

Armin nodded.

'But I thought ...? Did Jahan go back to Trebizond?'

'No. The Stewarts were in Gümüşhane.' He looked at her for a moment. 'They were leaving for America.'

Out at sea the ship had become indistinct. It grew hazy and pale, fading into the horizon until it vanished from sight. From behind her burqa Anyush watched it disappear, too far to identify any more. America was on the other side of the world, an unfathomable distance away, but Lale was alive. Nothing else mattered.

'There's something I would like you to have,' Armin said, taking the rucksack from his back. He opened it, took out a book and leafed through the pages. A photograph fell from it and Anyush picked it up. It was a picture of Jahan and his lieutenant. They were standing side by side, caps straight and uniforms buttoned. Lieutenant Kadri looked solemnly at the viewer but Jahan appeared to be smiling.

'And take this,' Armin said handing her a fistful of money. 'You'll need it.'

'No, you have done enough.'

He pushed it into her hand as the siren blew to board the ship. 'You'd better go. Get on now, before the others.'

'Thank you,' she smiled, though he couldn't see it. 'Thank you Armin Wegner.'

Ŭ Ŭ Ŭ

Five years later

Beyrouth, nestled in Saint George Bay, was clapsed like a lover in the arms of the Chouf Mountains. Beyond the boats and tin shacks of Batroun Harbour, tall buildings of pale stone and yellow brick lined the wide paved streets. The town was once grand, but when Anyush stepped off the boat and saw it for the first time, it was not as she had imagined it. Because of the blockade set up along the Lebanese and Syrian coasts, Beyrouth was in the grip of a famine. Hundreds of thousands of Lebanese had died of hunger before the end of the war, and a cholera epidemic had overrun the city so that bodies lay rotting in the streets as fodder for the rats. That first day it seemed to Anyush that she had returned to the scene of her worst nightmares.

For six weeks she slept under a bridge with three other Armenian families who offered her the protection of numbers. She was hungry and cold and never less than afraid, but a chance meeting with a woman from Trebizond resulted in her moving to the Armenian Refugee Camp. It was located on a patch of waste ground in the Beyrouthi suburb of Karantina, where jumbled-together shacks and lean-to cabins were fashioned from iron sheeting, old doors and loosely stacked concrete blocks as well as the remnants of Red Cross tents. A few chickens pecked at the dirt, and clotheslines stretched from dwelling to dwelling, crossing the spaces like a badly drawn spider web. At first, Anyush shared a hut with five children and three adults, but the removal of a bone from a child's throat brought her to the attention of Dr Altounyan, the Armenian doctor who ran the orphanage and held clinics at the camp. He offered her the job of nurse's assistant at the orphanage hospital, but by then word had got around that she had worked for Dr Stewart, and she found herself in the role of camp nurse and first-aid doctor. Dividing her time between the hospital and the camp, she was given the privilege of a shack to herself – one room, just wide enough that when she lay down her head and feet touched the opposing walls. She had a bed-roll to sleep on, an upturned crate for a table and a box to hold her tin cup, her plate and her old abaya and burqa. Food was cooked outdoors over fires or stoves, and a trench dug at one end of the site served as a latrine.

Anyush was happy in Karantina. Nobody in the camp spoke about what had happened but they were drawn to each other, to memories played out alone and in silence. On quiet nights when Anyush could hear the distant sound of waves breaking on the shore, she thought of the village. Of her family and the faces of her friends. Of her old school class-room and the first time she had ever seen Dr Stewart. She remembered the feel of wet sand beneath her feet and the taste of Gohar's lavash and the early morning smell of sap oozing from the pines. She thought of her old life like a story in one of Bayan Stewart's picture books, and, though she mightn't have wished to, she thought of Jahan.

The orphanage where Anyush worked took up one side of a sunny square in Bourj Hammoud. Known locally as the children's hospital, it had been housed in an abandoned convent of Catholic nuns. The building was three storeys high, made of cut stone and with arched and barred windows that faced onto a central courtyard. Surrounded on all sides by the city, a newly chiselled block of granite over the door informed the visitor that this was the Armenian Orphanage Hospital of

Beyrouth, funded by Near East Relief. Two security men sat in a small hut at the gate.

'*Günaydın*, Anyush,' Arshak, the younger man, greeted her.

Ohannes also lifted his hand and smiled.

Arshak had come from Adana on the Mediterranean coast and was almost completely blind. Matron Norton had nicknamed him Caesar because she said he reminded her of a bust of the Roman emperor she had once seen in a museum. He had a noble head, the shape visible beneath his close-cropped hair, but it was the white discs of his almost blind eyes that most resembled an ancient statue. Arshak didn't live in Karantina with the other Armenians but slept in the security hut on the hospital grounds and still managed to work as a messenger boy and handyman. He was devoted to Matron Norton who had taken him in even though he was over sixteen and should have been sent to the Home for the Blind. British soldiers had found him wandering alone in the Syrian desert where he had survived for two years on grass, roots and herbs. He had some sight in his left eye and none at all in his right but had the ability to hear what no one else could through walls and ceilings and doors. Arshak never spoke of how he had come to be in the desert, but it was said that he had lost his entire family in the concentration camp at Deir al-Zor. The older man, Ohannes, was Lebanese by birth, Armenian by birthright and a relative of Dr Altounyan.

'Matron wants you,' Arshak said. 'She has a letter for you.'

The mention of a letter set Anyush's heart racing. She never lost hope of hearing from Jahan, even though he had answered none of her letters. All she wanted was news of her daughter, or so she convinced herself. Despite everything, she was still curious about him. How did he look? How had he managed his injury? Was he happy? Was he married? She imagined him with a wife, certainly a woman of means, someone who would make him laugh the way she had done, a woman

346

who would bear him children.

Anyush thought then of Lale, precious Lale who would now be five years old. The loss of her daughter was more deeply felt and harder to bear with every passing year. Anyush ached for news of her, any news. The Stewarts were good people, but she wanted her daughter to know that her mother pined for her, that every child in the orphanage was a reminder of her and that she was tormented by her absence.

'Matron's in her office,' Arshak said.

Up a flight of stairs and along a corridor in a small room, Matron Norton was standing on a chair and talking to someone through the bars of the window. Matron was a small, well-built woman; she was wearing a white dress to just below mid-calf, a long white apron over it and a stiff headscarf that moved not an inch, even though her head nodded constantly as she spoke. On her left sleeve she wore an armband with a red cross, and she spoke with a pronounced American accent. Someone on the far side of the window was getting severely reprimanded.

'Anyush, I didn't hear you come in. That scamp has blown out my eardrums!'

'One of the children?'

'Spot!'

Matron's dog Spot was barking loudly in the courtyard below, the sound coming in through the open window. 'He followed me from home and I had to tie him to the railing in the yard. He's not happy I can tell you. What would you do with a dog like that?'

Spot was a small, wiry, mongrel stray with a liver-coloured patch over his left eye and ear and another on his rump. He was a clever little dog who liked nothing more than to perform tricks, and Matron adored him. She told him to be quiet, pushed the window closed and stepped down from the chair. Seating herself behind the desk, she dabbed a handkerchief to her upturned nose and invited Anyush to sit. On the desk was a letter with a local postmark, which she handed to her.

'It's your American visa. I knew it was coming because I met Mrs Jordan who told me that the Ambassador had got the list and you were on it. Well, don't look so downcast! I thought you'd be pleased.'

'I am pleased. It's just ... very sudden.'

'Six months is hardly sudden!'

Matron leaned across and patted her hand. 'Going by yourself is never easy but you've been through worse. You'll get to know people really quickly. Mrs Jordan tells me there are a number of people from the camp on the list so you won't be alone. I've heard that Vassak is already there and I'm sure he'll be in touch. Anyway, it will be easier to trace your daughter from there.'

They discussed the matter for a few minutes more before Anyush left to join Dr Altounyan's rounds. She was thinking of Vassak who had once been as essential to the running of the orphanage hospital as Dr Altoun-yan or Matron Norton, but in a different way. A second generation Leb-anese-Armenian, his family had come to Beyrouth, from Diyarbakır and set up as ironmongers and blacksmiths. Vassak's older brother looked after the business, while Vassak ran various rackets in the city. The embargo and the famine had wiped out the business but opened the way for a growing trade in black-market goods. When food supplies at the orphan-age ran low, Arshak suggested to Matron that Vassak could solve their problems. Sacks of flour, oils, bulgar wheat, lemons, in fact almost any-thing you wanted could be had through Vassak's network of smugglers. The only obstacle to filling the orphans' bellies, he explained to Matron, was the price.

Matron didn't trust Vassak but the Near East Relief food lorries had been grounded on the wrong side of the Mediterranean and she had no choice but to deal with him. Using her own money and donations she begged from foreigners in the city, she paid Vassak large sums to keep the orphans fed. Food stocks and medical supplies began to arrive at odd hours of the day and night, including medicines with the Red Cross stamped on them.

Vassak had noticed Anyush working with Dr Altounyan and plagued Arshak until he gave him her name. He began to appear at the Karantina clinics with bandages, liniments and medicines. He brought gifts of dates, figs and flasks of foreign perfume. There was nothing Vassak couldn't find and he laid them at her feet. Anyush accepted the gifts reluctantly. She had no interest in Vassak but needed the supplies for the refugees. She was polite and cautiously grateful but ignored his more obvious advances. Never a man to give up, Vassak tried a different approach. He was a gifted mimic, and his rendition of Matron in full flight made Anyush smile. Despite herself, she fell into the habit of him. She came to depend on him the way she depended on there being seven days in a week. She never asked about his life outside the hospital but knew more about him than he realised.

Arshak had told her that Vassak was a member of the Armenian Revolutionary Federation, a secret organisation whose aim was to assassinate all members of the Turkish Government and those involved in the Armenian Genocide. A Turkish general had been gunned down outside his apartment in Berlin and Arshak claimed that Vassak's cell had been responsible. In Arshak's eyes these men were heroes.

At the end of one very wet autumn, Vassak disappeared. People believed he was dead, a martyr to the great Armenian cause. Arshak claimed he was holed up in the mountains until the next assault, but Anyush knew better.

One night, as the rain fell in torrents and turned the lanes of Karantina into rivers of mud, Vassak came to her door. Water cascaded from him, and she brought him inside. He stood without speaking, dripping and shivering in the small space. Anyush helped him out of his wet shoes and clothes. His hands felt like the hands of a corpse and she placed them between her own, rubbing vigorously to make them warm. Suddenly he lunged at her, pushing her up against the wall and tugging at her night-clothes. His mouth was on hers, crushing her lips as he tore the cloth covering her breasts.

'No, Vassak ...'

Pulling the sleeves down over her shoulders, he pinned her arms to her sides.

'Not like this ...'

His knee was in her groin, pushing her legs apart and his cold hand between them. He rammed himself into her and groaned. The rain hammered on the tin roof as he pounded her hips against the wall, and then it was over. He slumped against her, water dripping onto his bare back.

'I have to go,' he said, pulling away.

Anyush never saw him again, but some months later a letter was pushed under her door. He had to flee, he said, to America. There wasn't much work but he was getting by, doing a bit here and there. He wanted Anyush to join him in Philadelphia as soon as she could. She went outside to the stove and threw his letter on the flames.

Jahan

'Another one, Papa. Tell me the story about Maman.'

'I'll be late, *ma petite.*'

'One more. *Je t'en prie.*'

'I'll ask Melike to read to you.'

'I don't want Melike. Please, Papa. A story about Maman.'

'The others are waiting, *chérie.* Tomorrow night.'

'Was she a real princess, Papa? Did she live in Topkapi Palace?'

'Of course she did. Haven't I told you she was the sultan's favourite? And all the beautiful gifts he bought her? The rarest, the most beautiful white tiger ...'

'Called Griffe.'

'And a talking cockatoo ...'

'Called Plume.'

'And enough jewels and gold to fill a thousand caves. And because she was the most beautiful, most clever princess in the whole world, she always went to sleep when the sultan told her to. So now ...' Jahan bent to kiss his daughter, 'you must do the same.'

'Why can't we go to the palace, Papa?'

'Because Maman's not there any more. Remember I told you? That she became ill?'

His little girl nodded.

'And that she's with Grand-père? And she's very happy there.'

'How do you know? Have you been?'

'No darling,' he smiled. 'Maybe when I'm old.'

'Can I go?'

He reached out and stroked Lale's dark hair. 'Your *maman* wants you to stay here with me. She would like you to be a princess just as she was.'

'But I'm not a princess. Tansu said I'm not.'

'You are to me,' he said, bending to kiss her forehead. 'Now sleep. I'll see you in the morning.'

Jahan tucked her in and leaned over to extinguish the lamp. In the doorway Madame Orfalea stood watching. She was dressed for the opera, tucking a pair of opera glasses into her *réticule*.

'Do you think that's a good idea?' she asked as Jahan closed the door. 'Talking about her mother like that?'

'How would you have me talk about her?'

'It might be kinder to describe her in more realistic terms.'

'You want me to tell Lale that her mother was murdered by men like my father?'

Madame Orfalea flinched as though he had hit her.

It had been almost three years since his father's death, but his mother still mourned for him. She had changed physically in that time, becoming more lined about the face, but she had also lost something fundamental to herself. Gone was the sparkle and the flirtatious girlish humour. She shrouded herself in black floor-length gowns while the nation's hemlines moved upwards and the passions of a demoralised post-war Turkey rallied around the young Kemal Atatürk. Madame Orfalea mourned not only her dead husband but a vanishing way of life. Because of the war the Empire had lost its territories in the Balkans and the Middle East, and those sources of income which had been poured into cosmopolitan Constantinople were also lost. Istanbul, as it was now called, had seen hundreds of thousands of its young men die in the war, and, with this sudden loss of population and wealth, its importance on the world stage vanished. Jahan had taken over the tannery after his father's death, but the demand for leather products had fallen dramatically and he struggled to keep the business afloat. Unemployment was rife and progress in what had once been a great world capital ground to a halt.

'We'd better go,' he said. 'I told Hanife I'd collect her and Madame Bey before seven.'

Ü   Ü   Ü

The following day, Jahan left the tannery and the old city, coming to walk along the Bosphorus. The sun was setting and mosques and minarets, tankers and hawsers all gleamed with gold. Only the water in the boatyards lay dark and still, and he found himself thinking of Anyush. She occupied his thoughts less than in those first months, but at moments like this, usually at dusk, she came to him. He walked on, crossing into Galata and making his way to the house on Grande Rue. Madame Orfalea had called him to her suite that morning, insisting he formalise the engagement with Hanife. There was no logical reason not to marry his sister's tutor. She would make an excellent wife and a wonderful mother to Lale, but there never seemed to be a good time to put matters on a formal footing. Hanife's father had fled to Germany after the war and her only brother was killed in an explosion at sea. Jahan's own father had died shortly afterwards, resulting in an uncertain future for the family and the tannery. But these had nothing to do with his indecision. It was no more than dishonest evasion. He wasn't sure what he wanted. He knew he didn't love Hanife, but he also knew he liked her. She was a favourite with his mother and sisters and Lale adored her. Reaching the house, he broke the hinge on his prosthetic leg and began to climb the steps. Madeline opened the door and admitted him to the hallway, taking his hat and coat. Lale came running towards him and he lifted her into his arms.

'What have you got in your hair?'

'Paint.'

'You were painting your hair?'

She nodded.

'I'm surprised Azize hasn't scrubbed you in the bath.'

'Mademoiselle Bey said I could show you first. It's a *papillon*,' she said, bending her head towards him.

He laughed. 'Well it's very beautiful. The most wonderful butterfly I've seen.'

She wriggled out of his arms and ran upstairs to find her grandmother. Standing in the hallway watching her climb, Jahan came to a decision. There would be no more prevarication. He would ask Hanife to marry him at the first opportunity.

Before he could think of the engagement, there was some business which needed attention as a matter of urgency. That evening, Jahan sat down with his mother and told her the true state of affairs concerning the tannery. She was calm and showed a quick understanding of their predicament, and together they agreed to keep the shoemaking plant and to sell the larger of the two businesses, the tannery. The family lawyer was to draw up the terms of sale.

The next day, the lawyer asked Jahan to find the title deeds but there was no sign of them at his father's office. Jahan guessed they would be with his father's papers in the bureau in his parents' suite, but his mother had the only key.

'Madeline,' he asked, 'is my mother anywhere about?'

'She is out, Monsieur. With Madame Bey.'

'Have you any idea when she'll be back?'

'Non, Monsieur, but she said she would not take *déjeuner*.'

'Thank you, Madeline.'

It would have been easier to wait for his mother's return, but he believed that if the process were set in motion then a change of heart was beyond reach.

The house seemed peculiarly silent. Tansu and Melike were at their lessons, and Azize had taken Lale for a stroll in the park. He stood in the doorway of his parents' suite, looking around him. Their two beds were just inside the door of the first room, and the sitting area was located in the far room with a bay window and balcony overlooking the Grande Rue. As a boy he had played in these rooms while his mother dressed for dinner. Jahan stepped inside, surprised it was still so redolent of his father and his illness. His father's dressing gown was draped over the armchair, and his silver shaving kit was laid out beside the ewer and basin. Old periodicals were neatly stacked on the marble-topped commode and a book lay open on his bedside cabinet. Jahan walked to the far room facing onto the street and went to the bureau-bookcase against the wall. Through the glazed doors he could see his father's collection of books and magazines, but it was the slope-front bureau beneath that drew his attention. He tried to open it but it was locked. A key and tassel hung from the doors above it but did not open the bureau. Jahan looked around. The key was probably in the room somewhere, but he was reluctant to rummage through his parents' things. He had decided to ask his mother when he saw something glinting on the architrave over the door. Reaching up, he felt for it and took down a small silver key that fitted the lock perfectly.

He found the deeds almost immediately. They were rolled into a scroll and pushed into one of the pigeon holes at the back of the bureau.

Taking off the ribbon that bound them, he glanced cursorily through the pages and satisfied himself that all was in order. It was only as he went to close the bureau that he saw the bundle of letters tied up with string. Olcay Orfalea had never struck him as the love-letter sort, and Jahan looked again. The addressee on the top letter caught his eye. Written in large cursive script was a name he recognised. His own.

The deeds fell from his hands as he began to look through the letters. The same name was written on all of them, Jahan Orfalea

The Letters

155 Linden Strasse

Helgenplatz

Berlin

January 22nd, 1921

Dear Jahan,

As I write this letter I am hoping that you have survived the war and that it finds you in good health. I am taking a chance that this address, given to me by an old friend of yours, is the correct one. Before I get to the purpose of my letter, let me tell you a little of my adventures since we last met.

Not long after you were discharged from the hospital in Sivas, I contracted cholera and became quite ill. Given the conditions we were working under, it was a miracle any of us survived. After my recovery, I was sent back to Germany and although it is a very different country to the one I left, I am enormously relieved to be home. I will shortly be demobilised and I cannot say I am sorry.

I have been in communication with the Peace Conference in Paris and they have expressed an interest in my Armenian photographs. I haven't yet been asked to testify, but they may still call me. Apparently Woodrow Wilson is sympathetic to the idea of an independent Armenian state, and I can only hope it becomes a reality. Which brings me to my reason for writing.

Just before I left Turkey I met with Anyush Charcoudian, through a series of coincidences, which I will not go into here. Let me just say that she was in real danger even then but managed to get out of the country on a ship to Lebanon. From a photograph I gave her, she found my address on the back and has written

357

to me a number of times. She tells me she is well treated and settled in her adoptive country with many other exiled Armenians. She also mentioned that she wrote to you on several occasions but has received no reply. I am aware, Jahan, how delicate this matter might be for you and that your circumstances have possibly changed. She asked me to contact you solely, and I stress the word, with a view to finding her daughter Lale. I was able to tell her that the child was given into the care of the Stewarts, and she believes they may have brought her with them to America. Anyush is hoping that they have been in touch with you or provided you with an address.

Let me say again that I understand, as does she, that it may not be possible to commence a correspondence with you, but any information you may have regarding the child can safely and discreetly be passed on through me. If it happens that you have had no contact with the Americans, then all I ask is that you write and tell me. For kindness's sake, I would like Anyush to know the truth. Hope can be a cruel master.

With every good wish,

I remain yours sincerely,

Armin Wegner

For a long time Jahan sat in the chair beside the bureau. The clock in the hall struck the quarter hour and then the half. After a while, he folded Armin's letter and put it back in the envelope. Taking the next letter from the bundle, he began to read:

Dear Jahan,

Forgive my writing to you again, but I am desperate for news of my daughter and you are the only connection I have with her. Believe me when I say that I have no expectations for myself. I wish only to know if you have had contact with the Stewarts or any information that might lead to my finding Lale. It is not in my nature to beg, but I will gladly do so for even the smallest crumb of news of her.

I want only to know that she is safe and well and to hold to the hope that I might one day see her again.

Respectfully,

Anyush Charcoudian

Dear Jahan,

I was wondering if perhaps your family no longer lived at this address ...

Dear Jahan,

I am writing to let you know that I am living in Beyrouth ...

Jahan picked up the next envelope. It was older, the writing faded and the corners torn.

Dear Jahan,

If you receive this and if it is within your power to do so I urge you to write ...

Dear Jahan,

It is becoming difficult for me to post letters from the village. It is overrun with gendarmes and soldiers, but there is something I need to tell you which will not keep ...

Dear Jahan,

I am writing this from our ruined church because it is where I feel closest to you ...

A board creaked and the light in the room dimmed. Jahan looked up to see his mother standing in the doorway.

'You knew,' he whispered.

'Jahan—'

'You knew all along. I thought it was only Papa who had betrayed me. I would have staked my life on it.'

He held out the letters clenched in his fist.

'Some of these were written after he died. The last one only two months ago. You kept them from me.'

His mother sighed and removed her hatpin. Carefully she lifted the hat from her head and placed it on the chest beside the door.

'Yes, Jahan, I did. I hid them along with all the other letters that woman wrote to you.'

'That *woman* is Lale's mother.'

'She's an Armenian! What did you expect me to do? Send Lale back to her? A stranger? This is Lale's home. Here with us. We're the only family she has ever known. Would you take her away from it?'

'It wasn't your decision to make.'

'Whose was it? Yours? I don't think so! You came back from the war like some impostor wearing my son's clothes. Have you any idea what we went through? The worry you caused? You weren't capable of making decisions. You weren't even capable of looking after yourself. I spent nights pacing the floors waiting for some gendarme to tell me you had thrown yourself under a train or drowned yourself in the Bosphorus. Did you really think I would let you decide my granddaughter's future?'

Jahan looked at his mother's still beautiful face. 'I thought better of you.'

She smiled sadly. 'You're a dreamer, Jahan. Intelligent like your father but a dreamer. Look around you. Everyone has changed. Everybody who survived the war is altered by it. It is the price we pay.'

She went and stood at the window looking down onto the street.

'You'll learn, Jahan, that certain things in life are beyond our control. The war ... the death of your father ... losing the business. Events greater than personal resolve decide our fate. There is a period of adjustment, and then you carry on as best you can. I was never surprised you fell for an Armenian. It was almost inevitable. No doubt she was young and pretty and you needed a cause to champion, but it's over now. There are harsh realities facing all of us. Your sisters depend on you, Jahan. They are your responsibility until the day they marry.'

Turning from the window, Jahan's mother walked back to the room and picked up the deeds from the floor.

'You have obligations, especially where Lale and Hanife are concerned. What happened with the Armenian is finished. It's over.'

She held out the documents and when Jahan didn't take them she placed them in his hand. Slowly, he got to his feet. 'This is not over. This is only the beginning.'

Anyush

The baths looked more like the foundations of a building site than a swimming pool. Two enormous holes had been carved out of the ground, the sides squared by large blocks of stone. A huge water-wheel and sluice in the middle pumped water from a well. Some of the older boys pivoted the sluice first into the bath where the girls were swimming and then over to the boys who they pushed and jostled to stand under the flow. The younger children splashed around naked while all the others bathed in their underclothes. Anyush stood in the girls' pool, her skirt tucked in at the waist and her hair bound up in a scarf. It was still warm but not so hot that pale skin would redden and burn. In her arms she carried two-year-old Dikkran, left on the hospital steps when his mother died of puerperal fever. Dipping him in the water, she swung him high in the air as he kicked his thin little legs and laughed with delight. Around her the girls shrieked and the boys shouted.

'Andranik, try not to drown your brother. And leave some water in the well ... eh?'

The early autumn wind blew across the pools, cutting through the heat and whipping around gates and walls. Anyush looked over to the group of children sitting on chairs in the shadow thrown by the main building. These were the TB orphans, the infectious children who were confined to their own wing and couldn't swim with the others. A lonely group whose number varied from week to week and whose hopes of a cure were slim. When Anyush had first come to work at the orphanage, these were the children she was drawn to, but in recent weeks Matron had forbidden her to have anything to do with them.

'You won't get into America if you have TB.'

America. It seemed she was going one way or another.

A sudden quiet had fallen over the baths. The girls were huddled together in a group and the boys stood silently beside the dripping water-pipe. They were staring over towards the main building at the path leading to the front door. Anyush followed their gaze and saw a stranger approaching, a man whose face was shaded by the sun at his back. Cautiously, he stepped into the sunlight. He was not that tall, wore a light grey summer suit and walked with a pronounced limp. A small girl tugged at Anyush's skirt, but she didn't notice.

The person who walked towards her looked like an older brother or uncle of the man she remembered. He made slow progress, without the aid of a stick but as if every step took an effort. His thick black hair had thinned at the temples, and his skin was the colour of someone who spent too much time indoors. Jahan had aged, the years of the war written on his face.

'Take Dikkran, Houry,' Anyush said, handing the child in her arms to an older girl. 'Ask the boys to empty the pools.'

Tugging her skirt down, she waded over to the edge of the bath where Jahan extended a hand to help her out.

'Can we go somewhere?'

They walked around towards the back of the hospital, followed by the children's curious stares. The formal garden of the original convent had fallen into decay but for the newly-dug vegetable patch which led down towards a disused side-gate. They kept to the path, stopping at a garden seat half hidden beside a bolted door.

'You haven't changed,' he said, as they sat on either end of it.

'I have. As have you.'

'Not for the better,' he smiled. 'I'm going to be bald like my father. Oh and of course there's this.' He pulled up his trousers to reveal a prosthetic leg. The metal was the colour of old soap and gleamed dully in the sunlight.

'From your fall?'

'With a little help from Murzabey.'

The name hung in the air between them.

'I never knew you were here,' he said. 'One of the men from my regiment told me no one survived.'

'Your friend knew. The lieutenant.'

'Ahmet was killed at Gallipoli.'

The sun slipped behind the buildings and they were thrown into deep shade. The children's laughter carried to them from the pools and the sound of water splashing from the pipe.

'I suppose I should say I'm sorry,' Anyush said quietly.

Jahan looked at her.

'His uncle took me in. I wouldn't be here without him,' she added.

Jahan nodded, leaning his elbows on his knees and staring at the ground between his feet.

'You forgot your shoes,' he said.

Anyush glanced at her feet, dirt and leaves clinging to her wet soles. She drew them under the bench as the wind picked up again, whistling through the gate and rattling the rusty iron on its hinges. Anyush shivered.

'Here,' Jahan said. He took off his jacket and put it around her. For a moment, his hands lingered on her shoulders and her face came very close to his. He began to say something, and then changed his mind.

'You're out of uniform.'

'Yes. I've left the army.'

'What have you been doing?'

He sat back against the seat, mossy verdigris staining his white shirt green. 'I'm running my father's tannery. Badly, but there's no one else to do it.'

'You're a businessman, then?'

'Not much of one. Not like my father was.' He looked at her. 'What about you? They told me at the camp you work as a nurse.'

'I help with the refugees. And the children here.'

He looked over at the hospital buildings and the lines of clothes flapping between. The paint had peeled from some of the walls and two of the top-storey windows were broken. Anyush watched him, his profile just as she remembered.

'Why didn't you answer my letters?' she asked.

'Believe me, Anyush ... I never got them.'

'Then how did you find me?'

'Armin. I wrote to him and he told me you were still in Beyrouth. When I got off the boat I went to the refugee camp and they directed me to the orphanage.' He smiled at her. 'It didn't surprise me to find you by the sea.'

She thought of Trebizond then, and the blue-green waters of the Black Sea. She thought of the cove, and the two people it had once belonged to.

'Anyush,' Jahan was saying, 'I met Matron Norton and I've made certain arrangements—'

'I don't want your money.'

'That's not what—'

'If you had read my letters you would know that I don't want anything from you. I've got my papers for America and I'm leaving as soon as I get my ticket.'

'If you would just—'

'The only thing I want is to find my daughter, so if you could tell me where the Stewart's are living—'

'I haven't heard from the Stewarts, but Anyush please, listen—'

A shrill cry came from the direction of the pools, followed by hysterical high-pitched screaming.

'Dikkran!'

Running along the path, Anyush rounded the corner where the children were huddled around the injured child. Behind her, Jahan called her name.

Dikkran was concussed and bled copiously from the cut on his forehead. Houry tearfully explained that he had wriggled out of her arms and hit his head against the iron sluice. Anyush cradled him on her lap while Dr Altounyan stitched the wound. There would be a small scar, he said, but the boy would heal.

Some time later, she sat by the child's bed, waiting for him to fall asleep. She wasn't thinking of the little boy any more, but of the conversation with Jahan. Dikkran's eyes closed, and she crept from the room, making her way along the corridor to the main door and the yard outside. The pools were empty when she passed them, and she took the path around the corner to the garden. The seat by the gate was scattered with fallen leaves, and the wind whined through the bars of the gate. Of course Jahan was gone.

Ŭ Ŭ Ŭ

Arshak was waiting for her on the hospital steps. She was to go to the matron's office, he said. At once. Climbing the stairs, she prepared to face Mrs Norton's wrath. A child in her care had been injured, and she should have been apprehensive, but as she approached the matron's office,

Anyush realised she felt nothing at all.

She had imagined this day for so long. Everything she would say. Everything she would hear. All those feelings of hurt and loss she would give voice to, and all the feelings of joy and happiness she would share with him. And how it would be to touch him again. To smell his hair, his skin, his clothes. To feel his hands on her. To remember what it was like to make love. But the man she knew had died in the war and a Turkish businessman had come to take his place. A man who would ease his conscience with money.

A dog's loud barking distracted her. The sound was not coming from the yard outside but from somewhere within the hospital itself. She realised that Spot must have managed to get into Matron's office and was making a lot of noise. Fearful of what she might find, Anyush stopped outside the door. Pushing it slightly open, she saw Matron Norton standing in front of her desk smiling and clapping her hands. Opening it wider, there was Spot performing his trick of standing on his hind legs and begging for food. But he was turned away from Matron, his attention on someone else, someone with a small hand holding out a piece of bread for the delighted dog. Anyush pushed the door open wide as Spot snatched the bread and dropped on all fours to eat it. A small, smiling face turned towards her. A little girl of about five years of age with silky black hair tied up in a bow, skin so pale it was almost white, and laughing brown eyes like her father's.

Jahan

Jahan willed himself to keep moving, to distance himself from his daughter and the woman he still loved. But his body felt uncoordinated, hampered by his leg and the weight of what he was about to do. And he would do this, no matter what the cost. The pain that squeezed his heart and whipped the breath from his lungs was evidence enough of his contrition. A first drop in an ocean of years. He drew in his shoulders and stiffened his spine against the wind blowing up from the sea. Heading towards the harbour and the port, he thought he heard his daughter's voice calling to him ... 'Papa' ... but he didn't turn around. Beyrouth was fixed in his mind. The light and cold and desolation of it. The broken hopes and misery of it. And the sea and the waves and the wind whispering of atonement.

Epilogue

Diary of Dr Charles Stewart

Springfield

Illinois

March 29th, 1922

I found my old journal in a trunk this morning and spent some time reading over everything I had written. As it was one of those wintry Illinois mornings, a fire was burning in the study and I thought I would throw the journal onto the flames. For whatever reason, I couldn't burn it. Instead, I find myself writing one last entry, a few words in the hope of ending what should never have been started.

We are back in Springfield, Hetty's home town, and I am discovering what it is to work as a city doctor. People have been so kind and welcoming that it's easy to forget why we left in the first place. My days are fully taken up with the practice now that the Armenian Relief Fund has folded and finally closed its doors. I wrote to Henry to tell him, and he wrote back that it was inevitable after the donations dried up. Still, it rankles with me. How soon we forget. Hetty believes it was only to be expected, that people's hearts and minds are drawn to other causes, other tragedies, and she's probably right. In my lifetime, Armenians and their story will be forgotten. On this side of the world, at least, it will only be amongst those of us who lived through that terrible time that anything of it will be remembered. That is the great irony. Those of us who might wish to, can never forget.

In my own family the legacy of our years in the Empire lives on. Thomas is an angry young man who intends to change the political world, and Robert is studying medicine and hopes to work abroad. The girls may marry or not as the case

369

may be, but Milly, who is quieter and more reflective of late, is studying law. They all miss their sister and talk about her sometimes which I suppose is a good thing. Of course it is.

Sometimes I try and imagine how life might have turned out if we had never gone to Trebizond, had never left Illinois. I wonder what I really hoped to achieve. As a young man I wanted to show Hetty the world, but a world as I had experienced it. Where right and wrong, good and evil conformed to my understanding of them. It was only after our return to America, when I became ill with a debilitating depression that left me unable to get out of bed or to eat or even to communicate with my children, that Hetty brought the world to me. I never doubted that I loved my wife, but it was during those long weeks and months of my illness that I came to understand the meaning of the words. My lovely wife, who lost her daughter, her innocence and her youth and who never blamed me. Who has forgiven me. I am trying, God knows, to forgive myself. Does she marvel, I wonder, at the arrogance of a man who believed he knew best? A man who thought his influence alone could save Trebizond's Armenians when, in fact, he could do nothing? Nothing that mattered.

We hear from Manon occasionally, a card at Christmas or on the children's birthdays. She is still living in Turkey, in our old house in the village, and claims she's too old to uproot herself and has nowhere else to go. The hospital lies in ruins and is unlikely to function as a hospital ever again, but Manon holds clinics at the house and does her best. I think she's happy, if Manon could ever be described as such.

Paul's body washed up on a beach ten miles west of Trebizond. It was too long in the water to know exactly how he died, but the authorities claimed that his injuries and broken bones were due to battering against the rocks. Manon buried him in the old graveyard next to Lottie, which seems fitting somehow.

In the years since our return, work has been a great comfort and distraction for Hetty and myself. I thank God for honest endeavour and for the people of Springfield who keep me busy enough that I don't think of the Empire for long stretches at a time. There are days when I'm convinced I'm done with it, even if Trebizond does not appear to be done with me.

I have a recurring dream where I'm in the village again. It is springtime and the lemon trees are in blossom. The square is crowded, full of people singing and dancing, much as it was on the day of Vardan Aykanian's wedding. There is music playing, the oud and the doumbek. People are happy and everything is as it should be. I am standing among them smiling and clapping when I notice the music grow quiet. To my right, I see the band players, all the old men, put their instruments at their feet and disappear into the lanes and side streets. They are followed by the women, and then the young girls in their summer aprons and scarves.

I am weeping now because I know they will come for the children next.

And even as the thought takes shape I see a child walk into a darkened alley.

All the children.

I call out but they cannot hear.

Try to hold them back but I cannot reach.

And there is silence.

Terrible silence.

I stand in the square alone, watching until the last child has gone.

And now these three remain: faith, hope and love.

But the greatest of these is love.

1 Corinthians 13:13.

Afterword

On 24 April 1915, the Armenian intellectual elite of Constantinople, the capital of the Ottoman Empire, or modern-day Turkey, was rounded up by order of the government and shot.

Known as the Three Young Turks, the men who governed Turkey through the Committee of Union and Progress proceeded to oversee the systematic obliteration of the Armenian people from the Empire. From then until the end of the First World War it is estimated that between 1.5 and 2 million Armenians were killed in what is believed to be the first genocide of the twentieth century. The twenty-fourth of April is commemorated by Armenians worldwide as Armenian Genocide Day.

Author's Notes

Although *Anyush* is a work of fiction, several of the individuals in the story are based on real-life characters or are a composite of several characters I came across during my research. What follows is a brief resumé of their actual life stories. I should also add that the village of Mushar is fictitious and that some dates in the novel were changed to make the historical events fit the timeline of the story, and so apologies to all historians. Finally, the American nurse, Ellen Mary Norton-Gerard, who undertook wonderful work for Armenian children orphaned in the genocide, ran the orphanage in Aleppo in Syria and not Beyrouth (Beirut) as in my book.

DR FRED DOUGLAS SHEPARD
REV. DR LYNDON SMITH CRAWFORD
(DR CHARLES STEWART)

The characters of Dr Charles Stewart and Hetty Stewart are based upon Rev. Dr Lyndon Smith Crawford and his wife who worked as missionaries in the Trebizond area of north-eastern Turkey, and Dr Fred Douglas Shepard and his wife who were missionaries in Ayntab in southern Turkey.

Rev. Crawford wrote extensively to the American Consulates in Trebizond and Constantinople about the plight of local Armenians and Christians which he witnessed at first-hand. Mrs Crawford ran the American

School for Christian Children and was allowed take Armenian orphans and babies into her care when their parents were taken to the concentration camps of Deir al-Zor in the Syrian desert, among others. As happened in the story, all her charges were eventually removed by the authorities. In an account given by an officer in the Turkish army, the infants were taken out in boats, stabbed and thrown into the sea in sacks. Considerably older than the character of Charles Stewart, sixty-four years of age at the time of the genocide, Rev. Crawford died in Trebizond on 22 September 1918.

The details about the life and work of a missionary doctor came from Alice Riggs' book about her father, Dr Fred Shepard. Charles Stewart's building of the hospital and his dealings with local people are based on accounts in this book. Fred Shepard was a religious man, much loved by the local population, who was deeply affected by the events he witnessed during the genocide. He contracted typhoid following the first wave of Armenian deportations and died shortly after.

ARMIN T WEGNER

Armin Theophil Wegner was born on 16 October 1886 in Elberfeld, Wuppertal in Germany. In 1914, at the outbreak of the First World War, he volunteered as a nurse in Poland and was decorated with the Iron Cross for assisting the wounded under fire. Following the military alliance of Germany and Turkey, he was sent with the German Sanitary Corps to the Middle East in 1915. Later that year, with the rank of second-lieutenant in the retinue of Field Marshal von der Goltz, he travelled through the Ottoman Empire where he witnessed the Armenian Genocide. A keen photographer, he disobeyed the orders of von der Goltz and the Turkish government by taking hundreds of photographs of Armenians on the roads and in the concentration camps, along with notes, documents and letters. Wegner was eventually arrested and sent to work in the cholera wards, where he became ill. In December 1916 he was recalled to Germany and smuggled his photographic plates and notes out of the country. Von der Goltz died from typhus in Baghdad that same year.

At the Peace Conference of 1919, Wegner submitted an open letter to President Woodrow Wilson, outlining the atrocities perpetrated by the Turkish government against Armenians and appealing for the creation of an independent Armenian state.

Between the First and Second World Wars, Wegner's success as a writer grew, reaching its peak in the 1920s with the publication of *Five Fingers Over You*, which foresaw the advent of Stalinism.

As the Nazis extended their grip across Germany, he wrote an open letter to Hitler, protesting the state-organised boycott against German Jews. He was arrested by the Gestapo in 1933 and spent the war in seven different concentration camps and prisons.

In 1956, the federal German government awarded Wegner the Highest Order of Merit, and the city of Wuppertal decorated him with the Eduard von der Heydt prize in 1962. Because of his advocacy for the rights of Jews as well as Armenians, he was awarded the title of 'Righteous among the Nations' by Yad Veshem in Israel and the Order of Saint Gregory the Illuminator by the Catholicos of All Armenians. A street in the Armenian capital, Yerevan, was named in his honour.

Armin Wegner, intellectual, doctor of law, photographer, writer, poet, humanitarian and defender of civil rights, died in Rome at the age of ninety-two on 17 May 1978.

After his death, some of his ashes were taken to Armenia, where a posthumous state funeral took place near the perpetual flame of the Armenian Genocide Monument.

COLONEL ABDUL-KADAR AINTABLI & JEMAL AZMI (COLONEL KAMIL ABDUL-KHAN)

The character of Colonel Kamil Abdul-Khan is based upon an amalgamation of the Governor of Trebizond, Colonel Abdul-Kadar Aintabli, and a man known as the 'Monster of Trebizond', Djemal Azmi. I first came across Abdul-Kadar Aintabli in a document from the Armenian National Institute detailing the eyewitness account of a Turkish army officer, Lieutenant Sayied Ahmet Moukhtar Baas, which was circulated to the War Cabinet on 26 December 1916. In his statement he talks of the Governor's infamy for his 'atrocities against Armenians' and how he had the Bishop of Trebizond murdered at night, which gave me the idea of setting the headquarters of the National Guard in the Bishop's Palace. I could find no specific information on what became of the colonel after the war, but had more success with the fates of Djemal Azmi and his superior officers, the members of the Committee of Union and Progress (CUP), a Turkish nationalist grouping. These were the so-called 'Three Young Turks' or 'Three Pashas' who were the instigators of the genocide and whose portrait hangs in Abdul-Khan's office in the story.

After the fall of Constantinople to the Allies in 1918 and the signing of the Armistice of Mudros, the leader of the CUP, Talat Pasha, resigned on 14 October and fled Turkey in a German submarine on 3 November. Sultan Mehmed VI instigated a court martial to punish the CUP for the Empire's ill-conceived involvement in the First World War and 'the massacre and destruction of the Armenians'. The three members of the CUP, Talat Pasha, Enver Pasha and Djemal Pasha were sentenced to death, but all of them had fled to Germany. British Intelligence pressured the Grand Vizier to demand that Germany extradite the Pashas to stand trial, but Germany responded that it would do so only if papers could be produced proving that the men had been found guilty.

On 15 March 1921, Talat Pasha was killed by a single gunshot as he came out of his house in the Charlottenburg district of Berlin by Soghomon Tehlirian, a member of the Armenian Revolutionary Federation (ARF), as part of Operation Nemesis to assassinate all members of the CUP and those guilty of crimes against Armenians.

On 25 July 1922, Djemal Pasha was assassinated by the ARF in Tbilisi.

The third member of the triumvirate, Enver Pasha, fled first to Germany and then to Moscow. Having had his services as ex-leader of the army rejected by Mustafa Kemal (Atatürk) in the Turkish War of Independence in 1921, he travelled to Russian Turkestan on Lenin's behalf to suppress a Basmachi uprising. After defecting to the rebel side, he was killed by an officer of the Red Army, a soldier of Armenian extraction by the name of Agop Melkumian, on 4 or 8 August 1922.

The 'Monster of Trebizond', Djemal Azmi, accused of drowning 15,000 Armenians, was sentenced to death by a Turkish court martial in 1919, but the sentence was never carried out. He was assassinated in Berlin by Arshavir Shiragian on 17 April 1922.

HENRY MORGENTHAU

On 26 April 1856 Henry Morgenthau was born in Mannheim, Germany, into a Bavarian Jewish family. His father, Lazarus, moved the family to America in 1866, and they eventually became naturalised American citizens. Henry attended the City College of New York as an undergraduate, followed by Columbia Law School, and set up practice, amassing a sizeable fortune in real estate. In 1882, he married Josephine Sykes, and together they had four children. He became a prominent supporter of the Democratic Party and served as their Finance Chairman in 1912 and again in 1916 during Woodrow Wilson's presidential campaigns. Wilson appointed Morgenthau US Ambassador to Turkey in 1913 where he served for three years. During the genocide he appealed both to Talat Pasha and the German military leaders to stop the massacre of Armenians but without success. He wrote to American and European newspapers about what he called 'The Murder of a Nation' and appealed for funds to support the refugees in concentration camps. After the war, he attended the Paris Peace Conference as an expert on the Middle East and went on to become involved in many war-related charitable bodies, including the Relief Committee for the Middle East, the Greek Refugee Settlement Commission and the Red Cross. In 1919, he headed the US government fact-finding mission to Poland on the treatment of Polish Jews, and, in 1933, he was one of the American representatives at the Geneva Conference. He wrote the first part of his memoir, *Ambassador Morgenthau's Story* in 1918, documenting his experiences in Turkey, and went on to write several more volumes covering his time in Poland and Greece.

Henry Morgenthau died of a cerebral haemorrhage on 25 November 1946, aged ninety.

ELLEN MARY NORTON-GERARD

Ellen Mary Norton-Gerard was born in Lake City, Minnesota, in 1883. She trained as a nurse and in 1918 volunteered with Near East Relief to serve three years in Lebanon and Syria. Working at the Armenian Orphanage Hospital in Aleppo, she had over a thousand children in her care, orphaned by the Armenian Genocide. In 1922, she married Frank RJ Gerard in India and moved to Santa Barbara, California, in 1941, where she worked at the Hoff Army Hospital. The Gerards had two daughters, Mary and Hélène.

Ellen Mary took many photographs during her time in Aleppo and Beirut and had more from her travels to Egypt, the Ottoman Empire and India. In 2000, an album of her photographs and some loose photographs were discovered in a military antiques shop in the Los Angeles area, which are now available to view online. Ellen Mary is often pictured surrounded by the children in her care and with her dog Spot. Two memorable photographs in the album are of the 'blind boy' and the 'desert boy', and the character of Arshak is a composite of both.

Ellen Mary died in 1966 at the age of eighty-three.

NEW FICTION FROM

AN IMPRINT OF O'BRIEN

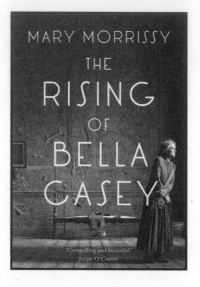

From a piano abandoned on the strife-torn streets
of Dublin at Easter 1916, Mary Morrissy spins
the reader backwards through the life
of enigmatic beauty Bella Casey, sister of the
famed playwright Seán O'Casey.

'Elegant and unadorned at the same time ... an intimate portrait of a
woman and a depiction of Irish history at its most extreme ... a wonderful
book from one of our finest writers.'

Colum McCann

'One of the most intelligent, well-written and well-researched
historical novels I have read. Mary Morrissy is the Irish Hilary Mantel.'

Eilis Ní Dhuibhne

'Mary Morrissy has a genius for lifting characters out of the dim
backgrounds of history and brilliantly illuminating them ... she evokes
the rich Dublin world of the plays of Seán O'Casey.'

John Banville

A tense thriller that stalks the urban streets of southeast London
and the bleak wilderness of the North Kent coast,
Hunting Shadows introduces the forceful, compromised
police detective, DI Ellen Kelly.

'Wonderful characterisation and a gripping plot. DI Ellen Kelly's
mourning felt so tangible that it was heart-wrenching. This debut pulled
me in straight away and I was hooked! A book that has stayed with me
long after the reading.'

Crimesquad

'Terrific ... compelling.'

Irish Examiner

'Truly a tour de force. Imagine a collaboration between Anne Tyler and
AM Homes. Yes, the novel is that good. This is great writing.'

Ken Bruen

'A most assured debut.'

crimefictionlover.com

BRANDON